HUNTED BY DARKNESS

COVEN OF SHADOWS AND SECRETS

CROWNS OF MAGIC UNIVERSE

ASHLEY MCLEO

MERAKI PRESS

GLOSSARY

* the Beinecke - a library at Yale
* the Covenant - the supernatural ruling body of the human world. It's made up of three individuals from each supernatural order (example: three vampires, three witches, three phoenixes and so on).
* the Darkborn - people in the human world who follow the Princes of Hell. Some are Hellblooded, but not all.
* Hellblooded - individuals with demon blood. They are usually born in the human world and are forced to register by the Covenant.
* Hellborn - individuals who were born in Hell. Nearly all of these creatures are demons.
* Isila - another realm where magical beings live. It's comprised of nine kingdoms (four fae kingdoms, mage, dragon shifter, elf, vampire, and wolf shifter). Many characters in the Coven of Shadows and Secrets have direct ties to Isila's courts.
* *Lapis caelesti* - the sacred stones made by angels thousands of

years ago and given to seven witches to protect. They are great sources of power that can defeat the darkest evil.

* Ordo Aeternum - Also known as the OA, Ordo, or the Order. An elitist group of supernaturals who believe those of magical blood should rule the world (many believe they should enslave humans too).

* Ouroboros - The symbol of the Coven of Shadows and Secrets. It is a snake, formed in a circle, eating its own tail.

* Wolvea - royal wolves of Isila

CHAPTER ONE

MEREDITH

WHAT EXACTLY DID ONE PACK FOR A JOURNEY TO HELL?

I stepped back from my duffel bag, examining the contents skeptically.

"I still think I should go with you," Benedict, my feline familiar, drawled from where he lounged on my pillow.

The muscles of my jaw tightened. I'd expressly told him not to touch my pillows, or even the bed, but the cat never listened.

Annoyed with my familiar, and without the energy to fight where he chose to plant his rear end, I ignored him. There was no point in reiterating what I'd already said anyway.

According to Hans, we had to fly to Romania and wouldn't be able to slip a cat across the border. Not with our strict time constraints, anyway. If we were going to save Luca from shade poisoning, we had mere days to get to Hell and back.

My stomach clenched. Poor Luca. The coven master had been poisoned with shade venom and currently lay dying in the infirmary . . . and it was all my fault.

"Meredith!" Benedict hissed insistently. "I made a vow to your parents to look after you!"

My parents . . . If there was one thing that could get me to talk to my familiar, it was that.

Veering away from the carry-on, my gaze landed firmly on the cat. "Speaking of my parents. I saw a vision—a memory—with my father in it."

It said a heck of a lot that I hadn't remembered that little nugget sooner. So much had happened during the meeting at the Shadow and Secret's tomb that it consumed me.

"Did you?" Benedict asked, though his tone was less interested than I would have expected, given the topic. Maybe he thought I was trying to distract him, so he'd forget that I was leaving his butt here. Not a bad tactic, actually. "What was the memory about?"

"Dad and I were on the Yale campus. It couldn't have been too long before their accident." I thought back, trying to recall every tidbit that I could of the precious memory. "We were supposed to meet Mom for lunch. They both worked on campus, didn't they?"

The cat's ears perked up. "They did."

"What did they do?"

"I can't tell you that."

My lips parted in exasperation. "But you just confirmed they worked at Yale!"

"Only after *you* said so. Those are the rules, Meredith. You have to remember your past on your own."

I glared at him, and though we hadn't known one another for long, I could read his expression. It said that he wasn't budging.

Insufferable cat.

Rolling my eyes, I turned to the spread of clothing and supplies I'd strewn over the quilt. "Fine."

Silence fell between us while I tossed a few more items into the bag and finally zipped it up. I was as ready as I'd ever be for the journey.

"You know I would tell you more if I could," Benedict added softly. "I don't like keeping your past from you."

A resigned sigh left me, and a teensy bit of the tension bunching up my shoulders left me. "I wish they didn't force that promise on you. I don't see the point."

"Neither did I, to be quite frank." His light amber eyes glowed sincerely, and in that instant, the frustration simmering between us disappeared.

Then the doorbell rang.

"Rooms!" Shay hollered from downstairs, the one-two punch shattering my moment with Benedict. "Can you get that? It's probably Hans, and I'm not decent!"

"Yeah!" I yelled back, since the nephilim had to be talking to me and not Harper, who she didn't dare call 'Rooms'.

If she wasn't "decent", that meant Shay must have been the one I heard hogging all the shower water. Harper was probably irate about that, which meant the nephilim would be avoiding the wolf.

I left my room, jogged down the creaky, wooden steps, and opened the front door.

All the breath left me as I came face-to-face with not Hans, but Tobias. I swallowed thickly, as stunned by his handsome features as I had been the first time I laid eyes on him in an Egyptian prison.

The vampire's skin glimmered in the pale moonlight and his jaw was strong, seemingly chiseled from stone. Like normal, he wore a suit jacket tailored to his compact, muscular form. The navy color of the suit brought out the evergreen in his eyes beautifully.

As I studied him, my blood hummed with desire. I wished it wouldn't, but around the vampire I sometimes found it difficult to control my emotions.

"Stone," Tobias said in greeting.

"Yeah?" I asked, trying to act normal, like I wasn't feeling something shift between us, something I didn't understand.

The vampire's attention raked over my face, his nostrils flaring. "Is Shay packed and ready?"

I was sure that wasn't what he'd been planning to say. In fact, he looked like he wanted to say something else . . .

But he didn't, and now I was on the verge of awkward-as-hell, so I shrugged. "Uh . . . I don't kno—"

"I'll tell her you're here." Harper breezed out of the hall bathroom in a towel.

I blinked at her sudden appearance. *Wait, so Shay wasn't the one in the shower?*

"Might I wait inside?"

Stepping back, I invited Tobias into Shay's home, shutting the door behind him. Briefly, an awkward silence hung between us, and though I didn't usually mind silence, I sought to fill it.

"I thought you'd be Hans."

Annoyance fluttered across the vampire's face. Or maybe I'd imagined it? The expression was there and gone so fast, that I must have. Had I said the wrong thing? And how so?

"Are you prepared for your mission?" Tobias asked, his tone tight. "It's rather risky, you know."

Yes, some might call a journey to Hell to find an herb a touch *risky* . . . or stupidly dangerous. But I'd committed and I wasn't a woman to go back on my word.

"I have a bit of the lucimisia herb from the healers to help with the seeking, and I've packed a bag," I said. "That's about as ready as I'll ever be."

Tobias nodded, though he didn't seem to like my answer.

For the second time that night, an uncomfortable silence surrounded us, but this one, I knew exactly how to fill.

"Hey, I wanted to thank you," I blurted.

"Pardon?"

I drew back, remembering who I was addressing. Tobias was a vampire. I had no idea how long he'd been alive, but it could have easily been thousands of years. Though he passed as normal most of the time, sometimes the way he spoke hinted that he belonged to another era.

"I never thanked you for saving me that night in the museum. So . . . thanks." I looked away, unnerved by the intensity of his stare. "I appreciate it."

"You are welcome," he replied, though conflict rippled through his words. "Giving mortals vampire blood isn't usually a good idea, but you wouldn't have made it back to the tomb had I not done so."

That was what the healer said too.

Another pause prompted heat to creep up my neck and into my cheeks. What in the world was up with me? Was he feeling this weird connection between us too? What was it? I hadn't felt it in the meeting over the stolen Opal of Heaven. Or in the infirmary. Then again, everyone had been pretty preoccupied with the theft of a *lapis caelesti,* and in the healing wing Luca dying in front of our eyes. Both matters made it impossible to focus on anything else.

"Meredith," Tobias said, in a way that focused all of my attention on him yet again.

"What's up?"

"I believe that you should not go to Hell."

I blinked. That was the last thing I'd expected. Not that I'd had any clue *what* to expect, I never did with him, but whatever it was, it wasn't *that*. "Why?"

"You're not ready."

I snorted. "Like *anyone* is ready to go to Hell."

"You even less so," he replied, his tone harsher than before.

A memory of Tobias and me training suddenly returned. The way he'd dismissed me . . .

The skin on the back of my neck grew tight as the obvious solution presented itself. "You don't think I can do it, do you?"

"Let Hans go. And Gunner, if he must. You, however, should remain here."

Oh, he totally thought I couldn't do this. I hated when people underestimated me, and always strove to prove them wrong. Even if I, too, was conflicted—which was kind of the case here. I mean, who actually wanted to travel to the underworld?!

I was going mostly out of a sense of duty, and guilt. After all, the shade that poisoned Luca had been sent to S&S's headquarters for me. Not the mage.

Still, what the heck? Tobias and I were on the same team. The vampire and the mage were friends, and I'd seen Tobias's desire to help Luca as we stood around his bed in the infirmary.

Most importantly, I was a seeker, a supernatural made for finding shit! I was perfectly suited for the task of finding an herb in another realm, and as Daphne had told us many times, we had to act quickly. Luca had two weeks to live—tops.

I tilted my chin up to meet the vampire's stare. "I'm going, Tobias. I can do this, and I have been through plenty of dangerous landscapes. Plus, we have vials of the invisibility potion. Demons won't even see us."

I was still reeling from the discovery that an invisibility potion existed, but I didn't let that show on my face. It would only make him consider me even more naïve.

His lips pressed together, whitening. "As you were told, the elixir can only be used once in a day, or the user suffers adverse reactions. And it lasts merely an hour. You'll be in Hell far longer, and in that time, I fear that you'll only endanger the others."

Air escaped my lips, like he'd punched me in the gut, and I glowered at him.

"I will *not*," I ground out. "I—"

"Oh, it's you," Shay interrupted, and footsteps sounded down the hall, coming closer.

A moment later, she appeared beside me, and immediately my frustration with Tobias shifted to confusion. I cocked my head.

Shay had showered, done her hair, *and* taken the time to put on makeup, including red lipstick. I'd never seen her wear red lipstick.

"Who were you expecting?" I asked. Did she plan on sneaking in a hot date before she and Tobias caught their flight to Switzerland? Who got so done up for a redeye flight?

"No one." The apples of Shay's cheeks grew pink, and she held up her bag. "Anyway, I'm all packed, just have to put on my boots. You got us tickets, right, Stiff?"

"We leave in four hours, but traffic is bad, so we must get moving." Tobias ignored the jab as the nephilim grabbed her boots from the hall closet and sat on the step to pull them on.

"I'll wait in the car." With that, the vampire left, his shoulders set in hard, unforgiving lines. When he reached the vehicle, he threw one look back at me, making my breath thin.

He looked like he wanted to say something else, like he might come back, but then he shook his head and eased himself into the vehicle.

"What crawled up his butt?" Shay asked, coming to stand by me.

"He thinks I'm going to ruin the mission to Hell."

She pursed her lips. "You're not going to *ruin* it, but I do worry about all of you. I—"

A car screeched to a sideways stop out front, nearly slamming into the back of Tobias's parked vehicle. The vampire shot out of his seat and glared at the offender.

"What the heck, Hans?" Gunner yelled, emerging from the passenger side of the second car as if he couldn't get out fast enough. "You're drunk, aren't you?"

"Only had a beer or two," Hans shouted gruffly.

"No way. Can't believe you pulled this shit." Even from where I stood in the doorway, I saw Gunner's jaw tighten as he hovered outside the vehicle, passenger door still ajar. "Give me the keys. I'm driving."

"Fine!" The wizard exited the car, hurled the keys at Gunner who caught them one-handed.

I watched, eyes wide as he stomped partway down the street like a toddler throwing a tantrum. Gunner shook his head, and in a shocking turn of events, Tobias was the one to follow the wizard. He forced Hans to stop, and placed both hands on his shoulders, like he was giving Hans a pep talk.

"What's wrong with Hans?" I eyed the pair, with furrowed brows. As a coven, we'd been out for drinks, but I'd never seen him act like this. Not even when he'd been pissed off that Tobias ditched on helping him train me.

"And I'm confused by this." I gestured to the guys whispering to one another. "I thought they weren't friends?"

"They're not, not really," Shay said. "But they're kinda Luca's right and left-hand guys, with Gunner as a close third. They all help the coven master lead the coven, so there's respect there—though you wouldn't always know it." She sighed. "I feel like Hans is hiding something. But what?"

I eyed her sidelong, unable to deny the yearning in her tone. The softness of her expression.

Does Shay have a crush on Hans?

Before I could ask, Harper barreled down the hallway in a robe, her hair wet and disheveled.

"Are you two leaving right now? Without saying goodbye?!"

I jerked back. She cared that we were leaving? Where was my aloof wolfy roommate?

"Sorry," I said, shaking off my shock. "Hans and Gunner . . . um, arrived."

She peered outside at the men, her green eyes narrowing shrewdly at Hans's askew parking job. Tobias was still talking quietly to Hans, while Gunner had turned his back on the wizard and was now marching up the walkway toward the house.

"Sorry you had to see that, ladies." His face was still pinched with anger. "Hans had a bit too much to drink. He told me it was just a beer, but now I know better."

Letting out a judgmental *'hmm'* Harper turned to me. "Something is up with Hans. I felt it in the infirmary."

"Same," Shay echoed.

"Be careful around him, Meredith," Harper added.

"I will," I promised.

They were totally right. I didn't know *what* was wrong

with the wizard. Nor did I plan on digging for that answer, but I would keep my guard up. Emotions clouded reason, and where Hans, Gunner, and I were going, we couldn't afford a single poor judgment call.

"Meredith, come on!" Hans yelled, twirling gracelessly out of Tobias's grip and stomping back to the car.

"Let me get my bag," I called back and spun to run up the stairs, but Shay caught me first.

"We need a roomie hug."

Harper groaned, but it sounded forced, like she was putting on a show. Considering she'd run out here to say goodbye, I suspected that was the case. The wolf put up a tough front, but she liked the nephilim more than she wanted to admit. Me too, I liked to think.

When the wolf threw her arm around me and Shay, my lips curled upward, touched.

"Good luck getting into the bank," I whispered to the nephilim and then twisted to Harper. "And don't you get behind in your classes."

The wolf snorted. "Never. I'm more concerned about you boiling to death in Hell."

We hugged it out, and Shay squeezed my hand before trailing down the walkway.

Tobias saw her coming, and apparently having had enough of Hans—who was leaning against our car, tattooed arms crossing his chest—got in his vehicle to wait.

"We're in a rush too," Gunner reminded me gently.

"Be right back." I took the stairs two at a time, but once I got to my room and grabbed my bag, I paused, taking in the area. "Benedict?"

No answer. My lips pressed together. Usually, he'd be

lounging on his luxury cat bed, but as I searched, I noticed the window was open.

"That little shit!" I muttered.

He had left without saying goodbye. I thought we'd semi reached a truce, obviously not. If he left, he was still mad about not getting to go on the trip.

That cat was savage.

"Fine." I strode across the room to my bed. "Bye, Benedict. Not that you'll know I cared to say goodbye!"

I ran out of my room, ready to begin my mission.

TWELVE HOURS, THREE FLIGHTS, AND ZERO MINUTES OF SLEEP later, I was exhausted, hungry, and more than ready to get to our destination.

"Stone, can you take Hans's bag?" Gunner grunted.

I glanced at the guys. Hans appeared to have fallen asleep while walking, and Gunner was trying to nonchalantly carry him through the Romanian airport. Behind them, the wizard's bag dragged across the ground.

"Does he usually drink so much?" I snatched the backpack out of Hans's hands and nearly passed out from the alcohol fumes wafting off him.

He'd downed drink after drink on each of our flights. The only time he wasn't imbibing was when he passed out from the booze.

"Never seen him like this," Gunner admitted. "But we *are* goin' to Hell."

While terrifying, that didn't seem like enough of a reason to me. After all, Gunner and I were holding it together.

"Try to wake him up," I urged. "I doubt that they'll let a

sleeping adult through customs. And we don't have time for a drunk tank. Or whatever they have here."

Gunner snorted and shook the wizard, who awoke with a grumble. "Bro, you gotta pull it together for ten minutes."

"Whatever," Hans mumbled, standing on his own.

Miraculously, we got through customs by the skin of our teeth. With acting worthy of an Oscar, Hans somehow managed to pull himself together for those few minutes, and even charm the customs agent by speaking fluent Romanian.

Only when we got the rental car did I relax. We climbed in the tiny sedan, and Gunner took the wheel because Hans was still way too drunk to drive. The wizard rode shotgun, which left me in the cramped backseat with my bag.

"This is where I need to go, right?" The wolf handed his phone to Hans, who gave it a cursory glance and nodded.

Gunner started up the GPS, and minutes later we were off. We'd made it only five miles before Hans passed out again. Loud snores rang from his lips, suggesting that he wouldn't awake soon.

I exhaled. He wasn't being a dick to us, but something about the wizard's vibe had me on edge.

"You want music?" Gunner asked.

"Whatever you want. If it's okay with you, I'm going to try and rest."

The wolf had slept on the flight, but I hadn't.

"Sure thing. I won't bug ya." He grinned in the rearview mirror.

"Thanks." I leaned my head against the car door.

Cold seeped through the metal and plastic as we passed snow-covered yards, then open countryside. Mountains loomed before us. Apparently, that was where we were heading. Specifically, to the Carpathian Mountains, a place associated with vampires.

A flash of Tobias flitted through my mind, making my heart rate accelerate. I frowned, hating the reaction and the memory of him telling me that I'd ruin everything.

Why didn't he believe in me? And why did he have to be such a jerk about it?

And why do I still care?

That, more than anything, was really bugging the hell out of me.

Why was I letting him, of all people, get to me? I rarely cared so highly of what others thought. I was capable and strong. I'd been in and gotten out of so many binds in my life. Who was he to judge me? And why did I—?

Next to me, my bag moved, halting all my thoughts.

What the heck?

When it moved again, I slowly reached over and unzipped the duffel. My clothes lay there, looking slightly rumpled from the hours of travel, but other than that, nothing was amiss.

Another shift of my luggage made me suck in a breath.

Okay, something was totally up here.

I began to dig through the bag, and soon enough, I found the cause—Benedict was curled in a ball, sleeping at the bottom.

"Oh, *hell no*," I muttered, and shook the luggage.

The cat awoke with a start, his amber eyes flashing to me in alarm.

"I told you not to come," I scolded. "How did you even get through security?!"

"Is that a *cat* I smell?" From the driver's seat, Gunner peered at me in the mirror.

"It is," I fumed while Benedict sat up, his posture haughty as ever even though he was in deep shit.

"Thought I smelled one before but didn't know it was *on* you. Hard to tell in airports. Lots of scents."

"It's my familiar, and he stowed away. Explain, Benedict."

The cat's chin tilted up defiantly. "You said you didn't want me to come, but I disagreed."

"But you're my familiar! Doesn't that mean you listen to me?"

"Again, you're mistaking me for a normal cat. One that has little respect for itself."

I cringed. That was exactly what I was doing, and he'd made it clear before that familiars and pets were two totally different things.

Still, would it kill him to do what I asked when I had his best interests in mind?

"Cats don't listen so well," Gunner cut in from the front seat.

Benedict ignored him. "As I said, I'm not here to be at your beck and call, Meredith. I made a vow to help you, to protect you as best I can. I came to do that."

"But how did you do it?!"

Surely, the TSA would have stopped me had they seen a cat in my carry-on! For crying out loud, they'd taken Gunner's shampoo because it was an ounce over their precious size restrictions.

"Familiars have magic," Gunner offered. "Didn't you know?"

"What's your magic?" I glared at Benedict, who didn't look at all guilty.

Freaking cats!

"I can do a few varied things. Like becoming invisible for

periods of time, which was how I got through the airport. I can also call other felines to my aid. And now that your magic is free, I can find you with relative ease, which I do believe I've already mentioned."

"I-invisibility!" I sputtered, unable to believe he'd left out his most interesting power. "Did you use a potion too? How'd you get it?"

"No potion. My power is all natural, and quite handy when I need to be at your side. I've even gone to the coven with you when you failed to invite me. Rude, by the way."

What a sneak! He'd never been interested in my classes and led me to believe that he'd stayed home and waited for me every day. Even made me feel bad about it!

The balls on this cat . . .

"He's here now, Stone. No going back." Gunner shrugged, clearly not as bothered by Benedict's appearance as me. "Maybe Hans's dad will watch over him while we descend into the underworld."

"No." I glared at Benedict. "If he's so determined to come, I say we let him."

Benedict's lips curled into a feline smile. "I knew you'd eventually see it my way."

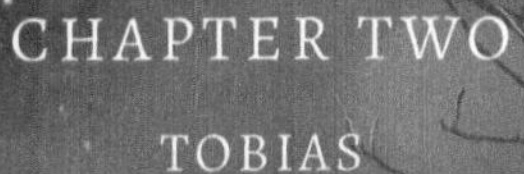

CHAPTER TWO

TOBIAS

Snow-dusted mountains rose on either side of the vehicle as Shay and I drove a winding Swiss road. Down the hillside, not so far away, a green-blue lake glimmered in the bright sunlight.

We were in a place of stunning beauty, but I couldn't enjoy a second of it. One thought, one person, occupied my existence.

The witch, Meredith. The person who was single-handedly responsible for me downing more blood in two weeks than I had in years. Since I was a newblood, to be exact.

Try as I might to banish thoughts of Meredith entering Hell and perishing amidst the damned, the visions had plagued me for hours.

"Dude, you need to chill. You're even more stiff than normal." From the passenger seat, Shay gestured to my knuck-les, now white from gripping the steering wheel tightly.

I hadn't even noticed.

"We're almost there. I need you to be relaxed, charismatic, and *convincing*," she reminded me.

Much to my annoyance, the half-angel wasn't wrong. The moment we entered *Le Bastion*, I had to be at my best which necessitated releasing all thoughts of the witch.

The coven had tasked Shay and me with gaining access to the looted vault, and hopefully, the name of the owner. Ironically, the former, though considered more invasive by most, would be easier. The coven was well known in supernatural circles, and if the elite bank had not made progress on their own, they might have wanted assistance in discovering who stole the Opal of Heaven.

Le Bastion would not, however, wish to give up the name of their clients. It was their first credo, their promise to anyone powerful enough to possess a vault inside their mountain.

But there was no denying that they were in a less powerful position than usual. Just the fact that the theft had been broadcasted on international television hinted that someone had tipped off the news stations. The thief? It was a distinct possibility. Whomever it was, they had forced *Le Bastion* to admit some of their faults. I couldn't recall a single other instance when that had occurred.

"So, you've been researching for a while. Do you know anything about the Opal?" the nephilim asked.

"Nothing," I said. "If I had, you know I would have shared it with S&S long ago. As far as I'm aware, there is no documentation on that specific sacred stone, nor its effects. Only the Pearl of Hell has stories attributed to it."

"That's what I thought too. But I hoped that after your research, you'd know more. Maybe even that you and Luca were making a quiet plan that we'd be filled in on later."

"Unfortunately not," I admitted, even though it killed me to have failed on such an important front. "Perhaps, if we can get the owner's name, they can shed light on the stone."

Shay stared out the window. "How do you know where to go, anyway?"

Her inquiry drew a sigh from me. The nephilim was a good partner, powerful in her angelic magic, which had the added benefit of being rare and therefore, unexpected. However, the downside to being paired with Shay was that she didn't stay quiet for long. And she asked *a lot* of questions. Some of which I usually hesitated to answer.

Like this one.

"Family obligations," I replied.

"Birth family or vampire?"

I cleared my throat. "Vampire."

When not in the company of my vampire family, I went by Tobias Blake Aston. From those in the coven, only two knew my vampire bloodline—that I was a royal. Luca, the coven master, and Hans, the half-wizard. The latter discovered my secret on the same mission in which I tasted the darkness flowing in his veins. As I drank from him, his blood revealed his truth. My lineage, on the other hand, had been revealed by a vampire who met his end shortly after.

On that same mission, we'd agreed to keep our secrets to ourselves. That had been years ago.

But now, in light of all that was going on in the world, I wasn't sure secrecy was wise any longer. At least not secrecy on my end.

The Laurents sought the celestial stones, and it was all too likely that, in time, the Blood would call me in to help. More immediately, the head of *Le Bastion* might voice my secret too. It would be best if I did so first.

"I'm a Laurent," I confessed, and Shay's gasp reverberated in the car. "My older brother has a vault in the bank, though

I've not been to that one. When I visited before, it was on behalf of my maker's family in Isila."

"You're a *royal* vampire?" She paused. "That makes so much sense! Damn, how did I not think of it before?"

Why would she? There were thousands of vampires in the world, and while they were all related to the Blood of Laurent—the original vampires, those born, not made—most were very distant relations. After three generations of separation from the original born vampires, the Blood wouldn't claim anyone, and no one would dare speak against them.

"I don't advertise it."

"Why not?"

"Baggage comes with being part of the royal family."

"Hmmm." Shay nodded, as if she understood. "You're going to tell the bank?"

"*Le Bastion* retains its employees for longer than most employers. My last trip here was twenty years ago, and I spoke to the head of the bank—*La Tête*. We might speak with the same person. Their positions are not exactly listed on the internet, so I can't be sure."

"That's why you told me."

"It would be foolish to make you look as if you don't have all the information."

Reaching a corner, we entered the town, and I turned down the snow-lined street and wound through the town. Though it had been years, I recalled the location of the bank like it was yesterday. When I got to the correct street, I drove all the way to the end of the lane, up to an old stone building abutting a mountain on the edge of a posh village. I parked in front of the building. "We're here."

"How cozy." Shay pulled her white, faux fur jacket closed around her and exited the car.

We'd purchased the coat in a duty-free shop at the airport. Unlike myself, Shay had not come prepared to enter *Le Bastion*, but for a regular mission. Underneath the jacket, she wore clothing more suitable for action—S&S members often had to make quick escapes—but *Le Bastion* required those who crossed its threshold to dress as though they belonged there. The luxurious jacket did well to hide Shay's attire, and had the added benefit of suiting the cold environment nicely.

"They built the vaults into the mountain," I said, joining her outside. The midday light was practically blinding, reflecting off the white powder. "It's secure."

"Usually."

"Yes, usually."

We walked to the front door, guarded by two men who were mountains unto themselves. Judging by their scents, one was a shifter and the other one of my kind.

"*Bonjour.*" The shifter held up a hand in greeting.

"Hello," I replied in English for Shay's sake. She spoke many languages, but French was not one of them.

"Do you have an appointment?" the man asked, switching languages.

"We don't," I admitted as we stopped before the pair. "We're from the Coven of Shadows and Secrets, here to assist *Le Bastion*, if *La Tête* will permit it."

The guards didn't appear to recognize the coven's name, but that didn't surprise me. The last time I arrived here, no guards stood outside. Were these two a result of the recent theft?

"Is Oskar Accola still *La Tête* of *Le Bastion*?" I pressed.

"He is."

"Please inform him Tobias Laurent has arrived on behalf of Shadows and Secrets."

The vampire's eyes flashed with recognition of the royal name, and he reached for his walkie talkie, murmuring into it.

I clasped my hands behind me and waited.

"Mr. Accola will wait for you in the lobby," the vampire said, not even a full thirty seconds later. He stepped to the side and opened one of the double doors. The shifter mirrored his partner, opening the other door.

I cast Shay a sidelong glance. She nodded, understanding. For us, getting inside the exclusive bank was the easy part. What we had to do next, however, would take much more persuasion than a powerful name.

We strolled into the building, down the long hallway that led to the heart of the bank. The corridor was grand, with white marble flooring veined with gold, glittering candelabras lining the wall, and paintings of past bank heads every few feet.

On the way, Shay and I also passed by the office of lower-level employees. From my previous visit, I understood those who truly possessed power held offices deeper in the mountainside.

The corridor opened into the lobby, and a soft gasp left Shay's lips. Though I was not as struck, I still recalled my first time here—I'd acted the same way.

We stood at the edge of a cavern, dripping with white marble and gold and candlelight. A chandelier the diameter of an eight-person dining table hung from the ceiling in the center, illuminating even the farthest flung edges of the circular space.

Seven doors rounded the lobby and from the one opposite us, *La Tête*, Oskar Accola, emerged.

"Tobias! It's been a long time!" Accola's power, prodigious among wizards, filled the room, and a smile as wide as the

Thames crossed his face as the Swiss banker swaggered our way in a refined bespoke suit.

I rolled my shoulders back and met him in the center. Shay followed, a half step behind me.

"I hear that you're here on behalf of Shadows and Secrets?" Oskar asked. "The outside guard claims you wish to be of assistance."

"If you'll have us." Clasping his hand, I firmly shook it. Accola's snow and rosemary scent washed over me, somehow reminding me of Meredith, even though he smelled nothing like her. "Oskar, this is my colleague, Shay."

"It would honor *Le Bastion* to accept the help of your coven." He beamed, clasping hands with Shay. "I assume you'll want to gain access to the vault that has recently been . . ." He cleared his throat, as if having to force out the next word. "Plundered."

My lips compressed before I caught myself. That had been too easy. I'd believed that we'd have to talk our way down to the safes.

Oskar's simple acceptance could mean only one thing. The bank had no leads on who had taken the Opal of Heaven, and though I doubted they understood the true nature of the gem that had been taken, they were desperate to retrieve the property. They needed to reinstate their reputation—as much as possible—and finding the stolen property would be a start.

"What are we waiting for, then?" Shay asked. "Lead the way."

"As you wish, *Mademoiselle*. Please, remain here." With a dip of his head, Oskar veered toward a door on the far left. He pressed his hand against the surface, and white light wreathed his body, extending five feet in each direction.

"Warder?" Shay whispered.

"Only the best for *Le Bastion*," I confirmed.

The magic pulsed, and the door opened to reveal a room filled with hundreds of keys. Closing the door halfway behind him, Oskar slipped into the depths of the space, his footsteps growing more distant.

"Keys, huh?" Shay mused. "How antiquated."

Truly, it was, but *Le Bastion* relied on many types of technologies and powers to keep their clients' assets safe. Even the most archaic kinds.

"Did the thief use that key?" Shay asked when the wizard reappeared with a gold skeleton key in his hand.

"They did not." Oskar's pleasant expression faltered, and he gestured to the room he'd exited. "No one breeched that space."

Not that the security of the key-room did the bank any bloody good.

Oskar waved for us to follow him across the circular lobby, toward the door at a 90° angle from his office.

"I'm glad you came prepared." Oskar nodded to Shay's jacket as he reached the door. "The vaults are quite cold."

"I've heard."

Once again, Oskar placed his hand on the door he wished to open. A light pulsed, causing a hidden panel to slide out of the wall. I eyed it. Facial recognition.

Leaning closer, Oskar brought his face in line with the scanner. A beam of red ran over his traditionally Swiss features, then a green light blinked to life.

As the door *snicked* open, frigid, stale air rushed out of the mountain's depth. Shay shivered, pulling the jacket tighter around her.

"Watch your step," Oskar said as he descended the stairs.

"Down?" Shay whispered. "Isn't it enough that the vaults are in a mountain?"

"Recent events would dictate not," Oskar's tone turned sour.

We followed him, every step taking us deeper into the belly of the mountain. Though it should have been dark, with each step, lights illuminated a few feet in front and behind us, lining the walls.

On the way down, we passed three barriers made of lasers crisscrossing at random. At each barrier, Oskar waved the key in front of us and the lasers disappeared, only to reappear once we'd passed.

Those had not been in use during my last visit. Had they been in place before the theft? After a moment of thought, I decided it was likely. Even *Le Bastion* couldn't implement new protections so quickly. So the thief had somehow rendered a key obsolete and gotten past the lasers. Intriguing.

After descending what had to be five floors, we reached the bottom and found ourselves in another circular landing. Ten heavy, iron doors lined the walls.

"How many clients does *Le Bastion* have?" Shay asked, her gaze sweeping over the doors.

"I cannot say." Oskar arched an eyebrow at her before walking to the one across from us. Again, an electronic panel appeared, and he placed his finger on it to open the door.

"How the hell did they get in?" Shay whispered.

To that, I shrugged. The feat did seem incredible.

"This way," Oskar guided.

The moment we were on the other side of the doorway, my heart gave a single hard beat as a person vanished into a wall. I blinked, but no, they were gone. Had I really even seen them?

"Oskar . . . Am I seeing things?"

In answer, a smirk tilted his lips. "They weren't quick enough to hide this time."

"And they are?"

"Specters. Only the oldest vaults have them guarding their possessions." He eyed me as if to say not even my family was worthy of specters.

Now that was of note. If the Laurents were not elite enough to possess ghostly guards, then who was? The desire to learn who this vault belonged to burned within me.

Eight vaults lined this corridor, and Oskar took us to the one at the very end—labeled 004.

"We're here," Oskar announced.

Shay shot me a look that plainly said *'finally'*, as Oskar placed the key in the old-fashioned lock, and the door clicked open.

"After all *that*, you use a normal key?" She gestured back the way we'd come. "Actually, worse, a skeleton key?"

"We enchant each key to work for certain people. Only the vault holder, certain *Le Bastion* employees, such as myself, and those in the vault owner's bloodline—should they perish before passing on the vault—be able to use the keys." He frowned. "Which makes it all the more infuriating that someone didn't even need the key to break in."

Oskar pressed the door open, and before us, a cavernous space filled with gold and gems was revealed. My eyes widened. I'd seen wealth. Possessed it too. I'd also stood in vaults larger than this one, brimming with treasure, but the fact that this wealth remained *here* only hammered home a single fact, the thief had known what they were looking for.

They'd passed up gold, easy money, for one gemstone.

Not just any gem, though, the Opal of Heaven.

"Take a look around for clues," Oskar urged. "I'll be right here."

I motioned for Shay to enter before me, which she did, her lips parting in awe.

Narrow paths cut through mounds of gold coins, and as we walked deeper into the vault, more treasures emerged. There were staffs that appeared Isila-crafted. A crown encrusted with red rubies, and a crystal ball that gleamed as bright as the moon on a starless night. The last item gave me pause. Few supernatural orders could use crystal balls.

Does a witch own this vault?

Dividing to conquer, Shay and I wound our way down the paths, scrutinizing the contents of the vault with each step. We were searching for any clues that might lead us to learn who the owner, or the thief, was. After we'd traveled the last pathway through the riches and come up blank, we turned to one another.

"I found nothing enlightening," I admitted. "Then again, I'm not sure we'd realize if they left something or not, considering how packed this place is." I gestured to the gold climbing from floor-to-ceiling.

"Agreed. Overall, this was a bust," Shay said. "Next stop, try to get a name from Oskar?"

"Let's wait until we get to the top."

"Duh. I'm not about to be stuck down here!"

We made our way back to the vault's door, to where Oskar was waiting. Hope glinted, plain in his eyes. "Anything?"

I shook my head. "No luck, my fri—"

Shay's loud gasp interrupted me. "Tobias!"

She darted to the door, and knelt by the threshold. One trembling finger showed me what we'd previously missed.

Etched into the wall of the vault, and illuminated by a patch of light seeping in from the hallway, was the Sigil of Lucifer.

"The same group," I muttered, kneeling next to her.

"What is *that*?" Oskar positioned himself behind us.

"The sign we were looking for. We found this same symbol at the site of another plundered location." I stood.

"Who is it? Can you apprehend them?" Oskar's tone rose with excitement.

"Actually, we're not sure yet," Shay replied, and I turned in time to see the wizard's hopeful expression fall.

"Why ever not?" Accola pressed.

"We don't know exactly who they are, but the fact that they stole an opal out of this bank and another stone from elsewhere," I side-stepped giving him the stones' true names, "is telling."

"That's all they took, right?" Shay pressed. "An opal?"

Oskar's face grew red. "Are you telling me you truly have no idea who these people are? That I let you down here for nothing?" Spit flew from his mouth and his professional composure cracked. "You led me on . . . allowed me to believe . . . Get out!"

"Oskar," I interjected, my tone firm, "we said we would *try* to discover the thief. Not that we had a hunch."

"I said, *get out!*"

Exchanging glances, Shay and I exited the vault which Oskar promptly shut and locked behind us. Once it was secure, he marched down the corridor. Keeping our distance, Shay and I followed, biding our time until our next ask.

La Tête didn't say a word as he climbed the stairs, breaking each defense with a glower or a punch of his finger into the fingerprint pad. When we reached the top floor, he was still furious, and whirled around to face us.

"I must request that you leave *Le Bastion*."

"Actually." Shay stepped forward, a sheepish look on her face. She was trying the innocent act, a good idea. "We wondered if you wouldn't be able to give us the name of the vault holder? We hoped to question him or her. Maybe they will recognize the symbol?"

Oskar's face turned three shades redder and he drew himself up until he appeared six inches taller. "Absolutely not. Our clients' identities are sacred to us! Now, I must insist that you leave *Le Bastion*!"

This would not do.

I placed a hand on Shay's shoulder, and she let out a sigh. She wasn't keen on compelling Oskar and making enemies with *Le Bastion*. Truth be told, I wasn't either, but we needed the information.

What must be done, must be done.

"Oskar," I whispered, making eye contact with him. "We know it's against the rules, but be reasonable. Your client might know what the symbol means. It's imperative that Shadows and Secrets discover this information, not just for *Le Bastion*'s benefit. For the world."

"*Leave*," Oskar simmered.

"Not until we get what we came here for." I closed in until our noses hovered inches from each other. I accessed my power of compulsion, looking straight into his eyes. "Tell me the vault holder's name."

But instead of spitting out a name, Oskar did not give into my compulsion. Rather, he smirked derisively. "You think I'd allow you on the premises, down into the looted vault, without defending myself against your powers of compulsion, Tobias? I drank an elixir to negate your ability the moment the guards announced a Laurent's presence. We keep it on hand."

Bloody hell.

"Oskar," I tried again. "See sense."

"I've already broken one rule in hopes that you two would find a clue we missed, Tobias. I won't tell you the name of one of *Le Bastion*'s most exclusive clients. That information is for me to know, and me alone." He clapped his hands right in my face and footsteps filled the lobby. "In fact, I won't do a damned thing more for you."

I twisted to find six armed guards closing in on us.

"Oskar!" I turned back to try again. "I—" The rest of my plea stuck in my throat as a sharp point dug into my back. A stake.

"You're coming with us, Laurent," a man growled.

Eyes narrowed, I glared at Oskar. "So, it appears I am."

CHAPTER THREE

HANS

MY EYES FLUTTERED OPEN TO REVEAL A LAND I KNEW IN MY BLOOD and my bones. A rough and rugged country so different from the place I currently called home.

Snow spread before me, only a couple of inches deep in this part of the mountain range, but it expanded as far as the eyes could see, intensifying the pounding at my temples.

I groaned. Why had I gone on a bender? It wasn't going to change the inevitable—my return to my village.

And now I felt like a donkey's asshole.

My eyes closed. How many times had I heard my father utter those same words, when Domnul Balan pressed him to have one too many ales at the tavern down the road? Only a few hours in Romania and I was already sinking back into village-speak.

"Need an aspirin?" Meredith asked from the backseat.

"Got a bottle?" Slowly, because moving hurt, I twisted toward her. "And water? Anyone—what the hell?"

Meredith's familiar sat on top of her duffel bag, blinking at me with his large, light amber eyes.

"How did he get here?"

Meredith huffed. "Stowaway. He can go invisible, so he hid in the car and then traipsed through the airport until he could sneak into my bag. Walked right past security! I need to pay better attention to my stuff. What if someone put a bomb in there?!"

I blinked. "That's a stretch. The drugs?"

Pulling a bottle of aspirin from a side pocket in the bag, she gave me two.

"Don't skimp." I thrust my hand out again. "Two more."

"That's not good for you."

"What are you, my doctor?"

"Give it to him, Stone," Gunner drawled. "The man's having a rough go. Judgin' by the drinking, I betcha' he's preparing to meet some demons. A couple of extra aspirin ain't gonna kill him."

Gunner had no idea how on point he really was.

"Don't blame me if your liver gives out." Meredith plucked two more pills from the bottle and placed them in my palm.

Down the hatch went the drugs, and I resumed my earlier position—cheek pressed against the cold window. These pills needed to kick in quickly, because we were less than an hour from my village.

Part of me felt bad for leaving it up to Gunner and Meredith to find their way there. We'd been traveling for nearly a full day, and they looked exhausted. Despite that, and them not reading Romanian, they'd figured it out though.

Thank the Goddess, because I hadn't been prepared to help anyone.

Coming home wasn't something I'd ever planned on doing. My village, idyllic though it may seem on the surface, changed when the moon grazed the sky. Under the light of *lună*, the village of Minim was the stuff of nightmares. Of course, some of those nightmares were only in my memories, but that didn't make them any less real.

Minim had been the Novak clan's home for centuries, but I didn't love the place. The village had made me hard, made me hate a part of myself. During my childhood there had only been a few lights that I could count on.

My family. The wolf pack on the edge of town. A couple of friends who didn't care what others thought. For the most part, the villagers had taken too much time to trust me, and that had done irreversible damage.

An aching hurt that would never go away, no matter how many miles I put between me and Romania, awakened. I swallowed, trying to down the pain, and succeeding only in dimming it to a low thrum.

"There's a gas station up ahead," I told them as we passed a mailbox painted red and in the shape of a chess pawn. The hermit who lived in the house down the twisted mountain lane was a chess master and recluse.

"We don't need gas," Gunner drawled.

"I need to pick up a few things." I might be reluctant to come home, but I was here and I wouldn't arrive empty-handed.

Ten minutes later, we stopped at the gas station and I bought half their snack aisle. I returned to the car, loaded with chocolates, gummies, and most important of all, marzipan.

Father adored marzipan, and though the sweets were against my personal dogma of *'sugar is poison'*, I hoped they would be a sufficient olive branch. Father, I wasn't so worried about, but *she* would require all the softening I could bring in the door.

"Did you leave any for others?" Meredith asked when I tossed the bag full of candy in the backseat.

"We'll need this. You'll see."

Gunner studied me in a serious way that didn't normally grace his face, before he began driving. "You gonna tell us what we're walking into?"

"You'll find out soon enough."

My insides turned to ice. When they learned the truth, could I count on them to keep it quiet? Gunner and I were pals. We shared beers from time to time and regularly played pool, so I could probably trust him. However, I barely knew Meredith.

Far too soon, we rounded a corner on the mountain road, and my village appeared. Snow glistened, and red roofs popped in the field of white.

Meredith leaned forward. "It looks like a storybook!"

"People in the city visit here for that sense of wonder," I admitted.

"The way you're acting, I was kinda expecting an ominous Dracula castle." Gunner chortled.

"Same," the witch admitted. "But this is beautiful."

"Looks can be—" A figure strolled onto the road, fifty feet in front of our car. "Watch out!"

Gunner slammed on the brakes, skidding to a stop on the ice. The back fishtailed, and Benedict hissed.

"Hold on!" Gunner grunted, fighting for control of the car. For a southern boy, he righted the vehicle with surprising speed.

I exhaled when we skidded to a stop five feet from where the person—a girl with long blonde curls—stood.

"Aw, hell!" Gunner drawled, his hand straying to the door, and starting to open it. "I feel so bad. I—"

"Stop." I pulled him back as the young woman's dark eyes latched with mine. The corners of her lips curled up ever so slightly. My heart raced.

"What? I nearly ran her over!"

"She wanted to get your attention."

"That's insane. How could you know that?" Meredith accused.

"Because that's my sister."

"Wha—for true?" Gunner asked, eyes wide as if he couldn't believe it.

I opened my door. "Stay here."

The other two began to argue, but I was already out of the car and casting a locking spell on the vehicle, trapping them inside. Ice crunched beneath my feet as I walked toward my sister, her intense glare never waning.

"Nicoleta," I greeted when we were face to face. "You sensed me coming?"

"I did."

"Why not meet us at home? You nearly gave my friend a heart attack."

A smirk curved her lips. "Waiting at home is never any fun."

My brows furrowed. The way she said it, sing-song-like but with a growl of darkness, made me think I wouldn't like her ideas of fun.

"Why are you here, Brother?"

"We have to go to Hell . . . for a mission."

My sister's eyes widened. "No!"

"Yeah, so I planned to stay in the village for the night, and then head into the woods tomorrow."

"Hans . . ."

I shook my head, needing to say what I needed to say

before we got off track. "Nicoleta, they don't know what I am, what *we* are, and I'd like to keep it that way."

"Why?" She frowned. "There's power in the darkness."

"I do fine without it."

My sister, younger than me by ten years, studied me with eyes as dark as a moonless night. In the time that I'd been gone, her childhood had flashed by, been used up. She was now a young woman of seventeen, and from what I could gather from my father's phone calls, a wild one.

"Please, Nicoleta. I know I haven't been the brother you deserve, but please keep quiet. For me? For our family?"

She grabbed my hand, assuring me. "My family means everything to me."

A relieved breath left my lungs.

"Speaking of family, Father will be happy to see you. You should go. I'll meet you there."

With that, Nicoleta walked across the road, disappearing into the woods surrounding the village. I watched the spot where she'd vanished into the trees, a chill that had nothing to do with the cold washing over me.

The sound of pounding broke my concentration, and I turned to the car to find Gunner and Meredith both glaring at me, the witch thumping her fist against the window. I walked back to the vehicle, already dreading having to answer for what I'd done.

"What the hell was that about?" Meredith demanded as soon as I slid into the car. "You locked us in here!"

I opted for the most basic of excuses. "I wanted a private word with my sister. You'll meet her soon."

"I better buy her a bottle of wine or somethin'," Gunner mumbled, still looking shocked that he'd nearly run over her. "Old Ones save me. I feel awful."

"She said not to worry about it," I lied. "And no wine. She doesn't drink."

Another lie, which he'd probably discover soon, but, if at all possible, I wanted to minimize the alcohol where my sister was concerned. According to our father, Nicoleta frequented the pub just as I had as a teenager. Unlike me, however, she got loose lips when she drank. It was one of the few traits she'd inherited from our father.

"Aw, hell." Gunner began to drive. "Well, I'll figure something out. I wanna walk in the town, anyway."

Cold trickled down my spine. There was always the chance nothing strange had happened lately in Minim, but I wasn't counting on that. Somehow, I'd have to make sure he was in our family's house before dark, without giving away one of the quirks of my home. Villagers had ways of protecting themselves, and recognized any signs of darkness lurking, but tourists didn't. They were often targets.

"I'll go with you," I said.

"I want to come too," Meredith added. "Can Benedict?"

I turned and eyed the cat, who had snuggled back into the witch's bag and was dozing again. "Might be cold for him after the sun goes down. We'll make it an early walk."

There, that ought to do it.

Once we reached the edge of the village, I began directing Gunner through the streets. When he made the last turn down my street, the breath gathered in my chest. My father's house looked the same—better, actually, than it had when I left. The paint was fresh, the windows no longer had ripples in the glass, saying that he'd upgraded to double-pane ones.

Pride bloomed inside me, a nice change from the anxiety tightening my lungs. He'd been using the money I sent him to spruce it up. At least I was doing some good for the family.

"Pull into the driveway. Next to those two cars." I motioned to the vehicles that my father must be working on for the neighbors.

He often tinkered with cars in his free time, and had taught me to love doing so too when I was younger. Days spent with oil slicking my hands and the sound of newly fixed engines revving were some of my most cherished memories. I wished we'd have time for such bonding this time.

The moment Gunner parked, Meredith opened the door and jumped out of the vehicle.

"I'm so sick of being in the car!" She stretched her arms and legs. "It is cold, though, isn't it? Glad I brought my thicker jack—"

The door to the home flew open, and a robust giant of a man appeared. "Hans! *fiul!*"

"*Tată,*" I breathed, jumping out too and going to hug my father for the first time in years.

His powerful arms wrapped around me, tears filling his eyes as he kissed me on both cheeks. "I didn't know you were coming! Look at your arms!"

He took in my tattoo sleeves, only slightly disapproving. I'd sent photos of the artwork I wore, but my father still did not approve.

"And you brought a girlfriend?" My father shifted gears, looking over Meredith. "Or a *wife*?"

I blinked, but why should that confuse me? Of course, he was going to go there. Father was a family man. He wanted a wife and kids for me. Truth was, I wanted those things too, but the timing had never been right.

"Meredith is a friend, a witch, Father." I did not mention she was a seeker. That was meant to remain hidden until we absolutely had to expose Meredith's power to the world.

"And Gunner," I motioned to the wolf who was last to get out of the car, "is also a friend, a wolf shifter. I work with them."

"Ah." A crestfallen expression flitted across his wide face, but, as usual, my father recovered quickly. "American?"

"Yes."

"I will get even more chances to brush up on my English!" He waved the other two closer. "Come in! Come in!"

"Father," I hurried, "they don't know all of what Nicoleta and I are. Please, stay quiet about that."

Unlike my sister, he nodded, understanding. The villagers accepted us now, but it hadn't always been that way. Surely, those early days of hardship were burned into my father's memory.

When the others approached, I introduced them to my father, Domnul Novak, the baker of Minim.

True to his good nature, my father ushered them into his home and set the table, offering them fresh-baked bread, butter churned down the road, and mugs of ale. Gunner accepted happily, and Meredith relaxed, sipping ale while my father bustled about the kitchen.

Only Benedict appeared on edge, and I thought I understood why.

"Father, I told you that my companions were supernatural?"

"Of course."

"The cat is too. This is Meredith's familiar."

"Thank goodness," Benedict breathed. "Being around normal humans is so difficult. I forgot to ask Hans and hadn't gotten close enough to determine what you were yet, Domnul Novak."

"A familiar! Haven't seen one of those in ages." My father

beamed at the cat. "I'm a wizard, like Hans, but I never had a familiar. No one in our village has one."

"We are not that common," Benedict replied, the tension in his body gone now.

"Hans, my man, where's your sister?" Gunner asked, stuffing a bite of bread into his mouth and closing his eyes briefly, in heaven. "I still need to apologize. Even though you said it was fine, I just gotta. My pa would kill me if I didn't."

Father gave me a curious look.

"Nicoleta walked in front of our car. Gunner had to slam on the brakes."

"Ah," Father said, not looking at all concerned. If my sister had wanted to, she could have stopped the car. She possessed enough power to stop a semi-truck barreling toward her. "She should return soon."

As though his words were magic, the front door opened and Nicoleta swept into the house—all confidence and twinkling dark eyes.

"Whoa," Gunner breathed, taken by my sister's beauty . . .

And the invisible dark magic flowing off her in waves.

I glared at her, and she pulled it back. A bit. My sister was never one to play by others rules, but she respected Father and me. Or at least she had respected me. I could no longer be sure of that.

"Welcome!" Nicoleta gushed, aiming for Gunner first, recognizing that he'd be more easily manipulated. "I thought our guests might like these!"

From behind her back, a bouquet appeared. The black tips of the red petals hinted that she'd conjured them.

Meredith smiled, but Gunner looked sheepish. "I should have bought you flowers, Miss. I nearly ran you over!"

"No harm done," my sister assured with a flirty, dismissive wave. "I should have checked the road."

Or not been lying in wait.

"What flowers are these?" Meredith asked, staring at the bouquet. "I'm surprised you can get any way up here, it's so cold. Does someone in the village have a greenhouse?"

Her observations impressed me as much as her interest in the blooms surprised me. Was Meredith a botanist?

"A neighbor grows them in a sunroom," Nicoleta lied, the words so convincing that if I hadn't been watching Father's growing frown, even I would have believed her. "I'll put them in water."

Swaying her hips, she hummed a Romanian folk tune on her way to the sink. From beneath it, she pulled out a vase, plopped the blooms in, and filled it with water. All the while, a faint sweet scent permeated the air, enchanting Gunner until he couldn't take his eyes off my sister.

My jaw ground from side-to-side. Normally, if anyone stared at my sister like that, I'd be pissed at them, but not now. Nicoleta was only seventeen, but she understood what she was doing and because of her powers, she could bait a man better than most women. Which was exactly what she was doing to Gunner, who didn't know a thing about her.

My poor father's cheeks glowed red. He didn't know how to handle his temptress daughter. He never had, even when she was a young girl able to curl others' desires to her whims. While I didn't know how to contain Hurricane Nicoleta either, I didn't need one of my colleagues falling prey to her, so I took the most direct route.

I marched over to the sink and leaned over her shoulder, close enough to count her eyelashes. My jaw was clenched so tightly the headache I'd gotten rid of threatened to make a reappearance. "Stop using your power."

"Why? They're magical too. Like us, Brother." Nicoleta smirked, knowing full well no one in this room was like us.

"Meredith is a witch, and Gunner a wolf, and you're trying to lure him. I demand that you stop using your powers."

Turning off the sink, she whirled, her blonde hair whipping me in the face. "You no longer make demands in this house!"

"*Nicoleta,*" Father warned.

"Why do you defend *him*?!" My sister threw her hands in the air, all pretense of being happy and sweet, gone. "He left us! He's been gone *ten* years, and thinks he can come back to tell me what to do?!"

At the table, my friend's charmed expressions faded to unease. They shared a wary glance. I wished that I could push them out the door, but that would lead to more explaining later.

"Hans immigrated to America for a better life," my father scolded. "He's a good boy and provides, so that we have a very good life."

"Oh, shoot me now! If I have to hear one more time how good the brother who abandoned me is, I'll vomit." She turned her eyes on me, and my breath hitched.

A ring of red curled around her normally black irises.

"Nicoleta," I pleaded, placing my back to Gunner and Meredith. "Stop."

"Stop?" she whined like a child. "You're asking me to stop? Grow a pair, Hans! I had to!"

"This once . . . think of me."

"Like you thought about me when you left a child, your little sister, all alone in a Romanian village that hated her?" Her gaze darted to the pair at the table, but I didn't dare look back. "You left us to learn to control your power. To get stronger. But what was I to do? Who else would teach me to control my demon magic?"

"*What?!*" Gunner shouted.

"Oops, did I let that slip?" Nicoleta sang, falsely remorseful. She sashayed around me, and I turned to find Gunner's tanned face had gone white, while Meredith looked confused.

Benedict, however, exhibited the most intense reaction. He glared at my sister, back arched and tiny teeth bared.

"Cool it, kitty," my sister growled, approaching the table. "I take it you two know nothing about my brother and me. How we're Hellblooded?"

"Uh," Gunner choked out, "no."

Meredith shook her head. She was too new to this world to understand the consequences of what that meant. Though she didn't have any trouble reading the room.

"Well, it's the truth. Papa here fell for our beautiful mother's graces." Nicoleta twirled, and ribbons of black magic spun from her, enchanting and horrible all at once, before dissipating into the air. "After all, few women can hold a candle to the famed Lilith."

"L-lilith? Like *Lucifer's* bride?" Gunner asked, his voice raspy. His eyes strayed to me for confirmation. "That's your mother?"

Why I'd trusted Nicoleta, I wasn't sure, but the truth was out now, and there was nothing to be done about it but own it.

I exhaled. "Yes, Lilith, the demoness of lore, is my mother."

CHAPTER FOUR

TOBIAS

I KICKED OPEN THE DOOR TO MY ROOM, TRYING TO IGNORE THE sensation of the *Le Bastion*'s guards' hands on my skin.

We'd gotten so bloody far! Learning that the same group that stole the Pearl of Hell plundered the vault in *Le Bastion*, was incredibly valuable information, but it wasn't enough. Shay and I had failed to obtain the most important piece of the puzzle, and that infuriated me.

Reaching for the hem of my shirt, I prepared to step into the shower and wash the guard's stench off, when a knock came at the door.

"Tobias! We need to talk!"

I snorted. The nephilim had also been furious over our failure. So much so that she refused to speak during our short drive to the hotel. But now she wanted to talk?

She's as irritating as the witch.

My eyes closed in frustration. Why did Meredith insist on popping into my head? Could I not get a moment of peace?

The knocking came again. "I'm not leaving!"

"Fine," I huffed and went to open the door. "You rang?"

"We can't take this lying down."

"What do you suggest we do, Shay? Accola will not see us again. Our only other option is to break into *Le Bastion* and we both know that's not happening."

Her eyes lit up. "Actually, that's not a bad idea."

A groan escaped me. "Truly, *it is.* You saw their security. Not to mention, if we got caught, they'd probably try to pin the first theft on us. Oskar is furious enough to do so."

My attempt at compulsion had no doubt tipped him over the edge. People didn't like being controlled. Men and women in powerful positions, even less so.

"Oh, screw him." Shay walked to my bed and perched on the end. A pensive look took over her face, one that I wanted to wipe off because it was sure to only cause trouble. "He wanted us to help him, without giving us anything in return. I hate people like that."

"Your kind really shouldn't hate."

"*Half*-angel."

"I doubt that more every day."

She rolled her eyes. "You can't tell me you're fine with not knowing who that vault belongs to?"

"Of course, I'm not. But I've been around long enough to know institutions like *Le Bastion* are not to be trifled with. Their clients are among the most powerful supernaturals in this world. In the other realms, too."

"You're scared."

"If you'd ever been to Isila, met my family, and the type of people who hold vaults in *Le Bastion*, you would hesitate to meddle in their affairs too."

It had been a long time since I'd visited the world where my kind originated. That was by design, and I was not itching to return.

"Who are you most scared of there?" The fury on the nephilim's face had lessened a touch, replaced by genuine curiosity.

"My kind. The mages. The Winter Court of the fae. Dragons." I snorted. "Even the wolvea that rule the Isle of Wolves. In truth, they're *all* deadly—some more than others."

"You think someone from there owns the vault that got broken into?"

"I can't be sure, but if they are the owners, be certain that we're courting our doom by needling without permission." My hand rubbed the back of my neck, trying to melt the tension away. "It's one thing to compel Oskar into giving us the information. Then, at the very least, the owner of the vault would see us as an ally to the bank. Oskar would be sure to *spin* giving up their identity that way. But by taking their personal information outright, we're little better than the thief who stole the Opal of Heaven. Royals hide things for a reason. I'd much rather the information be given."

"And put Accola to blame."

I shrugged. "Sure."

"I wonder if the owner even knows what they really had?" Shay mused.

In truth, I'd questioned that too. To own one of the seven *lapis caelesti* was a great honor. It also placed a target on your back.

Slapping the sides of her thighs, Shay stood, shattering my thoughts. "Whether they did, or not, we still need to figure out who the owner is. If someone broke into their vault, and took only the Opal, that means the thief knew exactly what they'd find."

"Yes," I agreed, not liking the glint in her eye.

"Well, how? Did the owner slip? Or was it the bank that

screwed up?" Shay shook her head. "Only the top bank officials see the deepest vaults, and I can't see Oskar slipping."

No. *La Tête* wouldn't slip.

"If he won't help us," Shay continued, "we have to do it ourselves."

The nephilim must be touched in the head.

"Shay—"

"If you're too scared, that's fine." My partner paused, blue eyes turning ice cold. "But I *am* going to break into *Le Bastion,* Tobias. With or without you." Spinning on her heel, she marched toward the door.

For a few seconds, I stared at the door, willing her to return, but it was no use. The members of Shadows and Secrets might disagree, but we stuck together. It was our code.

A resigned breath left my lungs before I followed my partner to learn what she had in mind.

THE SUN HAD FULLY SET BY THE TIME WE PUT OUR 'PLAN', IF IT could even be called that, into effect.

"Let's hope the concierge was right, and this is *the* place to see and be seen." Shay pulled the fur coat tighter around her body as we strolled into the village tavern, a few blocks from our hotel.

It was one of three pubs in the mountain town, the one the woman at the front desk assured us was a local's hangout spot. If the plan was to succeed, we needed to locate a bank employee.

I scanned the crowded space, ignoring the stench of stale beer and decades of body odor lingering in the very walls. The tavern was indeed lively, and judging by how underdressed for the weather people were, I suspected those must be locals. One man wore shorts, a foolish endeavor in the freezing cold for a human, which his scent confirmed he was. Some people didn't prize their skin enough.

"There!" Shay pointed across the room. "That's one of the guards who let us into the bank."

The vampire guard sat on a stool at the far end of the bar, drinking a glass of red wine and watching television.

"You can compel him?" Shay checked.

"He seemed shocked to learn I was a Laurent, which tells me he probably is not related to the vampire royal line," I considered. "As long as Oskar didn't give his staff the same potion he ingested, which I find difficult to believe, then yes, I should be able to." Assessing our surroundings, I straightened my jacket. "But we must act quickly. Otherwise, he might suspect our motives."

"Then let's move, Stiff."

We shuffled past tables packed tightly together to the other side of the tavern. The vampire proved quite engrossed in the hockey game. So much so that he did not see us coming until we flanked his sides.

"Hi," Shay greeted, and I swore a little angelic light wreathed her face. It was hard to be certain, because if the angel or nephilim wished it to be so, the power was visually undetectable, even among those beings with superior senses like me. But I'd felt angelic influence before, and sensed that same sensation now in the air. "Remember us?"

"I recall kicking you out of the bank." The guard snorted. "What are you doing here? Tourists prefer the pub across town."

"We have no need for that place," I said. "We came here to talk to you."

The man leaned back, his eyes widening a touch, as if slowly realizing that our visit could spell trouble for him.

"What's your name?" Shay pulled up the rickety stool next to our target and perched on it.

"Jakob. And I'm watching the game. Don't want to talk."

"That's too bad because we have some questions for you." Shay smiled, and against his will, the vampire became captivated. Struck by an angel. Shay was doing well; her influence would slow his reflexes. "Tobias?"

Her attention shifted to me, and under the angel's spell, which charmed and led people to follow their wishes—almost like compulsion, but not nearly as strong—Jakob turned to look at me.

My powers of compulsion unraveled, taking him fully under my control in an instant. Jakob stiffened, but it was too late.

"Remain calm," I murmured, aware there might be others of my kind, or shifters, in the tavern. "We need to get into *Le Bastion*. Do you have keys?"

"No."

Shay swore softly. We'd both been sure that a guard would have keys to the first door. After that, we'd have to deal with interior protections, but getting in the front door was the first step.

"Who does, then?" I pressed.

"*La Tête*. And the vice president."

"Who's that?"

"Ingrid Bolstrand."

"Where can we find her?" Shay asked.

"She's on holiday."

Of course, she bloody was.

"Anyone else?" I wouldn't stop until we succeeded, or ran out of options.

"A few support staff."

"Like?"

"The janitor. He leaves later than anyone else, so he locks up."

"Is he here?" It was almost too much to hope for, but the front desk had assured us that most locals drank here and the place *was* packed to the gills.

Jakob turned on his stool to scan the crowd with glassy eyes.

"In the back corner." Jakob almost pointed, but Shay slapped his hand.

"Describe him," she hissed.

"Long blond hair. He's wearing a neon green ski jacket."

My attention latched onto the man right away. He wasn't watching us, but rather finishing his second beer and reading a book.

"What powers does he have?" I demanded from the vampire. Humans didn't work at *Le Bastion*. Too risky. So, the janitor had to be something else.

"Hedge witch."

"Perfect," Shay whispered.

Hedge witches were the weakest sort of witches, capable of only producing basic magic. I could easily manipulate that man.

The bartender approached, and I waved her away before continuing. "His name?"

"Marc."

"One last question. Where does *Le Bastion* keep the names of their clients?"

"Accola's office."

"Not a vault?"

"They need to access the information when people call, and most like to speak with *La Tête* or the vice. These people are important, so Accola doesn't like to keep them waiting."

"Makes sense," Shay mused. "I think that's enough."

"Agreed. Jakob, go home. Tell no one that we spoke. Do not leave your house until tomorrow morning."

"Okay." Abandoning his wine, the guard left the bar.

Once he was gone, Shay eyed me. "Is compulsion forever?"

"If he was human, or a *very* weak supernatural being, it would be, but he's not. And I'm not a natural born vampire." Only the core royals of Isila were born vampires, rather than made. As such, they were the most powerful among my order. "Eventually his own powers will fight off my influence. He'll come to his senses and remember what happened."

"How long?"

I shrugged. There was no way of knowing for sure, since I did not know the extent of Jakob's powers, but it had been easy enough to compel him. "A day or two. On that front, we have time."

"Good. Moving on." Shay nodded toward the back corner, and together we rose to speak with Marc.

Except, he was gone.

"Bloody hell!" I swore.

"He couldn't have gone far. Let's go."

Hustling out of the pub, we scanned the area. There was no sight of the hedge wizard.

"Smell the air!" Shay urged. "Can you scent a witch?"

I tilted my chin star-ward and inhaled. All I could detect was a vampire, Jakob, and nephilim next to me. Shay's floral, angelic scent was so strong it tended to overpower everything within a five-foot radius.

I distanced myself from her and inhaled more deeply, my nostrils flaring. Finally, I caught the touch of rosemary and sage in the air, likely an indicator of a hedge witch. They usually smelled more herbaceous.

"I think I have something," I announced and proceeded to follow the scent.

With Shay trailing me, we strode down the streets of the village. The farther I went, the stronger the aroma of herbs became, giving me hope. When it led us to a street lined with small single-family homes, I felt sure that we'd taken the right trail.

"Second one on the right," I indicated, the door where the scent had congregated most strongly. "You knock."

Shay, while annoying to me at times, charmed others—especially if they didn't work with her. Or if they were human. Humans loved angels in the same way they feared vampires—with fervor.

My partner strode up to the white, squat home with red shutters and knocked. Right away, footsteps sounded, and seconds later, the door opened.

"Hi," Shay said quickly, to show that she spoke English.

"Hello," Marc replied, his accent thick. "May I help you?"

"Yes," I added, coming up behind her in a blaze of vampiric speed. "You work at *Le Bastion*, no?"

At the mention of the bank, Marc's eyes went round and the door began to close. Unfortunately for Marc, I was fast, and stuck my foot into the jamb. Then, not willing to draw this out further, I looked Marc in the eye and forced him under my influence.

My compulsion magic took easily, and his shoulders

lowered. As long as Jakob told the truth, things from here on out would be easier.

"Marc, you work at *Le Bastion*, correct?" I repeated my question.

"Yes."

"And you have a key to get inside?"

"I do."

Shay pumped her fist.

"Don't get too excited," I chided. For her plan to work, we needed the answer to one more question, and it had to correlate with Jakob's. "Where is the client list for *Le Bastion* located? In a vault?"

Marc blinked. "I expect that would be in Mr. Accola's office. The most important information is stored there. He wards it so well that he keeps hard copies, as well as digital."

"How sure are you?"

"Fairly certain. He only allows me to clean his office when he's present. But I can go inside the vice's office at any time."

I cut Shay a glance.

"We have to try," she whispered.

"Get your key to the bank and a coat, Marc. You're going to take us there."

Like a puppet, Marc did as I requested and joined us outside. From there, we walked to the bank, using back roads to draw less attention. When we got there, some fifteen minutes later, I was pleased to find that no night guards stood outside. It was a poor choice, but Oskar clearly believed the protections he had in place now were enough.

"This door is accessed by a key only?" I asked when we stood in front of *Le Bastion*'s entrance.

"Yes. Otherwise, I would not be able to get inside."

"What are the protections once we're in? Is there a passcode on an alarm system? A spell? And if so, can you break it?"

"There is an alarm system. The code is 358960. After that, each individual room has wards. I set them using a word when I leave for the day, but can't break them."

"That's fine. Get us in the building and turn off the alarm. We'll take care of the rest," Shay replied, still sure of her plan.

It was, truthfully, a good one, though it would leave traces that someone had broken in. Surely, *La Tête* would consider us, he'd be an idiot not to do so. That meant we had to make sure we were far away when he discovered what happened.

Marc pulled out his key and unlocked the door. Straight away, the alarm blared.

"Hurry," Shay hissed.

Darting inside, he opened a hidden compartment in the wall, and punched the numbers on the keypad. The blaring stopped.

I exhaled. Step one, accomplished.

"Will we need him to come with us for anything else?" Shay whispered.

"Marc, you're quite sure that you can't get us past any more wards or alarms?"

The hedge wizard shook his head. "There are none in the hallway or lobby. They're only on the office doors, the key room, and leading down to the vaults."

"Very good," I said. "Stay outside and keep watch. Yell for us if someone approaches."

Marc slipped outside while Shay and I made our way deeper into the bank.

As we'd seen Oskar exit his office to greet us that very day, we knew exactly which door to approach. Even from far away, I sensed magic coming off it in waves. That had not happened before. Had Accola increased his security after we left? Perhaps he put fresh wards in place every night, but it presented a dilemma.

I frowned. "Shay, you truly can handle this?"

Meredith will be furious if I return her roommate injured.

Catching myself, I shook my head, hating that I cared what the witch thought—hating that I pictured her in Hell and it infuriated me. All day, I'd done my best not to think of the witch. Distressingly enough, she'd still infiltrated my mind more often than I would ever admit.

"I have to try," Shay insisted, though there was a slight hitch in her voice.

"Don't push too hard. You'll—"

"I understand what my kind is capable of, Tobias. I don't need it vampsplained to me."

My lips clamped shut. Of course, a nephilim would understand that by pushing their angel magic too hard, they risked burning from the inside out—burning out. The prospect probably featured in their nightmares.

Yet, I feared Shay would have to push herself to the brink for us to get past *La Tête's* wards. He was not in his position by chance, his magic and how he wielded it played a role in him heading *Le Bastion.*

"Be careful," I urged when we stopped in front of the door. "I suspect that he put more protections in place."

"I feel it too. But few witches or wizards know how to hold back heavenly magic, and Oskar never asked what I was." Shay smirked. We hadn't offered that information on purpose. All too often, other orders mistook nephilim for witches or shifters, not because of their magic, but because being part angel was rare. Witches and shifters were far more common. "To beat back my magic he'd have to have very specific protections in place, and I doubt he did that. So I'll go as hard as I have to to get what we need."

Knowing better than to argue, I took a step back.

Angel magic, and nephilim magic, was varied and multifaceted, but Shay possessed a special kind from her father, the Archangel Uriel. She wielded the usual angelic light from her hands *and* could also call upon a sword of entwined fire and light.

Shay pressed her hands out in front of her, glowing with the purest, whitest light. Once a ball of light bloomed, a thin rod streamed toward the key slot in the door. The beam slammed into it, and the metal shimmered. The scent of hot metal filled the room, depositing the taste of pennies on my tongue.

My throat tightened but so far, no magical protections had been triggered nor had an alarm been set off. Had she been correct in thinking that Oskar hadn't warded specifically against a nephilim?

No sooner had the question popped into my mind, than a beam of blue magic shot out of the door—straight for Shay.

She gasped, dropping her power and whirling out of the way. The magic caught on the fur of her coat, singing it, and filling the air with a burnt, chemical stench, but she was unharmed.

"There will be more," I warned.

"That means I have to work faster." The nephilim's jaw set with determination.

Another flare of light streamed from her, this one more frantic, consuming half the door. The portal flung a second blaze of magic at her, but Shay was ready and dodged it. The third stream of defensive power came my way, but I too had been waiting for the wards *La Tête* set to attack and ducked so that it sailed harmlessly over my head.

More defenses came at us, and like a dance, we wove out of the way and Shay kept working to break through. If Oskar thought this would be sufficient to put us off, he was incorrect.

When the wood of the door finally cracked, and the bottom half fell away, I exhaled. Shay released her magic, bringing her hands to her heart. It was only then that I realized she was trembling.

"Are you alright?"

"Fine. I—" Her knees buckled, but I caught her before she hit the ground.

Holding her, I pulled up the sleeve of her jacket, and a stream of curse words left my lips. "You pushed too hard."

Her veins glowed red, the fire and light in her blood threatening to consume her. She might have only been minutes, perhaps seconds, away from burning out.

"I'm fine. Help me inside and let's search."

I also wasn't about to let all the work she'd done be in vain. So, I held her as we shuffled into Oskar Accola's office, determined to learn who had once owned the Opal of Heaven.

CHAPTER FIVE

MEREDITH

Hours after Mr. Novak had shown us to our rooms and we'd cleaned up and rested a bit, Hans remained pissed off.

His sister had blown his secret, and I didn't know what to say to him about that. Of course, I understood that demons were bad, but I was too new to the supernatural world to decide if they were *all* bad. Were there degrees of evil? Was it just that they got a bad rap? Did some run charities?

I snorted at that last one, but who knew? It could be a thing. People were always shades of gray. Why not magical beings too?

Nicoleta didn't seem monstrously wicked. Sure, she appeared mischievous, unwilling to let her brother tell her what to do, but *evil*? I wouldn't go that far.

Then again, I didn't know her well.

And from what I knew about him, I wouldn't put Hans in the evil camp either. Not even as he drank his beer and stared into space with a surly expression on his face. Clear from the other side of the room I could feel the 'I don't want to talk' vibes wafting off of the guy.

Trying not to disturb him, I turned the page of the book I'd brought with me extra quietly.

"Hey, Stoney," Gunner called, emerging from the hallway.

I exhaled, relieved that someone else was here to buffer Hans's bad mood. If there was anyone who could lighten the mood, it was party-boy Gunner.

"Hey." I cocked my head. "Trying a new look?" He'd pulled his shoulder-length hair up in a man bun.

"Yeah, you like?"

"Not really."

"Take it down," Hans growled. "The villagers don't like anything too modern."

Gunner scowled at our non-acceptance of the hair-style, but he did as Hans requested. "Y'all are hard on a guy."

"Sorry, it's not a good look for you." I shrugged. "Down is better."

"Put on your coats, you two," Hans grumbled, ignoring Gunner's worries about his hair. "Now that the wolf has graced us with his presence, we need to train for a few hours."

Train? That was news to me. I'd gotten cozy, thinking we'd be relaxing until we set out tomorrow. Apparently, the trek to the spot where we'd enter Hell would take a half day's walk, and Hans didn't want to be in the woods at night, so we had hours to spare.

"Hey, man, how 'bout first we talk?" Gunner countered, staring at Hans, who immediately stiffened. "You had a while to cool down, but I want to say, that half demon or not, you're still my bro."

Hans's shoulders lowered an inch.

"I feel the same way," I assured. "Not about being 'bros', but I don't care that you're part demon."

"Do you even understand what it means?"

I bit my bottom lip. "Uh, not really."

"Then how can you say that?"

"Because we care about you!" Gunner flopped onto the couch next to me. "So, do you have other magic you don't use much? Darker, like your sis?"

At the mention of Nicoleta, Hans frowned, but he answered Gunner anyway. "I get the caster blood from my father's side, but since I'm part demon, I *can* access dark spells. Those created in Hell. Though I don't like to use them." He paused to take a swig of beer. "I can also make people . . . hurt."

My throat tightened. *Hurt? Talk about ominous . . .*

"What does that mean exactly?" I asked. "Like a headache?"

"That. All the way up to torture, probably—I've never tried that hard." Hans shook his head, as if trying to dislodge a bad memory. "All I have to do is will it."

I cut Gunner a sidelong glance. His carefree expression was gone, and he looked paler.

"If they have demon blood, it's difficult," Hans continued, clearly caught in his thoughts. "Humans are the easiest, supernaturals all vary. I haven't used that power in years, but when I was younger, it just happened. Like when I got bullied. I didn't know how I was doing it."

"How'd you learn?" I asked, ill at the thought but still curious.

He shrugged. "Mother visited and explained what was happening. After that, I figured out how to control it."

"Snap, Bro."

"Yeah." Hans took another glug of beer. "Like I said, I don't use that side of my magic. Haven't for years. The less you use your demon powers, the weaker they become. And vice versa, if I used them more often. So, I don't know how my magic would react now, since it's been so long."

"What does Nicoleta's magic do?" I asked, ready to move on from the thoughts of Hans torturing people.

"You saw her tendrils. She calls them her army. They can do pretty much whatever she wishes. She also has strong manipulation powers from our mother. She uses them to get what she wants from others."

"And the witch magic?" Gunner asked, oblivious to the fact that the girl had tried to manipulate *him*.

A concerned breath left him. "We don't know. She seems to have smothered it in favor of her demon magic."

Oh, shit. So maybe Nicoleta was a tiny bit evil? I'd definitely be watching my six around her. "Did your dad know who your mother was?"

Mr. Novak seemed so kind, so jovial. It was hard to imagine him with a demon queen.

"When they first met, he didn't realize she was Lilith," Hans replied, his tone defensive. "And she didn't stick around after she got pregnant. Not until she was ready to give birth to me. Then she reappeared like she'd been in the village all along." Hans scrubbed his hand over his budding five o'clock shadow.

"I know it doesn't make any sense, but my dad loved Lilith, still does, I think. When she came to see me, and eventually Nic, they'd spend time together, but she doesn't belong here, can't be here."

"Why not?" I asked.

Gunner turned to stared at me. "Damn, Stoney. Sometimes I forget how new you are to all this."

"Gee, thanks." I stuck my tongue out at him.

"Lilith is Lucifer's wife," Hans explained. "His *property*. If he learned about me and Nicoleta, or my dad, he'd be furious."

"But your mom got pregnant *twice* by your pops," Gunner reasoned slowly as a realization dawned. "Is the devil blind?!"

"Female demons don't show their pregnancies like human women. Their stomachs stay flat, so it was easy to hide. After her first contractions, she ran here and delivered." Finishing his beer, Hans slammed the bottle on the end table. "Now, let's go outside."

Apparently done answering questions, he marched out the front door, wearing only his black t-shirt and jeans.

"The man's crazy," Gunner muttered, watching Hans go. "I'm gonna get my jacket."

"Same," I agreed, not about to turn into a popsicle.

By the time we emerged from the comfort of the Novak's home, Hans had already placed a line of daggers on the ground. Surprisingly, Benedict was at his side, pacing the lineup.

"What are you doing out here?" I asked my familiar.

"Spending as little time as possible around that she-demon. Her stench clogs the house."

"Rude!" I looked at Hans apologetically. "That's his sister, Benedict!"

"It's fine," Hans dismissed it. "Cats are known to be irritable around demons."

Yet, Benedict had never been like that around Hans. Did that mean Hans was less demonic than his sister? Or that because he repressed his dark magic, Benedict had not sensed it, and therefore had not spurred the wizard?

"These are all weapons made and charmed to kill demons," Hans said, clearly not worried about matters pertaining to my familiar. "Our village has a few of them because the portal in the woods is always open."

My brows knitted together. "Do demons come through all the time?"

"No. My mother made it in order to come here, and she did well in hiding it, but sometimes a demon on the other side discovers it and slips through. Usually, they don't realize what happened until it's too late, and they're in our world. When they stumble into the village, the villagers know what to do."

So, the portal Lilith made was how we'd be getting to Hell.

"Does your mother visit the village often?"

"Not sure." Hans shrugged. "I haven't seen her since I left Minim. She came about a month before that. I assume she does, but . . ." He trailed off, letting us know he didn't ask about that stuff and didn't want to talk about it. To be reminded of what he was.

I stepped closer to the blades, eager to end his discomfort. "They look like regular daggers."

"They are, except for the charms. My mother called them *aslinkis*, which she said translated to 'blades of darkness'."

"In demon language?" Gunner asked.

"Yeah. Any demon who touches these, except for the Princes of Hell and my mother, will turn to ash. We're taking them because we have to limit our magic in the underworld. Our powers don't belong there and might draw attention. The doses of invisibility potion the coven gave us don't count, but those will only last an hour. Tops."

"I wish we could have brought more potion," I admitted.

"It wouldn't do us a bit of good," Hans replied, parroting what Daphne had told us. "If you ingest the suggested dose of invisibility potion more than once a day you risk weakening yourself to the point of fainting. That would be detrimental in Hell."

I could imagine. Fainting, only to wake up visible and with a bunch of demons around us, wouldn't be good.

"Demons can sense our magic?" Gunner asked, circling back to the wizard's first point.

"The princes can, and since they command armies that's a big deal. They can conjure shades too, which these blades will help protect us against."

"Too bad Luca didn't have one when that shade attacked S&S's tomb."

"Agreed," Hans said. "But they're basically one of a kind. Bringing them to New Haven never even occurred to me, and considering the portal I wouldn't have done so even if it had. The villagers need these more than others."

I swallowed. Much of this information was new and unwelcome. To find the herb, using my magic was a must. This was the first I was hearing about our powers possibly giving us away, though it made sense. The underworld probably had a magic all of its own, and ours didn't belong. We'd stick out, like fish flying in the sky.

"How many princes are there?" I asked, wondering how many chances we had at detection.

"Seven."

An exhale parted my lips. That was a lot!

"But don't worry about them now. They're there and there's nothing we can do to change that, except prepare. Choose a blade." Hans gestured to the lineup. "We'll train with them before dinner. All three of us know our way around a dagger, but it's best to be familiar with these particular ones, just in case."

I snatched up the smallest one, eager to work my body

after so much sitting and traveling, but Gunner quickly called first dibs and set to sparring with Hans.

"Meredith, you should practice your magic while you wait for the next round. Call light."

"What's that going to do in Hell? Isn't using magic a bad idea?"

"We'll do what we must to survive, and if the beam is powerful enough, you can use it for offense. Blinding those of the underworld, even burning them. Get creative, Stone."

"But won't your neighbors notice?"

"They know about the Novaks. Why hide?" Hans shrugged.

"Alright." I moved off to the side with Benedict, giving the guys more room to spar.

It had been a few days since I'd worked with what Hans referred to as 'basic magic' the type most witches could accomplish. This was the power even hedge witches could access, and before, I hadn't been so great at tapping into it.

Still, my seeker abilities had grown in that time, so maybe the other types of magic had too.

Carefully, I removed my gloves. My magic might work with them on, but I figured it would be better to go easy on myself. So far, only seeking came naturally. Why put up more roadblocks?

Staring at my palms, I willed the energy to gather there. A flush of heat warmed the chill of the mountain air on my skin, and power seeped from my pores to illuminate my whole hand.

My heart lifted. That was easier than it had ever been. Not *natural*, but I hadn't needed to concentrate so hard. A step in the right direction. Trying to push harder, maybe even create a sphere like Hans could, I forced more light from my palm. The blaze intensified for a second, wreathing my hand completely before fizzling out.

I frowned. "Dammit. Lost it."

"Keep trying!" Hans called.

I twisted to find him leaping from a barrel as Gunner followed, blade whining through the air and an ear-to-ear grin on his face.

Dang. They were good.

"I don't know why he's so set on this session," Benedict muttered. "Not that I don't want you to practice your magic, but there's an evil presence in this very house, and Hans isn't even taking care of her. Makes me doubt this journey is well planned."

I rolled out my neck. "You need to chill. His sister can't help what she is."

"Nor can I help how I feel, and I don't trust her," Benedict argued.

A snort escaped me. "Fine. We won't be here long anyway, so it doesn't matter how you regard Nicoleta. Where'd you go when you were hiding from her, anyway?"

"I was *not* hiding!"

"Whatever." He so was. "Did you see the town?"

"I did. This place is . . . odd."

From what I'd seen, nothing was strange about it, except the fact that demons sometimes appeared, which we hadn't witnessed firsthand. Benedict was probably being judgmental, and I didn't have time for that kind of nonsense.

"Maybe you should have heeded my advice and stayed at home." I lifted my palms again, ready to conjure light once more.

"Quite the opposite." The cat glared up at me. "You might

be a witch armed with magic and a dagger, but I'm certain you'll need me now more than ever."

By the time darkness fell over the quiet village, my arms were sore as hell. Hans didn't want anyone down below to get the jump on us, so he insisted on sparring for *hours*.

After we'd cleaned up for the second time that day, the three of us met in the living room once again. Mr. Novak had returned from the market and made himself busy in the kitchen, but when he heard us, the baker poked his head into the living room.

"Dinner will not be ready for two hours. I have a pheasant roasting—an old family recipe! Remember that, *fiul*?"

"Your best, Father." Hans smiled at his dad, a rare moment in which the tension lining his face vanished.

"Do you need help?" I asked, semi-hoping he didn't take me up on the offer. I could handle the basics in the kitchen, but I was no chef, and roasting a pheasant sounded hard.

"No! Please, go to the tavern! Enjoy Minim! I will call Hans and Nicoleta when the meal is ready."

"Great idea," Hans agreed, from where he lounged in an armchair. "I need a beer."

My stomach twisted. We were going to Hell tomorrow and needed to be at our very best. I wanted to tell him to lay off the booze, but I also realized that beer might be the only thing getting him through this time.

As long as he slows down, it will be fine.

"I'm game too," Gunner said. "Where's that cat?"

I rolled my eyes. "Still outside."

Benedict had refused to come in with us. What he'd do

later, when the temperatures dipped to freezing was anyone's guess. Hopefully, I could tempt him inside and tell him I'd protect him under my blanket. Though, knowing my familiar, that wouldn't work. He was as stubborn as me, and I was a Taurus!

"He can come to the tavern," Hans offered. "It's very old style."

My eyes narrowed on him. "Didn't you leave town before you hit legal drinking age?"

Hans smirked. "The villagers let some things slide."

"Let's go y'all," Gunner urged. "I've never been to Romania and wanna see this place."

With a wave to the baker, we grabbed our coats, and left the home.

I shuddered as the night wind grazed my skin. Somehow, it had gotten even colder outside. As we crossed the yard, into the street, I rubbed my arms vigorously as I searched for my familiar.

"Benedict!" I called out, hoping he'd come with us to get out of the cold. "Where are you?"

"Here," a voice came from right behind me, making me jump.

"How did you get there so fast?"

"I saw you exit the home. Ran over."

So, he was staying close, even though he didn't want to be near Nicoleta.

"We're heading to the tavern. Hans said they'll let you in."

"Even if they didn't, I'd come and stay under the table. I'm pleased to let my paws thaw."

Oh, right. The invisibility.

Our foursome wove through the town, attracting the attention of many as we passed. Two people lifted a hand in greeting to Hans. An older woman stopped him to say hello, but most stared as he went past.

It gave me the willies, but I ignored them, and focused on taking in the scenery, which was pretty and peaceful, with a dusting of snow on everything and the darkness falling over the range. There was no denying that the village of Minim was charming, even if parts were slightly rundown. With a new coat of paint on a few buildings, she'd be a real stunner.

"What did you do before you left, man?" Gunner asked when another man glared at Hans while we passed him.

"Things were okay before I left, but I didn't hang out with those in town much, preferring to spend time with a wolf pack that lives on the outskirts. Plus, I haven't been back in a long time and people here are distrustful. They put up with tourists for the money, but other than that, they want to be left alone."

I could understand that sentiment. Often, I felt that way. Although, since I'd joined Shadows and Secrets, I was beginning to learn I liked being around people too. In small doses, anyway.

Turning down another street, I stopped dead in my tracks.

"What was that?" I squeaked. I swore that I'd seen a shadow dart across the narrow lane.

An annoyed huff left Hans' throat. "Nicoleta is around somewhere. Luckily, here we are." He stopped before a nondescript door. "The oldest tavern in this mountain range."

I took in the building, which looked like it might fall over at any minute, but other than that, at least nothing looked creepy. I just hoped the structure would stay up while we had our drink.

The moment we entered, heat from the hearth warmed my frozen cheeks. People milled about talking and laughter filled the air, making my shoulders loosen. This place might collapse, but it was homey. Nice. I could relax a litt—

"Brother!" A voice rang out, sharp as a crow's call, and I tensed all over again. "What brings you out among the commoners?"

Nicoleta stepped out of the shadows, from the crowd where she'd been hidden. She held a beer in one hand, a cigarette in the other.

A seemingly forced smile appeared on Hans's face. "Checking out old stomping grounds."

"Well, the village wishes you a merry night." Nicoleta spun, sloshing beer from the mug. People hooted and clapped.

They loved her here, a fact that Hans could not possibly miss. His jaw tightened, and as I glanced back at Nicoleta, I realized why.

Dark tendrils of magic twisted from her while she danced and others sang, danced, and drank around her. So, they didn't love her as freely as I'd first thought.

She was mesmerizing these people, probably did it all the time for fun. Clearly, they couldn't see her magic, but we noticed it.

Still, the town recognized that Hans and Nicoleta were different. Did they suspect she clouded their thoughts? Did the baker realize this was what his daughter did?

Again, my estimation of the girl lowered.

"Come on," Hans grunted as he turned to the bar. "Let's get a drink."

CHAPTER SIX

TOBIAS

SHAY GROANED AS I EASED HER INTO OSKAR ACCOLA'S DESK chair, hinting that no matter how much she insisted that she was fine, she wasn't altogether well. "You sit. I will do the searching."

"If I help, we can get out of here faster." She tried to lean forward and assist, only to nearly tip out of the seat.

I righted her, my gaze boring into hers. "You've already done more than enough, that's why you look like this." I gestured to her trembling arms and legs. She'd used a dangerous amount of angel magic to break through *La Tête's* office door and although her veins no longer appeared to burn from within, she still was not better. "It's my turn to earn my keep."

"Fine," she huffed, though when she leaned back, I thought I caught a glimmer of relief in her eyes. "I'd start with one of those two filing cabinets. Let me know if you need help breaking them open."

We couldn't use angelic light magic or her sword of fire here. Aside from the fact that any amount of magic would tip

Shay into burning out, a power like hers might set the cabinets ablaze. Then the identity of the person who owned vault 004 would be lost.

"A last resort," I said, moving to the cabinets with the intent to allow her to recover.

Of course, Oskar would also have his client's identities on his computer, but I was no hacker. If we could find the name of the owner of vault 004 in the cabinets, I'd be grateful to avoid the hassle of technology.

Unsurprisingly, the cabinets were locked. I turned to examine the rest of the office more thoroughly. Oskar had decorated his space in the minimalist style, with only high-end pieces and art.

His desk gleamed as the centerpiece, with two dark brown leather chairs opposite. The filing cabinets appeared custom made with gold hardware, and a bar cart brimmed with rare and expensive spirits. On each of the walls hung a single painting, all stunning. One, featuring a woman with a determined expression that reminded me of a seeker witch I was trying not to think about, was a true masterpiece.

"What are you doing?" Shay asked.

I gestured to the cabinet. "These take keys. He might carry them, but they'd be more easily lost then," I mused.

"He warded his office so well," Shay agreed, "I doubt he'd think many capable of breaking through those protections. To me, it's just as likely that he'd keep them safe in here." She popped open the largest drawer on the desk. The inside proved spartan—three pens, a pad of paper, and a pack of gum.

"Or maybe behind the painting?" Shay asked. "I'll keep checking for hidden compartments in the desk."

I took in the artwork again. "The painting does seem to fit his style."

"Why do people always think that's such a clever place, anyway?" Shay rolled her eyes.

"They haven't had to search for items as often as we have, so they don't realize how common a hiding spot it is."

Approaching the painting across from his desk—hence the one Oskar would view most—I pried the frame away from the wall. It was heavy, but I held it with one hand, examining the wall.

The wall proved smooth, not a single line there to give away a hidden compartment in the walls of *Le Bastion*. My gaze strayed to the back of the painting. Nothing there either, so I eased the painting back in place, and moved on to the next, with much the same results.

"Anything inside the desk?" I asked Shay.

"Not yet, but I'm double checking for hidden compartments."

"There are only so many places he can keep the keys," I said, hoping we weren't wrong about him storing them in here.

Would he go as far as to place the keys for the cabinets in the same area the bank stored the vault keys? Surely not. Having both a key to a vault and his precious client information in one place seemed foolish.

By the time I reached the fourth painting, the masterpiece, doubt that this would pan out had seeded deep inside me. Still, I lifted the painting softly, not wanting to harm it, and peered behind it.

My eyes widened. "Found something. I'll need help with this one."

"Okay." Grunting escaped Shay as she got to her feet and shuffled closer.

"See that?" I lifted the canvas a touch more, allowing her greater access. Behind the portrait, just within reach, was a square cut into the wall. Small depressions deep enough for someone to place their fingers in and ease the square open, stared back at me.

"That's got to be it."

"Perhaps," I hedged. "The compartment might hold many things. I'll support the painting. Can you reach that?"

Her arms were long enough, but could she lean over that far and not topple?

"I got this." Placing one palm flat on the wall, her muscles strained, still exhausted as she steadied herself. "One sec."

Shay leaned forward, reaching for the depressions. Her fingers fit inside them perfectly but instead of prying the door open, it popped open all on its own.

"Spring loaded." She grinned triumphantly, snaking her hand inside it.

The jangle of metal echoed like bells while she picked up whatever was in the depression, giving me hope. When I caught a glint of three keys on a ring, I grinned too.

Once Shay righted herself, she handed me the keys. "Gonna sit again."

"I'll take it from here." Two golden keys clearly matched the cabinet. I wasn't sure what the third, much smaller one went to, but at that moment, only the drawers mattered. Choosing at random, I stuck a key in the lock of the top drawer. It gave and clicked.

Success.

Smiling, I opened the drawer, shocked at the depth. They

went so far that they must dive into the wall behind the cabinet.

"He has to have a charm on that thing," Shay commented, watching my progress. "I bet he labels them by vault number. So 004 would either be at the front or the very back."

"Someone like Oskar might also arrange by prestige."

"Pompous, but true," Shay groaned. "What do you see?"

"Numbers, all larger than 004. Perhaps the one we seek is at the bottom." I knelt, unlocking the lowest drawer. Only ten folders hung inside it, each with inches of space between them, making them the more exclusive. The most important clients would be found there.

Quickly, I scanned the files, and when I found it my lips curled in triumph. "Got it."

"Bring it here! I want to see!"

Gripping the portfolio made of thick paper, a luxury stock, I spun and approached the desk, placing the file on the surface. "Go on then. We wouldn't be here if you didn't insist."

When Shay flipped the folder open, a name at the top leapt out at us. One I never would have expected. Not in a million years.

"No," I whispered. "How?"

"I have zero idea." Shay shook her head, as stunned as I was. "She didn't seem to know."

"Meredith couldn't have," I insisted. How on Earth was *Meredith Stone* the owner of vault 004? "There's a 'in care of' name too. That must be who put it in Meredith's name."

"Miriam Black . . ." Shay cocked her head. "Ever heard of her?"

"Never. Is there an address?"

The nephilim sorted through the pages, and together we

searched for an address. The closest thing we found was the name of a small village in England.

"We need to take a picture of this," Shay suggested. "Meredith will want proof when she comes back."

My shoulders grew tight. The trio would be preparing to enter Hell now. The reminder was most unwelcome.

"Document it," I gritted, trying my best to remain in the present. There was nothing I could do for the Hell-bound. My job was here. Unsurprisingly, kicking Meredith from my thoughts was more difficult than I liked it to be. "Then, we leave."

My partner snapped photos of every page. All the while, I still couldn't believe that our newest coven member was so closely tied to the Opal of Heaven. Though I didn't want her to join S&S, it seemed that her involvement with the *lapis caelesti* was more than unearthing the Pearl of Hell.

"Done." Shay stood, and this time she did not sway in the slightest. "Let's roll."

With great haste, I returned the folio to its proper place. Yet, before I could shut it, something caught my eye. A small box sat at the back of the cabinet, the numbers 004 engraved on the lid.

"This is hers too." I grabbed the box and attempted to pry it open. "It's locked."

"Try the smallest key on the ring."

"Brilliant," I agreed, sliding the key into the lock without resistance. When I opened it, another mystery appeared. "What is this?"

Shay's eyes briefly studied it. "Looks like a regular ring. Maybe a moonstone? I don't know, but take it. It belongs to Meredith, and I'm not sure Luca—or my roomie—will want to come here. Might be better for her to lie low." She paused, as if thinking better of what she'd said, and a conflicted expression crossed her face. "Remember all that money, Tobias? That's all hers. She could pay her debts to that Ringmaster guy!"

"I'll take the ring," I decided, disliking the idea that any of that money might go to someone who'd threatened Meredith.

However, that wasn't my choice to make. When the witch was ready, and it was safe to do so, she'd come forward and claim the money.

I slipped the ring into my pocket. "Now let's—"

A holler came from the front door.

"That's Marc!" Shay hissed, her every muscle tensing. "Run!"

We left Accola's office, not bothering to attempt to clean up after ourselves, and sprinted through the lobby. When we burst out the door of *Le Bastion* it was to find Marc fending off Jakob. I swore. It appeared that the vampire had shrugged off the effects of my compulsion more quickly than normal. Perhaps his blood was stronger than I'd thought.

He should have listened.

I zoomed over to the pair, ripping the vampire's head clean off his neck seconds before he would have landed a killing blow to the hedge witch.

Marc fell to the ground, a terrified cry flying off his lips.

"Stop yelling," Shay instructed, holding out a hand to help the wizard stand. "Get up and go home. Quietly!"

"You must," I agreed, looking him in the eyes, and strengthening my compulsion over him. Surely, the next day he'd be interrogated by *Le Bastion*, but once Oskar understood I placed Marc under my thrall, he'd likely be safe too.

Accepting Shay's hand, Marc rose. Then, without further instruction, he ran.

Once we were alone, I looked down at Jakob. "We'll move

the body inside, but there's no point in burying it as it will soon decompose. We can't hide our intrusion, anyway."

Picking up the corpse, I dragged him inside the bank. It wasn't much, but at the very least, this would save the body from being eaten by animals before decomposition began.

"Should have kept out of it, mate," I whispered, settling the vampire on the floor, only a few paces from the door.

I exited, and Shay pulled the door shut behind me. "I wish he wouldn't have fought your magic."

"I don't like it either, angel, but we cannot dwell on his choice. We must leave this village." I scanned the area, making sure no one else was around. "Once first light hits, they'll know what happened, and we need to be far, far away."

"ARE YOU SURE YOU DON'T WANT TO COME BACK WITH ME?" SHAY asked when I pulled up at the Bern Airport departure gate.

"I have a personal errand to run," I replied, putting the car in park.

Giselle, my maker, would be furious if she learned I was in Europe and did not stop by my brother's castle in Northern Italy. She'd already asked me to visit when we first received news of the Opal's disappearance.

Giselle claimed she feared he'd been alone too long, and since she was currently working as an undercover spy, she could not visit him herself.

"Are you going to Romania after? Or back home?"

My fingers tightened slightly on the wheel, but only for a second. "Why would I go to Romania?"

"To be there when Meredith comes out of Hell."

I looked out the opposite window.

Shay chuckled. "She's gotten to you, hasn't she?"

"We're colleagues, nothing more," I forced out the lie. I certainly didn't need others egging me on. No matter what I felt, I could handle it, I had to. The image of the last woman I'd gotten involved with was still etched in my mind, stone cold in death.

Never again would someone I love die for me.

"Keep telling yourself that, Stiff." Shay opened the car door and grabbed her bag from the back. "Did you know that she's from New Haven? Or at least, she lived there for a time."

I blinked. "No. How do you know?"

"She remembered it, and I happened to be there when the memory surfaced." Shay shrugged. "Apparently, her parents worked at the university. I might be able to dig up information on them. From that, maybe we can learn about that ring. It's a starting point."

"You do that." I tried to sound uninterested, even though I absorbed the information about the witch like a sponge. "Best to keep busy until they return."

She smirked, recognizing a brush off when she saw one. "Right. Well, see you back home, then."

"Safe travels."

The nephilim disappeared into the airport, and I wound through the maze of cars clogging the drop off area. As I drove, I couldn't help but wonder if others thought Meredith had gotten to me in a way few others had managed over the years.

Once, Gunner had said something of the sort. Giselle too, though her reasoning was laughable. My sire claimed we might be soulmates, but I still thought that was impossible. Creatures did not have soulmates of other races.

Except for Kora and her fae prince.

But that was an outlier. A once in a billion chance, perhaps even less. Even among those in one's magical order, soulmates, the fated ones, the bloodbound, were rare.

Meredith was a witch, so she simply couldn't be my mate. Not to mention, the woman frustrated me more often than not. That had to count too.

I'd left the boundaries of the city, and was well on my way south to my brother's castle, when my cell rang.

"Giselle," I greeted after glancing at the screen. "News?"

"I was hoping you had some. I heard through the grapevine there was trouble in Switzerland."

A line formed between my eyebrows. "How?"

"You don't think that Ordo Aeternum would learn of the break-in at *Le Bastion* and *not* go investigate? Representatives arrived at *Le Bastion* as it was opening. You're lucky I was not there, Tobias."

"Did you tell the OA my coven would be there?"

"After our talk, of course not. It wounds me that you'd think that."

Her hurt tone made me cringe. Giselle might be spying on the Order for the Blood of Laurent, but she held more loyalty to me.

"I apologize."

Giselle blew out a long breath. "It's okay. I might not like it, but I can see why you'd ask. As I said before, if we meet and I am with the OA, I must play my part. As it stands, I'm caught between a stiletto and the cobbles."

"And my time at *Le Bastion* has me on edge," I added, not wishing for her to shoulder all of the blame.

A pause. "So did you find anything interesting?"

There was no way I'd give her the news regarding Meredith. While Giselle was loyal to me, and her royal ties in Isila—

even when she did not agree with their aims, as was now the case—I had no illusions that she would not seek the witch if she thought Meredith might ultimately help the Blood of Laurent. As long as her actions did not directly harm me or her other children, Giselle would do as the Blood wished. For now, the less my maker knew about Meredith, including that she was a seeker, the better.

"We visited the vault," I admitted.

"Accola is desperate, then."

"Indeed. The newscasts didn't lie. There were still many treasures there, but we found nothing that pointed to the owner, or that they had other powerful items." Someone merged in front of me, causing me to break in my story. "Arsehole."

"Pardon me?"

"Not you. The driver. There's but a dusting of snow here and they act like they've never seen it before."

"What of the Sigil of Lucifer?" Giselle asked, ignoring my outburst.

"It was there. The same group that took the Pearl also stole the Opal of Heaven."

For a moment, Giselle said nothing. I pictured her pacing, her rouged lips pulled tight as she shook her head in thought.

"It would be bad for King Vladistrica to get his hands on the *lapis caelesti*. And the Order cannot wait to possess the Pearl and cause mayhem . . . but to not have a clue who has the gems? It is almost torturous. I wish I was blessedly ignorant of what was to come."

I shuddered at the thought of either the Order or the vampire king having more power. Neither possessed pure motives. The king wanted to push his power into this world, and the Order wished to bring about an apocalypse to subjugate humans.

"What would your coven master do with them if you found them?" Giselle asked.

"The darkest objects the coven possesses all go in a safe that only Luca and one other person can open. Both mages. He has not told us the name of the other person. Only that he trusts them implicitly."

"And you?"

"I trust Luca with my life. He's a good man. Not power hungry, which is why he makes a good leader."

"Very well. Then we can only hope your coven finds the culprits before the Order, or anyone else, does." Giselle sighed, sounding exhausted.

Vampires played one part or another for most of their long lives, but I imagined doing so when you did not support either cause would be exhausting.

"I'm going to Raphael's now," I said, knowing it would cheer her.

"Oh! Good! I'd hoped to check on him after Edinburgh, but the Order has another ideas."

"Where?"

"When I know, I'll tell you."

"And I you," I offered, comforted that though the world was in danger, I still had my coven and my family, people I could trust.

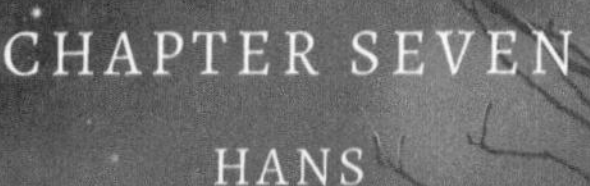

CHAPTER SEVEN

HANS

MY HEAD POUNDED AS WE TRAMPED THROUGH A FRESH LAYER OF fallen snow toward the portal. We'd already been hiking for hours, and I felt, once again, like a donkey's asshole.

One would have thought after I blacked out for most of our trip across the world, that last night I would have been smarter. Particularly, considering the journey we were about to embark upon.

One would have been wrong.

Beer was the only thing capable of numbing the pain as I watched my sister flaunt her magic. Her black ribbons twisting and turning through the tavern, right under the noses of humans.

Nic didn't care that we'd spent years being hated by villagers because of what we could do. She didn't care that our father had almost been run out of the town he'd grown up in. Nor that every use of her power brought her closer to her dark side.

All Nicoleta cared about was having a good time and

others adoring her. Which, thanks to her magical ability to manipulate them, they did, with gusto.

What would happen if they figured out the truth? Would they attack my sister? My father?

"Hans," Meredith called from behind. "What's that?"

I turned to find the witch pointing east, and followed her direction—a hand shielding my eyes from the brightness.

A wolf prowled closer, one with red fur and curious eyes. The rain cloud hovering over me lifted a touch.

"Hey, scoundrel!" I waved at the wolf. "Come talk."

"You know him?" Meredith asked, her tone cautious.

"Only all my life."

"Been sensin' him for a while. He was avoiding me," Gunner added as the wolf loped closer. The big southern man rubbed his hands together, his cheeks ruddy from the cold.

"Makes sense," I replied.

Gunner descended from the wolvea, royal wolves of Isila. Others of his kind would sense that powerful blood, the danger that Gunner posed, and keep their distance, unless called.

Or unless they had a death wish.

The red wolf, Mihai, wasn't that stupid though. Though he'd been born in Minim, and never stepped foot in Isila, he respected the old ways of the wolvea. He always had, and as my best childhood friend, I grew up watching those wolfish traditions. Mihai's cottage was my second home.

A refuge that I'd needed to survive growing up. My best friend's family and pack lived far on the outskirts of the village. Even when others hated me, the wolves didn't, likely because they were magical too.

As Mihai approached, he inclined his head to Gunner in a respectful gesture.

Gunner beamed at the wolf, no trace of threat on him. "Hey, man."

An instant later, Mihai shifted, standing in front of me, his red hair longer than ever and face more lined than I recalled. The harsh mountains of Romania stole youth quickly.

"People said you were in town," my childhood friend said. "Why didn't you come by the house?"

"We're here on a time-sensitive mission, and unfortunately, I can't stay long." I enveloped him in a hug. A sharp inhale filled my ear, but Mihai was kind not to rear back at the stench of alcohol rolling off me in waves. "Walk with us?"

My friend quickly introduced himself to the other three, and we set off again. Behind, Meredith whispered something to Benedict. Though I couldn't make out the words, from the cat's tone, I'd bet it didn't please him that another wolf had joined. He tolerated Gunner, who was generally good natured, even to cats, and hard to dislike. Benedict and Harper, however, did not get along. Other wolves probably fell strongly on the 'dislike' side of the spectrum too.

"Can you share anything about your mission?" Mihai asked after a few steps. "I can guess by the direction . . . but . . ."

The wolves knew something was very off with the land we journeyed toward. They didn't know exactly what it was, and were smart enough not to ask. The entire pack avoided the place.

Only my family could pass through and take others beyond the protections my mother had set around the entrance to Hell. Of course, beasts sometimes found their way from the underworld into *this* realm, but that was a different matter entirely. In this instance, directionality mattered.

Once the unwitting demons emerged from the protected

sphere my mother had created to hide the entrance to Hell, the demons never returned to their homes. The people of Minim and the wolves struck hard and without mercy.

"We're going exactly where you think, old friend."

"Why?"

"A life depends on it."

"That person must mean a lot to you." He glanced back at the others, who were giving us space to talk. "And you bring a wolvea descendant. I bet Nicoleta didn't like that."

That got my attention. My sister had pissed me off all night, but she liked Gunner. Because, again, most people did. "Why do you say that?"

"She's changed, Hans. Aside from the obvious, she's nearly a woman now, and has developed strong opinions of her own."

"She uses her magic openly," I added. "I saw it last night. Couldn't believe it."

"In truth, she uses her powers *liberally* on others. But they love her for it." A shudder rocked my friend's body, and since wolves ran hot, I doubted it was from the chill. "The pack stays away from Nicoleta. Even the alpha."

"Can you give me specifics of what she's done? I'm going to speak with my father about her behavior when I return."

Unease flickered across my friend's face.

"Mihai. Please."

"You can't let her know I told you."

What the fucking hell was Nic getting up to?!

"I promise."

"She enchanted the priest's son for a summer," the wolf said slowly. "Took his virtue and then left him crying. He was trying to wait for marriage. I think to your sister it was a game."

My stomach twisted.

"And once, I believe she urged a friend to set fire to their cottage."

"What?! Was anyone injured? Killed?"

Mihai shook his head. "They got out, and no one blamed Nicoleta. Your father might recognize her responsibility in his heart, but he denies the truth. Turns a blind eye to most of her actions."

I swallowed. Father had often said that he didn't know what to do about my sister. Now I was getting the feeling that he only told me about the lightest of her transgressions.

"She needs to respect the village better," I said finally, unsure what else to say.

Mihai nodded. "She does. But even if she changed tomorrow, some wouldn't trust her. The pack knows and we don't forget easily. She's undone so much of what you two worked to achieve, a peace, before you left."

"I don't blame you." A long, heated breath sunk my chest. Judging from how silent Gunner and Meredith had become, they were listening. I wished I could keep my family's darkness tucked close. Hidden away.

"Tell me of your family, Mihai," I urged, not sure I could bear to hear more of my own.

Thankfully, my friend acquiesced, catching me up on the pack, until the surrounding air grew thick and smelled of sulfur. That was our sign. The boundary was close.

I stopped. "Mihai—"

"I'll go no further." He gripped my gloved hand. "It was good to see you, friend. Come back to us soon."

We hugged, and the others waved to him. Then Mihai turned back into a wolf and disappeared through the snowy trees.

"We're close, aren't we?" Meredith asked, rubbing her hands on her arms. "I feel weird."

"The portal is about two hundred yards in that direction." I pointed left.

"No one goes beyond this area?" Gunner's keen eyes scanned the forest.

"Most wouldn't make it even this close. Lilith made journeying in this direction unappealing. Even animals avoid it."

"I can see why." Benedict's round amber eyes shone, luminous as he took in the area from where he rode, safe in Meredith's backpack. "I want to turn around."

"Well, we can't, so ignore that sensation," I said. "My mother's magic won't harm you. Not when you're with me."

Noon neared as we reached the portal, a circle of dead-looking trees deep in the woods. Nothing about this place seemed natural, and even though the hexes my mother had placed in the area didn't affect me like the others, they still made me tense.

"Shed layers, but remember to keep your blades handy." My hand patted the pair already sheathed and on my hip. "We also need to top off our water supplies with snow. For those of this realm, there's no potable water in Hell, and it's hot as balls there."

"You don't say," Meredith slipped off the pack in which she carried Benedict.

I began to prepare too, ditching my jacket and setting down my pack. Already hungry, I pulled out the homemade energy bars Father had given us. We wouldn't take everything he'd pushed on us—a generous dozen each—to Hell. We needed to travel light, and save room in our packs for the lucimisia herb, but we'd definitely bring a few in case this took longer than expected. The mere idea sent my pulse pounding.

"Eat a few energy bars," I suggested to the others. "Then stuff six a piece in your bag. If you have any left over, they can stay here for when we come back. And Meredith, don't forget to shift the herb you'll use to seek to a place you can reach. A pocket, but one with a zipper, so it doesn't fall out."

They didn't need me to micromanage, but I couldn't help it. I was nervous, and so much rode on Meredith using the herb to seek. We couldn't lose the lucimisia or this journey would be for nothing.

I'd taken all the superfluous items out of my pack, and was about to situate the energy bars in an easy-to-reach outer pouch, when a tendril of black magic eased past me.

I stiffened. "Where are you, Nicoleta?"

"You'd leave without saying goodbye to me?" Nicoleta stepped out from behind a tree, a pouty expression on her face. "That hurts, Hans."

I snorted. "I didn't think you cared much for what I did. You mostly ignored us in the pub."

"I was having fun! Try it on for size, instead of being miserable and getting drunk."

"Guys, can we not fight now?" Gunner interjected. "We need to keep a clear head, Hans."

"I'm sorry, but my brother is being *so rude!*" Nicoleta scowled. "He hasn't been around for years, and now he's leaving. It's like he doesn't even care about our family!"

My throat tightened. Did she really think that? Did others?

Nicoleta both worried me and pissed me off, but she *was* my little sister. I loved my family, and one of the primary reasons I left Minim was to protect them. One less half-demon around was sure to lighten the load. Or so I'd thought.

Had I really only hurt them by leaving?

"Nicoleta, I love you so much." My tone softened as I

assured her. "Though, I have to admit, I've been upset with you since I got here."

Lowering her gaze, she gripped her hands in front of her, the gesture uncharacteristically sweet. "I know. I'm sorry I told your friends about us. I was mad at you."

A weight, slight though it may be, lifted off my shoulders. I understood acting out because I'd done so many times as a teenager, and that's what Nicoleta still was—a seventeen-year-old girl.

"Brother, can we talk before you leave?"

"Go on," Gunner urged. "No one wants regrets."

What he didn't say was that we might not come back, and this talk might never happen.

Gunner had called his family before the flight across the Atlantic to tell them he loved them. Unfortunately, Meredith didn't have anyone to call. At that, a pang cut through me. I was lucky enough to have people who cared, and even if we didn't understand one another, I wanted to make things right.

Maybe if I did, my sister would stop rebelling.

"Yeah, let's walk," I said.

My sister and I left the other three, skirting around the circular portal and trailing through the woods. We hadn't made it far before she turned to look at me.

"I really am sorry; I've been a jerk, Brother. I just wish we could all be together."

"I do too, Nic," I confessed, "but I have a few really important things to do right now. After they're done, I can come back and visit for longer. The summer could work."

Pain shone out of her, as if from her very soul. "Hans, do you ever think about Mom?"

Honestly, I tried not to, but I wouldn't tell my sister that. "She's in my heart."

"I miss her so much. She hasn't been back for years." Nicoleta's dark eyes found mine. "I want us to all be together again. I worry about her."

"Lilith can take care of herself," I assured her. "She's been around for thousands of years. She's tough."

"Obviously. Where do you think you get it from?" She beamed at me, and I grinned back. It was nice to get a compliment from my sister. They were rare.

"Father misses her too."

Unable to add more to that, I nodded. Father had always loved our mother, and Lilith loved him in return—though she could never stay true. Their relationship had been one-sided in that regard, and it killed me.

"Hans, I wasn't sure I should say this, but I won't be able to forgive myself if I don't." Nicoleta's dark eyes met mine. "I'm positive that I can secure the portal and erase any trace of Mother slipping through. If she was here when I did that, she could stay."

I stopped walking. "What? How? And why consider this? It's dangerous, Sister."

"I don't care how dangerous it is . . ." Her tone became high-pitched, almost frantic; she'd never sounded more like a teenager. "I miss her! I love her! And I want her *here*, Brother." Nicoleta's hand found my wrist, and she turned me so that we stared into each other's eyes. "Can you bring her back for me?"

My heart lodged in my throat. Bring Lilith, Lucifer's wife, here? My sister had gone insane.

"The princes can't leave Hell," she argued.

"That doesn't mean they can't find a way." The seven princes were banished to Hell long ago and kept there by magic. Any Hellblooded now in this realm were distant descendants of demons who had long since been shunted into Hell, or monsters created with demon blood by sorcerers. Well, all except Nic and me.

"The last time Mother was here, she told me that her portal was the only exit. Every time she uses the portal, she fears Lucifer will find it. Then, he'll come here too." Nicoleta gestured behind us. "But I really think that I can seal it for good. Make it stick. If I do that, though, I need her on this side first."

"You're more powerful than her?" I arched my eyebrows.

If that's what she thought, my sister's hubris proved out of this world.

"Not *more*, but maybe equal. Mostly, we have different skills, but I really think she needs a counterpart to keep her safe. I can do that."

"You'd be putting the entire village in danger."

Maybe the world. Would Lucifer try to break through to this realm if his wife was here? How long would he wait? A day? A decade? For immortals, time ran differently.

"Please, Brother. I never ask you for anything."

It was true. Nicoleta did not ask much of me, and I owed her. I'd been gone so long. "I'll look for her."

"And bring her back?" My sister's eyes lit up.

"*If* I see her, which you know isn't likely." Our mother had taught us that the underworld was made of seven kingdoms, each ruled over by a prince. "Hell is vast, and I can't go questing about and sabotage this mission, Nic. A life is at stake."

She frowned.

"But that doesn't mean I can't try later."

"Try your hardest *now*."

Our eyes met, hers so dark they were almost black and hard, unyielding.

"Promise me that you'll try your hardest, Brother."

I swallowed, not liking what I was about to do, but about to do it all the same. "I will. And if I see our mother, I will bring her back."

With a squeal, Nicoleta leapt at me, her arms wrapping around my neck. As we embraced, I realized we hadn't done so since she stood on the cusp of seven years of age. My throat tightened with regret. Goddess, I was a horrible older brother.

I gave her another squeeze before we parted. Tears shimmered in my sister's eyes, and I patted her shoulder. "We'll be back as soon as we can."

"Safe journey, Brother. I'll be waiting for your return."

With that, I turned and stomped through the snow back to my friends.

"That looked like progress," Meredith said as I neared. "Did you two make up?"

"We did," I conceded, not ready to tell them about the promise I'd made. If we came across Lilith, an unlikely event, I'd break the news. Actually, that might be good. Lilith could help us out of Hell. Until then, we needed to focus on the mission at hand.

"That's great, man. Glad to hear it." The wolf tightened the straps on his backpack, looking pleased by my family's development.

"Are you two ready?" I craned my head to make sure Benedict was in the backpack. He could go invisible, or at least he could in this realm. Before we tested that premise in Hell, we wanted him to be secure and with Meredith.

"Ready," she confirmed, and Gunner gave me a nod.

"Both of you grasp my hands. You have to enter the circle at the same time as me."

"What happens if we don't?" The witch eyed the ring of dead trees warily.

"It will hurt," I admitted, choosing not to go into the murderous lengths Mom went to keep this area, and our family secret safe.

Without hesitation, the pair took my hands, and we stood in a line in front of the largest break in the trees. "There will be a lot of heat. Close your eyes to protect them." Giving them a sidelong glance, I inhaled deeply, steeling myself as they followed my directions.

"Together." I took a step, and the others matched me. When we passed through the barrier, a sizzle of flame caressed my skin, then washed away.

"You guys okay?"

They affirmed they were, and I was glad because that had been the easy part. "Keep a tight grip. Now that we're in the circle, I have to use the incantation my mother gave me. It will open the portal and take us to the underworld."

"Alright," Meredith replied, and for the first time, nerves laced her voice.

"Ready," the wolf grunted.

"Close your eyes again."

When they did, I too, closed my eyes, clenching their hands tighter. The dark magic I normally kept tightly locked up inside me surged. It knew where I was, where I would soon enter, and it hoped that now was its time.

Not today.

I inhaled and then breathed out the word my mother had taught me all those years ago. "*Otkrx.*"

The cold of the mountains disappeared, and heat—vicious,

searing heat—took its place. A gasp escaped Meredith, and I felt Gunner tense.

"Stay still," I murmured. "It will pass."

No sooner than I'd said it, the heat dissipated, and our feet slammed down into hard rock—the snow we'd trudged through gone.

An ear-piercing scream jolted through me. I opened my eyes and nearly vomited.

We stood in a shallow rocky depression, partially hidden by black stone jutting out in front of us. Though small, the outcropping would be enough to hide my mother from sight, but since there were three of us, it was not as effective. Hence, I had a clear view of the horrendous scene before us. Some yards away, a field of demons grew out of the ground, like daisies. Only a dozen of them were still alive, but each and every head was aflame.

"What the actual shit?" Meredith hissed as she peered around the jutting rock.

"This is the Field of Punishment," I said when another demon grew out of the ground and his ugly head ignited. "Mom told us about it."

Seeing it was so much worse. I hadn't been able to fully visualize the horror before, but now I had no question as to why my mother had placed her portal here. The punished demons just appeared. No one brought them to this place, and they were in no condition to tell anyone about her portal.

"That's nasty." Gunner's nose wrinkled.

"Get used to it, because that's only the beginning of the horrors we'll see," I murmured.

CHAPTER EIGHT

MEREDITH

A CASCADE OF SHIVERS RUSHED DOWN MY SPINE AS I FOLLOWED Hans and Gunner along the edges of the Field of Punishment. Though I tried not to look to the side, occasionally, a demon head would push out of the ground and ignite. Shrieks of agony followed, making my skin crawl. Between the screaming and the rotting stench of sulfur in the air, I was officially regretting signing up for this task.

Not that I would turn back. Luca depended on us, and I owed him so much. But *damn.* I wanted to get this shit over with and leave ASAP.

"This way," Hans guided, scaling a mess of obsidian rocks on the opposite side of the cavern from the portal.

Hoping he was as knowledgeable about where to go as he was seemingly confident, I followed, gripping the rocks and climbing. At the top, I was surprised to find myself at the opening of a tunnel. A few steps in, the screaming faded, and I could breathe easier.

"How do you know where to go, anyway?" Gunner asked. "Haven't seen you bust out a map."

"My mother burned a rudimentary map of Hell into my mind. Nicoleta's too. You know, in case we really needed her help."

"What's considered rudimentary?" I asked, surprised by Lilith's forethought. Then again, she'd been around for . . . Well, probably a long-ass time. Surely, she knew how to make sure those she loved were safe.

"I know where the most demon populous areas are," Hans replied. "Where the various sub-orders of demons live and work. And where the princes' primary palaces are located."

"How about where the herb grows?" I asked, hopeful.

"If I possessed such granular knowledge, I wouldn't have brought you," Hans assured me. "But I do have a general idea of where it might be. Down here, they can grow plants for potions and food in only a few places. I bet the herb is in one of those areas."

"And this will take us to one of those locations?" Gunner gestured to the black walls of the tunnel.

"This tunnel has many offshoots and openings," Hans said, "but the final one ends in a wide-open space. A valley where my map tells me food is grown. There's a castle nearby and dwellings, which tells me this area is probably actively growing stuff all the time. That's the direction we need to go."

"Should we use that invisibility potion?" Gunner asked.

"It will only last an hour," the wizard reminded us—as if I could forget. "We'll have to wait until it is absolutely necessary. At the edge of the field would be ideal."

"How long of a journey through this?" I gestured down the tunnel, into the darkness.

"A few hours?" Red flushed Hans's cheeks. "I have the map, but distance is hard to determine. There's no scale."

I scoffed. The anxiety rippling across his face said it all. He had a map, but no context. What if this took days?

Would we survive?

"Then, we should move," Gunner urged, and Hans nodded, leading the way.

I trailed at the back, my anxiety rising by the second. So much was left to chance, far more than I'd counted on.

"There should have been a better plan," Benedict whispered.

Though I agreed with the familiar, I wouldn't actually voice any negative thoughts. They might become our reality, and we could not risk anything going wrong. Instead, I focused on breathing to calm the heck down, and stayed quiet, as did the rest of the group.

It didn't take long for sweat to drip down my face. With each step, the heat amped up a notch or two, so I took a glug of water, attempting to stay hydrated in the land of fire and brimstone.

Try as I might, as minutes stretched into hours, I kept sweating, and my tongue grew heavier, drier, in my mouth. I was weakening and needed a jolt of energy. Reaching for my pack, I grabbed a bar, stuffing it in my mouth.

"Might I have a bite?" Benedict asked. His voice sounded faint, making my heart race.

I hadn't even thought to bring him cat food! Benedict preferred tuna, but Hans's father had purchased the high-quality wet cat food, and I hadn't packed a single tin. My stomach hardened with guilt.

"Sure." I pulled a sizable chunk from the bar and passed it behind me.

His feline paws grabbed it, and the sound of chewing filled my ear.

"Awful," he muttered, making me snort.

"It's all we have. Be grateful."

"I'd like down," Benedict replied, some strength returning to his voice. "I need to walk to wake up."

Without stopping, I slipped off my backpack and unzipped it. He leapt out, stumbling as he hit the ground. I winced. He'd been in there so long his legs were probably asleep.

"Sorry. I should have let you out sooner."

My familiar turned to me, light amber eyes gleaming in the relative darkness. His mouth open, on the edge of replying—

And then my vision clouded, the scene before me grew smaller, fading away until my familiar disappeared. Everything did.

"What the hell!?" I spun, trying to orient myself, to find my friends.

When my vision cleared, as suddenly as it had clouded, I stood in a home—in a wood-paneled corridor lined with photos. There was no more rotten egg smell, but rather the clean tang of sage and peppermint. Voices came from down the hall behind me, and I turned with a gasp.

A girl of about nine or ten stood at the end of the hall, her ear pressed to a door. Though I had no memories of my childhood, nor pictures, the girl had my mismatched colored eyes. One blue and one green. She had to be me.

I was spying . . . On my parents?

Something about the idea rang so true that I snorted out a laugh that choked to a close when a woman yelled.

"We can't take her to them! She's too young, Gavin! I won't do it. Not yet."

"Lynn," the man's tone sounded softer, appeasing, "her power is growing by the day."

"We've told her to keep it hidden."

"And she's a child. Did you do everything you were told when your magic appeared at the tender age of eight?"

Silence.

"No one does, honey," the man, Gavin, my *father*, reasoned. "I didn't. You didn't. And Meredith won't either."

"I don't want to lose her. The moment we take her to meet them, they'll want to hide her."

"Perhaps we go on a sabbatical and join her?"

Before my mother could counter, the girl—me—sneezed. She stiffened, eyes wide, and I sensed she was on the verge of scampering off, but it was too late. The door opened, and a woman appeared.

I sucked in a breath. Previously, I'd only seen my father in memories. This was my first time seeing memories of my mother, seeing the other half of what I'd lost. She was absolutely beautiful.

Light, glowing brown eyes illuminated her features, her hair dark and shiny. She held herself like a queen, tall, regal, and—my throat choked up as she knelt, pressing a hand to my childish chubby cheeks.

"Meredith, darling, it's not polite to listen through doors. You're supposed to be in bed."

"You were yelling."

"Daddy and I are talking about the future." Tears shimmered in her eyes.

"It's about me. I want to know."

"No, honey, this is for Mommy and Daddy to figure out." She stood, patting my hair. Two rings graced her fingers—her wedding ring, and another that glowed faintly white, like moonlight. "We'll choose what's best for the family."

"Meredith!" a voice that sounded far away, and deeper than my father's called.

"Stoney!" another male voice added to the mix.

Suddenly, I shook, and the hallway disappeared. So did the coolness, and the scent of sage. All of them were gone, and sulfur bombarded me once more. Then Gunner appeared in front of me, his eyes narrow, and his beefy hand on my shoulder.

"Stoney? What happened? You stopped. Are you hurt?"

My mouth opened, then closed, only to open again. "I saw a memory."

"Oh, wow. Kinda shitty timing, but good for you, eh?"

"Yeah." I chewed on my bottom lip. Normally, the understatement would have drawn a chuckle from me, but not here, not now. Not after what I'd heard and seen. "I've only had one before and it wasn't like that. This one was more immersive."

"We can talk about that later." Hans stood beyond the wolf, sweat pouring off his face. "We need to keep moving. Or—"

Whatever he said next was lost as a demon rounded a blind corner with a roar and sprinted our way. A scream threatened to rip from my throat, but I slammed my hands over my mouth, stopping it in time.

The beast was huge and disgustingly white, almost see through, except for the horns on his head, and the claws on his hands and feet, which ended in red tips.

The wizard whirled, a blaze of red light, magic, soared from his palms, slamming into the demon's chest.

The monster flew into the wall, and Hans ran up to it. He hauled the creature up by the horns and whispered something in his ear.

Gunner stiffened.

"What did he say?" I asked, all the while waiting for a horrible alarm to sound or something that announced our presence.

"Something about Lilith. I didn't hear the first part. Too shocked."

Did Hans think his mother somehow knew he was here and had betrayed us? The question was on the tip of my tongue when Hans sliced his *aslinki* blade across the demon's neck. Before my eyes, the monster began to disintegrate, turning to white ash. When he was gone, Hans spoke another spell and a strong breeze distributed the ash down the tunnel.

"He was alone," Hans assured, "but someone might look for him."

"Will your magic be enough to tip them off that we're here?" I asked, terrified that the answer might be 'yes'.

"I don't think so, but we should haul ass either way."

Gunner and I exchanged a glance. Hans didn't sound certain at all. He also hadn't mentioned his mother. As the wizard turned his back on us and began marching down the tunnel, my eyebrows knitted together. Something was off here.

Still, I followed. The wizard was acting oddly, but my trust in Hans was strong, especially considering I'd only known him a few days, but he'd been acting off since we learned of this mission. He was not at peace with his demon side, and I suspected that was affecting him in ways I couldn't understand.

What could I say to that? It wasn't my battle to fight, nor could I even pretend to understand it. So, I stayed quiet and alert as we continued down the tunnel for another unknowable stretch of time.

My legs told me that we'd gone maybe another mile when I started to hear voices. Another noise came, and the muscles in my jaw tightened.

Not voices. Wailing.

I sped up to stride alongside Gunner, Benedict glued to my right. "Are there more coming?"

In front of us, the wizard slowed, and though I couldn't see his face, I suspected he was reading the map his mother had put in his mind. "No. A river is up ahead, and there's an opening in the tunnel so demons can get to it. We have to go past the opening carefully."

The second he mentioned it, the gaping hole in the side of the tunnel came into sight. My steps became lighter, taking me ever closer to the sounds of wailing that only got louder with each step.

The hair on the back of my neck stood up as we closed in on the opening, and the smell of water filled my nostrils. If I listened closely, the slushing of running water echoed too. Yes, that had to be the river.

"Look." Hans reached the door to the outside first and pressed his fingers to the tunnel wall.

Etched in the black stone was the word "Lethe".

I sucked in a deep breath. *I've read about this before!*

Because so many of the items the Ringmaster's clients desired had roots in lore or history, my old boss insisted that his thieves be knowledgeable about mythology and legends of other cultures.

"Lethe is a river in Hell," I whispered, which earned me *'duh,'* looks from the guys, but I wasn't done yet. "It's Greek and one of five waterways documented in literature. They called it the river of forgetfulness."

"What does that have to do with us?" Gunner asked, eyes trained on the opening, ever prepared for someone to enter the tunnel.

"It's supposed to flow around the cave of Hypnos, and by Hades's palace," I replied, teasing what I'd read from the recesses of my mind. "And whoever drinks from it experiences complete forgetfulness. It's so new souls will forget their lives. Is that all true?"

"According to my mother, Hades actually goes by Lucifer. And yeah, you're right. Personally, I think the river is another punishment," Hans muttered with a shrug. "Like the field."

I shrugged. That was an option, but down here the river might just as well be a salvation. Who would want to recall their lives when they were stuck in Hell? I could see it going both ways.

"No matter what it is, or where it goes, I don't want my head dipped in that water. We gotta get past this door without anyone seein'," Gunner said. "I hear a lot of wailing, which I expect is from the drinkers, but they might have supervisors around. Those who don't have to drink."

"Definitely. There's a hierarchy in the underworld." Hans's blue eyes went to the opening. "But I still don't think now is the time to use invisibility. We really need to save that for when it matters most."

"An illusion?" I'd seen him make one before, it was one of the few castings I was certain Hans was capable of accomplishing. His previous illusion had covered the street outside the coven headquarters, so members could shuttle in blood. This should be cake.

Hans nodded. "I'm wary of keeping my magic up for too long. Don't want anyone to sense me. But at least the gap in the wall is fairly small."

"Let us know when it's in place. We'll run so you don't have to have it up too long," the wolf said. "Have your blades at the ready in case a prince senses it and sends his minions after us, though."

I unsheathed my blade from where it hung at my side. Our

group clumped together, right at the edge of the opening, while Hans worked his magic.

I held my breath, hoping no one sensed a wizard was traipsing around the underworld. When Hans gave the signal, we darted across the threshold. As we did, I stole a glance at the river, and pity stabbed through my heart.

Lines and lines of people stood before a figure in black robes. The robed person had their back to us, but in full view were the faces of the hundreds of people who waited to drink at the banks of the Lethe.

They waited to forget their lives, only to live out their eternity in Hell.

A shudder gripped my spine. I hoped that we weren't caught and forced to join them.

CHAPTER NINE

TOBIAS

DARKNESS WHISPERED OVER THE COUNTRYSIDE, AND AS I TURNED down the drive to my brother's estate on Lake Como, a weary exhale left me. The drive had taken longer than it should have, and I was bloody tired of being stuck in the car.

I'd always hated lengthy travel, whether it be by horseback, vehicle, or plane. Only standing on the deck of a ship, carving through the ocean waves, could I stomach long journeys.

Though, I supposed there was one good thing about driving so far. The road demanded my mental faculties, so I couldn't wholly focus on those coven members in Hell. Couldn't worry about if they lived. Couldn't picture the witch being assaulted by the Hellborn.

My grip on the wheel tightened and I forced myself to loosen. *They will get in and out. Hans wouldn't offer to go if he didn't believe he could escape.*

And it wasn't just up to Hans. Gunner was a fierce and capable warrior, and Meredith was a fighter who possessed a bunch of lucimisia. The dried herb she carried would guide her to where the rest grew.

They'd find the lucimisia. The trio would return. Luca would live.

I exhaled, trying to believe the tale I'd spun.

A gate presented itself about thirty yards down the drive. Off to the side, within view but not so obvious as to put people off, a small gatehouse loomed. The keeper would perch inside, ready to fire a weapon should I prove to be an intruder.

Stopping in front of the intercom, I rolled down my window, and pressed the call button.

"*Sì?*"

"Tobias Aston, here for Raphael."

The air on the other end of the speaker crackled, going dead for a few seconds longer than normal. Then the gate buzzed open.

I pulled through, coasting down the drive. Castel Romono appeared slowly, in bits and pieces, as the cover of trees thinned. In the setting sun, it was as magnificent as the first time I'd laid eyes upon it. Grand and imposing, just as my brother wished.

The castle was larger than the Palazzo Medici-Riccardi, where Raphael had worked during his youth, serving one of Italy's most famous families. In addition to the monstrous home, my brother had purchased much land—giving him the largest lot on the lake, expanding for miles on each side of his castle.

A lover of the finer things, my elder brother had spared no expense. He showed his wealth like a peacock presented its feathers. He loved it, but in my opinion, his home was ostentatious, bordering on that of the Imperial Russian-style in their most gaudy periods.

The road curled into a circular drive which I eased into, stopping the car before steps that led to a front door. Quickly, I grabbed my bag from the back, and patted my pocket, checking yet again that the moonstone ring was still there. By the time I exited, a man had appeared. He stood by my door, waiting open-handed for the keys. As I faced him, he bowed, and I cocked my head, sniffing the air.

This was not a human, but a vampire. And a servant.

Interesting.

"Who are you?" I asked, not recognizing the vampire. He looked young, and couldn't have been over eighteen when turned.

"Valet," the young one answered in a thick accent born in the villages of Northern Italy.

"How long have you been working here?"

"A decade."

A punch to the gut. When was the last time I'd visited?

"If it pleases *Signore* Laurent, I will park your car. Wash it too."

"Thank you." I handed over the keys. "Where might I find my brother?"

"His den. His butler will show you the way."

"Thanks," I said, willing to be coddled, though I recalled the way. Then again . . . *a decade* had passed . . . Raphael might have remodeled the entire castle a dozen times over in that span of years.

I climbed the steps to the front doors, which opened as I crested the staircase. As promised, a butler stood inside, also a vampire, turned in his fifties and clearly Italian by birth, like my brother. He bowed at my approach.

My eyes widened. So bowing was common in Raphael's castle now.

Like my brother, I descended from royal vampires, and other vampires respected my line in this realm, but they didn't bow. I never would have expected it, but apparently, my brother did.

"Master Laurent is waiting for you, sir," the butler greeted, giving me another tidbit of information.

Though the castle bore Raphael's birth family's name of Romono, he now used his royal name.

"You may set your bag down, *Signore*. Someone will see it to your room." The man paused. "That is, if you're remaining with us for the evening?"

"I'd hoped to." I was in no hurry to get back on the road.

"Master Laurent thought so. The moment the gateman called, we began preparing your quarters." The butler smiled, revealing crooked teeth, an uncommon sight on a vampire. The change usually shifted our teeth into perfection. His teeth must have been even worse as a human. "I'll show you to Master Raphael."

I followed him, still surprised that Raphael had hired our kind to serve him. Were all his servants vampires now? Before, they'd been humans and regularly compelled to forget the stranger aspects of my brother's home. Like why they sometimes left with a sore neck, but no markings, because after feeding my brother gave them drops of his own blood to heal quickly.

A trickle of cold washed through me. Had Raphael indulged too much, and the humans in the area grew wary?

A memory of when Raphael had over-indulged in feeding upon young starlets at a French film festival surfaced. That night he had been caught on camera. He'd remained in hiding until Giselle and Serena could take care of the evidence. We'd spent two weeks together, golfing, sampling from Raphael's cellar, discussing literature. Now that I thought about it, that was one of the last memories I had of my brother.

The butler halted before the door to the den and opened it. "Master, your brother, Tobias Aston, has arrived."

"Show him in."

My jaw tightened. From the tone, I deduced two things— my brother was a touch drunk and not pleased to see me. Was he in one of his *moods?* Those would drive away a dragon.

And yet, they didn't stop me from stepping into a room as moody and brooding as the vampire I was visiting. My lips curled into a smile. "Brother."

"Tobias," Raphael replied, lifting a glass from where he stood by a window overlooking the lake. His face was steely, as it so often was if there was not a party to be had.

The soft click of the door behind me, announced the butler's retreat, leaving us alone. Only a few lights lit the study draped in dark woods, rich fabrics, and old money.

"I didn't expect your arrival."

"Apologies. I should have called, but I thought I might surprise my elder brother. You used to enjoy surprises."

"Only in the form of bosoms, drink, and money."

I chuckled. It was true, and funny, though by the look on Raphael's face you'd never know it. "I'd hoped that *long absent family* would make the list."

"But you still call yourself Aston."

"Am I to throw off my past as you've done?" I arched an eyebrow. "Does calling myself Aston, rather than Laurent, make us less than brothers?"

"Of course not. I was merely making a point."

"Taken," I said lightly, a playful smirk on my lips. "Have you, by chance, taken up the study of law?"

Raphael snorted. He despised lawyers, always had. "Have

a seat, Tobias. We have much to catch up on." His steps took him to a bar at the edge of the den. "Wine?"

"You know what I like." I reclined in a burgundy armchair by the window, looking out over the vast expanse of lawn. Night had now fallen in earnest, and darkness settled on the land outside the castle.

He poured me a glass of what I was sure was his best vintage, and I stared out the window. Beyond an expansive lawn, Lake Como glinted in the moonlight, and in my mind an image of Meredith materialized, bathed in the same silvery light.

My throat tightened. Were they out of Hell yet? Shay had promised that when she got word of their return, she'd text me.

It might be days.

"Barolo." Raphael approached, handing me a wine glass. "The vineyard no longer exists. A shame."

With the first sip, my eyes widened as notes of rose, licorice, and leather swept my tongue. "Agreed. Did you buy the lot?"

"You know me well."

"You love the best. Always have."

"A lesson you could learn. So do you still hide your royal name in the coven of yours?"

"Luca knows. And now Hans has known for a while too."

"Only because your blood told him."

It was true. I shrugged. "A couple of others know too, but I don't flaunt it."

"I used to think the same, but perhaps you should."

What did that mean? I sipped my wine again, determined to change the subject to protect S&S's secrets. "This is exquisite."

Swirling the wine in his glass, my brother sat in the chair next to me. "Did Giselle send you?"

"She suggested I visit, but I would have come anyway," I admitted. Perhaps not at this exact moment, if it weren't so convenient to travel here, but that was better left unsaid.

"She should come too."

The ease gracing his face fell a touch. I often got the sense that my older brother believed our sire did not pay him enough attention.

"I tell Raphael he's my favorite child to mollify him. You know how moody he gets . . ."

Giselle's words came back to me, and for the first time, I wondered if maybe he wasn't a bit right.

"She will," I promised. "She's working on something for the Blood right now and can't get away."

"Why she bothers with them is beyond me."

Another touchy subject. Decades ago, Raphael spent time in the Royal Vampire Court of Isila, and they did not celebrate his presence. As a result, his regard for our royal kin had diminished. Best not to dwell on them.

"So, Raph, what have you been up to these long years?" I used his nickname cautiously, and didn't miss the look of surprise my brother threw at me. "I see you've replaced your staff with our kind. Shocking, that."

One of many surprises, to be sure.

"The humans stopped coming."

Raphael *had* driven them away.

"Do your neighbors suspect anything?" I gestured to the large homes on either side of his castle. Due to the size of Raphael's estate and the trees surrounding it, one couldn't see much of them, but they were present, looming aside Castel Romono.

"They're both American celebrities. Never there, nor would they listen to those from the villages. Ideal neighbors."

"Still, it's good to be careful."

"I don't see why we have to. We're more powerful than humans by a long shot." He focused on the wine in his glass. "I bore of bowing to them."

This wasn't the first time my brother had expressed such views. Taken a touch further, he was a prime candidate for the Ordo Aeternum. That was, if they didn't want to create an apocalypse to maintain their New World Order. My brother would loathe an apocalypse. All that luxury, gone. How would he survive?

"I jest, Tobias."

"Truly?"

"Yes," he replied, a lie tainting his tone.

Unsure of how to proceed, I took another sip of wine. For a brief spell, things had become lighter, more like in the days when I was a young vampire and Raphael didn't see me as a thief of our sire's attention. One more drink and the wine was gone. I looked at the glass, sad that I'd paid it less attention than it deserved.

"There's more," Raphael offered knowingly. "Help yourself."

"I will." Thankful for the break in our conversation, I rose and strolled to the bar, taking time to appreciate the pieces furnishing my brother's den along the way.

A hand-crafted cabinet with quartz handles that, on my last visit, I'd learned cost millions to acquire. My brother's Fabergé egg, once owned by the Russian Imperial family, now rested— nearly innocuous—on an end table by a settee.

My eyes swept over a Renaissance painting of Raphael's hometown, done in the style of da Vinci, and focused on the gold plaque that glinted at the bottom. The painting wasn't in the master's style, it was *by* the master.

"Where did you acquire this?" I asked, gesturing to the painting while I continued to the bar. "I've not seen this before."

"Two years back. It was a privately owned work, but the moment I saw it, I had to have it."

"Of course, it's of your home."

"*This* is my home."

I shut my mouth. Raphael might have wanted the painting because of who created it, but perhaps there was something about it that bugged him too. Perhaps it reminded him of his downtrodden roots.

Finally slipping behind the bar, I searched for the bottle. First, however, my gaze snagged on something else.

A pair of sunglasses, flat at the top, black, and so modern that they stuck out amidst the finery or the past. My head tilted as I plucked the pair up with my fingers. They were nothing special, definitely not designer glasses—hence, not Raphael's. Yet, they seemed so familiar. Where had I seen those before?

"What are you doing?" Raphael's tone hardened, and I looked up to find him watching me with a stern expression.

"Are these yours?" I held up the glasses.

"Of course."

His tone was the same as when he'd lied, and I wanted to call him on it, but refrained. Tonight was my time to speak with my brother, bond. Now that I was here, guilt over staying away for so long swarmed me.

I placed the glasses down and reached for the Barolo. "Not your usual style."

"An impulsive and poor choice, I admit," my brother

conceded, with a hint of a smile. "But enough about me. What have you been doing of late, Brother?"

Shocked, I blinked. Raphael didn't ask about me often.

"Don't look at me like that. You and Serena have always acted like I didn't care about you two."

"Not exactly. More like . . ."

"I'd rather discuss myself?"

I had nothing to say to that, which apparently hit my brother hard. A sheepish shadow crossed his expression, the sight strange on his strong, classic Roman features.

"For a while, I've been thinking it's time to change my ways. And it must be a sign that you drove all the way here to check in." He waved me back to him. "So please, tell me what Tobias Blake *Aston* has been doing these past years."

Taking the bottle back to where we sat, I reclined in the chair. The ring in my pocket felt suddenly heavier. There was much I couldn't discuss with Raphael, but I had many facets to my life. I'd only have to steer clear of those regarding the *lapis caelesti*. Easily done.

So, I dove into my personal studies, mostly focusing on various sciences, which evolved so much over the years that they held me captivated. Raphael listened intently and asked questions. We laughed. We drank. We discussed literature like old times. And before we realized it, the night slipped away and the sun climbed the sky, shedding light upon the lake.

At nine, a knock at the door finally interrupted us, and the butler poked his head into the room. "Master?"

"Yes?"

"The human from the museum in Florence is here to appraise your latest acquisition. Do you wish to speak with her?"

"I'll be right there." Raphael's eyes fell on me. "This has been quite an evening, Brother."

"It has," I said, a little drunk from the many bottles of wine we'd gone through. And tired. More tired than I had been in ages. Though vampires didn't need sleep in the same way that mortals did, we still required rest. "I think I might lie down."

"When you wake, perhaps we can hunt?"

I arched an eyebrow.

"Pheasant. Or buntings. Your pick."

"Sounds like fun. I'm waiting for a message from my employer, but if I don't hear from them, then yes. I'll stay the day."

Raphael rose. "I'll see you later, then."

The master of the house exited the den, but the butler remained. "I'll show you to your room, *Signore* Aston."

"Tobias," I corrected.

"Very well."

The older vampire led me through the castle, up the stairs and down a narrow corridor. While we walked, I stole a glance at my phone. Shay still hadn't contacted me, then again, she couldn't have been in the States long. There was no call or text from Luca either, which was more telling. The trio who'd quested to Hell had not returned.

My fists clenched, but I forced myself to shrug off the frustration from not being able to help Meredith, Hans, or Gunner. I'd done my job, discovered who the vault in *Le Bastion* belonged to, and that the theft was connected to the mystery group of thieves. Now, I had to trust that the other team could handle their jobs too.

Forcing my attention away from that which I could not change, I focused on the paintings and other pieces of artwork we passed, many Italian in provenance. The palace was abnormally quiet, seemingly empty of souls, though I suspected most were just out of sight. Raphael was probably of the belief that unless he required their assistance, servants should be neither seen nor heard.

The corridor ended in another hallway. When we reached the T, the butler went left—but I stopped. A few of the windows in this corridor were open, and a scent hung in the air—faint, yet strong enough to catch my attention after bottles of wine.

Smoke? A hint of brimstone?

"Signore?"

I turned to find the butler waiting. "Is someone burning incense?" That would be most unusual in a vampire household. We avoided strong smells.

"Not that I'm aware of. If it displeases you, I can find the source and eliminate it."

Lifting my nose, I sniffed the air again, but the scent had disappeared. It must have been passing, blown away by a lake breeze. Perhaps Raphael was incorrect, and one of his celebrity neighbors was at Como, practicing morning yoga.

"That won't be necessary. I can barely smell it now," I admitted to the butler, even though something still felt off. Best not to rock the ship in Raphael's home, and a faint whiff meant little. "Carry on."

"Very good. This way, *Signore.*"

CHAPTER TEN

MEREDITH

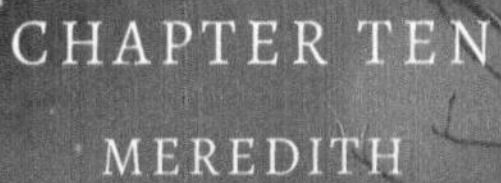

Time had officially become meaningless in Hell.

The heat shimmered in the air, oppressive, pulling sweat from our pores so that it dripped down our chins. Benedict had lost the pep in his step the energy bar had given him, and my own steps resonated as heavy, achy too. Though we were careful to conserve water, I was growing ever more fearful that our supply would not last.

At the thought of water, my throat itched and burned. I reached for my canteen, needing a sip, but became distracted when Hans stopped.

"The opening into the farming fields is around an upcoming bend. Are you two ready?"

I was dying to get out of this tunnel, but was I ready to seek amidst a field of demons? Who in their right mind would say yes to that?

Still, when Gunner nodded, I did too, not about to be the weak link in our chain.

"Time for these babies then." Hans slipped a hand in his pocket, pulling out the vial of invisibility potion.

Goosebumps dashed up my arms.

Finally. Gunner and I mimicked Hans, extracting our potions from our packs.

My bag was soaked through with sweat, only driving home the fact that I was dehydrating quickly, so I also grabbed my water and took two large gulps. Finally, I extracted the small bundle of lucimisia herb Daphne had given me. This bunch of herbs was the one thing I needed to seek.

Though tempted to call on my magic right away, to feel how strong the pull was—hence, how close the herb—I didn't. Any use of magic put us in danger, and unlike Hans, I had less skill at controlling the fluctuations in my power.

It was best to wait until we entered the farming area and got the lay of the land. Until we absolutely needed my seeker magic.

"We have an hour to find the lucimisia after the potion takes effect. Bottoms up." The wizard popped the top off his vial and downed its contents.

I followed suit, delighting in the moisture and the taste of mint.

"How long do you think we walked for?" I asked.

"Time runs differently here," Hans explained. "But my legs say hours."

My body agreed. That meant we'd be trekking for hours back. On autopilot, I pulled my second to last energy bar from my pack, gobbling down two-thirds of it. The rest I gave to Benedict.

Hans nodded his approval. "Good thinking. Keeping up your energy. You good, Gunner?"

"Yeah. Stone, give me a whiff of that herb. Maybe I can help scent it out while we're in the field."

The instant I offered him the bundle, the wolf put it to his nose, inhaling deeply. Then he returned it. "My first order of business is to watch your back. But if I catch the scent of the lucimisia, I'll tell you."

"Thanks." Having help would be welcomed, if it meant we could get the hell out of dodge quicker. "I—"

Cold washed over me, and out of nowhere I felt . . . wispier? Like a strong breeze might blow me away.

"My potion kicked in," Hans announced. "You're blurry."

"What?"

"Your edges are blurred. Daphne told me that's a sign that you're invisible to others," Hans said. "Are you two cold and kinda weak?"

"Yeah," I murmured, super confused. "But we can still see each other."

"That's because the potions are from the same batch. If you're cold, not quite feeling all there, and fuzzy-looking to other potion-takers then you're invisible. I'm blurry too, right?"

"You are." I turned to Gunner. He too seemed fuzzy. This was so odd. "Both of you."

"Then let's not waste any time," Hans said, gesturing for us to follow.

We set off, and soon enough, rounded the bend. The tunnel opened before us, light spilling into the ring of obsidian we'd been walking through for hours. I sucked in a breath. As Hans had predicted, a field spread out in front of us.

A field filled with *hundreds* of monstrous-looking creatures working the soil. I scanned the valley, fear gripping me tighter and tighter by the second. There were more types of devils than I ever could have imagined, and during our walk I'd been imagining a hell of a lot.

Some of them loomed over others, massive brutes, all

muscle and mean red eyes below their curled horns. The largest among them looked like pure meat shells, with plows attached to their bodies while they trudged down the fields to dig up the earth.

Most sub-orders were smaller, many with black wings, and carrying cans of water in clawed hands.

The supervisors looked the most human though with barbed tails and horns. They walked up and down the paths between plantings, whipping anyone who didn't move fast enough. Or maybe just because they wanted to? Every few seconds, the sound of a whip cracking on flesh, and a growl or shriek of pain filled the air. Excessive and disgusting.

On the far side of the valley, miles away, steam rose. From the dripping of lava down one mountainside, I suspected a river of lava flowed over there, bubbling and boiling hot.

Please don't let the herb be close to that. It was so far away that it would take us the better part of the hour to get there. Returning to the relative safety of the tunnel would be impossible.

"Stay close," Hans whispered. "Benedict, that means you."

The cat peered around the corner and glared up at Hans before turning invisible with his own magic. Truth be told, the wizard had a point. Benedict often trailed off, separating himself from the group. He couldn't do that here.

We rounded the edge of the valley, steering clear of the demons working the fields. As we trod, I gawked at the massive, black castle on the opposite side of the valley. Which Prince of Hell did that belong to? Were they in residence now? Close enough to feel my magic when I used it?

"Gunner, can you smell the herb?" the wizard whispered.

"Not a whiff. Can't smell much over the stink of demons though. It's way stronger in the field."

"Let's hope they can't detect us over *their* stench, then."

My stomach dropped. Did demons have enhanced senses, like wolves? There were so many kinds that surely, they did, right? Oh, God.

"Okay, Meredith." Hans twisted, catching my eye and ripping me out of what would have likely become an epic mental freak out session. "Are you seeking? We can't put it off any longer."

Oh crap! I'd been so caught up in the demons and the castle and, well, *everything else*, that I'd spaced.

My hands grew clammy. So far, it didn't seem that Benedict's invisibility had set off any alarms, but would adding my magic be the tipping point? Would mine be more powerful, more noticeable?

An image of Luca, clinging to life in the infirmary bed, swam in my mind and my throat tightened. No matter the risk of using magic, I had to do it. My power was our best chance to find the lucimisia and get the heck out of here.

"On it." I gripped the bunch of herbs in my hand and called my magic. It sprang to life inside of me, as if it, too, had been waiting for this moment.

Tingles rippled across the skin of my hand holding the lucimisia, flew up my arm and into my core. I took in a steeling breath, no longer noticing the stench of sulfur, but instead waiting for the sensation that would tell me if we were on the right track.

One more step. Two. Then three.

The pull struck behind my breastbone, and suddenly I sensed the lucimisia, knew it was here. Not close enough to bend down and pull it from the soil, but here. Somewhere . .
.

"It's in this field," I whispered.

"Thank fuck," the wizard breathed, hinting that he might have been more uncertain than he'd shown.

"Can we stop for a second? I want to get a clear read." For the time being, there wasn't a demon *too* close to us. The nearest one was about fifty feet away, a hulking beast pulling an old-fashioned plow to create new furrows in the soil.

Obliging, Hans paused, and Gunner followed in line. As Benedict was using his own magic, and not our potion, I couldn't see him, but hoped he was listening.

Not about to waste a second, I honed in on the direction of the pull and scanned the field. As my magic searched, I did too. Daphne had informed me that living lucimisia looked a lot like dillweed, and when she showed me a photo, I agreed. Though, the herb from the underworld had purple flowers with spiky petals on the top, which my dried herb did not have.

I hoped the flowers would stand out in the field, but there were a lot of colors out there. Mostly red, but enough blues and purples to make me doubt if I was looking at a patch of lucimisia or not.

The tug of seeker magic yanked me to the left, and I twisted, eyes widening when I caught a patch of purple amongst a bunch of red. That had to be it. Thank goodness it wasn't by the river of lava.

"There!" I pointed for the guys. "See the purple?"

"Yup." Hans looked at Gunner and I was struck by how weird they looked, all fuzzy around the edges of their body. As my extremities were blurred, I knew I looked the same to them too, but still . . . how bizarre. "I'll take front. You stay behind her. Meredith, if your magic changes direction on you at any time, do not hesitate to tell us. There might be more crops and if we need to, we'll make a couple of stops. Filling up the bags is imperative."

"That row of crops has some of the bigger monsters hanging around," Gunner considered, sizing up a demon who was indeed standing two rows over from the one we needed to pick.

"When we harvest, we do it carefully. Not too much from one place. Like we talked about earlier," Hans added, clearly as worried as I was that the smallest thing would give us away. Shit, I was trying not to even breathe too loudly. "And Benedict?"

"On Meredith's left," the cat replied.

"You stay behind Gunner. We can't have anyone tripping over you. But that means if we have to do a quick retreat . . ."

"I best be quick about it."

"Yeah," Hans confirmed. For a second a thoughtful expression crossed his face, but it seemed he had nothing else to add, so he rolled his shoulders back and gave the signal to move. "Let's go."

I fell in line behind the wizard, my magic still tugging me in the same direction. Steady. Strong. Reassuring. We were at the point where every minute counted. I didn't want to get halfway there, only to realize that I'd misspoken and the herb was actually a mile in the other direction. The tunnel might be relatively free of demons, but this field was crawling with them. We could not be in the open when the invisibility potion stopped working.

We scurried down the row I was pulled to, our steps halting when two demons passed, talking to one another in a brutal-sounding language full of hard sounds and guttural noises. As soon as they passed, we were on the move again, reaching the patch of herbs a few minutes later.

A relieved breath left me, seeing that the plant in front of us matched the dried lucimisia in my hand. Just the fresh version with flowers still attached.

"This is it." Kneeling in front of it, I opened my bag, taking care to keep touching the fabric of the backpack so it wouldn't become visible.

The guys did the same. We knew the drill. This was the moment that counted. With a gentle shake to vanquish the nerves, I wrapped my hands around the stem, as close to the root as I could get.

Healer Daphne told us that if we got some root, the supplier in our world *might* be able to use the roots to replant his crops. It was a long shot, but we had to do our best to harvest properly.

Every handful counted, and no one needed to undertake this quest again.

I gripped and pulled. The herb came free of the dirt—which was loose and dry—easily. Slowly, I shifted the plant into my bag.

"Reposition," I whispered, and as a team, each of us moved down two spots. We had to spread out what we took, so we wouldn't leave obvious patches in the field.

Steadily, we worked together like machines, pulling and shifting down a few spaces, moving as fast as we dared.

"Behind you," Benedict hissed, and the rest of us froze when one of the supervising demons strode our way, about four rows behind. The whip in his hand dragged along the ground, like a snake poised to strike. My pulse pounded, so hard and fast that I feared he might hear it.

Once the creature passed, and got far enough away, I exhaled a breath I hadn't even known I was holding.

"Too damned close for comfort," Gunner whispered.

"For sure," Hans rasped. "My bag's half full. Yours?"

I nodded, as did Gunner.

Relief dashed across Hans's face. "Five more minutes. Get as much as we can. Then we leave."

I'd never heard sweeter words.

I went to work, counting the seconds as I harvested, hitting sixty and starting again at zero. When I'd done so five times, I looked at Hans, and blinked.

He'd stopped harvesting altogether, and was turned the other way, his shoulders rigid, his gaze on something in the distance. The castle? A foe?

My attention drifted up and I shifted so that I could see around him. Catching his view, I sucked in a breath.

A woman stood off the fields, her hair a brilliant red, her beauty striking in a landscape of demons and darkness. A strength wafted off of her, unlike anything I'd ever seen. But he couldn't just be looking at her beauty. Nor because power radiated from her.

Was that Hans's mother? She didn't look old enough to be . . . but Lilith was eternal, a demon prince's wife. She might not age.

"Hans?" I whispered, trying to break him out of his trance.

In answer, he zipped up his bag, rose, and began walking toward the woman.

"What in the hell is he up to?" Gunner asked, too loudly, and a nearby demon turned our way.

Eyes narrowed, the brute grunted, though it sounded like a question—like he wondered who had spoken—but I couldn't spare the demon another thought.

Hans was getting too far away. We had to stop him before he blew our mission.

Securing my bag, I darted after the wizard. The sound of

footsteps told me that Gunner jogged at my heels. Unable to see him and check, I hoped Benedict trailed us too.

As we ran after Hans, he picked up speed. The red-haired woman had entranced him, so much so that he didn't even look back at us. I watched, in horror, as he stopped in front of her, reached for her.

He's giving away that we're here!

Hans's hand landed on the woman's shoulder and she jerked back, but he must have said something too because an instant later, a smile bloomed on her face. Her shoulders loosened.

Okay, she knows him. It has to be his mom. She—oh shit!

Hans had not just announced himself to someone, thereby risking our mission, he'd also stopped looking fuzzy, an indicator that the invisibility potion was wearing off. But we couldn't have already been out here for an hour!

"Stoney," Gunner whispered.

"I know," I shot back, unable to take my eyes off Hans and the woman, who stared at where he stood—though the blur around the edges of his body had reappeared so I didn't think she saw him—pure shock on her beautiful face.

We had to get the hell out of dodge. Fast.

With a burst of speed, I sprinted toward them, nearly colliding with the wizard. "Hans!" I hissed, which made the red-haired woman jump. "What are you doing, you idiot!? We have to get out of here!"

"Mother, you have to come with me." Hans ignored me, redirecting Lilith's attention to him.

I stiffened as again, for a heartbeat, Hans became solid and therefore visible.

"Nicoleta needs you."

The demoness stared right at where Hans stood, now invisible once more, but who knew for how long. Her expression was loving yet pained. I expected that she couldn't see him, but she envisioned him there. With her. "Son, your friend is right. You must leave. Now."

"But—"

I slammed my hand onto his shoulder and whirled Hans around to face me. "You're flickering back to solid! No one has noticed yet, but they will. We have to—"

The blur around my arm vanished and returned.

Oh no, now I was flickering into sight, too.

"Intruders!" someone roared from deep in the field. "Queen of Darkness! They're right next to you!"

We'd run out of time.

Lilith's eyes hardened. "I can't join you, Son. Go. *NOW*."

"But I promised Nicoleta I'd bring you back!"

He'd done what?! Heat that had nothing to do with how unbearably roasting it was down here, flared within me.

"It was a foolish promise, my son. I'll visit when I can." Lilith's eyes trailed to something behind me, and my blood ran cold as terror flashed in her eyes. "I'll cover for you."

Fire bloomed in the queen's hands, and she blasted it over our heads. "Go, Son! If you don't, you and your friends shall perish!"

Gripping Hans's arm, I pulled him. He didn't budge an inch, but Gunner butted in, and when he grabbed Hans, he couldn't fight the alphablood's strength. Gunner dragged the wizard across the crops, rustling them as he went, but considering our time constraints I figured that was the least of our worries. I ran after them, sweat pouring down my face.

"Benedict!" I yelled, panicking and forgetting to stay quiet.

"Right next to you!"

"Jump into my arms!" I held them out, urging him to make

the leap. A second later, a furry weight landed. I clutched him to my chest, holding on for dear life. We had to make it to the tunnel. If we could stay invisible and do that, there was no reason to believe the demons would go there. The tunnel had been empty before, unused. I had to believe it would be that way again—that we wouldn't have a hoard chase us . . .

A vicious roar came from behind, and against my better judgment, I twisted. In that second, the glimmer of hope I'd been clinging to crashed and burned. Three of the skinny, winged demons were already chasing us.

"Faster!" I gritted out. We were fuzzy around our edges, so the demons couldn't see us, but we were leaving a trail through the field. Once we got in the tunnel, we'd be much more difficult to follow. "Guys, we have to—"

A rope of fire, lashed from behind the winged beasts, lassoing them and ripping them in half.

What the heck?

My questions were answered as I caught sight of Lilith pulling the lasso of flame back. I exhaled. Hans's mother had our sixes, and I had to trust that she would do everything to allow us to escape.

"We need to pick up the—" When I turned to face my team, the words died in my throat. Two rows down, coming from the side, a muscular, horned demon charged toward Hans and Gunner, the latter of whom was focused solely on forcing the wizard forward.

"Guys!" I yelled, but the beast ran at an astonishing speed, and had already launched himself at Hans, claws extended, mouth gaping.

By some miracle, the demon miscalculated, hitting the ground before he could grasp our friend. Yet, his claws were so long that they still sank into Hans's leg. The wizard roared, and magic flew from him, sending the demon soaring back the way he'd come.

If our flickering invisibility and me yelling like a mad woman hadn't given us away, that surely had. Not that I was angry at Hans for fighting back. That demon was out for blood and he'd gotten it too, but Hans had made him pay for it. Thankfully, the wizard could still run, though now with a limp.

My heart began to beat frantically. If only using more invisibility potion was an option! That would save our butts! As it was, it would be a miracle if we got out of here alive.

A screech shot another surge of adrenaline through me, and I glanced behind us once more.

Again, Lilith was wielding fire, but somehow, she was even fiercer than before. With astonishing accuracy, she hurled fire at anyone who was close or chasing us—including the flock of demons. They dropped from the sky, rolling through the crops, and setting row after row aflame.

I found it almost impossible to tear my eyes away from Hans's mother. She was so powerful; it was like she *was* the flame.

Better yet, her attacks were causing other demons, probably the ones for which tending the crops was their occupation, to give up on following the intruders. They were now focused on trying to save the plants. I'd bet money that if the crops died, they did too. This was Hell, after all.

Determined not to let the Queen of Darkness's actions be in vain, I put on a burst of speed and raced for the tunnel.

CHAPTER ELEVEN

HANS

Regret tore at every fiber of my being as we rushed through the tunnel.

Though it was lunacy, with each step my heart urged me to return to my mother, to pull her behind me.

To make good on my promise to Nicoleta.

But somehow, my brain stayed in control. As the only one capable of working the spell to open the portal, Gunner, Meredith, and Benedict were counting on me to get them back home. I couldn't risk their lives. Not again. I'd already royally screwed up by blowing our cover. My mother had had to save our asses.

What made it even harder was that I'd seen how much Lilith wanted to come. The yearning to be with my father, the man she loved, and her children, shone plainly in her eyes. The moment I flickered out of invisibility, however, that desire had vanished, replaced by the fierceness of a lioness.

My fists clenched so tightly that my nails cut into the skin of my palms. If only I'd spotted her five minutes earlier. If that had been the case, we all might have been able to sneak out of Hell.

As it stood, I'd return only with a broken promise. With lives put at risk, and my covenmates ire upon me. Worst of all, my mother was likely now in danger because she'd protected us.

A burning sensation flared in my dry throat when I swallowed, my body begging for water. Was this the day my mother came clean about her family in my world? Would Lucifer kill her for her adultery? If so, it would be all my fault.

My soul cracked in half, and my breath ripped out of me, leaving me feeling empty save for the pain washing through my body.

"We're close, right?" Meredith wheezed, just before we burst out of the tunnel and scrambled down a mountain of black, shiny rocks. She hitched her bag full of lucimisia higher, shifted Benedict's weight in her arms, but her attention remained trained on me, demanding an answer. "The portal entrance is close?"

"Yes." I gestured toward the Field of Punishment as it opened to our side. "We're close. Do you hear anyone?"

"No," Gunner replied. He'd been listening for trailing footsteps for hours.

"Good. I'll go first," I offered, while Meredith and Gunner slowed so that even with my limping gait, I overtook them. We were within twenty feet of the portal, a hidden niche in an otherwise black expanse of wall, when I held out my hands. "Grab on!"

Meredith grunted, shifting Benedict's weight yet again— from both arms to one. Then, one of her hands latched on to mine while Gunner took the other, and we shuffled into the depression in the rock wall.

"Otkrx."

Hell disappeared, and a bitter cold wrapped around me, sucking away the stifling heat. The abrupt change in temperatures shocked my body, and I was unable to brace myself as we entered the human world. I fell like a rag doll, snow shoving its way up my nostrils when I face-planted in the center of the circle of dead trees.

A moan escaped my lips, half from exhaustion, half from relief. The oppressive heat was gone. We'd retrieved the herb.

Against all odds, and despite my idiocy, we'd survived.

Thank the Goddess.

Meredith shifted to her side, groaning as she did so. "You okay, Benedict?"

"F-f-fine." The stutter, so unlike the pulled together feline, betrayed the truth. No one here was fine. We were all reeling from what we'd seen, how we'd almost died, and the marathon sprint back to safety. How we'd run so far for so long, I don't think I'd ever know. It had to have been the adrenaline pushing us through.

"Well, I feel like hell," Meredith grunted. Another shift in the snow, another groan. "Gunner?"

"Wish I had a cold brewski to calm the old nerves."

At that, a strangled laugh worked its way up my throat, and I pushed myself up, grabbing a handful of snow and shoving it in my mouth. Damn, that was good. Cold and wet.

My vision, which I hadn't even noticed was cloudy from dehydration, cleared a touch and I looked around us. The forest was still, stars glinting in the pitch-black sky.

So, it was night. What day? What time?

Somewhere in the distance, a wolf howled, then another, only to be joined by a third. I scrubbed a wet hand over my nape.

"That's a real one," Gunner rasped from where he lay, face up, staring at the sky. "Not my kind."

"Uh, we should go then?" Meredith asked, already sitting up and looking worried that a wolf might jump through the circle of trees and attack.

"It won't come here," I assured her. "Nothing does."

"But we have to walk a long way back to the village. That's plenty of time for a wolf pack to find us."

Meredith sounded like the very thought of walking to Minim might do her in. I didn't blame her. With my limp, I wasn't looking forward to the hours of hiking through the snow either. But at least, we had plenty of water and the extra energy bars we left here to sustain us. The plastic baggies filled with goods were half-buried in the snow. We were beat, but strong. Get some calories in us, and we'd be fine.

"The wolves won't bug us as we walk either," Gunner added. "The pack will sense me and stay away." He rose to sit, his shirt soaked through with sweat.

The first brave soul to attempt walking around was Benedict, which he did as if he were a kitten trying out his legs for the first time.

When I tried standing too, I nearly fell over. The dehydration was real, more serious than I'd let myself feel in the underworld, so I ate five more handfuls of snow. Slowly, my energy rekindled to where I thought moving might be an option. I took a tentative step toward the edge of the trees.

I blinked. Someone was walking toward us. Wiping my eyes, I focused on the shadow again.

Is that Nicoleta?

"Sister?"

"It's me."

"What are you doing out here? It's late!"

The woods were dangerous at night. The spot we stood in was safe, but she would have walked for miles to get here, and the rest of the forest was crawling with animals.

"Waiting for you, Brother. I didn't go home."

"What?! How long have you been out here?"

"It's the day you left. A few minutes before midnight."

We'd been in Hell for twelve hours. It felt like so much longer.

"Where's Mother?"

"She's still in Hell," I admitted to Nicoleta. "I'm so sorry, Nic. I tried to bring her. I really did."

My sister's face turned hard as stone.

"He tried so hard it nearly got us killed," Meredith spat out. "Which, by the way, I have questions about. Why didn't you tell us you were on the lookout for your mom?"

I turned to the other two. "I'm sorry. I told Nicoleta I'd bring our mother back if the opportunity presented itself, and it did so . . ."

"You did see her then?" my sister asked, her tone twisted with venom and steel.

"Yes." She'd come closer, and now stood right in front of me, her hands clenched at her sides. "I spoke with Mom, Nic. She was so happy to see me, to hear of you."

"You saw her, you *spoke* with her, and you didn't bring her?!" Tendrils of darkness, illuminated by the moonlight, spooled out of Nicoleta.

My eyes widened, and I took a step back. Clearly, she was so upset that she couldn't control herself right now. It had been a long time since that happened, and spoke to how badly my sister had wanted our mother back. "We ran out of time and were in a dangerous position. I—"

"You broke your promise! You're *worthless!*" Black wings

unfurled from her back, whipping the wind around me and stealing all the breath from my lungs.

What the hell? She'd never had those!

"Nicoleta!" I called, taking a faltering step back as she beat cold wind into my face. "What are you doing?"

"What I should have done when you showed up here, you worthless piece of *rahat*!" A blade appeared in her hand, one I recognized from Father's collection, the silver glinting in the moonlight.

My heart rate kicked up as I dove into the snow, only to be caught by black tendrils of magic. I struggled, but they wound their way around my body, my neck, covering my mouth and stealing my air. Flat on my back, my sister sneered viciously down on me.

"Leave him alone!" Meredith screamed, to which my sister laughed, a lyrical crow's laugh.

In the dark, Nic's eyes glowed red. "He failed me, failed our family. Hans is *weak*, he always has been. It's why he ran away instead of facing those in our tiny village." She spat on the ground.

The pressure around my throat tightened, and I began to choke. I reached up, pulling at the ribbons of darkness, and failing. Nicoleta's smile widened, a cruel slash in an otherwise angelic face. She was strangling me with her tendrils.

"He—!" I tried to cry for help, but only managed part of the word.

It was enough.

The air shifted in a way that I recognized. Gunner was transforming, but my vision was already going fuzzy. The alpha wouldn't be fast enough to counteract Nicoleta's assault.

Benedict, however, was. With shocking viciousness, the cat

leapt toward my sister with a hiss—claws extended. He struck true, clawing at my sister's cheeks and slicing her skin open.

A pain-filled scream ripped from her throat, and her tendrils released me, allowing breath to swoop into my lungs once more. I gulped it down, and slowly the world shifted back into focus.

"Vile beast!" Nicoleta screamed, and the cat wailed, disappearing from my starry field of vision. A *thunk* told me he'd been hurled against a tree.

"*Benedict*!" Meredith screamed.

Desperate to help, I drew in another breath and staggered to my feet, calling on my magic. I faced my sister, who was now sneering at Meredith while she kneeled outside the circle of trees, cradling her unconscious familiar.

"How could you?!" Meredith spat, her free hand reaching for her *aslinki* blade.

At the sight of the dagger, my sister snorted, shooting a dark tendril at Meredith. It struck her square in the temple, and the witch collapsed with the cat in her arms.

"Nicoleta!" I roared.

"She's knocked out," Nicoleta sang. "I don't need to kill. My prince will eliminate all the weaklings when he takes over! He will be the great decider of fates!"

Was she *insane*? What was she talking about?

Gunner's vicious growl called my attention, his wolfish silver eyes glinted with a warning that he was about to strike, but I held out a hand.

It was my failure that had upset her, and I knew firsthand how hot the darkness burned through us when we were in that state. I had to control her, to make her see sense, and get answers. She'd done damage, but she could still come back from it.

I just needed to talk sense into my sister.

"What are you talking about, Nicoleta? Why would you, or some prince, want to," I swallowed, recalling her cruel words, *"eliminate* anyone?"

Nicoleta's wings beat, lifting her higher into the air, and as she rose, her eyes glowed red in the center.

The sight froze my every muscle. No . . . This couldn't be real. Nicoleta had embraced her demon side more than I'd known, more than I thought was possible.

"You didn't really believe I sat in Minim for a decade, waiting for my stupid big brother to return? For Mother to make an appearance?" My sister sneered. "No, Hans. After a year, it became clear you weren't coming back, so I took matters into my own hands. I sought mentors. Practiced my magic."

"You understood how to use magic when I left," I countered. "I made sure of it. And Father could have helped you too."

"Father can help with my *witch* magic. *Weak* power, unworthy of someone of my line." Nicoleta spat into the snow. "Your line too, Brother, if you weren't too cowardly to claim the blood in your veins."

The moonlight fell on her back, illuminating the tendrils that spooled out of her, both mesmerizing and threatening as they twisted toward the heavens.

My teeth gnashed together. "What prince are you talking about?"

"A Lord of Darkness, of course."

Gunner growled again, but I kept my arm out, hoping he'd stay put. If he wanted to, he could push past me. He was, after all, an alpha wolf—the strongest of his kind. But I had to get to the bottom of this, had to understand.

"Impossible," I argued. "The Princes of Darkness are all banished to the underworld."

For a brief period during the Second World War, the princes had figured out a way to escape their underworld prison. They flitted in and out of Hell. Their minions had too, and all had wreaked havoc on humanity. Once the human war ended, supernaturals banished the demons, and locked them up tight.

This included the worst of their kind, the seven Princes of Darkness, Lilith, the other royal brides, and the royal heirs.

Until they weren't . . .

Dread exploded inside me. Mother had returned and she wasn't just a royal bride. She was the strongest among them, her power equaling the princes's. But Lilith always swore that she worked alone.

Still, had other demons escaped too? Wouldn't supernaturals have noticed?

"You're finally using your brain." Nicoleta sneered. "Mother isn't the only royal to have created an escape hatch. My lord, Orien, did too, and he's putting things in place for when his brothers arrive. For when we blow the Eyes of Darkness open wide!" She threw her arms out to the side, reveling in the horrible idea.

"You can't," I ground out. "If you do—"

"I know what will happen!" Nicoleta shrieked. "When my lord rules, all those who doubted him will bow before him. The Darkborn will stand at his glorious side while we purge the Earth!"

At that ominous proclamation, Gunner lunged, teeth bared, claws ready to dig into my sister's skin, but Nicoleta retaliated just as fast, her tendrils snapping out. They seized the wolf, lifting him forty feet in the air.

"Let him go!" I ordered.

"If you insist."

Nicoleta dropped Gunner, and as he fell, his silver eyes flashed with fear.

"*Baestu.*" I hurled the protection spell at the alphablood to slow his fall before facing my sister.

Her eyes narrowed on me, the irises burning crimson. Off to the side, a *crash* and a whimper announced Gunner had hit the ground, but I couldn't turn away from Nicoleta to check on him. It was far too dangerous to turn my back on her.

"Hide them though you might, Brother, you have wings too, buried in all the weakness. You could have flown to get him. Or used these."

Her tendrils surged my way once again.

"*Baestu!*"

The dark wisps slowed but kept coming, so I flung another spell, another protection. Sweat dripped down my face as I tried to stop my sister.

Her sinister laughter split the night. "Can't you see? The dark side is where the real power is!" Nicoleta paused, as if realizing something for the first time. "You've failed, but you do have the same potential as me. So, I'll make one more request of you, Brother."

I drew in a breath, not liking where this was going.

"Join me, Hans. We'll have to stop in the village before we meet my lord, but he'd welcome another warrior. Another of our bloodline."

"Why the village?" I asked. "You can't take Father. The prince will kill him!"

"I'd never endanger Father." Nicoleta shot back. "And don't you worry about him. Orien will appease Lucifer. But we must stop in Minim for you to feed before you meet my prince."

My stomach dropped to my knees. "Feed?"

"How else do you think I gained so much strength? Mother's blood could only do so much. I feed on the life-forces of those who mocked us and called us monsters. You will too, and then my lord will be less likely to discard you as one of the weaklings he so despises."

She called off her tendrils with a wave. "You might have failed me in returning Mother to my side, but as I said, I love my family. So, I give you this chance, Brother. One more chance to pair with our kind, to serve my lord. Will you join me?"

Ice crawled through my veins. My sister fed off the life-forces of those we'd grown up with? Mihai had mentioned that the wolves kept their distance from her. Did they know this? Did she do it to them?

"It doesn't hurt the villagers," Nicoleta added, as if reading my mind was part of her arsenal too.

Could she? If one thing was clear to me, it was that her powers had grown. I didn't know my sister as well as I once had, not well at all.

"And I make sure they are happy afterward." Her black wings lowered her from where she'd hovered to land on the snow, a hand still extended for me.

I couldn't bear to watch my sister spiral into darkness. She sounded like a lunatic, and though even our mother had a dark side, she never spoke like this. Never acted this way.

No, I'd be damned if Nicoleta went full dark.

Striking like a viper, magic sprayed from my hands, meant to stun, to disarm, but my sister anticipated my move.

Twirling out of the way, she retaliated by sending a blaze of black power my way.

I braced a half second before it hit, and I soared backward ten feet. I slammed into a tree, groaning when I slumped onto the ground.

"Get away from me, you filthy witch!" Nicoleta shouted.

Meredith! I shot up to find the witch stumbling away from my sister, a dagger in her hand.

"Hans! Her shirt!" Meredith screamed.

I squinted to find the witch had torn a part of Nicoleta's shirt, and through the tear, a necklace from my paternal grandmother gleamed, the moonlight reflecting off the central black-blue stone.

"The symbol!" Meredith roared.

The what?

I squinted and this time, I saw it. A breath of frigid air filled my lungs, freezing my body as it plunged.

The Sigil of Lucifer was branded on the right side of my sister's chest.

Meredith slashed her again, and determined to help, Gunner rose from where he'd hit the earth. The wolf lunged.

Nicoleta moved as fast as a serpent, wings unfurling again. Tendrils swam through the air, but she thought twice about taking on the three of us alone, instead throwing me a glare.

"Tell Father I'll keep him safe. The Darkborn will stay away from him, from Minim. But I make no such promise to you, Brother." Beating her wings, she lifted from the earth and soared into the night sky.

CHAPTER TWELVE

MEREDITH

"I'll drop you here." Hans pulled over, as close to the entrance of the S&S tomb as he could get, given all the cars parked on the street side. "You good?"

"Yeah. I'll be fine," I mumbled, bones and muscles aching as I looped the duffel containing my clothes, a sleeping Benedict, and the lucimisia herb around my body.

Only Gunner, who we'd already dropped off at home because it was on the way, was physically fine after hiking so far through the Romanian woods and practically running a marathon in Hell. I was envious of his shifter abilities, but I'd heal in a day or two. Or at least, that's what I kept telling myself as I slid out of the car, stifling a groan.

"I'll bring in the other bags. See you there." Driving off, Hans went to find a place to park.

Mentally, I wished him luck. The blocks surrounding campus were more packed than usual. *There must be a concert going on or something tonight.*

Hobbling down the sidewalk, my ankle twisted, making

me winced. Okay, maybe I'd need more than a day to feel normal again. A week of sleep should do it.

Had I pulled my Achilles tendon? As if to really stick it to me, my lower back spasmed. Groaning, I pressed my palms into the muscles around my spine.

This must be what getting old is like.

Finally reaching the alley that hid the entrance to head-quarters, I turned, and a wash of cold air rushed over me. A shiver gripped my spine, but the cold disappeared before I even got to the door.

Though students passing by on their way to their evening courses couldn't see me, I still shot a wary glance to the road before extending my hand and whispering the password. The single word, in combination with my unique magical finger-print, opened the door to S&S's tomb. Slipping inside, I exhaled and made my way to the healing wing as fast as my body would permit.

Thankfully it was late, so the hallway was empty, as was the atrium. In all, I only passed one person while I climbed the stairs to the infirmary wing.

When I reached the healers' wing, Shay was there, and at the sound of someone entering, her head swiveled toward the door. Her blue eyes lit up.

"Rooms! You're back!" she shrieked and leapt off the empty bed next to Luca's. As she ran my way, Shay typed on her phone.

"Shay! Remember where you are!" a voice I recognized as Daphne's yelled from the back.

"Oh, my God, Meredith! I'm so happy to see you. Where are the others?" She threw herself at me, arms wrapping around my aching body, phone still in hand as she squished me and my bag.

Inside the duffel, Benedict squirmed and hissed.

"Hey." The girl didn't seem to know her own strength, so I pulled away softly. "Hans is coming. Benedict is in here." I unzipped the bag, and the cat poked his head out, his light amber eyes narrowed.

"Oops! Sorry, Benny." Shay reached out to pet the cat, who batted her hand away. He hated being treated like a normal cat. "I was wondering where you were. Thought maybe you went mousing."

That earned her a hiss.

"The little shit snuck into my bag and came to Hell with us." My gaze traveled over my roommate's shoulder, landing on Luca. "How is he?"

Shay swallowed thickly. "Not any better. You got the lucimisia, though?"

"Tons."

"Good. And well within the week timeframe." Daphne appeared from the back room. Sara, the necromancer, trailed behind the lead healer, her strawberry blonde hair a mess. I squinted. Was that a twig sticking out of it?

Once in front of me, Daphne extended her hand. This close up, I could see the dark circles beneath her eyes. Had she been here all day? Since Luca was admitted? "I have the potion half prepared and will give it to him as soon as it's ready. This gives him the best chance to wake up."

I pulled out a bunch of the herb and passed it to her. As I did, Benedict hopped out of the bag. He stretched and loped toward the line of beds, where he hopped onto one and curled into a ball.

I snorted. The lazy ass cat was going to snooze again! He hadn't even run to the portal or trudged through the snow back to the Novak's home. I'd carried him! *I* was the one who needed sleep. Days of it.

"Is there more?" The healer asked, pulling me from my ire with my familiar.

"Oh, yeah. Two bags full," I assured her. "Hans had to illusion them to get them past security at the airport. He'll bring the rest in."

"Did you harvest them as I specified?"

"Pulled them out by the roots. Your supplier will hopefully be able to replant his field, and no one will have to journey to the underworld again for lucimisia."

"Thank the goddess." Relief washed across Daphne's face. "You did a splendid job. I'll have the elixir out as soon as possible and will want to get the roots in water quickly. Bring the rest back when Hans arrives."

I nodded, and she disappeared, leaving me with Shay, Sara, and Benedict.

Sara smiled at me. The beams of sun coming in from the skylight above really made her freckles pop. "So glad you guys made it back safely."

"Me too," I agreed. "You okay?" She'd come from the back of the infirmary but to my knowledge, she wasn't a healer.

"Okay?"

"You're in an infirmary."

"Oh, yeah. Right." Sara gave me a soft grin. "I'm applying to medical school, so I sometimes hang out with the healers."

Since she was a necromancer, the idea of her being a doctor surprised me. That conflict must have shown on my face, because Sara grinned good-naturedly.

"I get that a lot, but healing has always been a passion." Suddenly, a timer on her watch went off. "Oh no! I'm late to meet Josiah for dinner. I have to go." With an apologetic look, she turned. "I'm glad you're back. Joe will be too. See you two later!"

When the door shut behind Sara, I faced my roommate. "How'd your mission go?"

Shay's eyes widened, but she quickly masked the expression and replied, so I didn't question it. "It was pretty good. A few hiccups, but Tobias and I work well as a team. He worries about you, you know."

My heart spasmed, and oddly, my blood warmed at the thought of the vampire. *Weird . . .*

"That's who I texted. Tobias wanted to know when you guys returned."

Her eyes studied me intently. Yet, even though my heart had done an odd sort of stutter when she said the vampire's name, I refused to acknowledge or dwell on it. Tobias had been so rude, so unsupportive before my mission, and that still stung.

Actually, Shay's admission only confused me, and I didn't need that. Right now, the best thing for me was to move on to something else, rather than ask why Tobias would care so much.

The vampire, though frustrating most of the time, affected me in ways no one else ever had.

"So, did you get inside the vault?" I asked, trying to change the subject.

"We did. The Sigil of Lucifer was there. Same group that took the Pearl of Hell took the Opal too."

"No way!" The memory of the symbol on Nicoleta returned, but I pushed it to the side for later. It felt wrong talking about Hans's family without him present. "What about the identity of the vault owner?"

Shay's mouth opened, but she closed it quickly, shaking her

head.

I got the sense she might be holding something back, and for a moment, annoyance flared. Yet, as quickly as it burned, the heat dimmed. Even if they did learn who the owner was, she probably wanted to tell Luca first. As the coven master, he deserved that much.

"Have there been any episodes of madness?" I moved on so I wouldn't dwell on the vault.

Besides, seeking the Pearl—and I supposed the Opal of Heaven now too—affected me. I needed to be prepared to move when the first bouts of mass madness started cropping up in the world. That was a sign that the Pearl was in play and my cue to go find the stone. Hopefully, the Opal would be with it and the coven could retrieve two at once.

"That's what I was researching when you showed up." She gestured to the bed where she'd been sitting. Newspapers spread across the blanket.

Crossing toward the bed, I scanned the papers, my eyebrows knitting together. Publications in Italian, Spanish, German, Arabic, and what looked like Japanese stared back at me. "You can read all these?"

"I'm fluent in German and Arabic. The rest, I know enough to get by." Shay shrugged. "Remember, I'm not as young as I look. Angels, even half angels, age really slowly."

"Strange that you're so immature then." That earned me a slug to the arm, and a groan parted my lips. I rubbed my upper arm. "Damn, Shay! Why you gotta do me like that?"

"I don't act immature!"

"Truth hurts, girl." I shrugged, which also made me wince.

Concern wrinkled Shay's features when she noticed the gesture. "Seriously, though, how are you?"

"Super sore," I admitted. "We walked and ran a long way. But don't brush off my questions. The cases of madness?"

"So far, nothing has cropped up. Be sure that when anyone finds something suspicious, you'll be the first to know."

"I hope Luca is awake by then." I turned to the coven master. He'd become almost a father figure to me in the short time I'd known him and I felt a crapload of guilt over his illness. That shade had been sent for me—by who, we didn't know—and Luca had taken the brunt of its attack to save my butt.

For a few seconds, only the sounds of Daphne bustling in the next room filled the vast space, then the door opened again. Expecting to find Hans, walking in with the other bags of herbs, I faced the entrance. Instead, green eyes met mine.

"You're back," Harper breathed. "If I'd known, I would have picked you up something for dinner!" She held up a greasy bag as the scent of burgers filled the air. "Shay, why didn't you text me?"

"She *just* got here. You can share mine, Rooms. I got two burgers anyway," Shay offered, leaving me to wonder where the heck she put it all.

The wolf joined our group, and we worked around Benedict's sleeping form to clear the papers off the bed. Once there was enough space, we sat side by side and dug into the greasy fast food.

With the first bite, I let out a moan—I hadn't realized how hungry I was. By the time Hans stomped in, carrying the bags filled with lucimisia and muttering about the parking being ridiculous, my burger and allotment of fries were gone.

"Is Daphne already making the potion?" Hans asked, eyeing the food with unmasked hunger.

"Yeah," Shay replied, her tone higher than normal.

I stared at her, amused. Before I'd left, I'd gotten the sense that she had a thing for the wizard.

Oh noooooo.

My eyes widened. Hans wasn't just a wizard, though. He was part demon, and Shay was part angel, and I was pretty certain she liked him.

I swallowed the lump rising in my throat. That couldn't work, right? Or could it? Did magical beings not distinguish in the way someone like me, a person new to this world, might assume?

"I'll get these to her," Hans held up the two bags. "You got any more of that?"

Harper frowned. I was learning that her love language was related to food. In our home, she was the cook, the maker of tea, the one to decide what was for dinner. She'd probably hated it when people went hungry.

"No," I answered, not wanting her to feel bad or blame Shay. "But we can order some."

"That's okay. I won't stay too long and can grab something on the way home." With that, he went to the back, where Daphne worked.

Once Hans was out of sight, Shay's shoulders loosened. Yeah, she totally liked him. How had I not seen it before we left for Hell?

Had I been too focused on my own stuff and issues—of which there'd been plenty. Or was I more in tune to the nephilim now because I cared about her more? Considered her a friend, even?

My throat tightened at the realization. That had happened so fast, and that it had happened at all for someone like me was sort of . . . magic.

"So," Harper broke the silence that had come over us, "how was it?"

"Hell?"

"Yeah."

"Pretty much as expected. Hot, it reeked of sulfur, and was filled with monsters." An image of the Field of Punishment filled my mind. "Absolutely horrible."

"But you got in and out with no issue?" She scanned me. "You look alright."

"She was limping when she came in," the nephilim announced.

"We ran into a few snags . . ." I was of the mind that what happened was Hans's story to tell. Still, Shay and Harper were staring at me hard core, so I had to say something. "We were almost caught."

"No," Harper breathed, her fry stopping an inch in front of her lips.

"Yeah. We—"

Hans slipped back into the room with Daphne on his heels. She held a glass like it was pure gold, her eyes trained on Luca.

"Is it ready? Extra strong, right?" I asked, heart pounding as I leapt from the bed. My ankle rolled for a second time in an hour, the pain making me wince.

"The strongest I can make it," she affirmed, her gaze darting down to my feet, though she said nothing about it. "If this doesn't work, then all I can do is keep making the same thing and hope it will take before . . ."

Before he died.

I shook myself. That wouldn't happen, I refused to believe it. We were here way before the week was up, and we'd brought enough of the herb for the healers to make tons of doses.

"I'll prop him up." Hans eased his arm around the coven master and lifted him.

Though he wasn't conscious, Daphne still got Luca to swallow. Hoping he would wake instantly, I stared at him, as if my attention would somehow help the matter.

"It will take some time," Daphne said, her attention locked on her patient. "I'll check on him in the morning." Then she turned to me. "You need a checkup too. I caught that ankle roll. And Hans told me that you got hurt on the way back from Hell."

I glared at Hans, ungrateful. Sure, I ached, but I wanted to sleep in my own bed.

"Sorry, Meredith," Hans shrugged. "I'm going to be examined too, but that's a pretty obvious injury."

"How bad does it hurt?" Daphne prompted.

"My Achilles tendon is pretty sore," I admitted.

"After hearing part of your team's story, I am not surprised. You put in a lot of mileage and might have pulled it. Normally, that can take months to heal, but lucky for you, I have a remedy that is much faster. Though, if you take it, you must stay here. It knocks people out for days at a time, and I'll need to give you the potion again in the morning. Plus, check your gait before you leave."

I sighed. Before I signed on with the coven, I never went to the doctor. And definitely not the hospital. I'd rarely relied on others and all that was changing quickly. While I found it difficult to accept help, I had to get over that quirk and fast because the coven had made it clear that they'd never leave me hanging.

"Fine."

"I'll go whip up that potion, then." Daphne disappeared into the back once more, leaving the four of us, an unconscious Luca, and a sleeping Benedict, to our own devices.

Harper turned back to me. "So, how were you almost caught?"

Across the bed from Luca, Hans stiffened. *Geez, Harper, way not to miss a beat.*

"We, uh—" I looked at Hans. In two seconds, his face had grown red. "It just happened."

Harper's eyebrows pinched together. "Like, you were careless? Or was it worse than you thought?"

"I guess it was—"

"It was my fault," Hans blurted.

The girls turned their attention to him, and I exhaled. Though I'd been pissed about his detour in the Underworld, I didn't want to push him into anything because I also hadn't wanted to lie to my roommates.

"You're so practiced, though." Shay seemed shocked that our team's issues could come from the wizard.

"None of that matters when you run into your mother in the pits of Hell," Hans muttered. Unable to look Shay in the eyes, his face tilted to the floor.

I sucked in a breath. He'd gone there right away, despite how much it tore at him. My heart broke for Hans.

"Your mother died, and you found her soul there?" A pained expression crossed Shay's features. "I'm so sorry, Hans."

Oh, God. She didn't get it. Of course, she didn't. Who would assume that Hans's mother helped rule the underworld?

"Hans . . ." I whispered, wanting to save him from the humiliation he experienced when he told us the truth. No one should be backed into a corner like this. "You don't have to."

"I do." His pained blue eyes lifted to catch mine. "You saw my sister, Meredith. You understand what's happening, what group she's a part of, and everyone is going to learn, eventually. I'd rather it come from me."

He turned his attention to the other two and he rolled his shoulders back, perhaps trying to release the tension obviously building there. "My mother hasn't died. My mother is Lilith, Queen of Hell, and I'm half demon."

CHAPTER THIRTEEN

HANS

Especially Shay's.

Her angelic visage, so concerned for my plight seconds before, crumpled. Now the nephilim's lips pinched painfully, her pert nose wrinkled in disgust by my bloodline, like I was a fart in the room that she couldn't avoid.

My stomach rolled. Of course, someone with angel blood—archangel blood, no less—would act like that. Most people considered those with demonic lineages untrustworthy. And as much as I hated to think it, most of the time they were right to do so.

"Are you sure?" Shay's voice ground against me like brake pads pushed to the edge of viability.

"Positive." At my word, her irises brightened, became bluer than normal. Was she tearing up? "I've known my whole life who my mother was. That's how I knew where an entrance to Hell was located."

"Who else knew?" Shay's chin tilted upward.

"Tobias. That's it."

It had always been a source of annoyance to me, something the vampire held over my head, even if he never spoke of it. Even if I knew his secret too. Even if he never hinted at using the leverage the knowledge of my bloodline could give him.

I didn't enjoy that someone else was aware of what I was, what I could become.

Well, if he'd ever wanted to, now his chance was wasted. He no longer would be the only one in on the secret.

Shay cleared her throat, the sound pained. "I have to go."

Without another word to her friends, she strode to the door, slamming it closed behind her so loudly that Daphne called out for quiet from the back room.

Seeing Shay so upset unleashed something unexpected in me. I wanted to chase her, to assure her I wasn't bad, just as much as I wanted to stay away from the half-angel. Not because of what she was. I simply didn't want to make her uncomfortable, to see my own discomfort with my lineage reflected in those azure eyes.

"That's how you got in," Harper mused, ripping me back to the wolf and the witch. "I wondered how, but figured there must be a spell that you are forbidden from sharing. Or maybe one that no one else could handle. So, now we understand how you saw your mother, but what's this about your sister?"

"Hans," Meredith said again, her tone gentle, "we don't have to go into all of it yet."

Fuck it, why not? I'd already begun unraveling my lies, my omissions. This would never get easier.

"I'm fine," I lied, focusing on the wolf listening intently. "My sister wanted me to bring our mother back. Lilith is Lucifer's wife, and through all our lives she's had to return to him, leaving my sister and I behind. It was for our safety more than anything. If she stayed in the village, she was sure Lucifer would turn Hell upside-down to hunt her. And one day, he'd discover us too, probably murder everyone in my family out of spite." My lips tightened. I'd had that nightmare often as a kid. The one of a faceless, evil man breaking into our home, wiping us all out with a snap of his fingers.

"Why would your sister want Lilith to come to this realm if that happened?" Harper asked.

"Nicoleta didn't want our mother to be separated from us anymore, so she made me promise to bring our mother back if I found her. She also thought that she'd be able to seal the portal by our village permanently once Mom was Earth-side."

Harper let out a low whistle.

"Yeah," I said. "More than that, I screwed up the mission by approaching my mother in the middle of a field with hundreds of working demons. The invisibility potion stopped working. Mother saved our asses, but clearly, I didn't bring her back."

I took a steeling breath, hating that I had to say the next part.

"When I told her what happened, my sister attacked us and revealed that she's in league with a demon prince on Earth. The prince leads a group that Nicoleta referred to as the Darkborn. They want to take control. And get this, my own flesh and blood had the Sigil of Lucifer branded on her chest, which makes me believe the Darkborn are the ones who got the Pearl."

"What?!"

"It's true," Meredith confirmed. "And get this Hans, Shay said they found the Sigil in the vault at *Le Bastion* too."

I blinked. So, it was likely that the Darkborn took the Pearl of Hell *and* had the Opal of Heaven. That was unwelcome news.

"What I don't understand is why she'd have that symbol if she's working for Prince Brian?" Meredith asked, her eyebrows pinched. "Or Orian? What the heck was the name?"

"Orien," Harper breathed. "Isn't that it, Hans?"

"Yeah, that's it." I didn't know all the prince's names by heart—why would I when they were locked in the underworld?—but I sure as hell knew that one. "I don't understand it either."

For a moment, silence fell, then Harper shook her head. "I'm sorry that happened to you. I want you to know that I don't look at you differently." Her eyes darted to the door. "Really, I don't think Shay does either. She was just shocked. After all, she's . . ."

"On the other side of the heavenly divide," I finished for her, my tone strained. How often had I wished I stood on the opposite side to the one I'd been born? To exude light and not darkness, death, and despair? "I get it."

"But we work with necromancers and vampires, and some might say they're creatures of darkness," Harper insisted, clearly not believing me. "So, I bet she'll get over it. Eventually."

I nodded, as if I believed it. "I'll have to tell others."

"Wait until Luca wakes up," Harper suggested. "He has a way with words and can help."

"Good point."

My attention shifted to the mage. When I'd dropped Meredith off on the street, all I'd wanted to do was go home and drink myself into oblivion yet again, but not anymore. Now I wanted more information on the symbol branded into my sister's chest and the group it represented.

"I'll go to the Beinecke for a while," I announced.

Harper's eyebrows pulled together. "Why?"

"To see if there's anything on that symbol, because Meredith's right. It makes little sense that Orien would brand Nicoleta with the symbol of his brother."

Unless she worked for *both* princes, but Nicoleta hadn't mentioned that. And she'd sounded devoted to Orien alone. Plus, we'd both always despised Lucifer because he kept our mother from us.

There has to be more to the Sigil of Lucifer than we know.

"How will you get inside?" Harper asked. "The Beinecke is closed."

"Some of us have special privileges," I confessed. Namely it was just me, Luca, and Tobias.

The wolf gaped. "You have access at any time?"

"I do."

"I want those too, and a chance to get into the supernatural section. On my own," the wolf clarified.

"I'll see what I can do." Luca had extended the privileges to me and Tobias because we were his right and left hands, but Harper was wicked smart. She'd have to pass the test the hedge witches who acted as librarians to the elite section gave to those who wanted access, but I was sure Harper would succeed on that front. Plus, with all the trouble looming on the horizon, it would be good for more people in the coven to have access to the texts on supernaturals.

Feeling as though I had nothing else to say, I took a step away from Luca's bed. "I'll check with you ladies tomorrow. Heal up, Meredith."

She frowned. "Thanks."

The witch sounded a touch annoyed to have to stay in the infirmary, but it really was for the best. She had classes to get back to, and a mission that might start at any given moment. We needed her to be ready when signs of madness, of the Pearl of Hell's influence, began cropping up. Demons and those who followed them possessed it, so there was no longer a question of 'if' insanity would strike, but 'when?'.

Leaving the infirmary, I walked through the halls of the empty coven headquarters. Shay was nowhere in sight—both a relief, and oddly, a disappointment.

Where had she gone? Home? Was she crying?

Something about the thought tore me up inside. I hated when women cried, and though I couldn't explain it, the idea of disappointing Shay hurt more than I expected.

Slipping onto the streets of New Haven, I breathed in the chilled autumn air. The stench of sulfur still filled my nostrils, though that had to be all in my head. I'd showered and changed at my father's, desperate to get every speck of Hell off me before we drove to the airport.

But some things proved more difficult to shake than one would imagine. Though miles from the portal, the presence of the underworld, how it smelled of sulfur and rot and death, how the heat of the place seemed to caress my skin, struck me at random times.

I might never be able to deny the darkness inside of me, but I hoped to learn how to win the fight of good vs. evil that was sure to come, and get my sister back on my side.

I swallowed. Nicoleta's face when she'd flown away was burned into my mind. Crushing and devastating. I had to win her back, for her sake, and for our father's. The kind baker of Minim had shattered when we told him his daughter had gone dark—that I failed to save her. She surely wasn't going to waltz back into Minim and rejoin society.

That village girl was gone. In her place was a half-demon who'd embraced the darkness and teamed up with a Prince of

Hell. Now I needed to learn about the devil who'd stolen my sister from my family.

Then I could take down the bastard.

My feet guided me through campus on autopilot. When I reached the door to the library, I scanned the area. Just because I could get in, and wouldn't be detected on camera, didn't mean random students needed to see me slip inside late at night. Thankfully, the coast was clear. With my hand on the door and a whispered password leaving my lips, the door opened.

Once inside, light appeared in my hand with a snap of my fingers. Quickly, I descended the stairs to the bottom level and kept going all the way to the very back, an area where few students ventured because a persistent draft plagued the space.

When I reached the charmed entrance, I turned to it and pressed my hand into the wall. A jolt of magic rushed through me as the library made sure I was, in fact, Hans Novak.

Here, passwords were not used. Every person with access to the supernatural section had to be vetted and approved by Wisteria and Bellamy, the elderly hedge witch and wizard— who ran the place. They were husband and wife and lifelong librarians. Both were committed to excellent curation and academics. Though, during the time that I'd waited for my acceptance to access the library, I'd found their pickiness annoying, it was actually a good thing.

The supernatural librarians let no one pass who didn't deserve it, and those who gained access could only bring one guest—ever. That person did not have to go through such a rigorous search as those with memberships, but if they acted out, the person who'd invited them would have their own privileges revoked. With an exclusive entry on the line, few extended invitations. I never had.

Maybe, if Luca doesn't think Harper is ready, I can use my invitation on her.

Harper deserved it, and if it meant Shay, her roommate and friend, wouldn't hate me, I was tempted.

Suddenly, the magic that had been checking my identity ceased flowing, and the wall opened. It had taken longer than normal. Was it because the trip to my village brought out my demon side more? Was I confusing the identification process? I frowned but dismissed the idea, entering the exclusive library.

Currently, I was hyper focused and sensitive, but really, not everything was about my lineage. I was the same as before: a wizard, a Romanian immigrant turned American, a mechanic, and Jeeper. Those aspects would always be the same, just as my heart would be. I had to work on owning how I perceived my demon blood.

"Starting with figuring out what the Sigil of Lucifer actually means," I muttered, heading to the demonology section.

Since magical beings could enter and leave at all hours of the day and night, enchanted candles came to life when they sensed motion in this part of the Beinecke. Enchanted, protective lanterns kept the sacrilegious flames in check. Letting the conjured light in my palm die, I exhaled, allowing the candlelight to soothe me as much as the scent of old tomes.

Books dating back all the way to the period writing developed lined the shelves. In all, that comprised a few millennia's worth of knowledge. It was no Library of Alexandria, but this hidden portion of the Beinecke was the closest thing magical beings possessed. Only two or three other libraries in the world rivaled it.

Passing a slew of desks, I turned down an aisle of shelves—

one of three marked for demons and creatures of the underworld. Since I'd gained access to this library, I mostly avoided this area. It brought up feelings I didn't want to acknowledge.

But now I have to . . .

My keen eyes scanned the shelves. There might not be a book on demon symbology, but something on the royals would be a good choice.

It was too much to wish that we'd have a book labeled *Darkborn*, but soon enough, I did come across a tome with promise. The tome was titled *Noble Lords of the Underworld*. I plucked it and backtracked to one of the desks I'd passed earlier.

Carefully, I opened it to the beginning. There was not a table of contents, nor an author name. Yet, seeing as the book was very old, I deduced that a monk had probably written this —a supernatural tasked with creating *extra*-special tomes that most believers would never see.

I flipped the page, the paper dusty beneath my fingertips. The first portion of the tome documented the geography of Hell. If I'd had more time, I would have compared it to the map my mother had implanted in my mind, but I didn't, and not seeing the Sigil, I continued.

It wasn't until I hit about a quarter of the way through the book that I got my first sighting of the Sigil. I paused, reading as fast as the old-fashioned script would allow.

"Though many villagers call it a sign of Lucifer, the most feared of all Lords of the Underworld, the King of the Princes, the Darkest Fallen Star, the Sigil does not belong to Prince Lucifer alone. In actuality, it is a symbol of the princes' brotherhood—their bond and family. Their crest. It's a sign of devil worship on a greater scale than humankind has ever seen. One that believers pray will not come to light for if the Sigil arises, it is a portent that the end is nigh."

So that symbol was actually something signifying the princes's brotherhood. Was it still? If so, did Nicoleta know that? Or did she believe it was the symbol of Orien, the prince she served, and that he used it for the Darkborn? And did Orien recognize her as Lilith's child?

If he did, would he hold that over my sister?

My jaw clenched. I had to learn more about Prince Orien. After skimming a few more pages, I began flipping them faster. When I struck individual entries of the princes, I exhaled. The author listed Orien right after Lucifer.

According to this text, Prince Orien ruled the second largest swath of the Underworld. Actually, in many things he was second—only Lucifer could seem to best him. His one claim to the top was that Orien controlled those underlings who patrolled the River Lethe. Hence Prince Orien controlled the newest sinners entering Hell and got his pick over those he wished to subjugate.

His sin, because each prince claimed a sin as his own and the sinners as their people, was wrath.

At that, my mouth went dry. The Prince of Wrath walked the surface of the Earth, most likely stealing sacred stones and amassing followers like my sister.

Strong supernaturals.

I shuddered to think what that meant.

CHAPTER FOURTEEN

TOBIAS

Midday was threatening to crest into evening as I rushed into Shadows and Secret's Hall. The moment I read Shay's text that Meredith, Hans, and Gunner had returned with the lucimisia, I'd left Castel Romono. I hadn't even gotten to say goodbye to Raphael, likely a slight he wouldn't forget.

And yet, I found it difficult to care, for forces pressed me to leave, to return home.

I had to be here. To lay eyes on Luca, hopefully alive and well.

And then, once I was sure of that, I'd request a bag of blood from Daphne and go see *her*.

My eyes closed, confusion flooding me. Though I did have a reason to see the witch, the ring from Le Bastion sat heavy in my pocket, waiting to be given to her, that wasn't truly why I wished to lay eyes on her.

Meredith had been on my mind for the duration of my flights. Why? I wasn't sure, but I did know that once I checked in on Luca, I had to see her. This odd twisting of bloodlust, how it presently resembled infatuation and caring for the well-being of the witch rather than the burning thirst of days before, was almost enough for me to believe Giselle's theory: that we were bloodbound. Fated. Soulmates.

Had Meredith been a vampire, it would have made sense.

Alas, she was no vampire, so it made no sense at all. Fated mates never occurred outside one's own magical order. This was nothing more than a different kind of bloodlust for the witch. It had to be.

"Tobias! Hey! How was—"

"Not now, Silas!" I barked, interrupting the silver-haired fae trying to flag me down to talk.

Silas stared, and as I passed, I felt his unwavering gaze on my back—sensed many eyes on me, in fact.

No doubt they wanted to know of *Le Bastion*—a place shrouded in mystery—and they would. In time.

Only when I reached the infirmary's floor did I slow. I was still a fair distance away, but Josiah was outside the healing area, pacing and muttering to himself.

I was halfway to the necromancer before he noticed me, stopping in his tracks. His dark brown eyes widened. "Oh, hey, Tobias."

"Is something wrong?" I gestured to the door.

"What?"

"You were pacing." Trying to be kind, I omitted mentioning the muttering as I took in his face. Only then did I notice the bags beneath his eyes. I'd never seen the necromancer so exhausted.

"Oh, right . . . Just worried."

"About? Is Luca okay?" The skin on the back of my neck tightened. Had the other team been too late?

"What? Oh! He's in there, resting, I think. They gave him a potion and he should be fine." Josiah shook his head, but the words relieved me greatly. It also gave me a moment to be more compassionate—a quality Giselle had told me many times that I tended to lack.

"Then what's wrong?" I asked. The necromancer was normally so steady. This was odd behavior.

"It's Igbo, one of my ravens. She ate something bad. She's always sneaking into places she shouldn't be and helping herself to whatever is there. Anyway, she got sick last night, and I know the healers aren't vets, but you try taking a raven like that to a normal vet. So many damned questions."

His eyes darted to the door, then back to me.

"I dropped her off and was thinking about going back in, but the healers have their hands full." With a resigned breath, he shrugged. "I guess I'm an overprotective raven-dad." At that, he managed a weak smile. "Sounds lame when I say it like that, but I do think of them that way."

"I suspect they'll be fine," I assured him, regretting that I'd stopped, over bloody birds of all things, and desperate to go inside. "Ravens are resilient, and the healers have many remedies to ensure the expulsion of poison."

"That's what they said too." He swung his arms so that his hands clapped in front of him. "You're right. I shouldn't take up more of their time. Igbo will be fine under their care. I'll go . . . Thanks for the words of wisdom." With that, Josiah turned and walked down the hall, out of sight.

Now, back to business. I went to the infirmary door, only to pause. Something beyond it warmed me and made me feel . . . good. Comforted.

Which an infirmary certainly shouldn't do.

Strange that, I thought, opening the door.

As expected, Luca reclined in a bed, his eyes closed, his

chest rising and falling. My steps halted when I saw that she, *Meredith*, was in the bed next to him.

My usually still heart gave a single, hard thump, and concern tightened my gut. Why was she here? Was she hurt? Shay had mentioned nothing of the sort. Only that the witch had returned to New Haven.

Still on the edge of the room, I remained frozen. Bloody hell, I shouldn't be here. I had not prepared myself for seeing Meredith. Usually, I needed at least a bag of blood to curb my bloodlust.

But then . . . I didn't feel it now. Did I?

A quick scan assured me that no, I didn't. Odd that. I hadn't eaten properly in days, but there was no urge to go to Meredith and drink from her.

And now that I'd laid eyes on her, I couldn't turn back.

Proceed with care.

Muscles tensing, I approached the beds, unable to take my eyes off the witch. Judging by her breathing, the witch was sleeping heavily. My eyes feasted upon her face, enchanted by how angelic she looked—nothing at all like the sassy witch who loved to get a rise out of me. Nor did she have the pallor of the ill.

Stopping by Meredith's bedside, I waited once again for bloodlust to strike. When it did not, I took a seat on the stool, telling myself that at the first urge to drink from her vein, I'd run out of the infirmary. A bottle of potion was on the night-stand, so I read the label. It was an elixir to help regrow and strengthen tendons.

At that moment, the witch murmured something in her sleep and rolled to face me, her lips parting softly. Skylights allowed sunlight to filter in from above, and yellow beams dappled her cheeks, dancing on her smooth skin. Meredith's hair flowed behind her, so long and silky I yearned to touch it.

In the back, noises arose. A clanging of metal. A bubbling of liquid. Someone asking a question. The healers were hard at work, but instead of going to inquire about Luca, as I should have done, I merely sat there, transfixed by the witch.

Annoying though the witch could be, she radiated beauty. In truth, she was one of the loveliest women I'd ever set eyes upon.

As if she could hear my thoughts, her lips curved into a smile. In response, my jaw tightened. What was I doing sitting here, and watching her like some besotted fool?

The last time I'd been so taken with a woman, she'd perished horribly. I'd sworn to myself that would never happen again, but presently, I walked a thin line.

I needed to ask about Luca and leave. Determined to do just that, I stood, the stool I'd taken pushing back and scraping the floor.

With the sound, Meredith's eyes—one blue, one green— flew open, and landed on me. "Tobias?"

I swallowed, aware of how close I stood to her bed, how this looked. How I couldn't leave now, or even look away. Bloody hell, what was wrong with me?

"Yes?"

"Where have you been?" Her hand lifted to wipe the crust of sleep from her lashes.

Meredith's voice sounded smaller than usual, tired of course, but also sweet. Though I remained standing, I could no longer find it in myself to leave. "Italy. My sire requested I visit my brother."

"Oh." Meredith sat up, and her hand fluttered to her heart. Only days ago, she'd had my blood, needed it to live, which would affect how she felt in my presence. Was that why she hadn't hurled her normal allotment of sass my way?

Was it also why I did not feel compelled to drink from her though I hadn't had blood in days? That made a certain amount of sense.

"Are you well?" I asked, my protective instinct surging as it sometimes did with this witch.

"Yeah. I've been here for . . ." She peered around the room. "Hey." She looked about again. "Where's Benedict?"

"Why are you here?" I asked, my tone a low growl. I didn't care about the cat, but rather why she was in the healing wing.

She met my eyes, her eyebrows knitting together. "I pulled my Achilles. We had to run to get out of Hell and then walk back to the village." She seemed like she wanted to say more but stopped. I had a sense of what might be on her mind.

"Did Hans's blood call to him there?" I pressed. Her answer had eased my anxiety, but now I wished to know why the running had been necessary.

She exhaled, relieved. "That's right. You know about him. Thank goodness. I didn't want to spill the beans."

The witch ran her hands through her long hair, a careless gesture that intensified her tempting scent. "Hans got us there just fine, but in the end his demon side almost cost us our lives though, and instigated the running."

I'd worried that something would snap in Hans if he traveled to the underworld. How spot on had I been?

"But we're okay," Meredith assured me, her focus darting to my fists, clenched into tight balls. "Everyone got out. We harvested enough of the herb that the supplier should be able to regrow in this realm. There's more, but I'm going to let Hans tell it."

Nodding, I exhaled. They'd been in danger, but they were fine now. I needed to calm down, but feared I was failing because her gaze continued to study me intensely. Almost like she was trying to peer into my very soul.

Suddenly, I had the ridiculous notion to cup her face in my hand and kiss her. The warmth inside me heated even more . .
.

Was the fact that she had ingested my blood affecting me in this manner too? What was happening between us?

"Were you really that worried that I'd screw everything up?"

I blinked, the spell that had lingered in the air broken by her words. "Pardon?"

"Before I left, you told me not to go. You said I'd put everyone in danger, which, for the record, I didn't. And now you look so relieved." Hurt flashed across her face. "You thought I'd fail them. That I wasn't good enough."

Did I believe that Meredith put them in any more trouble than Gunner and Hans? No. Though I'd let her think that, hoping it would keep her here—relatively safe.

"I underestimated you," I offered, knowing that admitting the truth, that thinking of her in Hell physically pained me, wouldn't do either of us a bit of good. "It won't happen again."

Her shoulders lowered. "Well, thanks." She reached for her glass of water and took a drink before setting the cup back down. "So, how was your mission? At the bank?"

My entire body froze. "Shay has told you nothing?"

"She said you got into the vault and found the Sigil of Lucifer, but stopped there. I think she was waiting for Luca to wake up."

I swallowed. Perhaps. Or she wasn't sure how to break the

news to Meredith that it was *she* who owned the plundered vault. That, somehow, this seeker witch who'd found the Pearl of Hell, was also tied to the Opal of Heaven. That she owned a bloody *lapis caelesti*.

Meredith's ring, the one we'd found in Accola's office, burned in my pocket. I'd kept it safe as I traveled Europe. On the flight home, I'd patted the ring in my pocket so many times people likely thought I had a tic. Nonetheless, if Shay had mentioned nothing of the vault, then I didn't feel right about doing so yet. I'd wait until Luca woke up too, then I'd share the news with them both.

"We came across shocking information," I started. "But I agree with—"

Suddenly, Luca coughed and shot straight up in bed.

"Healers!" I called when Luca grabbed his throat and gasped for air. "The mage awakens!"

A thundering of steps met my ears, and a duo of healers burst from the back. Daphne was there, a small rubbish bin in her hands.

"Stay back, he'll vomit the concentrated poison!" she warned.

Indeed, Luca appeared ready to be ill. Thankfully, the healer was fast and reached the mage in time for him to bury his head in the bin. Sick exploded from him, and the stench of rotted meat plumed in the air. I stopped breathing, thankful that I could do so without repercussions. Meredith and the healers, however, had no such skill, and each began to gag.

"Tobias." Daphne gestured to the can. "When Luca's done, take this to the back. There's a cauldron there filled with blue liquid. We brewed it specifically for this purpose. Dump the poison in so it can neutralize."

After a full five minutes, the coven master ceased heaving and pulled his head from the bin.

"Are you quite finished?" I asked, approaching quickly for the sake of the others. The stench had started to make their eyes water.

"Water," Luca rasped.

"Tobias, be careful with it." Daphne gestured to the bin. "That's a lot and very dangerous." Daphne pivoted for a pitcher. "I'll get water."

With care, I took the bin and strode to the back where healers kept their herbs, potions, and the like.

Immediately, I caught sight of something odd. Josiah's raven, Igbo, stood on the counter—uncaged. That didn't seem right. Josiah had mentioned that she got into things. Was she an escape artist too?

As I walked deeper into the room, the raven's dark eyes blinked at me as if asking why I was back there.

"Got a job to do," I muttered, feeling ridiculous for talking to the bird. "Don't muck up anything back here."

The cauldron was easy to locate, and in went the poison, immediately turning the blue liquid black. I set the rubbish bin down next to the cauldron, and with my job done, ran back into the front room. Upon my return, Luca was already breathing easier and Daphne was in the process of taking his vitals. Not wanting to be in the way, I stood back and waited.

Finally, an age later, the healers stepped away, relief lining their faces.

"That extra strong dose of potion finally did the trick. I'll make you another batch, which means you'll need to stay the night again, but your heart and lungs are much stronger than when you arrived."

"I sure don't feel strong," the coven master admitted,

though I had to agree with the head healer. Despite just vomiting, the gray tinge that had plagued the Italian's face in the days before he passed out was gone, warmth taking its place.

"You will soon," Daphne assured him and gestured to me and Meredith. "I assume that you have coven matters to discuss with these two, so I'll begin with that batch of potion."

I cleared my throat. "Don't know if you realized, but Josiah's raven is loose back there."

Daphne rolled her eyes. "The necromancer told me his ravens can't be caged. That they'll make a ruckus if they are, and eventually get out anyway. Guess he's right."

"You'll allow it to be loose?" A poor choice in a sick house.

"It's not protocol in an infirmary." Daphne flung up a hand as if to say *I give up*. "I didn't even want it here, but what was I going to do? Let the creature die? Josiah was beside himself. I couldn't say no."

That he had been. "I don't mean to pressure you. It simply shocked me."

"That makes two of us," Daphne replied. "I never thought I'd be taking care of a raven. I'll go check on it and get that potion going."

The healers retreated to their workroom as Meredith's cat loped in from the back.

"Hey!" Meredith called. "Where were you?"

"Hunting. I heard a mouse in one of the sick rooms. This coven should keep a feline on staff."

"So, you got enough sleep?" Meredith snorted.

"I apologize if I left you in a bind. The journey to Hell and back taxed me greatly."

My eyes widened. The familiar had gone with them?

"It wasn't planned," Meredith explained. "He snuck in my bag and followed me for protection."

I appraised the cat, liking him a bit more.

Meredith, though, twisted to face Luca. "Anyway, welcome back. How do you feel?"

"Better by the second."

"Honestly?" I glowered at him. The coven master had downplayed the shade poisoning for far too long, and it almost cost him his life.

"Truly this time," Luca promised. "Have there been sightings of madness?"

He'd always been one to get down to business quickly. It was a characteristic I appreciated about Luca.

"None that Shay has found," Meredith answered. "She was here with you, reading a bunch of papers, when I arrived with the herb we needed to revive you. The sheer number of papers she had makes me think that she would know pretty well if madness is spreading."

"And I presume someone traveled to *Le Bastion*?" Luca turned to me, dark eyes appraising.

"I did, with Shay, while the others journeyed to Hell for the herb."

"Hell," Luca breathed. "You didn't say . . . I'm so sorry."

"We couldn't leave you hanging," Meredith replied. "It was my fault you got sick to begin with."

"Hardly," I said. "There's a traitor in the coven. There has to be."

The witch eyed me. "Explain."

"Someone sent the shade for you, but it injected poison into Luca. And then, days later, the only crop of lucimisia herb in the world burns? They may not have gotten to their target, but clearly, they didn't want Luca healing either. Mages are powerful adversaries." My lips compressed. "There has to be foul play at hand."

"You're right," Meredith mused. "Do you suspect someone?"

Looking overwhelmed, Luca waved a hand. "Can we back up? I need time to digest what happened, regarding the trip to Hell while I was gone, but I really wish to hear about the vault. Did we get into *Le Bastion* and learn the identity of the owner? Did *La Tête*, the head of the bank," he added for the witch's benefit, "allow you to view his client roster?"

Meredith studied me with interest. Shay hadn't told her much at all. Maybe she believed we should be together to do it, but Luca was asking, and he was the coven master. I wouldn't say no to him.

"*La Tête*, Accola, allowed us to enter the vault," I answered. "And it's almost a certainty that the same group that took the Pearl now has the Opal. The Sigil of Lucifer was there."

"And while I won't say why, because Hans should tell you," Meredith interjected, "the Sigil was spotted during our excursion, too. It might mean more—or at least, something different from what we think. Hans was going to do research."

"I'll ask him later." Luca nodded, absorbing it all at a speed most in his situation couldn't manage. Rapid assimilation and making quick connections were both characteristics the mage was known for, and I was glad to see that the poison hadn't changed that. "The owner of the vault, Tobias? Did you obtain a name?"

"Meredith owns the vault."

"Meredith?!" the witch asked, her voice high with disbelief. "As in *me*, Meredith?"

"Precisely."

Luca leaned forward. "Are you sure?"

"Absolutely." I faced the witch, to find her mouth had

dropped open. "Your name was on the paperwork, along with another. A woman in England. You had no idea?"

"I—What?—No!" Her head shook adamantly, her attention shifting from Benedict, who also appeared shocked, to Luca. "I remember almost nothing about my past, and that definitely does not include a vault. Were my parents' names on it? Gavin and Lynn?"

"You recall their names?" Luca asked. "Your memories are returning! That's wonderful!"

Meredith managed a small smile. It had never been a sure thing that her memories would return after her magic was unbound. I suspected the retrieval of her past was both joyous and confusing for her.

"It first happened the day you fell ill," she said. "Now, I've had two distinct memories come back to me. One with my dad. The other with both parents." Her two-toned gaze found me. "Was it my mom's name on the paperwork?"

"The woman's name was Miriam Black. Does that name mean anything to you?"

Meredith shook her head. "No. How about you, Benedict?"

"I'm sorry to say I'm of no help in this matter," the cat said. "I've never heard of the woman. Nor this bank. If you own the vault, your parents must have secured ownership long ago. Perhaps right after your birth?"

"The vault is much older than that," I said. "One of *Le Bastion*'s first, which means it's centuries old. It must have been passed down through your family."

"Another dead end." Meredith huffed. "I don't remember anyone named Miriam right now. Maybe that will change in time?"

She sounded hopeful, and I suspected Luca felt the same

way. Whatever Meredith Stone was when we first learned of her existence, she was proving to be much more to the coven— to the world.

"There's more," I said, easing my hand into my pocket. Perhaps the ring would jog her memory. "When we found Miriam's name, we also found a box in the cabinet. One with the same vault number that *La Tête* showed us. Shay and I took it, since it's yours." I pulled the band out and handed it to her.

Recognition flashed in her eyes. "That was my mother's!"

"Are you sure?"

"I saw it in the memory I had in Hell. She wore it."

"It appears to be moonstone," Luca said. "Pretty, but they generally are not of great monetary value, which means there has to be something else significant about the piece. Why would Accola hold it in his office?"

"That, I don't know. Do you, Meredith?"

She shook her head. "No. Benedict? Surely, if I saw this, you did too?"

"To me, it was always a normal ring."

"Well, I can sense it's not. And you can bet your ass that I'm going to do my best to remember." Meredith slipped the ring on, a look of determination on her face.

The band fit perfectly, like the artisan made it for her hand, and the center stone gave off a soft glow that dimmed after a few seconds.

She turned her hand, examining the ring from different angles. "A stone at the base is gone. There are six below the moonstone, but there should be seven. Did you notice that, Tobias?"

I leaned closer and discovered she was right. In the center, the moonstone glimmered, so large that it attracted the eye the most, but other stones, smaller white opals, it appeared, were embedded in a gold base, barely noticeable.

"I didn't take notice," I admitted. "Shay and I found it not long before we had to run and leave the village. And I have not examined it much since."

"I didn't notice the base-stones in my memory either," Meredith breathed softly, examining the ring with wonder. "They're very small."

Luca watched the seeker with a million questions in his dark eyes. I had many too, and knew only one thing for certain.

This ring wasn't normal, just like the witch who owned it.

CHAPTER FIFTEEN

MEREDITH

I HITCHED MY BACKPACK UP HIGHER AND RUSHED DOWN THE sidewalk, on my way to my first class of the day.

"For someone who recently pulled a tendon, you're moving fast," Benedict drawled from somewhere at my side.

He'd decided to tag along to my classes, which meant he was invisible. It also meant I'd stumbled over him twice in as many minutes. Super awesome, as to others, I looked like a girl tripping over her own feet.

"Particularly for how early it is." Benedict yawned loudly. "I wish you'd go in for the afternoon courses."

My lips curled up slightly. It was after nine in the morning, but if given the chance, Benedict would snooze for half the day. "My Achilles is like new. Daphne's potion was pure magic."

"Is school that interesting, though? Why not relax? Luca only needs you at Yale as a cover, right?"

"I haven't been to some courses, but the classes I attended on the first day were interesting. That's all I have to go on."

My heart hammered at the admission. I'd missed almost the whole first week of school, and I was at Yale.

Me, a high school dropout, at *Yale*. Like, how?! Would I be able to make up what I missed?

Then again, Benedict was right. Would it really matter?

Luca had pulled probably a million strings to get me enrolled. Surely, he could move mountains to keep me here. As soon as the thought arose, I hated it.

If I were going to get a degree from Yale, I wanted to *earn* it. I wanted that accolade. Wanted to have something I'd worked for that was mine. Even if it took me a decade to do so, I'd graduate.

No shame in that. Earning it, is earning it.

"What's on the agenda today?" Benedict asked, oblivious to my inner turmoil.

"I have Bio Lab and Introductory English later. But my Women Who Ruled elective is the one I'm rushing to now," I said, ignoring the weird look I got from a passing student and hoped most others would buy that I had earbuds in because I was on the phone. "I'm looking forward to the last one most."

"Sounds . . . so human."

I snorted. Whatever that meant. "Is that why you're volunteering to come? Because you're interested in human culture?"

"I'll nap during the lecture."

Of course, he would.

"Will your invisibility stay in place while you sleep? It didn't when you were sneaking across the world in my duffel bag."

"That's because I released it *before* sleeping. I was under a mountain of clothes. I thought myself safe until we got to our destination."

Another person passed by and gave me a strange look,

clearly having heard the invisible Benedict. I waved, trying to look friendly, and most of all, distracting.

"I won't do that today," Benedict added.

"Kay. Well, I have a meeting with Luca, Hans, Shay, and Tobias later, so if you sleep past the end of my last class, I'll be at the coven tomb at 3:00 for my meeting. Then, we're having dinner at the house before going to Josiah's place. He's having a birthday party and invited the entire coven."

I wasn't the most social person, and it had been *ages* since someone had invited me to a birthday party, but I had to admit I was excited. After the journey to Hell, I was ready to let loose and have some fun.

Benedict snorted. "How you believe I'll sleep through a herd of humans stampeding from a room is beyond me. Most humans are *not* light of foot."

Once we reached the campus, I checked my phone. This place was still so new, maze-like. "I think it's that way," I said to Benedict, who didn't reply.

Hoping he was still next to me, I followed the map, and found the correct building. I filed into class as the professor called her students to order. Softly, I shut the door. If Benedict wasn't with me, he'd have to wait outside.

"Take a seat." The instructor, Professor Lambeau, my schedule indicated, gestured to the wider room.

I ducked my head, embarrassed to be cutting it so close to time, especially when the class was small. Only thirty people— one of whom I recognized.

Josiah, the necromancer who commanded the ravens that watched over me when I first arrived in New Haven, was here. I hadn't expected that. Sara, his girlfriend, graduated last year, and I'd assumed they were in the same class.

Guess not, I thought as he waved at me.

I returned the gesture and then, trying not to draw any more attention, took one of the two empty seats near the back of the room.

"As promised," the professor began, "today we begin our section on a woman who is, arguably, one of the best-known leaders of the ancient world, Cleopatra. She was actually the seventh of her name, and more than the vixen modern media likes to depict. Cleopatra—"

The door flew open and in walked another latecomer. At the sight of him, my eyes narrowed.

No. Freaking. Way.

"Mr. Sloan, so good of you to grace us with your presence."

"Had to grab a cap." Bentley lifted his coffee and grinned, probably thinking he looked cute and that a charming smile would get him out of trouble.

The professor only scowled, which made me like her immensely.

"Take a seat." The instructor pointed to the empty desk— the one right next to mine.

Bentley's eyes narrowed to slits as he climbed the steps.

Heart rate spiking, I scanned the room again for a different desk. Nope. These were still the only open ones, a fact that Bentley Sloan the Third, King of Dickwads, a total douche-canoe, didn't look too pleased about either.

When Bentley reached me, he threw down his bag and slid into the chair. "Why are you here?"

"I'm in the class," I growled back.

This, out of all the courses I'd chosen, was the one I'd been looking forward to the most. Now I had to put up with Bentley?

I must have pissed off a god in a past life.

"Drop it," he demanded.

Oh, he did not say that.

"Want me to claw him?" Benedict whispered, which made Bentley jump, nearly toppling his cappuccino. Swearing, he looked around us. When he found nothing, he glared at me again.

"What was that? A ghost? Are you using magic?"

"I wouldn't waste it on you. Why are you even here, anyway? And don't tell me you're a feminist."

He'd followed me to the ladies' room once, and tried to force himself on me. Bentley didn't give two flips of a fry basket about women's rights.

"It will look good when I run for office. So, I need to be here. Why don't you enroll in something more your speed? Underwater basket-weaving or whatever?"

"*Excuse me.*" Professor Lambeau clapped her hands to get our attention, so I turned her way, slumping.

"If you two can't be quiet, I'm going to have to ask you to leave." The professor arched her eyebrows. "And you'll want this information for when I discuss your upcoming project. Both partners will be required to contribute and show evidence of their work."

A partner project?

My stomach dropped. I didn't like the sound of that. Instead of focusing on the fact that I'd have to work with someone I didn't know, I resolutely ignored the mainstream asshole beside me, and listened as the professor gave a riveting lecture on Cleopatra the Seventh.

Halfway through the class, I'd almost forgotten I was in school. Though I'd studied ancient history and culture a lot during my time as a tomb raider, I'd never focused on this queen. And I certainly hadn't learned half of what the professor taught.

Cleopatra was one badass woman, someone to look up to for sure. Modern portrayals and the few snippets I'd read about her had never given me that impression, but they were dead wrong. Sexist and misogynistic. They expected the queen to play by the same rules as men in a world not built for her to rule, but she hadn't done so, had refused, and I loved that.

I enjoyed the lecture so much the class flew by, and I was shocked when at ten-till the professor turned to her desk.

"We'll resume our segment on Cleopatra next time, but for now, I'd like to get you started with your partner project. I've assigned your partners alphabetically. Here they are."

My mouth went dry. Oh no. Not that. Stone was much too close to Sloan.

Maybe someone else's name was closer? There had to be a Smith, right? There was always a Smith!

With each name she read, my breath tightened my chest a little more. There weren't many people in the class, and they were dwindling, but Bentley's name hadn't been called.

And then there it was. Paired with mine.

"We need to work on your karma," Benedict whispered.

A groan of agreement escaped me.

Once Professor Lambeau finished, she held up a stack of papers. "Find your partner and exchange numbers. Then grab one of these on your way out. It's instructions for the project, which will need to be completed by midterm."

"This has got to be a fucking joke," my partner growled, marching out the door.

I exhaled. For the first time, perhaps ever, I agreed with Bentley.

HOURS LATER, SO MUCH GLORIOUS KNOWLEDGE FILLED MY HEAD I'd almost forgotten about being paired with Bentley on a project. *Almost.*

Benedict had brought up the idea of asking the professor for a new partner, but I didn't want to do that. I was certain the professor knew I'd skipped the first two sessions, so I didn't want to draw more unwanted attention to myself, especially not in my new favorite course.

More than that, I didn't want to show weakness to Bentley. He was used to getting his way, and being my partner was sticking it to him as much as it was sticking it to me. However, unlike Bentley, *I* was used to being put in shitty situations, and could even thrive in them. I doubted he was like that.

According to the paperwork the professor had handed out, our project could probably be completed in a couple of weeks. It was a half-hour long presentation on one lesser-known female leader in history.

Determined to get started as soon as possible, after my classes were over, I stopped by a bookshop and picked up a few volumes on female leaders who might be interesting—one on Cleopatra too, of course. She was officially my new girl crush.

Currently, I was moving on to the second part of my day. Already at the Shadows and Secrets headquarters, I climbed the stairs to Luca's office, where our meeting would take place.

Along the way, I ran into Josiah.

"Hey." Josiah smiled a blindingly white smile. "I didn't get to ask at class, had to run to my next course, but are you coming tonight? I asked Shay to tell you."

"She did." I nodded. "I'm coming with her and Harper. Thanks for the invite."

"You're part of the team now. Wouldn't want you to miss out." His lips stretched into a grin again, so warm and friendly. It was unfortunate that necromancers brought to mind some nasty stuff, cause Josiah hadn't been like that at all.

"Thanks. Well, I have a meeting with Luca, so I'll see ya around."

"See you, Stone."

Turning, I ran up the stairs. When I arrived at the door to Luca's office, it was closed. Voices drifted through the wood, and a memory of me as a young girl listening through the door to my father's den came rushing back. My lips curled up, and I ran my thumb over the large moonstone in the ring Tobias had taken from *Le Bastion*. My mother had been upset that night, but I still cherished the memory.

Thankfully, though, I no longer had to listen through doors. I belonged here. Luca invited me, so I knocked.

"Come in!" Luca yelled.

As expected, the coven master, Hans, Gunner, and Tobias lounged in leather armchairs when I entered, a wall-to-wall bookshelf stood behind the scene. A coffee table, centered between the chairs, littered with glasses filled with various beverages, but Shay wasn't there. Had her class run late?

"We can start now if you're ready, Stone?" Luca offered. He looked a million times better than yesterday, when we'd been released from the infirmary. The color in his face had returned and his cheeks even seemed fuller.

"Sure." I set my book bag on the floor by the door. They weren't worried about Shay, so she was probably just running late. "Benedict is here too, somewhere."

At that, my familiar appeared by my side, glancing up at

me. "I don't see the appeal of classes. Save for the first. That was intriguing. I suspect that queen you learned about was a cat person."

"Agreed," I said and decided against pointing out that Benedict routinely claimed that he wasn't a regular cat. This wasn't the time or place. "That one is the best. Even if Bentley is in it."

"The Sloan kid?" Tobias barked from his chair by the book-shelf, a wine glass filled with red liquid—likely blood—in his hand. He leaned forward, annoyance sharpening the strong lines of his face. The replay of the day he'd tossed Bentley through the air flashed in my mind. "Is he bothering you again?"

"No." Not compared to before, anyway. His mere existence annoyed me, but there was nothing I could do about that. "We're in the same class, though."

"And partnered on a project," Benedict added.

"*What?*" Tobias asked, his tone a low rumble.

"The prof alphabetically assigned us partners," I replied, semi-surprised by how much Sloan annoyed him too.

"Do you wish it to be unassigned?" the vampire offered.

I did. I also appreciated Tobias having my back. After his non-vote of confidence before the journey to Hell, this felt like him reaching out a hand.

However, I also liked to handle my own shit, so I shook my head. I could get through this, and in doing so, I'd show Bentley once and for all that I wasn't a woman to mess with. "I've got this."

"Then, let's begin with matters at hand." Luca gestured toward the other chairs. "Join us."

I sank into the seat next to Hans. The wizard looked like he hadn't slept well. Was it because he was toiling away, researching the Princes of Hell? Or was he drinking too much again?

"Hans has already informed everyone here about what happened in Romania, his heritage, and his sister," the coven master explained, for my benefit.

A relieved breath left me, glad I didn't have to witness Hans baring his soul again. It was painful to watch.

"I wish to discuss our plans for what happens next concerning the Pearl and the Opal," Luca continued.

"So, will I be going to the vault?" I asked.

That I owned a vault at *Le Bastion* still shocked me. I wanted to see what was inside of it; if there was anything from my parents. Also, I'd be lying if I said I didn't want to see how much money I possessed.

Although my old boss had been keeping a low profile, I wasn't stupid enough to believe that he'd just forget about me. Just let me vanish and start a new life. Just leave me alone.

Seeing as vampire-Denz had said the Ringmaster could fuck off, I assumed my old partner was no longer working for our boss. So perhaps the Ringmaster simply hadn't found me yet, but one day, he would. And when that time came, he'd demand what I owed him. Paying off my old boss and getting out from under his thumb, never fearing those ice-blue eyes in a black mask again, would be a dream come true.

I hoped I wasn't too late.

"Not yet," Luca replied. "There's no need for anyone from the coven to return to the bank. Actually, it would be dangerous. After Tobias and Shay broke into his office, *La Tête* is sure to be gunning for us."

My shoulders slumped, but I perked up again quickly. "Then England?" I was *dying* to learn the identity of Miriam Black.

"I plan to send a team ahead of you," Luca replied.

Feeling like I was being blocked at every turn, I frowned.

"You'll go there," the coven master assured me. "Whoever Miriam Black is, she's sure to have information on the Opal. Perhaps she even possesses knowledge on how it reacted to other stones, or what the powers of the other stones are, but we can't risk you getting hurt again. Not with the Pearl and the Opal missing, and the threat of someone using them growing by the day."

"Basically, we need to vet the woman," Hans concluded simply. "What if she's in league with the demons?"

I looked at my ring. Why would the woman's name be on my vault if my mother didn't trust her? "I doubt that. My parents put her name down for a reason. I can't know what that is, but they wouldn't do anything to endanger me." Even having few memories of my family, I knew that much to be true.

"But things change, Meredith," Hans retorted. "Miriam might have been a good woman then, but a lot has happened since your parents died."

I yearned to argue but couldn't. Not without sounding like a child, anyway. Besides, he had a point. The last time he saw his own sister she was a child. Now, Nicoleta was in league with a demon prince.

"In general, the area is poorly documented," Gunner added, his drawl softening my disappointment. "It's all woods for miles and the road doesn't seem to be too big. We need to send shifters—I'll go if no one else wants to—to make sure it's safe."

"You and Silas will go," Luca agreed. "A wolf and a fae should be a good team."

"Sweet," Gunner conceded with a nod.

"Are you amenable to that, Meredith?" Luca asked. That he wanted my opinion warmed my insides, and the last vestiges of annoyance at not being able to leave right now left me.

"Sure. I could use the time for coursework anyway. But if I'm not going anywhere, why am I being included in this meeting?"

"Because of what Hans learned," Luca explained. "He's spent almost every hour in the supernatural section of the library, studying demonology. He has much to share. Hans?"

So, Hans *had* been researching. Were others? My gaze shifted to Tobias, a self-described researcher, and found him staring at me with such intensity that heat flushed my face. I glanced away.

"Most of the texts are obscure," the wizard picked up the imaginary talking-stick. "But I've pieced some stuff together, and I want us all to be in the loop. We'll tell the rest of the coven soon too, but we were on the ground, putting our lives on the line, and deserve to know first."

"What about Shay, though?" I asked. "She was with Tobias. If she's running late, we should wait for her."

Hans frowned. "Shay is—not willing to talk in my presence."

"She's havin' a hard time dealin' with Hans being a half demon," Gunner added. "She's part angel. And they've been in an eternal war since the beginnin' of time or something' like that. Might take a while for her to get over."

My eyes shifted to the wizard, my trainer, and someone I considered good at heart. "But you've known her for years, right?"

Shame washed over Hans in waves, and he stared at his lap. "Yeah. But that doesn't mean much. I'm not going to force someone to talk to me."

I recognized that tone. My old raiding partner, Denz, had used it a few times when I'd tried to learn more of his past. No more pushing. Case closed.

"She'll come around," I assured him. "So, what did you learn about the Princes of Hell?"

Hans exhaled, apparently glad to move on from the topic. "Demonology has never been a strong suit of mine. I avoided it because it felt too close to home. Of course, I knew there were seven princes, and the basics surrounding them, but I never went deeper."

A few papers littered the shelf on the bookcase behind his chair. Grabbing one of them, he set it on the coffee table between us.

I leaned forward, reading the names listed:

Orien - Wrath

Lucifer - Pride

Bale - Gluttony

Asmodev - Lust

Belhor - Sloth

Levi - Envy

Mon - Greed

"They have ancient names, but two accounts claim these names are what they have gone by most recently, when they were in this realm in the last century. During World War II."

"What's next to their names?" I asked.

"Each demon prince represents a sin," Hans explained. "As I studied, I learned Lucifer is known as the King of Princes, and represents the sin of pride. One brother seemed to hate that the most. Guess who it is?"

"Orien," I breathed. "And he's wrath."

"But wouldn't envy make more sense?" Gunner asked.

"They're demons," Luca replied. "And they only *represent*

the sin and feed upon it. They can *experience* all sins. Likely, they do."

"Rumor has it they manipulate their given sin too," Tobias added. "Though I can find no proof of that."

"I read that too," Hans admitted. "And yeah, Gunner, Orien is *absolutely* envious of his brother. Though there's not much info on the princes, other than Lucifer, there *are* noted cases of Orien and Lucifer warring. Putting it mildly, they have a tempestuous relationship, and both want to be seen as the strongest. Lucifer always wins out on that. Hence, he gets all the fame."

"That would suck," I mused. "Considering they've been around for . . . forever."

"Agreed," Hans nodded. "And obviously, Orien has a ton of pride too—as Luca said, *all* the princes likely do. But, most applicable to us, Orien is the Prince of Wrath and he is hunting stones. I can't imagine that a god of wrath having stones of immense power is a good thing."

"Nicoleta said that the Darkborn and the prince will purge the Earth," I breathed. "That feels like war, and the stones will help."

"That's what we're thinking," Hans agreed. "He'll destroy our world, and then bring his old world here. And in doing so, he'll show his brother who should be the King of Princes."

CHAPTER SIXTEEN

HANS

"I think that's enough for today," Luca said, calling our small meeting to an end. He stood and stretched, working out the kinks of sitting, and moved to his desk to jot down notes on what we discussed. "I need to consider matters."

"And I gotta study," Meredith said, her tone unnaturally high. "See you guys later." As though her ass was on fire, the witch rose and beelined to the door.

My eyebrows knitted together. She'd been fidgety most of the meeting, which wasn't like her.

I was just about to comment on Meredith's odd behavior, when Tobias cleared his throat loudly. One look at him, and the day just got stranger. The vampire was still in his seat, his eyes pinned on the door the witch had just disappeared through like he wanted to beat it down. Or run after her. In my head, alarm bells started ringing.

"Tobias?" I ventured.

He blinked, as though I'd broken a spell he'd been under. "Yes?"

"Are you . . . okay?" I substituted the last word for what I was really thinking. Was he trying to dominate the witch again? I'd thought he was getting better around her? Was I wrong?

Protective of the witch since the day Tobias had nearly bitten her during training, I made a mental note to ask Meredith. No matter what the vampire said, I needed her side of the story.

"Fine. Just thinking," Tobias said, rising to stand.

"Actually, I've been thinkin' too," Gunner drawled. "Can I talk to you about something, Toby?"

The vampire frowned slightly, his gaze flickering to the door again. "Let's walk and you can tell me what's on your mind."

Gunner, never one to take a hint unless it was strong as hell, nodded and started talking Tobias's ear off. The pair left, and only when I could no longer hear Gunner's voice did I rise and approach Luca's desk. There was something personal I wanted to discuss.

"We're not done?" Luca asked looking up from the notes he'd been writing.

"Not unless you have something to get to."

Luca studied me before gliding to the bar cart on the other side of his office. He poured a scotch and raised an empty tumbler, offering me one. I shook my head, declining. "I assume you want to discuss your sister?"

On point as always, Mage.

"She's clearly our enemy—"

"That's a strong word, Hans."

"She's part of the Darkborn," I amended, though I had no doubt I was correct the first time.

I understood demon emotions, how they struck deeper and hungrier and darker than others could imagine. Nicoleta would experience the same volatile emotions that I once had, before I repressed that side of myself.

"From what I know of your sister, she is young. Impressionable." Luca lowered himself into the chair behind his desk, and tented his fingers. "And I suspect, a Prince of Darkness would seek her because she's also powerful? More so than you expected?"

A breath dripping with tension left me. "Yes. It shocked me, Luca. What she could do—I don't think I could muster the same powers if I tried."

Not that I wanted to.

"She's young," I added. "Which means she might not be done growing into her magic. What I saw could just be the beginning."

"I see." Luca stared at me, a million questions in his deep brown eyes. "Only one thing matters to me, really. Is she redeemable?"

I swallowed. "I want to say yes."

"Then once we find the stones and send the Prince of Wrath back to Hell, we'll offer her protection. A place here, tutoring and support, if she wants it."

Hope loosened the tension on my shoulders. "You mean it?"

"I do. You've been a valuable asset to the coven for years, Hans. I'm sure Nicoleta could be helpful, given the chance."

My throat tightened. Since we'd returned to New Haven, the question of how to save my sister had burned in the back of my mind. One moment, I doubted it was possible. The next, I was determined to extract her from the clutches of the Darkborn. This offer was more than I'd dared to hope for.

"Thanks, man," I breathed. "I have a million doubts, but I really hope that she can turn to the light. I—"

The phone on Luca's desk rang, a landline number that only a few people possessed. The mage's eyes grew wide. "Excuse me, Hans."

He lifted the receiver. "Luca Moretti."

Not for the first time I wished I had the super hearing of a vampire or a shifter, but I didn't, so I waited. Muscles tensed as Luca nodded. Whatever the other person was telling him, wasn't good.

"I'll be there soon," Luca said finally, one of his few contributions to the conversation. He hung up and stood. "That was a member of Wolf's Head. A new recruit is acting strangely. They suspect magic." Luca arched an eyebrow.

"Strangely? As in . . . crazy?"

"That was the gist. I'll admit the person I spoke with was rather hysterical and rambling."

"Do you think the Pearl is to blame?"

"There's only one way to find out. I want to assess their tomb in person. Join me?"

Together, we left his office. Headquarters was uncommonly quiet for late afternoon, though someone did seem to be brewing a potion somewhere in the tomb. It reeked of patchouli, a scent I despised. Give me gasoline and metal any day over that hippie shit.

Luckily, no one emerged from the rooms Luca and I passed and we slipped through the halls and out the doors with no one stopping us. Once on the street we became just two guys and melted into the flow of students, professors, and New Haven natives alike.

"We'll take my car," Luca said, waving for me to follow.

"Sure," I replied, marveling at how much stronger he looked. Days ago, the coven master had been on death's door, but he was already back to normal.

Sometimes it was difficult to remember that though the trip to Hell pained me, it had really done a lot of good. Before our descent into the underworld, S&S had assumed it was the Ringmaster or a dark sorcerer from OA who'd sent the shade. As Meredith believed the Ringmaster was human, I'd been partial to the second theory.

But now I was pretty sure we'd all been dead wrong. It was far more likely that Prince Orien sent the shade. After all, the demon princes could command armies of the vile creatures, or so the texts told me.

Which led us to another massive issue the coven had not gotten around to addressing. After Healer Daphne informed us the world's lone crop of lucimisia was burned, necessitating our journey to Hell, a single word popped into my mind.

Traitor.

The possibility that there was one in our midst seemed great. Only a few people were aware of this, and for right now, it would stay that way. The slightest hint that we were wise to the lucimisia crops burning might send the traitor running. We could not abide that. It was best to wait, to hope for a misstep. To keep watch. In time, we'd catch the traitor.

After we got our hands on the Pearl and Opal. After we figured out how to kick a Prince of Darkness back to the underworld.

"Here we are." Luca stopped in front of a black Fiat, the mage's pride and joy.

I slipped inside the sports car, running my hand over the smooth leather interior. Not my style. I preferred my vehicles larger and built for rougher terrain, but I had to admit it was pretty sweet. My fingers itched to play around under the hood of this baby.

The engine started, and we were off, zipping down the

streets of New Haven to the home of Wolf's Head secret society. As we drove, women stared while men nodded in appreciation.

As we pulled up to Wolf's Head, a young man and two women waited on the lawn. All three looked like they might lose their shit at any second, but we had business to attend to, and this was no place for my anxieties.

"Luca, Coven Master of Shadows and Secrets." The Italian approached the students—all Yale seniors, and thus, in on the secret of our society—that we were actually a coven of supernaturals.

"Thanks for coming," one of the young women said. She had long black hair braided down her back, and eyes lined heavily with kohl. "We didn't know what to do, but an alumnus told us to call you."

"That's the proper protocol," Luca agreed, his tone soothing. "Tell me what happened. Slowly, this time."

Pink stained the dark-haired woman's cheeks. Apparently, she'd been the one to speak with Luca and was only now realizing how frantic she must have sounded.

"We came here to have a drink with a friend. Another new member," the guy explained, his foot tapping rapidly. "When we got here, Binita," he gestured to the woman with the long braid, "heard something weird."

"I did too," a blonde confirmed.

"Yeah, Suze was actually the one who investigated," Binita said. "Tim and I shrugged it off cause the sound was kinda rhythmic. I assumed old pipes or something. So, we started making drinks, but then, a couple of minutes after she went looking for whatever was making the noise, Suze screamed."

"We ran to her and saw our friend, Julio, sprinting away."

Tim gulped, looking green. "Blood was *pouring* from his head."

"Because he'd been pounding it against a wall," Suze added, swallowing thickly at the memory.

"Yeah, and as he ran, he looked crazy," Tim shuddered. "To be honest, he's been acting off since he got back."

"From where?" Luca asked.

"New York," Binita answered. "He visited last weekend, to see some friends from home."

Was this the clue we'd been waiting for? New York wasn't far, and spreading madness there would cause catastrophe. Was this a hint as to the Pearl's location?

"Did you see where he went?" I asked.

Tim swallowed. "Yeah, we were worried about him, so we followed, but he's fast as fuck—he runs track—and he lost us really quick. When we got back here, we called an alumnus, cause we didn't know what else to do. They said to ring you, that you'd take care of it. Can you?"

"If they suggested my coven, you must have given the alumni reason to believe magic was involved." Luca said. "What made you think magic?"

"His eyes *glowed*," Suze said. "Like a weird ring of light around his irises." She shuddered. "So freaky."

"Indeed." The mage rubbed the back of his neck with his hand. "And if that's the case, you were right to call. Which way did he go? Can you tell us anything that might help us locate him? Do you have a picture?"

The three students exchanged glances.

"What about your phones? A locator app?" I prompted.

"OhmaGod! Yes!" Suze gasped. "We added each other during a party once, but I totally forgot. One sec!"

She dashed into the secret society's house, and was gone

only a minute before reappearing, phone in hand. Her eyes were glued to the screen as she brought up the app. "Says here that he's by Harkness Tower." Her eyebrows pulled together. "What could he be doing there? I don't think he has a class nearby. Or one at all, right now."

An image of the tall masonry tower came to mind. "Show us a picture of Julio."

Quickly, the girl pulled up an image of a group of people. She zoomed in on a man with dark brown skin, a black and red mohawk that I suspected was a wig, and a grin that spread from ear-to-ear.

"That's not his normal hair," Suze assured me. "He has a buzz cut. Black hair."

"Give me your phone."

Suze jerked back. "Why?"

"Because if we're going to find him, we need to track him. Unless you want to come?"

She shook her head and handed over the phone. "He scared me. The unlock code is 1234."

"You should really change that to something better."

"Yeah, girl. You should," Binita echoed, looking unimpressed with her friend's shitty password.

"We'll return your phone right after we find Julio," Luca assured Suze, who glared at me.

Standing by what I said, I shrugged. The girl was just waiting to get hacked.

"Let's go, Hans."

We hopped back in the car, and Luca pulled away from the house before speaking. "What do you think?"

"I think he's going to high ground," I muttered. "Hope we get there in time."

We sped back toward campus, and Luca didn't hesitate

when he found a parking spot semi-close to Harkness Tower. The moment we hopped out of the car, I had Suze's phone in hand.

"He's still there. Actually, I think he might be inside."

"*Merda,*" the mage hissed and broke into a sprint. "We have to stop him."

Campus wasn't as crowded as it might have been, but that still left a fair amount of weaving and dodging through students and faculty. With each step, my heart pumped harder.

What if we didn't make it in time? If that happened, I hoped whatever force gripped Julio would weaken, that he'd see sense, or someone would notice the young man, stopping him from doing anything that might cause him harm.

As we neared the tower, I squinted. Was it my imagination or was someone up by the bells? Could people even get up there? We'd passed Branford College when a scream ripped through campus.

My heart lunged into my throat. "Luca!"

"Run!"

Except, now others were going the same way as us, and by the time we got to the Tower, a crowd had gathered. They stood a few yards from the building but blocked our view. My stomach sank, yet there was no stopping now. We had to know, to see.

"Excuse us." Luca pushed past the students.

"Dude! You shouldn't go in there!" one kid called, deepening the pit in my belly. "It could be a crime scene."

It wasn't. Not like they were thinking. Yet, even though I was expecting it, the moment I laid eyes on Julio—smashed against the pavement with blood pooling around him—my whole body tightened. We were too late.

"Do you sense magic?" I whispered.

As a mage, he was even more receptive to sensing it than me. I'd have to use a spell to figure out what happened, and we couldn't do that here. Not with so many eyes around us.

"I do. Dark magic." Luca shook his head, staring at a boy who not long ago had the world at his feet. "I think it was the Pearl's influence, but I can't be sure. I'd have to touch the body."

"Back away!" a voice filled with authority boomed.

I turned to find police running our way. Without saying a word, Luca and I melted into the crowd, distancing ourselves from the students.

"I will inform Tobias and Gunner," Luca said when we were far enough away that no one would hear, "but that's it."

"Not Meredith? Or Shay?"

"Not yet. Meredith will want to act, to seek the Pearl, but there's not enough proof of location to get her involved. And not a word of this to anyone at Josiah's party, Hans. Not until we can be sure this is a result of the Pearl's power."

"I'm not goin—wait, *you're* going to the party?" I gaped. "You just got well."

"All the more reason for me to live again."

After seeing Hell, I really couldn't argue with anyone who wanted to live life to the fullest, but I didn't completely agree with not telling our coven about what had happened. "Keeping it a secret will mean more incidents."

"It will." A veil of stone covered Luca's face. "But this is only one isolated incident. We can't act on that and risk letting our enemies know we're coming. It's best to keep watch, to wait."

"Nicoleta already knows I'll find her if bad things happen. And she understands the coven involves themselves in matters of dark magic. I never hid that from my family. Since it's a pretty damn sure thing the Darkborn have two *lapis caelesti*, she's likely expecting to see me again."

"I understand, but my decision is the same. *No action.*" Luca locked eyes with me. "Not until we're one hundred percent ready. From today, until the day we make a move for the stones, we watch the news. Focus on New York City, but we search for signs everywhere. And only when enough crop up in one area, we strike."

CHAPTER SEVENTEEN

MEREDITH

I WALKED DOWN THE SIDEWALK, TUCKED BETWEEN MY housemates, equally excited and nervous to be attending a birthday party. My first one in years.

Would there be cake? Did adults do that? Was that a stupid question to ask?

Yeah, probably . . .

My lips tightened, determined to trap the questions. I had no desire to look like the sad sap of a friend, who hadn't been to a party since she was a tween.

I'd survived a freaking trip to Hell. I'd started to recall my past. My magic was growing stronger by the day, and I was enrolled at *Yale*. When I considered all I had going on in life, things I never could have imagined, it was easier to pretend to be a woman capable of navigating a social scene like a pro.

Feeling it was a different matter, but I was a decent actress. I'd fake it until I made it.

Above, a raven cawed and launched itself off the telephone line, swooping toward us and circling our trio.

"We're coming, Josiah." Harper laughed at the raven.

"Can he see through any ravens' eyes? Or just certain ones?" I asked as the bird did another circle and soared into the air, cawing loudly again.

"Josiah has ones he favors and those he can use at any time," Harper said. "But technically, he can inhabit any raven. They have to be close enough for his magic to attach."

"Can all necromancers do that?"

"No. They have varied powers. Sara doesn't possess ravens."

Shay remained silent as Harper answered me, her eyes locked on the ground. Normally, she was bubbly and fun, but tonight, we'd had to pull her out of the house. I had a hunch why she might be acting that way, but I hadn't broached the subject of Hans yet.

Harper cleared her throat and gestured three doors down the street. "That's his place."

If she hadn't pointed it out, I would have known anyhow. Music blared from open windows, not loud enough for the police to be called, but on the cusp of acceptable. Through the windows, I spotted Luca, and my lips parted.

"The coven master is here?!"

"I'm not surprised," Harper admitted, glancing at Shay. I sensed the wolf felt an obligation to fill the empty conversational space left by our nephilim friend. "He loves a good party, and probably wants to assure everyone he's okay."

We walked up the path to the house, and Harper knocked. Josiah appeared as if he'd been waiting right behind the door, one raven on his shoulder and an easy smile on his lips.

"Glad you girls came. Come on in! Tobias was telling us about *Le Bastion*, Shay."

At the mention of the vampire's name a shiver rocked my spine. I blinked. For the time being, Tobias and I were on good terms, but I still found it strange how my body reacted to him. More than strange actually, it confused the hell out of me.

I clenched my hands into fists, rubbing my thumb over the moonstone in the ring. The gem glowed when I first put it on, but since then, nothing. Still, it comforted me, brought me back down. As it stood, this was the only thing I had left of my parents. Perhaps when I finally got around to visiting my vault that would change, but that could be a while.

Josiah showed us where to pile our coats in the guest bedroom, and as he did so, the raven on his shoulder stared right at me.

Tossing my jacket on the bed, I swallowed. "Is your bird okay? The one in the infirmary?"

"This is Igbo, actually." Josiah stroked the raven's feathered head. "She left before you and Luca did. Flew out a window once she healed up."

"Oh, that's good."

He shut the door to the coatroom. "Yeah. Daphne freaked out when she found her missing, but Igbo has a mind of her own."

"I'm glad she's okay." I tailed the necromancer back to the living room and pulled a bottle of wine from the oversized purse I wore. Harper did the same, but Shay just stood between us, gaze raking over the party as if she was looking for someone.

"These are for you." Harper said, and we handed over the party favors.

"Thanks," Josiah grinned. "I'll go put them on the table. There's more in the kitchen—a keg, cause I didn't want it on the carpet. Help yourself to anything that's out."

"Great," Harper said. "Where's your restroom?"

Josiah pointed it out, and Harper excused herself to use the restroom just as Josiah was called into the kitchen. Once alone, I looked to Shay.

"Wanna get a drink?"

She shrugged, which was at least something, so I gestured to the other side of the room, where a table had been set up with drinks. We ambled over, Shay still not saying a word. Was this how she'd be all night? Should we leave? I didn't want to, but Shay had always been loyal to me and if she wanted to leave, I would.

"Hey," I whispered to my roomie after we'd each filled our red cups with wine and found a spot to chill in the living area. Except for when they came out for drinks, most people gathered in the kitchen. "You doing alright?"

With my question, Shay glanced up, just as another raven swooped around us and settled on the back of her chair.

"Oh, uh, you don't have to answer," I offered, glancing at the raven.

Shay shrugged. "He's not using it now. When Josiah uses the ravens, their eyes go kinda milky."

I hadn't noticed that. Now I'd be on the lookout.

My roommate huffed out a long breath. "And I don't know. If I'm okay, that is."

"Do you want to . . . talk about it?"

Oh, hell. I sounded so awkward.

Shay gave me an amused look. "That's what friends do."

"Yeah," I answered slowly.

"Does that mean we're friends, Meredith?" The first smile I'd seen on her face all day bloomed.

An uncomfortable laugh flew out of me. Who asked that?! Then again, who felt unease at such a question? Me, that was who.

Shay popped an eyebrow, demanding an answer.

I swallowed, and hoped she didn't hear it. "Yeah, I guess so."

Shay snorted. "Making you uncomfortable is one of the lights of my life. Lucky for me, it's so freaking easy." She sipped her wine. "But seriously, though, I'm glad to hear that. You haven't been here long, and I know you have a hard time opening up, but I consider you a friend, too. Not just a roomie. Harper does too. She won't say it, though."

Tears sprang into my eyes, and I looked away, unused to the emotions rushing through me. "Thanks." I wiped the moisture away. "But I asked about *you*. So why are you making this all about me?"

"It's easier."

"She doesn't want to admit she likes him. Always has." Harper appeared from behind, drink in hand, and sat next to the nephilim. "And now it's common knowledge that Hans is half demon—what we call a Hellblooded. Angels and demons, even nephilim and the Hellblooded, don't mix."

As I'd thought.

"Way to analyze me, Harp." Shay sounded annoyed and another gulp of wine flowed down the hatch.

"Well, it's true. I know it. Meredith does too. Everyone does. Even Hans knows you're uncomfortable around him. Hence why he texted me and told me he wouldn't be here."

Shay relaxed at the news that she wouldn't see Hans. "Okay, I admit that I was smitten. Attracted to the bad boy with tats because I'm part angel and that feels *so* taboo." She waved her hand dismissively and snorted. "Turns out the tats weren't shit, and he's more bad boy than I ever expected. Now, I don't know what to do. There, I said it."

I exhaled. "Why do anything?"

"I'm part *angel*, Mer," Shay repeated. "Demons, Hellblooded even, if they go dark, are my enemy. This isn't something I take lightly."

"But he's never been evil before. Flawed, like any other person, sure, but not evil." I pointed out, picturing Nicoleta as her black ribbons tried to choke Gunner in wolf form. I shuddered.

At first, I'd given her the benefit of the doubt, but I'd been wrong. *She* was evil. Not Hans.

"His actions should count for a lot," I pressed.

"They do. I'm having trouble coming to terms. I'll get through it . . . eventually." She tilted her chin up so that her head rested on the back of the couch. "Can we pretend like this isn't an issue right now? I'd love not to think about it for an hour or two."

After exchanging glances with Harper, I shrugged. At least the truth was out in the open, and we didn't have to tiptoe around it.

"Sure," I agreed. "Actually, I'm going to go say hi to Gunner. I can hear him in the kitchen, and I haven't had time to check up on him one on one. I'll be a few minutes."

"We'll chill here." Harper waved at a trio of giggling women as they strolled in the front door without knocking. "I don't enjoy being in the middle of a crowd."

"See ya later." I stood and walked through the house, lighter than I'd been. Shay would have to work out her issues, but I had to admit it felt good to be trusted. We really were friends, and my heart lifted at the idea.

Before I reached Gunner, Daphne exited the kitchen, on her way to the drinks table. In true healer fashion, she stopped me and asked about my Achilles. I assured her I was fine, and the interaction left me with what was probably a dopey-ass smile on my face.

Three weeks ago, I hadn't been sure I could ever fit in anywhere, but the coven had proven to me they cared about me. They were good people. I could count on them—trust them.

When I got free and entered the kitchen, I found the wolf right away. He was on the far side of the fairly large kitchen regaling an enraptured group with a story. He seemed to feel me watching him though, because he caught my eye and waved me over.

"Stoney! How you feelin', girl?"

"Good." I took a step his way, but before I got to him, Josiah appeared in front of me.

"Hey!" he beamed.

"Uh, hey," I took a step back as he was sort of in my bubble. "What's up?"

"Seeing how you're enjoying the party."

"I just got here," I reminded him gently. "But it's great. Thanks again for inviting me."

"Sure thing. I wish Sara had come tonight. She's been wanting to get to know you better."

"Bummer," I said, meaning it. Sara had always seemed nice to me. "I thought she would be here."

"She's been busy with her volunteer gig." The necromancer shrugged, then his eyes lit up. "Actually, oh shit, this is perfect!"

"What's that?"

"Can I ask a favor?"

"What's up?"

"Sara and I have been dating for a while now, and I got her a birthday present." His expression turned sheepish for a beat. "You guys are about the same size, and I really want this gift to be perfect. Can you try it on? Give me your opinion?"

"I don't know her well enough to know if she'd like it, though. Would Harper be better? We're close to the same size too."

Josiah's nose wrinkled. "Harper is too prim."

I cocked my head. I'd describe Sara's style as preppy, not rocker, my personal style.

"It's in my room and won't take long," Josiah pressed.

"I—" The sensation of someone watching me grew tight on my skin, and my attention shifted from Josiah's hopeful expression to land on Tobias on the other side of the room.

I hadn't seen him before, probably because the vampire stood in a circle of women, one of whom was even taller than Tobias's towering frame and had blocked him from view. Now, however, he was in plain sight. As were the other women openly flirting with him. One drop dead gorgeous redhead even rested her hand on his shoulder, as if laying claim. She laughed loudly and spun a ball of magic in the other hand to get his attention, but Tobias wasn't obliging.

Just as I couldn't look away from him, the vampire's gaze was locked on *me*. Practically predatory in its intensity, his stare made the hair on the back of my neck rise. I'd never seen this exact expression on Tobias's face, and yet, it still gave me only one impression.

Tobias was hungry.

No, not just hungry. He looked like he was tracking my every movement, watching his prey. Urges flooded me, warring inside, washing away the rest of the room.

I'd have to be blind to not see that Tobias was sexy, and in that vein, I wanted to march up to him, take his chin in my hands and kiss that dominant look right off his face. To show him that I'd grown beyond the day he'd threatened me with his fangs. That he couldn't intimidate me anymore, and I was a force to be reckoned with.

An image of what sort of reaction that might elicit sprang to mind, and I snorted. My laughter only appeared to intrigue him, for Tobias immediately detached himself from his group and strode toward me. I stiffened.

"Meredith?" a voice asked. "Do you need to lie down?"

I blinked and found the necromancer watching me. Josiah was still standing there, waiting for my reply! How long had I been watching Tobias and him studying me? Seconds? Minutes? I had no idea. Time had seemed to stop . . .

"Sorry, Josiah, but can I check out that gift later? I really need to talk to Gunner."

Before the necromancer could respond, I turned to join the wolf, a safer option than the vampire. Yet, I didn't even make it a step before Tobias appeared, stopping me in my tracks.

"Meredith . . ." His rumbly and rough English accent, with a hint of posh, cut through me, reminding me of the day I met him in that Egyptian prison. I hadn't known how hard he could be then, how frustrating, but somehow his voice still had that panty-melting effect.

"Meredith?" the vampire pressed, coming around to face me with concern written across his face. "Are you well?"

I took a step away, still feeling a bit like prey. "Fine."

Josiah remained a few paces away, his eyes wide as he looked from me to Tobias, and back again. "Uh, I'm gonna bounce. Find me later, Meredith?"

"Sure," I assured, even though I had no intention of doing so.

"Were you trying to avoid me?" Tobias asked when we were alone.

"No," I lied. "You looked busy with the ladies, and I was

going to see Gunner. I wanted to check up on him after our mission."

"The ladies?"

"That ginger woman with magic. Witch? Mage? Fae?" I had no idea.

Recognition flashed in his evergreen eyes. "Lola. A hedge witch."

"Is she in our coven?"

"She's part of a local coven called The Night Circle. Josiah has many friends in that coven, and Lola likes to be in our company."

Was that his way of saying she liked to flirt with coven members? That she was attracted to power? According to Hans, hedge witches didn't have strong enough abilities.

"In any case, it's a good thing I stopped you. Gunner seems *quite* occupied. I doubt you'd want to interrupt."

The vampire's gaze broke from mine, and I turned to find Gunner *was* totally occupied. A young woman was in his arms, stroking his jawline.

"Uh, I see that now." My face was warm when I turned to face the vampire once more, and I jerked back. Had he gotten closer? Was it warm in here? Taking another step backwards, I found myself up against a wall. Cornered by a hot vampire.

"Would you like to take a turn in the garden?"

I blinked and then burst out laughing. An expression of embarrassment crossed Tobias's face.

"I meant would you like to go outside?"

"I understood you," I clarified. "But sometimes you sound like you're from Downton Abbey. It catches me off guard."

"Yes, well." He shook his head. "Sometimes the language of my human life returns when I least expect it."

My spine straightened. I loved history and anthropology,

and though I'd known Tobias was old, I'd rarely thought to ask him about his past.

"Actually, yeah. Not sure there will be a garden large enough to 'take a turn in.'" I twirled my hand at the fancy phrase. "But let's go outside."

His lips twitched ever so slightly, as if he was holding in a chuckle. "After you."

We made our way to the back of the house, and I caught a few intrigued glances being tossed our way. Sure, I was new to the coven, but I'd have to be blind not to see that Tobias wasn't overly social. He mostly socialized with Luca, Hans, and Gunner, and even then, he only seemed to enjoy talking to Luca. Then again, he had been here and flirting with girls.

But he'd left them all when I walked into the kitchen. So that begged the question, why did he want to isolate me?

To drink my blood?

I rolled my eyes at the stupid idea. Honestly, I didn't believe that, but our dynamic did feel uneven. Like he was a predator and I was prey.

"Is everything alright?"

Oh, crap. He'd caught the eye roll.

"Just thinking."

"Hmmm."

The instant Tobias opened the back door, cool air rushed in to meet us. As expected, Josiah had a porch and a normal suburban yard, not an expansive garden filled with hedges and roses to waltz through. Still, I breathed in deeply, happy for the extra space, and slipped out in front of him—replaying every syllable of that *hmmm* with such detail one would think I was trying to decode Ancient Greek.

Speaking of Ancient Greek.

"I have to ask," I started as he came up beside me on the edge of the porch. "How old are you?"

Outside, the night was quiet, and as he stared at me, it grew even more so. Had I asked something offensive? Was there vampire etiquette for this sort of thing?

"Should I not have asked that?" I added, feeling foolish.

"It was merely unexpected. I'm not used to being surprised."

There was something he was leaving off there, but I didn't push. Allowing him to decide if he wanted to answer or not, I paused on the edge of the deck and tilted my chin upward to soak up the night.

New Haven experienced light pollution, but tonight the stars shone brighter than usual. The air was cool on my skin, and the scents of fall—of newly decaying leaves, roasts in neighbors' ovens, and even a pumpkin-spice candle being burned somewhere nearby filled the air. It was a sweet neighborhood. Peaceful and clean. One that I, with my Yale-employed parents, might have called home.

Would I ever remember something like that?

"I was born in London, in 1855. I'm 167 years old," Tobias said suddenly, surprising me.

I turned to face the vampire, looked him up and down. "Damn, boy. You look good for your age."

As intended, that got a smile out of him, eliciting a flutter in my stomach.

"And how old were you when you were . . . transformed?"

An amused expression crossed his face.

"We call it being turned. And I was twenty-five. My sire noticed me when a ship I was working on returned to London. I was ill, fighting a sickness that eventually took many lives in my time. She was certain that I wouldn't have survived the sickness naturally, but Giselle saw something in me. Something worth keeping around." He gazed upon the stars too.

How different had the night sky looked to him all those years ago? Had he been able to navigate ships by the stars?

"She turned me when I was an inch from death."

He sounded both grateful and . . . sad?

"Did you ever see your family again?" The words popped out before I could stop them, and I slapped my hands over my mouth. Talk about private! I would hate it if someone I barely knew asked me about my parents. Even around Shay and Harper, I had a difficult time discussing them, and I trusted my housemates more than most.

Tobias didn't look irate though. "My mother was a deeply devout woman and my new *condition* would have threatened her. Newbloods have little control over their actions, so their sires must watch them closely."

A sad look crossed his face.

"I didn't dare return to our neighborhood in London, for the people there live too close to one another. A single visit might have endangered them all, and while I wasn't a saint as a newblood, far from it in fact, I somehow knew better than to test myself in that way. I grew up among the bottom of the barrel, and never clawed my way out. Not in my human life, anyway. Though I'd have loved to see my family, to tell mother that perhaps I could provide better in this way, I did not dare return home when I had such weak impulse control."

"Like in drinking blood?" It was probably obvious to other supernaturals, but I was new to all this and was darkly fascinated.

"Exactly. Bloodlust is strong in newbloods, and the most downtrodden in society did not need another burden to bear."

That I could understand. Though I'd acted a part many

times, usually to gain access to high society and steal their shit, in reality, I'd been indebted nearly all of my life.

"It's hard to imagine you as poor," I admitted, since now he wore expensive clothing and had the bearing of a prince.

"Is it? Before I enlisted in the navy, I had to scavenge for items to sell in the mud of the Thames. In my era, we were called mudlarkers. We found treasures in the muck and mire." He arched an eyebrow. "Not so posh, is it?"

"Guess not." It was still hard to picture, though. "When you could go places without your sire, did you go home? Like years later?"

Tobias's head shook. "As I said, my mother was devout, and word had spread that I'd died of a plague—my body burned before she could say her goodbyes. Returning would have only haunted her. We went to Paris as soon as I was capable of sailing."

"I'm sorry you didn't get to see them again." I understood a thing or two about not getting to say goodbye to those I loved.

"It was better that way. And while I missed them, still do from time to time, Giselle gave me a new lease on life. Another family." He shrugged. "We try not to dwell on the past, my kind. If you do, it might steal your sanity."

A cheer rang from inside, the party sounding like it had gotten larger. Wilder too. My lips curled at the lighthearted fun.

"I want you to know, Meredith, that I truly regret underestimating you," Tobias offered, and my lips parted in shock as he reached out and plucked a fallen leaf from my shoulder.

An electrical shock ran from where his fingers touched me, to my very core. Tobias paused, eyebrows dipping closer together.

"Where is this apology coming from?"

The vampire's gaze stayed on my arm for a beat longer before he removed his hand, meeting my eyes. "At first, when you joined S&S, I didn't wish for you to be here. I didn't believe you could handle it, but now I see that I was wrong. I respect your abilities and what you've done, Meredith. Can we start over?"

"You already apologized in the infirmary."

"Well, I've learned to be quite *thorough* with you." His lips tugged up at the corners, and the day that I'd demanded a second—admittedly, rather petty—apology from him rushed to the forefront of my mind.

Inwardly, I cringed at my behavior. Ugh. Why was I so stubborn sometimes?

"We can start over," I conceded. "That would work well for the both of us. I—*oh!*"

As it had in Hell, my vision clouded, and I braced myself, knowing what was coming. Distantly, I heard Tobias asking if I was okay, but before I could respond, I found myself standing in a bedroom painted lilac and cream. I shook myself, shocked at how vivid these memories were becoming, more like I was an active participant—rather than just viewing, like I had in the first one.

Along the walls, childish drawings began to appear, interspersed with photographs of my parents and me. Tears sprang to my eyes. This was my room as a child. As that sank in, two figures appeared in front of me, stealing the air from my lungs.

Mom sat in a chair next to my bed, reading to me. I looked to be about eight this time, and from the sour look on my face, I was not digging the book.

"I want your ring," I whined snottily.

A breath filled with barely restrained annoyance left my mother's lips, but she forced a smile and took off her ring, the moonstone one Tobias had given me. The one on my hand.

"Be careful with it, my darling."

"Why? It's mine, isn't it? I can do whatever I want with it!" I wrinkled my nose in a way that made me want to scold myself.

Why was I being such a brat?! Clearly, I didn't realize how good I had it. Or what would be taken from me in a few short years.

The idea made my throat tighten. I would give anything to go back to this night, body and soul, and hug my mom.

"It is yours, Meredith. But not yet. You're not ready for it."

"Why not?" I lifted my arm away from her, taunting her with the ring, even though my mother made no move to take it from me. Moonlight beamed through the window, and somehow, the ring looked even more luminous than it did in real life, on my hand.

"That ring, and the eight stones in it, will lead you somewhere. To someone who will teach you many things. And that," sadness filled her face, "means you have to go away. Somewhere you're not ready to go yet. Daddy and I want time with you first."

"I'm a big girl!" I yelled. "I'm ready! And I want to go. I bet whoever lives there will give me a puppy!"

"Meredith." My mother sighed as if she'd been over this a million times. She probably had. "Your father is allergic to dogs. Do you want him to be in pain?"

"I want a puppy!" I demanded.

Mother's fingers rubbed at her temples. "We'll talk about other options later. I know we had a hard day, but maybe it's best that we all go to bed. Can I have the ring back, Meredith? Darling?"

"It's mine!" young me shrieked.

The sound was so ear-splitting that I covered my ears and closed my eyes. A second passed, and the pressure of a hand on my shoulder alerted me that someone had spotted me. My mother? Could she see me this time?

When my eyelids flew open, my heart sank. Tobias stood there, watching me, so close, his hands pressed into my shoulders as if he was trying to bring me back through touch. Slowly, I lowered my hands. He followed suit, though the intensity in his eyes did not leave.

"What happened?" he asked.

"A memory." Recalling how much of a brat I had been made me wince. "With my mom and this." I lifted the hand which bore the ring. "My mother was wearing it, like in another memory I had, but this time, I demanded it from her. God, I was a terror. Talk about effective birth control."

At that, the vampire let out an amused, superior sound, ripping me from my pity for my mother.

"What was that?!"

"Let's just say I can imagine it."

"Excuse me! I'm having a serious moment here!" I glared at him, and Tobias rearranged his features from haughty to neutral.

"*Anyway,* my mother talked about this ring." The moonstone captured my attention once more. "She said that it would lead me somewhere, to someone. But she specified that the eight stones would, and as we talked about before, there are only seven."

His expression went still. "Do you believe she also referred to the ring showing you to Miriam Black?"

I hadn't had time to consider such a thing, but it made sense. They *had* found the ring in a bank that connected me to the enigmatic Miriam.

"I don't know the woman, so I can't be sure."

Tobias pondered. "It seems likely, though Luca will still want to send Gunner and Silas to scout before you journey across the pond. In case this Miriam woman is dangerous."

I shrugged. "Fine by me. At first, I really wanted to go, but I'm not quite ready to risk my life again so soon."

"Nor am I ready for you to do so," Tobias said, and then stiffened, as if he hadn't meant to speak the words out loud. "I only mean . . . You were quite injured."

I had been, and yet, there was something else, something more beneath his words. But like a coward, I wasn't ready to dive that deep yet. I took a step toward the door. "I should head back inside and check on Shay."

"Right. Very well." He cleared his throat, visibly relieved.

"Thanks for the chat, Tobias." I gave him a small smile. "See you inside."

Walking away, I listened. No footsteps followed, though with each step I took, I swore the vampire was watching me leave.

CHAPTER EIGHTEEN

TOBIAS

She slipped through the backdoor and, bearing down, I resisted the growing urge to follow the witch.

I'd prepared myself for the evening, drinking so much blood that my hunger had remained in check while I spoke with Meredith.

Or, at least, *one* type of hunger had remained sated. It had taken all I had not to kiss her during our chat. Particularly after she returned to the present, her two-toned eyes blinking innocently, my hands firmly on her shoulders, a finger gracing her bare skin.

A snort escaped me. This had to end. How much longer would my blood stay in Meredith—thereby connecting us in ways I'd never experienced. Making me care for her.

Subconsciously, my eyes went to the door that she'd vanished through. Her scent, more floral than earthy tonight, still lingered in the air. The aroma was a phantom, whose only purpose was, seemingly, to haunt me. Again, the urge to follow mounted. What was happening to me?

Giselle's reason swooped into my mind, unbidden.

It simply cannot be.

Although Meredith's features pleased my eye, and she made me want to engage in activities I'd forsaken decades ago, I knew better than to believe I was an exception. I was no silly human. Individuals of their kind always thought they were outliers, but not me.

Outliers were rare and exceptional. It would be too much to think Meredith and I, two supernaturals of different orders, were fated in the stars.

Most importantly, my staunchest reservation remained true. I couldn't give Meredith the life many mortal women wanted. A family—a legacy.

Of course, Giselle had also pointed out that not every woman wished for a child, but I found that so difficult to comprehend. In my time as a human, children were the greatest blessing. A way for a person with such a small span of years to become immortal.

Tipping my chin to the sky, I exhaled, recalling the stars of London in the 19th century. They were different, but would a person's desire for a legacy change that much?

I would not subject a mortal woman to that chance. If she felt similarly, like something was budding between us, even bringing up the idea of being together was doing her a disservice. What if I took her heart, and she forsook what she wanted to make me happy? Meredith might even do it without telling me.

"What's got you so down?" a voice asked, and I turned away from the heavens to find Luca standing on the porch. I hadn't heard him come outside. "It's not every day someone can sneak up on a vampire."

Not even every year.

"Just reminiscing."

Dark caterpillar eyebrows arched. "Don't go too far down the rabbit hole, Tobias. I need you to be alert."

I eyed the coven master. "Here? And why are you here, anyway? Shouldn't you be resting?"

Luca's hand waved dismissively at me. "Daphne is inside and has already scolded me. I'm a free man. If the healers are so worried, they should have made me stay in the infirmary."

"Don't go looking for trouble."

Luca looked away.

Too bloody late, apparently.

"What happened?

"An incident at Wolf's Head. A member perished."

"Okay?" Abnormal, but also not our concern. Humans died daily. It was a fact of life as a mortal.

"Hans and I suspect the Pearl of Hell influenced him. Drove him to jump from a building."

At his mention of the Pearl, a muscle in my jaw twitched. I stood corrected. Anything having to do with magical artifacts was the domain of S&S.

"Why didn't you call me?"

"Nothing to be done about it. The young man jumped from Harkness Tower before Hans and I arrived on the scene." Luca's hand ran through his black hair. "But I want you to be informed. We must be on the lookout for more signs of madness."

"Did it start here?"

That would be too coincidental, wouldn't it? New Haven wasn't a small town, but why would the Darkborn come here? Nicoleta knew her brother lived in New Haven—reason followed that the coven was here too. Wouldn't they stay away from people who would wish to stop them?

"The Wolf's Head members claimed their friend came from

New York. I'm sending three members there to scout while you, Hans, and I keep eyes on the news. As you know, we cannot act until we're absolutely sure."

For if we acted too early, and those who stole the *lapis caelesti*, those in league with a demon prince, got wind of us, they'd leave the city. We had to be sure of their location before striking. Then we could take the Pearl. Hopefully the Opal too.

"Was there evidence of the gems interacting?"

"Not that I can tell," Luca admitted. "It's hard to tell since no one has knowledge of what the Opal can do. Not to mention the other five stones."

"That is an issue," I muttered, annoyed. I'd spent years trying to find information on the *lapis caelesti*. Of the seven, only the Pearl of Hell was documented in any way that mattered. The rest, while listed as certain types of gemstones, were largely mysteries, their powers unknown. However, it was rumored that the stones would be drawn to one another, and that together, their powers might be altered. No one could say for certain though.

"But the Pearl brings on madness, and the man who jumped exhibited that. Dark magic cloaked the area," Luca added. "That is telling enough."

"Have you told Gunner?"

"He was otherwise indisposed." Luca chuckled. "He wouldn't want to be interrupted, and as there's nothing to do at the moment, no need either."

So, he was still making out with one of the hedge witches. Suddenly, their presence, usually benign, dripped with risk. "We need to warn Josiah to be more careful of who he hangs out with. All the covens, in fact. The Night Coven is fine, normally. But what if someone spoke too freely, and that's how the shade appeared in our headquarters? I hate to cut us off from the supernatural community, but—"

"These are abnormal times." Luca nodded in agreement. "Even among our own, we must be more careful. Tonight is a wash, but I'll make such an announcement tomorrow."

He said nothing of my loose insinuation that perhaps the presence of the shade had been the work of an outsider to S&S, and not a traitor to the coven. It was a topic we'd pushed away to focus on more important issues, but we could not continue to do so for much longer.

Like the witch, and that mysterious ring she wore. *Speaking of . . .*

"I have something to tell you," I began. Though this was not my tale to tell, it was also coven business. "Meredith recalled another memory. Of her ring. Her mother told her that the ring with all *eight* stones, it would lead her somewhere. Makes me think we need to find that missing stone to get the most out of the piece."

"Perhaps it would take her directly to the mysterious Ms. Black?" Luca asked, his mind on the same track mine had pursued. "That would be handy."

"I'm not sure. Either way, she needs to find a missing gem in the base."

"Should be easy work for a seeker."

"Once we get her in the right place. She can't bloody well search the whole world, now can she?" I paused. "Did you know her parents worked at Yale?"

"I did."

His answer shocked me.

"Well, perhaps they hid it on or around campus," I offered, trying not to take it personally that he hadn't shared that information. That I'd had to hear it from Shay.

"It's an idea, one I hope is true because it would make things easier." Luca stared across the yard, where an unkindness of ravens had landed to rest on the lawn.

Was Josiah watching us? Or were these birds natural? I turned my back on the birds.

"I can help Meredith search," I assured. "She wishes to learn about Miriam Black, and the ring might lead her to the woman. It would be faster if I assisted."

"Is that so, Tobias?" Luca asked amusedly, his lips slightly pursed. "You're much more involved regarding Meredith than with most new recruits. Any reason?"

I stiffened. Caught.

"None." The reply came out harder than intended. "I merely—"

A scream cut through the night, high-pitched and close. Too close.

I cast the mage a glance, and without another word, we sprinted to the side gate. The scream had come from in front of the house, and going through the party would only slow us. It would draw a crowd too.

What if the Pearl had struck again?

We reached the street and scanned the area. No one was outside. No one had even poked their heads out of their doors. Were we really the only two who'd heard such a thing in this quiet suburban neighborhood? How?

"Can you smell anything out of the ordinary?" Luca murmured.

I inhaled, and my shoulders tensed. "Blood. This way."

Like a lion on the hunt, I followed the scent all the way to the end of the street. At the corner, about four homes down from Josiah's place, sat a yard rimmed with waist-high hedges.

The house beyond loomed dark, all the lights off inside, suggesting that the owners were probably not there.

"Behind those," I whispered, pointing to the hedges.

"Careful," Luca replied as I sensed magic flaring in the night. The mage was prepared to attack should the need arise.

We crept closer, but no sounds hit my ears. Not even that of a heartbeat, so unless a vampire lurked behind the bushes, I didn't believe we'd find anything.

I was wrong.

A woman I recognized sprawled out on the other side of the greenery, dead, her red hair splayed behind her and one of her arms bent at an unnatural angle.

"Lola," I whispered, staring down at the hedge witch. A hole gaped in her chest, and blood covered her face and hands.

Luca's eyes widened. "She was at Josiah's. Do you think one of our own did this?"

"I—we need to check the body." Aside from the tang of blood in the air, there was something lingering around Lola, something magical.

"Go to the other side. The hedges provide suitable cover."

That had to be why the killer had brought her body here. What had Lola been doing out there, anyway?

Who would have done this to her?

Rounding the yard, we walked up the path, jogging through the lawn. No one was outside, and I didn't spot a single pair of eyes peering out the windows. The owners of this home were out, but what of the rest of the neighborhood? Those at the party had an excuse. The music was loud, but every other home appeared quiet. It wasn't so late for it to be unthinkable that someone else was awake.

How could Luca and I have been the only ones to hear the scream?

We reached Lola and crouched behind the cover of greenery. Again, the strange smell filled my nostrils, stronger. More familiar too. Where had I scented that type of magic?

Luca's hand pressed against the woman's wound but came up unbloodied. He must be using his power to create a sort of invisible protection. "There isn't just a hole. Her heart is *gone*."

Everything clicked into place. "Someone was trying to steal her magic."

The coven master met my stare. "Necromancer. You sense the magic in the air too, don't you?"

"I do." There were only two necromancers in our coven, Josiah and Sara. They rarely used their power in the tomb, there was no need for it. "Someone was trying to steal Lola's magic? But why?"

Luca sat back on his heels. "There's a home full of powerful supernaturals and they choose a hedge witch? It makes no sense."

"Unless the necromancer was practicing," I added. "And they failed."

It had been decades since I'd witnessed someone steal another's magic, but I'd never forget that night. The thief had to expose the heart, though the opening had been much smaller than this one, little more than a cut near the heart. A hired necromancer had taken the magic through the wound.

Yet, Lola's heart was gone, ripped viciously from her chest, hinting that either the person who desired power, or perhaps the necromancer, hadn't known what to do. That the person was one and the same was too far-fetched. A necromancer could, theoretically, steal another's power, but it made them ill —eventually killing them.

An image came back to me. "Did you see the unkindness of ravens in Josiah's yard?"

"Yes," Luca replied slowly. "Why?"

"What if someone knew we were the only ones who might hear the murder because we were outside, and they sent the ravens as spies? Don't you think it odd that the homes appear empty? That no one else came? There are wolves at the party. Surely, they'd hear the scream?"

"I see your point. A necromancer wouldn't be able to get close to us without one of us noticing, but ravens could." Luca glanced around at the houses. "They might have used magic so others didn't notice—but we'd have sensed that too."

"A potion? Sprayed on the yard to deter the other neighbors from leaving their homes? Or perhaps dampen outside noise?"

The coven master seemed troubled. "Possibly."

"Luca," I began carefully, "do you suspect Josiah or Sara? Or could this be connected to the Pearl too?"

A pained expression crossed his face, but it had to be said. To my knowledge, Sara did not control ravens, not all necromancers did, but Josiah was among those who could. "I'm not sure of the Pearl, and as far as Josiah and Sara, why would they do this?"

Why indeed.

"We must return to the party and investigate," Luca added. "Plus, Lola's sisters will want to take care of the body. We can't call the cops."

"No," I murmured, not looking forward to what came next.

Hedge witches might be magically weak, but they could still cause a ruckus, and I liked both Josiah and Sara. I didn't want to believe either of them to be capable of murder.

But a traitor lurked in our midst. Would we find them tonight? Was it one of our own necromancers? If so, what were their motives?

Something told me that whatever magic had been spread in the area, to ensure that no one peered out their windows, would continue to work. However, we wanted to be careful, so we tucked Lola tightly against the greenery.

Once she was well hidden, Luca and I walked back to Josiah's. Music still blared, and inside, Gunner roared with laughter.

That gave me an idea.

"Maybe have Gunner check for scents? His nose is more sensitive than my own. It might also placate the hedge witches."

"As if that would be possible," Luca retorted, "But I will suggest it."

We entered the home, and right away, my attention went to Meredith, Shay, and Harper on the couch. "Have you three been here long?"

"All night," Harper replied. "Well, not Mer."

The witch's cheeks grew rosy. "I came here right after we talked. Why?"

"Did anyone leave?"

"No." Harper cocked her head. "Why? What's going on?"

Luca clapped his hands then, magic spewing from them, and racing through the small house. "You'll see."

The mage's power silenced the crowd. Drawn by the force of Luca's spell, one by one, people crammed into the small living room. Josiah entered alongside a bleach blonde hedge witch, the pair taking the piss at the person following them, who didn't look upset by it.

Internally, I cringed. *Bloody hell. This will be a nightmare.*

"What's up, guys?" Josiah gestured to the door. "Did a neighbor come over and complain about the music? Sorry, I didn't hear them knock."

"Not quite," Luca replied. "Tobias and I stumbled across a body down the street."

Gasps rose all around us.

"Where?" Josiah asked, eyes wide.

"Down the street, the corner lot." Pausing, Luca cleared his throat. "There's no good way to say this, so I'm going to come out with it. The person who died was in attendance at this party."

More gasps echoed, followed by a few horrified glances.

"Who?" Harper demanded, her spine ramrod straight.

"Lola." Luca cast a glance at The Night Coven witches. "And there's evidence that whoever killed her also tried to steal her magic."

Silence shrouded the room, only to be broken by a shrill screech.

"Steal her—what?!" The blonde witch next to Josiah stared murderously at him. "That's what your kind does!"

"But . . . no! I—I was here." Josiah took a step back.

"Not the whole time!"

I blinked. Harper told us that no one left, and she'd been by the door almost all night.

"I went to the *bathroom* after my keg stand to wipe myself off and change! I had beer all over me!"

The bleach blonde shoved him, and bedlam threatened to break loose as others of her coven made moves toward the necromancer.

Meredith stood. "He didn't walk past us. He's innocent!"

"Yeah! I am!" Josiah darted toward me and Luca, almost as

if he were going for the door, but Luca's hand shot out to seize him.

"Witches of The Night Coven, please, go see to your dead," Luca instructed. "She's tucked out of sight against the tall shrubbery at the corner house. That way." His other hand gestured the way we'd come. "Gunner, accompany them and search for a scent to follow. Silas, you go too. Perform a glamour to hide the witches from sight so they may move their dead in their own time."

"And what about *him*?" One of the hedge witches pointed at Josiah. "You can't let him go free."

"If you do, we'll contact the Covenant!" another witch yelled. "We demand justice!"

I cleared my throat. "Josiah, did anyone see you enter your room and change?"

"I—what?!"

I looked to the crowd, but no one spoke up on behalf of the necromancer.

One of the hedge witches stepped forward, anger lining her face. "He has no proof. You have to keep him contained until we know for certain."

"I'm afraid you're right," Luca agreed to which Josiah's face fell. "I'm sorry, Josiah, but you're coming with me."

"And has anyone seen Sara?" I asked, curious to know if the other necromancer had arrived yet.

"I haven't seen her in days," Harper offered.

"She wasn't planning on coming. Right, Josiah?" Meredith asked.

"Too busy," he replied, his tone hollow.

That didn't make things better or worse, just more difficult. All signs pointed to a necromancer being involved in this murder, so not only did we have to lock up Josiah to appease the hedge witches, we had to find Sara and question her, too. When I glanced at the coven master, he nodded.

"We will check her apartment. I do not take a murder in the magical community lightly. We will investigate all leads."

The blonde hedge witch lifted her chin, as if to say *'damn straight'*. One by one, the witches of The Night Coven marched out, two swearing revenge for Lola. Gunner and Silas followed, disappearing down the street.

"I swear I didn't do it," Josiah repeated.

"We need proof," Luca replied. "You know we cannot have them contacting the Covenant."

S&S did all that they could to keep the supernatural ruling body out of our affairs—and right now that included Meredith's magical talents. Those needed to stay hidden for as long as possible.

"Too much is at stake, Josiah," Luca added. "So come along. Once we find the killer, you'll be let go. I promise."

CHAPTER NINETEEN

MEREDITH

All too soon the first party I'd been invited to in a decade ended with a bang. One I'd never forget.

Harper, Shay, and I walked to the car, lost in quiet thought. Behind us, other coven members strolled to their vehicles too, quiet murmurs flitting between them.

Part of me couldn't believe what had happened—a body found so close to Josiah's place. Someone tried to steal magic from a witch and killed her in the process.

What the actual hell!

I didn't understand exactly how necromancers took magic and transferred it to another person. Hans told me that most often, humans were the culprits. They learned of the supernatural world and wanted a piece of the pie.

I was dying to learn more, but it was poor form to gossip on the street about the dead. Holding my tongue, I let the questions build with each step. Finally, we got in Shay's car, and she started the ignition.

Unable to hold my curiosity back any longer, I leaned

forward between the front seats. "Do you guys really think Josiah could do that? Or Sara?"

I couldn't see either of them as killers. Josiah was chill, and Sara seemed so nice. Normal. A strawberry blonde from the Midwest. Neither struck me as a psycho—and I had a bit of experience with assassins and thieves for hire. Arguably, both of those camps had a little crazy in them.

A perplexed breath left Harper's chest. "I don't see it. She's sweet, and he's a good guy."

The nephilim pulled out of the parking spot, shaking her head. "Same. Sara is a total pacifist. Though, of course, the coven forces her to act when we need a necromancer's magic."

"So true. She doesn't take assignments if there's a possibility there might be violence," Harper added. "Still, someone of their supernatural order must have killed Lola."

"How does a necromancer take someone's ability and put it into another person?" I asked, hoping Harper or Shay could shed light on this form of magic.

"I don't know how, but I'll tell you what I think. It had to be a *human* who hired the necromancer," Shay replied, echoing Hans's belief that humans most often employed necromancers. "If they hired someone to do that and they're already magical, then why would they target Lola? Why wouldn't they take out someone stronger to add to their powers? Luca, me, or even you, Meredith? You're not trained fully, but you have a lot of raw power that many would kill for."

That made me squirm.

"Lucky for you Harp, shifters are safe," Shay added, oblivious to my inner turmoil.

"Why?" I asked.

"Shifting magic can't be taken," Harper explained. "No one understands it, but that's how it is."

"Okay," I whispered, "but this still makes no sense to me. They didn't need to take out the heart, right?"

"No," Shay confirmed emphatically. "Which makes it clear that whoever was doing this doesn't understand the process at all."

I leaned back, my gaze landing on the seat in front of me. How many necromancers were there in the world? How many would allow themselves to be hired by someone to perform such a foul deed?

Who would want murder done on their behalf?

Lola's face, the way she'd been clinging to Tobias when I entered the kitchen, flashed in my mind. She'd been so full of life, having fun and flirting.

A couple hours later, she died.

The sounds of whoops and roars cut through my musings. I blinked, turning to the window.

"Looks like it's frat party season." Harper's hand slipped out the window, pointing at an enormous house with an expansive yard spreading in front of it. "I'd hate to clean that mess up."

People hooted and hollered, dancing on the lawn, many dressed in togas and masks, some with laurel wreaths around their heads. Two wore antlers, probably in devotion to the Goddess of the Hunt.

Hundreds of red plastic cups littered the grass, and multiple rounds of beer pong were abandoned for the revelry the frat was partaking in now.

It looked chaotic, and admittedly, like fun. Maybe I'd go to a frat party once or twice. It wasn't something that I thought I'd ever do, but when in Rome.

"What frat is—?"

The words died on my lips as my blood froze.

No . . .

Slowly, I pressed my face to the window.

Most of the masks the partiers wore could be attributed to some sort of ancient god or goddess. One girl even had plastic snakes writhing on the top of her head. Medusa—one of the most misunderstood figures in mythology.

Yet, I spotted one mask that didn't belong to any god or goddess I recognized—and from my time studying ancient cultures, I'd learned about a crapload of them.

The person, an oversized toga swimming over their body, stared at our car. Their mask was all black, hard with geometric lines. In the moonlight, a silver sheen gleamed off it.

Their eyes locked with me, and the color, ice-blue, threatened to shatter me as they waved.

A shriek tore out of my lips as I ripped my face away from the window, unbuckled, and slid to the floorboards.

It can't be. It can't be. No . . . But they waved! I swallowed, replaying the scene again in my mind, trying to banish it.

No, no, no, it's impossible. That person is just drunk!

"Mer, what's going on?" Shay asked, twisting in her seat. "Are you okay?"

"Drive!" I yelled, my limbs shaking while the image replayed over and over in my head. Each time it replayed the scars on my back radiated with pain, as if preparing me for another crack of a cane on my skin.

"What? I am," Shay said, confusion dripping from her tone. "Rooms, what's going on?!"

"She's freaked, Shay. And you're not driving very well if you're not watching the road," Harper chided. I peered up to find her looking down at me, face tight with concern. "Get us home."

Shay pumped on the gas, and we sped down the street. Even though, logically, the frat house was long gone, the image of the masked person waving at our car, their ice-blue eyes focused on me, stayed in my mind—as if tattooed into my brain.

My roommates tried to get me to talk, but the words wouldn't form. Every time I tried to speak, bile climbed up my throat, and I forced myself to swallow it.

When we finally parked, my shoulders lowered slightly.

"Home," Shay announced. "Do you need help getting out?"

"No, I got it."

My arms trembled as I rose from the floorboards, exited the car, and shut the door. On shaky legs, I darted toward the house. Harper came up behind me, eyes wide while Shay let us inside.

"Should I get tea?" the wolf asked quietly.

"Liquor," I mumbled.

I didn't even like hard alcohol, but tea wasn't going to cut it. I needed to feel something stronger rushing through my veins. Needed to dull the fear feeding upon me. Needed to burn the image, the memory of that black mask and those eyes, out of my head.

Harper's teeth dug into her bottom lip, but she nodded and ran into the kitchen.

A hand, Shay's, landed on my shoulder. "Mer, what happened?"

"I—I saw something. Someone that reminded me of the past."

The nephilim's eyebrows pulled together, then her lips formed an O. "Denz again?"

I wished. Even as a vampire, I'd rather go toe to toe with

Denz again. Swallowing, I went to the couch, still trembling from head to toe. "No. The Ringmaster."

Shay joined, watching me with uncharacteristic quiet. Perhaps she sensed I needed a moment.

A few minutes later Harper emerged from the kitchen. She'd set the teapot on the tray, but also a bottle of whiskey and three tumblers. Baked goods were present too, and I remembered that she'd been baking when I returned from my meeting with Tobias, Luca, Hans, and Gunnar.

"Brownies," Harper announced. "Whiskey, too, but I made tea anyway. It's healthier."

Shay snorted. "*Screw healthy.* Bust out the whole bar and all the chocolate in the house! She saw the Ringmaster, Harp!"

The wolf nearly dropped the tray. "*What?* I thought you didn't know what he looked like?"

"I don't. Not really. He always wore a mask, even when I first met him. And then, after that, we didn't ever meet in person again, but video chatted."

I didn't add that sometimes, in the few instances that I'd screwed up a job, the Ringmaster would send messengers to deliver painful messages. He'd watch from a computer as the message sunk in. The scars on my back were a testament to how vile and cruel he could be.

"Every single time I saw him, he wore a mask. The exact same one that I saw." I took the whiskey Harper offered and shot it back.

The liquid burned like fire going down my throat, but the scary image remained locked in my head.

"Are you sure?" Harper insisted, sitting down on the other side of me to grab a brownie, and stuff it into her mouth. "There were so many people outside. Most wore masks. What if it was just something that reminded you of your old boss? We were driving, and it's dark, hard to see."

Everything she said made perfect sense. Yet, that mask had been the same one I'd seen for years on the other end of my video chat. The same sharp planes, the same tone of blackness and sheen of silver.

The same ice-blue eyes behind it. If that wasn't the Ringmaster, the resemblance was uncanny.

"I can't be sure," I admitted, "but it seems like an enormous coincidence. That mask showing up in New Haven at the one place where wearing a mask wouldn't be strange? When I'm here! And while I owe so much damn money!"

Once again, my thoughts returned to the vault in *Le Bastion*. *My vault*, which according to Tobias and Shay, brimmed with treasure.

Would it have enough for me to pay back my debt?

Was it too late?

Was the Ringmaster scouting me, preparing to send his assassins? Shit! Surely that was worse than him sending others to scout. I'd offended my old boss so thoroughly that he was personally seeing to his revenge.

I groaned, poured more whiskey into the tumbler, and tossed it back too.

My roommates exchanged wary glances.

"We need to tell Luca," Shay suggested softly. "And you need to be on watch again. It will be more obvious this time though. Both of our necromancers are under surveillance, so Josiah's ravens can't do it."

Closing my eyes, I shook my head. This was too much. I'd seen some serious shit in my life, done things I wasn't proud of, but being chased by the Ringmaster was my worst nightmare. He was a monster, capable of things that haunted my nightmares.

"You know what? I want to go to bed." I stood and wobbled. The whiskey had gone straight to my head. "The house is secure?"

Previously, Shay had told me that between her and Luca's magic, her home was impenetrable, but I had to be double sure.

My old boss had wriggled people like me in and out of situations that seemed impossible. The Ringmaster always succeeded in getting what he wanted, whether it was the head of someone who crossed him or a priceless jewel to sell to some Russian oligarch. And though the Ringmaster didn't usually do his own dirty work, he could.

At this point, I was certain he could do practically anything, no matter how terrible.

"You said he was human?" Shay double checked.

"As far as I know."

Harper poured me a cup of tea. "The house is secure. Now, take this upstairs. You said you wanted whiskey, but . . ."

I took the cup. Tea wasn't appealing, but she was looking out for me, and I'd had so little of that in my life. I appreciated the gesture.

"I'm gonna call Luca now," the wolf added. "Expect a message when you wake up. He might be busy with the necromancers right now, but he won't let this slide. He'll probably demand to pay your debts."

"And this time you should take it," Shay urged. "Don't be too proud."

My stomach clenched. The nephilim was spot on with that accusation. Before, I'd been too proud to take money from the coven. I wanted to claim my power and pay off my debt the right way, by myself. In no way did I want to transfer what I owed from one person to another. I wanted to stand on my own two feet. However, if the Ringmaster was here, surely time was running out for me.

It might already be totally gone.

"Sure." I threw them a wave. Without looking back, I climbed the stairs to my room, dreading falling asleep that night. Knowing that in my dreams, a black mask would haunt me.

"How was the party?" Benedict asked sleepily once I entered my room.

I didn't bother to turn on the overhead light. The street-lamps provided sufficient illumination for me to see, so I crossed the room and set the tea down on my nightstand. "Fun. Until it wasn't."

My familiar sat up, light amber eyes flashing in the darkness of my room. "What happened?"

"The Ringmaster. I saw him."

"What?!" Benedict exclaimed, his face horror-stricken

I shuddered. "He wore a mask, and I only saw him from far away, so I might be wrong. But I doubt it."

Suddenly, my body that had become cold since I'd spotted the mask, felt a million times more frigid.

"I'm going to take a hot shower. Try to calm down."

"I'll wait right outside the door."

I highly doubted a cat, magical or not, would stop the Ringmaster. Yet, his gesture was sweet, caring.

"Thanks." I closed myself in the ensuite bathroom, undressed, and turned on the water.

Not bothering to make sure it was the perfect temperature, I got into the shower. Right away, scalding hot water streamed down my body, chasing away the chill. Forcing the tears to stay in my eyes, I stayed under the stream. I wouldn't cry. No matter how much this sucked or how terrified I was, I refused to lose it. Instead, I closed my eyes, and let the stream beat down on me, pretending that it could wash away all my troubles.

If only life were that easy.

Once the water ran cold, I turned it off and reached for the towel on the rack. My hand found a soft fluff, and I wrapped it around me, quickly drying off and going to the mirror.

My hand wiped away the steam-induced fog as I shook my head. I looked like I'd seen a ghost.

"Worse," I muttered to myself. "A psycho with access to the best thieves and assassins on the planet.

"Meredith? Are you all right?"

"Fine," I lied to Benedict.

"Your phone has been beeping quite a lot."

"Shay told Luca what happened. It's probably him."

My familiar didn't answer.

Changing into my pajamas, I left the sanctuary of the bathroom, half expecting the Ringmaster to be there when I opened the door—perched on my bed and waiting to end me.

Of course, that didn't happen. Only Benedict sat on the ground, staring up at me with concerned eyes.

"You must have used all the water in the house." His tone was light, teasing. He was trying to be comforting, so I'd try too.

"I actually did."

"You probably want to avoid what happened, but you should really check your phone and reply to Luca. Messages that come in quickly usually mean someone is deeply worried."

With a nod, I brushed aside how odd it was for people to

care about me. Until I joined the coven, no one had worried about me for a very long time. Well, unless I had something they needed—then they were persistent, and only really worried about the item in my possession. But I'd never made anyone wait if I could help it. As a thief, I'd been excellent. I'd delivered every time, on time.

Until Egypt.

My stomach swooped as I padded to my bed, picking up my cell to find twenty missed messages. I blinked. The texts were not from Luca, but Tobias.

Why?

I opened the app to scan the messages. The vampire had many things to say, including demanding confirmation of my location, asking if I was alright, and if the house had been searched upon arrival.

Tobias had been worried.

He was also with Luca, which might explain why the coven master had not texted me. Still, it was unlike Tobias to show so much emotion.

The picture of him when I woke up in the infirmary crossed my mind, how he'd been staring at me like I was the most important person in the world. I thought I'd imagined that expression in his evergreen eyes, that it was a figment of my sleepy brain, but now I wasn't so sure.

The last text caught my eye.

> Tobias: Please call me or text me when you get this. We need to hear that you are okay.

As much as I desired to avoid thinking about the Ringmaster, I also did not want anyone to worry on my behalf, so my fingers raced across the keyboard, typing a reply.

> Meredith: I'm fine. Was in the shower. Sorry to worry you.

The bubble icon appeared, and a new text came in from Tobias.

> Tobias: Are you home? Is everyone present and well? Did you lock every door and window?

> Meredith: Home. Everyone's here. Locked up tight.

> Tobias: Thank God. We were worried.

My eyebrows knitted together, and I opted for a change of subject.

> Meredith: What's up with the necromancers? Any leads?

> Tobias: Not yet. I'll fill you in tomorrow, when I come to your house.

Surprised by him once more, I blinked.

> Meredith: Why're you coming here?

> Tobias: I will escort you until we can discern if the person you saw is, in fact, the Ringmaster.

My throat constricted. *Tobias* would be escorting me. The girls mentioned someone would, but I imagined one of them would be chosen, since we lived together. Maybe Hans. Not the vampire who'd sometimes looked at me like I was a snack, other times like I was his mortal enemy.

And then those *other other* times—I wasn't sure how to interpret how he looked at me.

So confusing.

> Meredith: You don't have to if you don't want to.

Send.

> Tobias: I'll be there in the morning, Meredith. Sleep well.

CHAPTER TWENTY

HANS

"I promise! I had nothing to do with Lola's death!" Josiah called out as Luca and I left him in the coven dungeon, locked behind magically reinforced bars. "Guys! I swear!"

"We need to show The Night Circle we're taking this seriously," Luca replied, weariness in his tone.

It was plain to see that, like me, Luca wanted to trust the necromancer, one of our own, but he was a leader of a powerful coven and had to be seen acting. The Night Circle was fully capable of calling in the Covenant to perform an investigation, and truthfully, it would be well within their rights. Just as much as he hated barring Josiah, Luca did not want the Covenant Seats to enter S&S's tomb. We housed far too many secrets that would interest them and not all the elected supernatural Seats were noble. In this instance, I did not envy the mage. He walked a thin line.

"Don't worry, Josiah," Luca added. "You should be out in no time and we won't mistreat you. Press the button and you'll have whatever you need. This will all be over soon."

"Argh!" the necromancer roared.

I didn't look back, disbelief clouding my head at what I'd learned when the coven master and Tobias arrived at S&S's headquarters with a furious Josiah in tow—waking me from a restless sleep. As I had every night since we returned from Romania, I slept at Headquarters, on a cot in one of the empty rooms. Going home was fruitless. I wouldn't be able to rest there, not with so many reminders of my sister.

And I won't sleep well tonight either.

I was still struggling to come to terms with the fact that there had been an attack on a hedge witch at a coven gathering. An attack meant to steal Lola's magic . . .

Why? Two years ago, Lola and I had gone on a couple of dates and eventually decided we were better off as friends. She was a fun girl, but was not a powerful witch. If a human wished to steal magic, there were plenty of options in the city. Lola should be a last choice.

Tobias waited for us at the top of the stairs, staring at his phone and looking more relieved than when I'd last seen him.

"Did you get a hold of Meredith?" Luca asked.

"I did. She's at home with Shay and Harper. All are safe. I told her I'd be there in the morning. She needs to go to classes."

"Yes, she does," Luca agreed.

"*You're* going to be her escort? What about what happened in training?" The day Tobias's fangs had come much too close to puncturing Meredith's neck would forever be emblazoned in my memory.

"Do you have the right to be concerned with her safety after what you pulled in Hell?" Tobias shot back, eyes flashing with fury. "Putting a mission in danger for personal reasons, Hans? You should be better than that."

My teeth ground together, the day of the meeting, how

Tobias's eyes had followed Meredith, came back to me. "There has to be someone else who can hang with her."

Tobias sneered. "Gunner is presently assisting The Night Coven and leaves for England tomorrow. Luca is far too busy to escort members to class."

"Then I can help," I countered, still not convinced that Tobias following Meredith around was a good idea. The vampire was usually calm and collected, but something about the witch set him on edge.

Luca's dark eyes landed on Tobias. "Let Aston. He volunteered and will take care of his basic needs beforehand. Right, Tobias?"

"I swear it," Tobias replied, his tone serious as the grave.

I shook my head, not agreeing with Luca's choice, but recognizing that I wouldn't sway him. Tobias better get his shit together, and I'd sure as hell be texting Meredith later to make sure things were going okay. "Fine. I take it we need to search for Sara as the next course of action?"

"We do," Luca agreed. "That's your job. Along with keeping track of the news for signs of madness."

My attention turned to the vampire.

"He already knows," Luca explained. "I told him at the party, before all hell broke loose. I still need to inform Gunner, but will wait until he and Silas return from England. That team will require focus while searching for Miriam Black."

The assignments, all except for Tobias watching over Meredith, made sense. "I haven't run into Sara since I came back from Hell. Have either of you seen her recently?"

"Not for days," Luca admitted. "She is busy preparing for medical school though, so I had not thought much of it.

"Nor I," Tobias said. "She wasn't at the party."

Ice trickled through me, but I told myself that it wasn't that unusual. Sara was a busy woman with obligations outside the coven, but still, alarm bells were ringing.

"I'll ask around." I pulled out my phone to text a few of the people Sara hung out with most. It was a small crowd, mostly Lisha, Dan, Gus, and Josiah. As we'd just locked up Josiah, I'd start from the top. I scrolled to Lisha's name and was about to send a text when Tobias cleared his throat.

"Lisha is not in New Haven. She has been on a mission for a month."

"Can you not snoop on me, Stiff?" I asked, annoyed.

I'd known that but forgotten, and though Tobias no longer had anything over me, no longer was the only one to know of my demon blood, I still felt tension between us. It was only natural. We were two alpha males, and the only people who could smooth over the roughness that stretched between us were Luca and Gunner—ironically enough, two other alpha males of different magical orders.

"I wished to save you time." Tobias shrugged. "The sooner we find Sara, the better."

"Dan and Gus? They didn't attend the party, right?" I looked at Luca.

"No," Luca confirmed.

I texted the twins, and an answer came right away, almost as if they'd been up and waiting. Which, even at the late hour, might be the case. Word of what happened at the party had to have spread.

"They haven't seen or talked to her for two days," I said. "They say that's not like her, but she booked herself up with volunteer work and school, so they didn't question it before."

Another text came in.

"Hold up. The guys say that this is the night she sometimes works at the senior center for community service. She sits at the desk in case one of the residents ring the help button."

"That's right," Luca murmured. "It's one of her many volunteer positions. She assists the nurses too. Believes it will help her get into medical school."

"They sent me an address," I shared as a third message arrived. "I'll go there, right no—"

"Okay, so what the heck is going on?"

A sharp feminine voice cut through me, tightening my throat.

"Please tell me you three have a plan to deal with this Ringmaster. I hate seeing Rooms like this."

I turned to find Shay, but she looked away quickly, a recent quirk that was becoming much too common.

"I haven't sent people out to look for the Ringmaster yet," Luca replied. The weary tone of his voice had multiplied tenfold since we left Josiah. "We're dealing with the necromancer matter first."

"Sure, that's important, but my roommate nearly shit her pants today, Luca."

"That's a bit—"

"No. It's not," Shay retorted, crossing her arms over her chest. "None of you saw Meredith. She was terrified!" Shay's voice lifted defensively, but before she could go further, Tobias stepped forward, his whole body taut as a bowstring.

"You should be with Meredith."

"Stuff it, Stiff. She's at my house and it's safe there. Plus, Harp is with her, and we both needed to know what you guys planned on doing about this." Shay's hands landed on her hips. She was not about to be intimidated by the vampire. "I think she should take priority over this necromancer issue."

"A hedge witch died, Shay," Luca reminded.

"I know! I was *there*, and I know I'm supposed to be all heavenly, so forgive me when I say that if I have to choose between making Meredith feel safe, or learning about who killed that witch, I'm choosing Meredith. I'm choosing her every damn time."

Tobias's shoulders loosened, and an intense look passed between them. "I feel the same."

The nephilim tilted her chin up at him, a thoughtful expression crossing her face. "Good. So, what's the plan?"

Luca scrubbed his hand over his stubble. "We've only gotten as far as tomorrow. Tobias will escort Meredith to her classes. As for who will search for the Ringmaster tonight . . ."

"I'll do it," Tobias said. "I'll search."

"Are you sure?" Luca asked. "That's around the clock duty."

"My kind doesn't need much sleep. Once I'm done, I'll return to Shay's place and wait for Meredith to go to class. Does that work for your household?" He peered down at the angel.

Shay's lips curled up, and it was the first time I'd seen her smile since I returned from Romania. "For sure. Look for a person in a black mask with a silver sheen, ice-blue eyes, and of short stature. She said the mask had many planes on it and he was by the frat house, so I'd start there."

"Good to know."

"You can text me after you search and get to the house. Just *please*, not before six. I have classes too and need sleep. Or I have to try to sleep. Doubt I'll be able to, I'll be worrying about Rooms too much."

"I will." Tobias inclined his head.

The muscles in my hands tightened. Something about their

interaction got to me, struck deep. Was it because Shay was looking at him with genuine warmth? Kindness?

Like she didn't loathe him as she did me?

"I can help too," I blurted. "When I'm done at the center."

Shay turned to me, lips pursed. The warmth I'd seen in her face vanished. "Tobias has it handled."

My blood hit boiling point. That she hated me brought up a million self-worth issues. I wanted to prove her wrong, but a small part of me—the darkness that never died—kind of wanted to prove her right too.

No. Don't be stupid.

Before I could say something regrettable over emotions I didn't understand, I decided better of it. Instead, I shoved down the turmoil inside me and stormed off to do my job.

I PARKED MY BLACK JEEP GLADIATOR, A CAR I APPRECIATED AS much for the name as the manliness it exuded, close to the front of the senior center, in a visitor spot.

As I hopped out of my vehicle, someone spied me out the front window. The woman looked to be in her early forties and from the twisting of her lips, she was not quite sure about me. Not that I blamed her. A dude driving a massive, souped-up SUV and covered in tattoos had rolled up to her place of employment in the middle of the night.

I'd never seen the woman before, and I doubted she'd seen me around New Haven. We were fairly far from Yale, and the townies who weren't employed by the university steered clear of the campus.

Still, I had to talk to someone here about Sara, so I moved slowly, giving the woman time to assess me as I trudged to the automatic doors. When they did not part for me, I knocked on the glass.

No one responded. Apparently, she was going to pretend like I wasn't there. That would not work for me. At the very least, I needed this woman to speak with me through the door.

I lowered my hands, knowing just the spell. "*Konfia.*"

Magic unspooled from my palms, crept under the doorway and into the senior center. Pasting a smile on my face, I waited a minute for the spell that enhanced trust to take effect. Once I thought it had seeded, I knocked again. This time, the woman appeared, no tension lining her face.

She came to the door, though she didn't unlock it. That was fine. I'd rather the lady be careful. A word was all I needed.

"Hi." I gave her a friendly wave. "I'm Hans. I'm a friend of Sara's."

"Oh! Hello. It's kind of late for a visit." The woman didn't offer her name, and looked around. The spell was working, but she might be extra untrustworthy by nature.

"I know. And I don't mean to interrupt you while you're at work. I was wondering if Sara was here? If so, can you show her down?"

The woman's eyes widened. "She's not."

There was more, something she wasn't saying. My palms itched to try the spell again. A double dose might make her more receptive, but something in me urged me to refrain. I didn't want to leave this lady in a bind if something happened after I left.

"Is there something else?" the woman asked.

How do I play this?

"I'm surprised. I thought she was supposed to work tonight."

"Well, that's because she was."

What?!

"So, I'm not crazy. Did she call in sick? I've been trying to reach her but couldn't."

The woman's eyebrows knitted. "You're just her friend, right?"

She knew that Sara and Josiah were together then. Did she suspect Sara of two-timing Josiah? Or did she think I was a stalker?

"We're studying for the MCAT together," I fabricated. "She missed a meetup, so I was checking in on her. It's unlike her to miss our study sessions."

The woman's shoulders softened a bit at that. "I shouldn't tell you this, but if you're trying for med school, you're probably a lot like her. Ambitious. Don't want to fail. And yes, missing engagements is unlike her." The woman trailed off on an exhale. "Sara was supposed to work tonight *and* last night. She never showed. Or called."

"And no one has gotten ahold of her?"

"Afraid not."

The skin on the back of my neck prickled. Josiah had mentioned that his girlfriend was busy. Not that she'd been laid up or MIA. Did he know? Were they the kind of couple who didn't speak for a few days and everything was fine?

No . . . at the tomb, they're inseparable.

"Sorry I can't be of more help," the woman added. "But I have to run. A resident is calling."

A beeping from inside met my ears. She was telling the truth. There was no need to pry any longer and make someone else suffer. I'd gotten what I needed.

"Thanks for your time." I waved and walked back to my truck, hopping in and starting the engine.

Next stop, Sara's apartment.

I drove on autopilot, recounting the events of the night. This felt bigger than the pieces we held in our hands. Possibly connected to the Darkborn. Had Lola's death opened a whole other can of worms that the coven didn't realize yet?

So far, no obvious signs of madness had cropped up in the city. Our only data point remained Julio and the dark magic radiating around the area where he'd died.

Yet, every bone in my body screamed that this was the calm before the storm. Soon, something would happen, and then, I might have to confront my sister.

At least now I had another option to present to her. I'd do my best to convince Nicoleta to ditch the Darkborn. To come to the light. I'd do practically anything to save her, even brave Hell again, and go after my mother. That, though, I'd do alone next time. There was no way I could risk other lives again.

After a short drive, I reached Sara's garden-style apartments. Taking in the quiet neighborhood, I walked down a path that cut through the shared front lawn. It was a nice getup, well-lit even at night, and tidy. I could see Sara here with Josiah, chilling on the lawn, having lunch.

I neared her apartment and exhaled. Lights were on inside it. She was probably awake. Trying to make extra noise so as not to catch her off guard, I stomped up the two steps leading to the door, opened the screen, and knocked.

The door creaked inward, making ice run through me. It had been open.

"Sara?" I called out loudly. "Hey, Sara! It's Hans from S&S. Are you there?"

In answer, a cat meowed. Glancing around, I found a kitten perched on the back of the couch. His tiny claws had torn the fabric to shreds. Recently too. The bits of sofa were all over the floor. As if the kitten knew he'd be in trouble, he darted out of the room.

"Sara?" I took a step inside, yelling louder. "Are you here? It's Hans. Your door was open, and I don't want to freak you out, but I'm coming inside!"

Still no reply. The cat had darted toward the back of the apartment, where lights blazed. Following a hunch, I followed in the kitten's tiny paw prints through the living room and into a small dining area attached to a kitchen.

A kitchen that had been tossed.

"Dammit all to Hell," I muttered, taking in the broken plates and glasses. Dried noodles were everywhere, and a wilted salad sat in a bowl—one of the few untouched items in the room. Most tellingly, a spaghetti sauce-stained handprint smeared across the countertop.

A struggle had taken place.

The necromancer wasn't skipping out on community service, or *busy*—as Josiah had said.

Sara had been taken.

CHAPTER TWENTY-ONE

TOBIAS

Footsteps echoed inside as Shay approached the door. It was ten minutes after 8:00 a.m. and I'd spent the entire night searching New Haven for a man wearing a silvery-black mask —a losing prospect, if there ever was one, but it had to be done. In matters of safety among members, S&S left no stone unturned.

"How'd it go?" Shay asked, opening the door.

"I found nothing." I considered mentioning what Hans discovered at Sara's apartment, and Josiah's denial at having anything to do with it, but promptly decided against it. So far, the wizard only told me and Luca, and the coven master wanted to personally assess the apartment before informing others about what happened. "I've scanned your neighborhood and completed a perimeter sweep of your home. There is nothing of note around here either."

"Annoying, but good, I guess," Shay muttered and gestured for me to come inside.

I stepped over the threshold, and the scents of three

females smacked me in the face, though of course, one stuck out most. Jasmine. A fresh spring forest.

Meredith.

"Mer's room is upstairs." Shay walked past me into the living area. "She's sleeping longer than usual, but given the events of last night, I can't blame her. I'm sure she'll be up soon, though. I know she doesn't want to get behind, and she always eats before class. You can wait down here. I have class to get ready for too."

"Very well."

"Do you want anything before I go? I don't have blood, but we'll swing by the coven and stock up on bagged blood for you while you're escorting Rooms. Do you drink coffee?"

Coffee. Ugh. How mortals drank hot bean water was beyond me. Though I despised the beverage, my face told nothing of my disdain. I was well-practiced at accepting many mortal foods and drinks I found repulsive.

"I ate beforehand. Thank you."

After my search for the Ringmaster, but before I ventured into Meredith's neighborhood, I'd stopped by S&S's tomb and downed two bags of blood. Of late the cravings to drink from her had dimmed, but counting on that to continue was perilous and foolish. It was best to be prepared in every way possible.

"Okay. You are going to camp out here tonight, right?"

"I'm staying here until we figure out the Ringmaster scenario. Luca has others searching for the mystery man while I escort Meredith to classes."

A relieved breath escaped the nephilim. "Thank goodness. The wards around my home are excellent, but something in me is niggling. I'd put good money on the idea that the Ringmaster is more than what he seems. But at least with you around, my chances of getting a full night's sleep are better."

Her note that the Ringmaster could be more than just a vengeful human struck me as interesting, but I said nothing. The nephilim took it as her cue to return to her room.

After Shay left, I remained alone in the living room, studying the decor. It wasn't the first time I'd been here, though this was the first visit in which I'd planned to remain for any significant length of time.

The home had once belonged to Shay's mother, Angelina Ramos, a business mogul and Covenant Seat who sold the estate to her daughter for half of its value. I suspected Shay had not taken the time to redecorate, as Art Deco furnishings dominated the room. Or perhaps she liked her mother's taste, but, to me, it did not seem like the nephilim's style.

I went to the dining room table. Papers and books lay scattered across its surface. The ladies appeared to use this part of the house not to reunite over a meal, as had been customary in my human family, but for study sessions.

One book, a smaller one on Cleopatra, caught my eye. The instant I picked it up, Meredith's scent filled my nostrils. Unable to help myself, I brought the book to my nose, inhaling, savoring the sweet, fresh scent. It was hers. Was she interested in the famed seductress and leader?

"I would have taken you for an old book guy. Not one fresh off the press." Her voice came from behind me, catching me off guard. I'd been lost deep in thought.

And she'd caught me sniffing her belongings. How inane.

I cleared my throat and turned to face the witch. That same perplexing warmth flooded my body, but I brushed it aside. "I appreciate all books, but thought there was a unique scent on this one." The lie slipped from my lips. "I was mistaken. You like the acclaimed Pharaoh?"

"We studied her in class the other day. I guess you could say I've developed a low-key obsession."

"She was extraordinary. And often misrepresented."

The witch's lips parted, her eyes lighting up instantly. "I totally agree. Not that I'm surprised that others didn't get her."

I'd known many strong women in my long life and heard their tales. Even the most 'normal' of women, if there was such a thing, seemed to be undervalued in society. Instead of going further down that path, however, I pivoted to a lighter topic, one that might keep her mind off her current predicament.

"Will your familiar join us?"

Meredith let out a humorless chuckle. "I stayed up late, and Benedict was up even later, watching over me. Once he heard you were going to hang with me today, he slept in." She rolled her eyes. "He's loyal, but also a touch lazy."

"So, a cat."

"Don't let him hear you say that."

I made a motion of zipping my lips, which got a small smile out of her.

"I'm gonna grab a coffee and muffin before we go."

"Very well." I set the book back on the table. "Did you eventually sleep soundly?"

"Uh, kinda."

So not at all.

"What's your first class?" I asked instead. Dwelling on lost rest only made people grow more anxious. With her old boss in the area, Meredith did not need to add to her anxiety.

"Psych." She took a muffin from a plastic container and popped it into the microwave. "The intro course."

"Do you enjoy it?"

"I like the Women Who Ruled class better, but sure. Psych is in the middle, I guess. More fun than Bio, especially the lab portion. That's three hours a week! Can you believe it?"

In my day as a human, students apprenticed with masters, often living with the master of their choice of trade. The hours were brutal, but for those who pushed through, their new life was usually worth it. I didn't mention that, though. The world was so different now. Back then, a cobbler would have no reason to even glance at a book of Alchemy. Nowadays, a well-rounded education was prudent.

"Which is your least favorite course?" I asked, noticing that her shoulders seemed lower, her energy lighter. My tactic of distraction was working.

"English. Which is weird cause I love to read, but from the syllabus I can tell we're going to read boring stuff in there. Books from the dark ages."

My lips twitched, a movement she caught.

"Oh, right. You were probably around when some of those were current, huh?"

"A few classics were penned in my day. Society was different then, so at that time, many of the classics were intriguing. Salacious even."

"I prefer a good thriller. Or fantasy—though now that I'm living it that feels weird."

"I enjoy thrillers too."

"Not too fast paced for you? Shouldn't you be all mopey and stuck in the past?" she teased.

"Not all my kind sit on their coffins day and night and obsess over lost centuries," I brandished a bit of snark back.

"I wouldn't expect that. Coffins are uncomfortable! Your butt would probably fall asleep."

I laughed at that, which earned me a brilliant grin.

The microwave beeped, and Meredith pulled out the muffin. To me, it smelled awful, but judging by the way her face brightened, she did not agree. After a liberal slathering of butter to the center, and a pouring of coffee into a travel mug, she faced me. "All ready."

We left the house and walked toward campus, which wasn't very far at all.

"Thanks for offering to hang out with me, today," Meredith offered suddenly, puffs of white breath blooming from her full lips.

The chill from the night had not yet left the air, and I suspected it would not until much later. We might be in store for an early winter.

"I know you have other things to do," she added. "Plus, I don't like to show weakness and ask for help, but it will help me relax to have you around. And focus in class."

"That's what we hoped." I gave her a small smile. "Others are looking for the Ringmaster."

Meredith let out a long breath. "I appreciate everyone help-ing. I should have taken care of this earlier."

"Not that you have had the time, between recovering from our mission and then going to Hell."

"Yeah. Guess you're right."

Silence fell between us for the rest of the walk, finally reaching campus. Meredith wove through the crowds as if she'd been in attendance at Yale for months, not just a couple of weeks. We arrived at the building where her class was being held five minutes before it began.

She turned to me. "Are you coming in? It's a large amphitheater style room. I bet the prof wouldn't notice that you're not enrolled."

With a step forward, I surveyed the room. Windows lined the opposite wall, but there were no latches on them, and not a single door beside the one we hovered next to. This was a terrible layout for safety purposes, but it was ideal for keeping track of those coming in and going out. I retreated and met Meredith's two-toned eyes.

"Take a peek," I encouraged. "Does anyone appear threatening to you?"

Her head poked in, and she scanned the room. "No. I've seen all these people."

"If you feel safe, I'll stand out here to monitor those coming in and out. But if you see someone who raises your alarm, leave the room and tell me."

Exhaling, she nodded. "Got it. See you in an hour, then."

The witch slipped into her classroom and took a seat. The moment we were separated an odd longing, a sad desire, filled me. Shaking my head, I tried to fight down the emotions that the blood exchange bolstered inside me.

"When will this end?" I muttered, watching her settle in before I eased away from the door.

A few last-minute students rushed down the hallway, entering the same class. Each passed me a confused look, but I smiled and their defenses fell quickly. A simple friendly grin or wave usually did the trick, and not because I was extraordinarily inviting. In general, humans were quite susceptible to vampiric charms—making them easy prey. A power-hungry faction of my order claimed that our ability to manipulate humans indicated they should not be on top of the food chain.

Raphael, my own brother, might even be among those vampires now.

Since leaving his castle and returning home, I had had little time to think about the stint spent in Italy. Though it had not surprised me when Raph said he was bored of bowing to humans, and I'd not believed him for a second when he claimed he spoke in jest, I also hadn't the time to mull over it.

With thoughts like that, I would have pegged him as an OA member. Would Giselle know if he was, and if so, why didn't she tell me when she requested I go to Italy? As I was stuck here with nothing to do but watch the classroom door, this was the perfect time to investigate.

I pulled out my phone as someone turned down the hall at the far end of the corridor, and halted, making a skidding sound on the linoleum. It was a short, muscular woman in sneakers and athletic wear—athleisure wear, Shay had recently informed me. The woman appeared to be in her late thirties or early forties, and she stared at me with murder in her gaze.

The effect was jarring. Cold. Calculating.

But why? Was she actually looking at me?

Slowly, I lowered my phone and glanced behind me to check that I was alone. As I'd thought, there was no one, so I turned back to inquire if there was an issue.

The woman was gone.

My eyes narrowed. *How curious.*

Instincts told me to follow her, but I couldn't. Not now. I was Meredith's protector and no matter what happened, I would not leave this post.

Instead, I merely did as I'd meant to before the woman showed up, and dialed Giselle. My sire picked up on the second ring.

"Tobias. So good of you to call."

"Do you have a moment?"

"I'm alone," she replied, reading between the lines.

"Still in Edinburgh?"

"Oh, no. I'm back in Paris, awaiting my next assignment, which no one is happy about."

I presumed that included King Vladistrica Laurent of Isila and the OA, as well as Giselle. She didn't want to be a spy for such a deplorable organization, but did it out of loyalty to the royal vampires—whom she also did not want acquiring the stones, but blood ran thick in the vampire court. Not to mention outwardly crossing the royals was a danger few would undertake. Giselle rooted for me, but she could not let our otherworldly kin know that.

"I have news on the front we've been speaking of," I said. "Shall I tell you? Or remain quiet?"

A pause expanded between us. "Keep quiet. The king's advisor in this world will come by any day and I do not want to involve you. Not if I can help it."

The muscles in my neck tightened. Giselle remained loyal to her children even more than the royal vampires. What would happen if the Blood learned that she was withholding information? Information she could extract from me because she was my sire. Actually, that would be the better deal. Far more agreeable than the royals paying me a visit themselves.

"How was your trip to Castel Romono, Tobias?"

"That's the second part of the reason I called." My eyes swept the hallway again for the strange woman. She had not returned. "Raphael was antagonistic."

"Nothing new."

"No, but toward humans. He spoke as an OA member would."

"How banal," Giselle uttered on the back of a breath.

I chuckled humorlessly. I supposed she was well over that message of hate and imperialism. The OA likely held chanting circles to keep their members brainwashed.

"Quite, but it got me thinking. Do you have any reason to believe that he's part of the OA?"

"Not at all. It's no secret that he's my son, and someone would have mentioned it if another Laurent was in the Order."

"Unless they don't completely trust you."

She snorted delicately. "I've played my part well, Tobias. As far as they know, I'm a lower-level royal, ready for her own taste of power. Be assured, I'm quite believable."

I didn't doubt it, but there was still something about Raph that unsettled me. "See if you can double check. Perhaps he's a member, but not active? It's worth looking into."

"Perhaps I should send Serena to investigate?"

Our sister was the smartest of Giselle's vampire children. Beautiful and charismatic too, which meant she often got what she wanted. In short, she was much like our sire, but I didn't believe she'd be able to pull any more out of Raphael than I had been able to.

"If you wish." My back leaned against the wall. "Though I'm uncertain that it will help."

"She might see something you did not. Or wheedle her way into Raphael's affairs. Trust your sister."

"With my life."

"Then it's settled. I'll call her straight away. Anything else, Tobias?"

"Nothing."

"Then I bid you *adieu*."

"*Adieu*, Giselle."

We hung up, and I allowed my thoughts to drift as the minutes stretched. Before I knew it, the hallways flooded with students once more. I remained by the wall, staying out of their way, and sensed when Meredith neared.

My spine straightened at the hint to her presence before I laid eyes on her, or even before I scented her. That was new, but it didn't take a genius to figure out why I was feeling it.

The bond of my blood flowing through her remained strong, warming my cold body to the core in a pleasing way. I yearned to know how this change, the exchange of my blood, felt to her. Did she even notice it? Did she sense me when I was near too? Did she like the feeling? I did, though I tried not to get too attached because it would surely fade with time.

She neared, and instead of asking the questions swirling in my mind, I pushed off the wall and walked to meet her. "That was fast."

"I agree." She rolled her neck. "I don't have another class for hours and am dying for a coffee. Want to swing by the cafe? I can buy you a cup for being my guard."

"It's not to my taste," I admitted. "But I'll join you all the same."

We began to amble through the crowded campus paths. As we passed, humans stared. Magic beings often drew attention, but this was more than usual, making me uncomfortable.

For her part, Meredith seemed lost in thought, and I was content to let that be. To take in the autumn air scented with spices from lattes and the faint decay of leaves that had yet to be cleared. These days, the world was filled with too much chatter. The strongest relationships were often between people who didn't need to fill every second of dead air.

But we're not in a relationship, I reminded myself. *Too dangerous and pointless when she'll perish, and I'll persist.*

Once, I'd coupled with a mortal woman. Never again. The loss devastated me. If I felt half as much for Meredith as I did for my lost love, and if I lost the witch . . . I wouldn't live through such a tragedy again.

Meredith halted, shattering the morose thoughts of my past. "Tobias. I sense something."

"What?" My eyebrows pinched together. "Danger? Do you feel the Ringmaster?"

"No."

She lifted her hand, decorated with the moonstone ring. Her eyes were wide as they scanned the campus green and the buildings surrounding it.

"My ring got warmer, and then pulled me this way, almost like my magic does when I'm seeking stuff."

I drew in a breath. "Do you think . . .?"

She nodded slowly, as if the realization was dawning on her as well. "I bet you anything that I'm sensing the gemstone that's missing. The one I'm supposed to find."

CHAPTER TWENTY-TWO

HANS

My Jeep jostled as I drove over the train tracks to the grittier side of New Haven.

After discovering Sara's apartment, and concluding that she had probably been taken, Luca decided we had to share this information with The Night Circle—Lola's coven. Not because it was any of their business what happened to our members, but rather a kidnapping appeared to clear Sara of guilt. On the flip side, it perhaps provided motive for Josiah, though when confronted with Sara's disappearance, he maintained his innocence.

As much as I hated to think he was guilty, right now things weren't looking good for my man, Joe. An initial survey of New Haven revealed there was only one other necromancer living in the area. We'd been quick to visit her, only to discover she was an old woman and had an airtight alibi for the night of Lola's murder. She'd hosted a party for her grandchild at her home, and at least a dozen people could vouch for the woman.

Joe was still a prime candidate.

With the hedge witches placing so much blame on Josiah specifically, and him being a member of S&S, we needed to be as upfront as possible with them. If they thought we were hiding things that had to do with The Night Circle, they would talk. They'd inform the Covenant, which would bring in a powerful ruling body. The Night Circle might even spill coven secrets they'd pieced together over the years. And S&S had many secrets that should never, *ever*, see the light of day.

Slowing at a stop sign tagged with graffiti, I took a right into a neighborhood filled with squat, rundown homes. Not everyone in Lola's coven lived in this area, but she had called this neighborhood home. As did her mother, Glenda Marigold, the leader of The Night Circle.

Though it had been a long time since I'd been over here, I drove on autopilot all the way to the one-story blue home where Lola had been born. I parked in front of Glenda's house, right next to the truck I'd once spent hours working on for Lola. Just the sight of it made my heart clench. We weren't close, but she and I had shared some fun times and she was a sweet woman. She hadn't deserved to die.

By the time I exited my car, Lola's mother, a red-haired woman with fire in her eyes that reminded me of her daughter, burst out of the front door.

"You've got a lot of nerve coming here!" Glenda thrust her finger at me. Her eyes were puffy and red. I expected that she'd spent all night and morning crying.

Tread carefully.

With my SUV between us, she couldn't see all of me, so I held my hands up, hoping to assure her I came in peace and to dissuade her from trying anything. I wouldn't fight the witch, but I would defend myself, if need be.

"Glenda, I—"

"One of you killed my daughter, tried to steal her magic, and now you drive up to our house like you have the right?! Explain yourself, boy!"

"We're trying to be open with you." I inched around the car to face Glenda. Somewhere down the street a door slammed, and from the corner of my eyes, I saw two more people approaching. My stomach sank. They, too, belonged to The Night Circle.

"If you wanna talk, you should call," Glenda scolded, her voice breaking with the words. "I can barely stand to look at ya! You should thank the Goddess that I don't get my athame and stab you right where you stand."

The words resonated as threatening, though the fresh tears streaming down her face made it very clear they came from a place of hurt rather than a thirst for violence. Glenda wasn't really like that. Neither was Lola. None of the hedge witches I'd met were.

"Coven Master Luca wanted you to know that Josiah has been indefinitely detained while we investigate. And I went to Sara's apartment last night," I said softly, determined to do the job I'd been sent to do. "She's—"

"The other necromancer in your group," the man who'd approached, I thought his name was Greg, spat. "Unnatural, you keeping so many of them around."

Most people my age or younger didn't consider necromancers unnatural, but for the older generations, the prejudice against that magical order was real. Greg's words sent waves of unease through my body. If he knew I was Hellblooded, he would probably try to gut me where I stood.

"Our coven celebrates diversity, and everyone has a place," I explained calmly. "Unfortunately, when I went to Sara's, I found evidence that someone removed her forcibly from her home."

The anger on Glenda's face faltered for a second, but then her eyebrows pulled together and her body stiffened. "You saying she was kidnapped? If you think that's anything compared to what happened to my daughter, you've got—"

"I'm *not* saying anything to diminish what you're going through. Lola's death is a tragedy, and nothing I can say or do will erase that or make it easier."

The words hung in the air, testy. In truth, *one* thing could erase Lola's passing and restore her to this world. Necromancers possessed the power to bring the dead to life, but the perished would never be the same. They returned to Earth as shades of themselves, ghosts among the living, an imitation of what they'd been in life.

Theoretically, if a heart was acquired to replace the one ripped from Lola's chest, Josiah or Sara both had the power to bring the hedge witch back to life. But I doubted The Night Circle wanted that. They would consider it unnatural, sad. An aberration.

I had to agree. I would never want that for someone I loved.

"What I *am* saying," I began again, hoping that they wouldn't start attacking, "is that if somebody took Sara, it might be connected to Lola's death. Josiah and Sara were close."

"So he *confessed?!*" Glenda screamed. "Lola told me those two dated, and it made me squirm. The girl, well, she was unnatural, but kind. That boy, though, always had a shifty look about him."

I shook my head. Unbelievable. They twisted my words

because they were so ready to deem Josiah guilty, with no proof at all.

"He did not confess. And this is not proof that he did it," I assured them, even if Sara's presumed abduction had launched doubt into my heart. "But we're trying to put the puzzle pieces together and be open with The Night Circle. We don't want to hide anything from you, but for all we know, the person responsible might be someone unrelated to S&S."

Greg spat on the ground. "Your group always hated us. You think us the scum of the earth."

"We think no such thing," I retorted truthfully. Most did think hedge witches were less powerful than specialized witches, but not that they were less than because of it. "I'm here on behalf of my coven master, sharing news because he wanted me to keep you informed. I repeat, we want to be open with your coven."

"But what if it is true?" Glenda's chin jutted upward. "What if that nasty necromancer killed my Lola for her power?"

I swallowed. "If we discover this is true, the coven will take measures against Josiah. I'm sure you all can agree that S&S knows how to provide an appropriate punishment."

That got to them. For a moment, all three were silent, and I didn't have to guess why. Twice, a traitor had been found in the coven, and twice, our society punished them so harshly that they probably wished they were dead.

"If it's someone out of your coven, we want to deal with them," Greg demanded, and the other man nodded vehemently.

"Fine. If we discover another necromancer, or anyone else, is guilty, we will bring them to you."

Glenda scowled. "You bet your ass you will. We—"

A motorcycle skidded around the corner and barreled down the street, coming to an abrupt stop in front of Glenda's home. A young man hopped off the bike. "Aunt Coco! She's dead!"

"What?!" Glenda's hands flew to her mouth. "How?"

The young man shook his head. "I couldn't get into the house cause Coco locked it up tight. She was an ace with her charms. But I saw her face through the window. It was so blue! She mighta choked on something!"

Glenda snapped her fingers at me. "You, come with us. You can get us inside."

"What if the necro is guilty over this, too?" Greg snarled.

I wanted to deny it was even possible, wanted to leave, but that would look bad for S&S. So instead, I'd stay quiet and help.

"I'll follow you," I said rounding my Jeep.

All except the young man piled into Glenda's car, and I trailed them through town. With each stop and turn, I wondered what we'd find. Would this implicate Josiah? Though I didn't want Coco dead, if she was, I hoped she was newly deceased. That way, Joe couldn't be a suspect.

Trying to ease my anxiety, I turned on the radio. Looking out for more signs of madness in New York would be a welcome distraction. Things had been slow so far, but the way my day was going, it wouldn't be long until I heard something horrible had happened.

As it turned out, it didn't even take two seconds.

"I apologize for interrupting your scheduled show, but this just in," a reporter announced in a somber tone. "Ten, no, wait! *Twelve* people have jumped from the tops of their buildings today."

The reporter seemed to pull her face away from the mic, and soft indiscernible murmurs filled the radio.

A cleared throat indicated their return. "Oddly enough, they all jumped at the same time. To the second, eyewitnesses say."

A shiver spider-walked down my spine. This had to be case number two of madness. The humans would debate about the root cause—cults, a full moon, mushrooms, whatever they guessed would be wrong.

None of them could foresee that an ancient, evil stone was responsible.

Luca would tell me it wasn't the stone that was evil, that it was the person who controlled it, but in respect to this, I didn't give a shit what Luca said. Out of all the seven sacred stones, the Pearl was the only one with a bad reputation. The one that, even though the angels created it, was supposedly born of Hellfire.

The radio announcer kept talking about the suicides, mentioning every person and giving a brief rundown of their lives and accomplishments. Most sounded career oriented and ambitious, Type A in the extreme. I listened trying to decipher other patterns, but when the motorcycle at the head of our follow train stopped in front of a home, I turned off the radio.

The hedge witches might know about what was happening in the city, but if they didn't, there was no way in hell I was going to be the one who told them. They would probably blame the suicides on S&S, and in a way, they would be right.

After all, Meredith had unleashed the Pearl, and she was part of the coven now. It would be stupid to outright blame her, but these people were grieving, and their accusations were all over the place as it was. Best to stay silent.

Once parked, I got out of the Jeep. All the while Greg and

the other man glared at me, still not wanting me to be around, but Glenda jerked her head toward the door.

"Get us inside. But be careful. I don't want to bust down anything and cost Coco money."

If she's dead that won't matter, I thought. "Will she have defensive charms in place?"

Glenda snorted. "Just protections. We don't do that."

She didn't say that was because they didn't have the power for defensive spells, but I suspected that might be the case.

I strode up to the door, and laid my hands on it, making sure that Glenda was right and there weren't any defensive spells as well. She was correct. Only a basic ward could be sensed—nothing strong like what a specialized warder produced. With a single word, I fully dismantled the protection.

The deadbolt clicked open, and I slowly turned the handle, checking for another lock, but none provided resistance.

"You should go in first." I turned to the hedge witches standing behind me. "It's open."

The younger guy on the motorcycle ran forward, his face frantic. Seconds later, a strangled cry sounded, and Glenda swore and ran in after him.

I followed last, wanting to make sure none of them thought I believed I should be there before them. By the time I got inside, they were crowded around the body.

The witch lay dead on the ground, and though the young man was right, her face was horribly blue, it was obvious Coco had not died from asphyxiation. No. Like Lola, her chest was carved open.

"Her heart is gone!" Glenda screamed.

"She's cold and stiff as a board," one of the older men said. "Must have been dead for hours!"

"It was that necromancer then!" Lola's mother glared at me. "I demand that you put him down!"

I jerked back as if she'd slapped me. "There's no proof yet. And he's not a dog."

"He's a monster!"

My throat closed up, knowing I could say nothing to these people that would make their losses hurt less. I'd seen what I needed to see, and I'd done what I needed to do.

"I'll speak with my coven master," I offered softly, knowing that Luca would want to investigate this death more thoroughly. Perhaps we could even get an exact time of death, something I was not capable of. "We will be in contact with your coven. We promise."

Glenda scowled at me once again before turning away.

At that, I left, feeling like a piece of shit, and hoping we could get to the bottom of these murders.

CHAPTER TWENTY-THREE

MEREDITH

Taking in the campus's green, I spun, trying to pinpoint where the guiding pull was coming from exactly. Not only did I sense my seeking magic telling me that something I sought, even if only subconsciously, was near but the ring I wore had warmed slightly too.

Would it continue to get hotter as I pursued the stone? I peered at the moonstone on my finger.

What would happen if I found the missing piece and put it together with my ring? How would that work?

My teeth dug into my bottom lip. Surely, it wouldn't be that easy. I'd probably have to visit a jeweler to get the stone set in place but . . . I inhaled slowly.

One thing at a time. Find the gem first.

"Is it close?" Tobias asked, his tone nonchalant.

For a moment, I was offended by his casual manner, but then I remembered we were in the middle of Yale's campus. Hundreds of students streamed by us, many stealing glances our way—our supernatural energy luring them in a way they did not understand or notice.

Tobias was acting as if this didn't matter for show. Not because it wasn't important. As far as the coven was concerned, and for me personally, the location of this missing gem was one of the most important mysteries to solve.

"My magic woke up, so I think it's pretty close," I confirmed, "but it's hard to tell."

"How do the gem and the artifact Skull and Bones hired you to find differ?"

Other than the obvious that one was a femur bone and the other a teensy gem, I had no idea. "Size?"

His eyebrows tugged closer together. "The Pearl of Hell is not large, and your power wasn't even fully released, yet you felt that in the tomb you raided, correct?"

He was right. Though of course I hadn't recognized what I was feeling back then as magic, it had been. And it had been relatively straightforward too.

I frowned, confused. During that tomb-raiding session, I hadn't even known I was a witch! Or had my magic fully set free! So why, after I'd trained up a little, *was* this more difficult to pinpoint?

"Are there other parts of campus that are warded, like the S&S tomb?" I asked, wondering if the problem wasn't me at all. "The wards might be throwing me off."

An expression of surprise flitted across the vampire's face. "A few, actually. But one is quite close by."

"What is it?"

"The library."

"The supernatural section?" I asked because though I hadn't spent a lot of time in any of the libraries at Yale, I'd heard of this one many times.

"Precisely." Tobias nodded. "Both of your parents were witches?"

"Yup. And they worked here, so they could have had access to many places." My heart raced as things started to click. "Will you show me where that part of the library is?"

"It's not so easy," Tobias countered. "First, we must locate the librarians to be allowed inside."

"Where are they usually?"

"In the Beinecke, which is the shell for the supernatural section. Though *finding them* is not truly what I'm concerned about. They will have to document you, and ensure that you're worthy, which will take a bit of time."

"*Worthy?!* That's some elitist bullshit."

"I'll vouch for you, so it will be nothing like the background check I underwent to gain access," Tobias assured me. "But you must understand that they cannot simply let anyone inside. There must be some test. The materials within the supernatural section are too precious."

"Let's start at the beginning," I offered, trying to move on from such blatant elitism. "Take me to the entrance. Once we're closer, I'll let you know if I sense something. Maybe the missing gem isn't in the library at all."

"Follow me." The vampire started walking.

I fell into step with him, doing my best to pay attention to my seeker's magic and the ring at the same time, all the while appearing like a normal student. It was more difficult than I would have imagined, but the magic did seem to be guiding me in the same direction we walked. Within minutes he stopped before a building.

"This is the Beinecke." He pointed to a strange looking structure.

I narrowed my eyes. Did that place have no windows? How depressing!

"Do your seeker senses tell you this is a place worth investigating?"

Once more, I tuned in to my power. "There's definitely a pull coming from this area. But it's not much stronger than before. Probably because we didn't go that far."

"Also there are wards, both around this larger library and the supernatural section, that could be dulling your senses," Tobias whispered.

I glanced at the building that might help me uncover my secrets.

"Why does it look that way? There are no windows. And it seems kinda like honeycomb, but square." My nose wrinkled. "It's so ugly. Who would want to study there?"

"Many, but few are permitted," Tobias replied, the reverence in his voice was undeniable. "We must protect the past, and this library is for rare books and manuscripts only—they are of great value and fragile. The section we're looking into is even more hermetic. Come along and see for yourself."

We entered the building, and my eyes widened. An amber glow filled the room when light passed through the seemingly solid marble walls. In the center of the building, a show-stopper glass tower stood, filled floor-to-ceiling with books.

"Incredible," I breathed. "But how? There are no windows."

"They chose a special marble that filters light from outside."

"Well, then I take back what I said. I'd totally study here."

"It is a marvel, isn't it? We'll have to check you in first, which means finding the normal librarians." He walked to a set of stairs and descended, leaving me gaping at the tower of books. "Meredith?"

"Coming," I replied and began to follow—only to have

heat sear my ring finger. "Ow! Mother effer!"

"What happened?" In an instant, Tobias stood next to me again.

A passing person blinked, probably having noticed the blur Tobias caused using his vampire speed to get to me. My protector didn't notice the person's confusion, and a moment later the onlooker shook his head, clearly thinking he'd imagined it.

"The ring burned me." My eyebrows knitted together as I gripped my hand to staunch the pain. "But it's not hot anymore, just warm. Like it flared and now is a pleasant temp. Do you think that means we're close to the missing gem, and the ring wanted to get my attention?"

"Perhaps. Are you using your magic?"

Crap! I'd been momentarily mesmerized by the library and had spaced out on using my power. Quickly, I called on my seeking abilities, doing another internal check. "It is stronger in here. We're getting closer." A smile split my face. "We found it so fast!"

"We haven't succeeded yet, so do not assume we will." His words were intended to be cautionary, but he sounded proud too. "Follow me."

I reigned in my optimism and trailed him. Two floors down, we entered a sub-chamber and came upon a desk. The librarian asked Tobias for his credentials, which he supplied. When it came time for me to show an ID, I got my university card ready, but Tobias leaned over the desk.

"She's with me. You will let her in."

I drew in a sharp breath. *Compulsion.* I recognized it from when he'd used his power on the guard in Egypt, but this time, I knew what was happening.

The librarian waved us in without requiring my ID. Only

when we were out of earshot did I broach the question on my mind. "I take it that won't work with the magical librarians?"

Tobias arched an eyebrow. "I wouldn't dare try. For hedge witches, they have extraordinary connections. I would not risk my membership."

Hedge witches ran the fancy part of the library? Interesting. So, one *could* make it in this magical society with little power. Then another thought hit.

"Speaking of hedge witches, what happened after the party. Did anyone find Sara?"

A muscle fluttered in the vampire's jaw. "Hans did not locate her last night. It appeared that there was a scuffle at her apartment. No word on that yet."

My heart rate kicked up. A scuffle? Did the hedge witches seek Sara out for revenge? Or was it someone else?

"Did she have enemies?" Unlikely. She was so sweet and wholesome. Still, I had to ask.

"Not that I'm aware of." Tobias turned down an aisle between shelves. "This way. I scent a librarian. She's nearby."

"You scent—Oh." My eyes widened, and I resisted the urge to sniff my pits. "Uh, how far away can you smell people?"

Another chuckle, this one light. A flash of heat cut through me, and I smiled as the warmth spread, the sound of his laughter lifting my spirits.

"You smell good, don't worry. It's more that I am quite familiar with the scents of this witch and wizard."

We wound through aisles of books, and as we went, I caught glimpses of their spines. Those books didn't seem that old. I'd bet the oldest ones were in the glass tower we passed in the lobby. Or maybe elsewhere, like a cage devoid of light and moisture. I'd only been here a few minutes and already my skin was dried up, my lips too. If the strange marble that acted as windows told me anything, it was that this library took preservation seriously.

"Ah, I believe I've found her," Tobias said, pulling me from my thoughts. "This way."

When we turned down the next aisle, a steel-haired woman appeared.

At our approach, the lady's head lifted. She glanced past Tobias sighting me, and she dropped the book she was holding.

"You've come," the witch announced.

Over his shoulder, Tobias threw me a curious look.

I shrugged. I'd never seen her before in my life, and I'd certainly never been inside the Beinecke.

"Wisteria, this is Meredith Stone, a new member of S&S," Tobias offered, stopping before the woman.

"I'm aware of who she is." Dark brown eyes lined with many wrinkles raked over me, as if measuring my worth. "Gavin and Lynn's girl."

"You *knew* them?"

"I did, child. Your mother came to the library all the time. And now that you're here, I expect you might be looking for something?"

"I am," I confirmed, brushing off the child comment. This woman was probably in her eighties, so I supposed that to her, anyone under forty was a child. I should probably be happy she didn't call me an infant.

I held up my hand and showed her the ring. "I think I'm supposed to find the missing gem. We have a hunch that it might be in the supernatural section."

Wisteria's lips curled. "Perhaps. We will have to undergo the routine test to see if you're allowed in the section that Bellamy, my husband, and I protect."

I frowned. "I'm pretty certain it's here. I sense it."

"Well, then you'd better get started, no?" Wisteria arched an eyebrow. "After, of course, you procure a sponsor." Her unwavering stare went to the vampire. "Tobias? I must officially ask. Are you willing to use your invite on this witch?"

"I am."

"I shall document it."

"Very well," Tobias agreed.

The exchange struck me as weirdly weighted, but I didn't have time to dwell on it.

"Now," Wisteria addressed me, "as you're not asking for membership and have a sponsor, I will allow you access to the library today. Provided, of course, that you pass the aforementioned test."

"Which is?"

"Find the entrance to our clandestine section of the library. If you are successful, I will grant you access." The hedge witch glanced at Tobias again. "You will remain with me while she searches. Not only does she need to accomplish this without assistance, but we can fill out your paperwork now, detailing your use of your guest right." Wisteria looked to me again. "Whenever you're ready."

I tried not to let my expression turn smug. I was a seeker and my ring was definitely hinting at something—the missing stone's proximity, I hoped.

Surely, this would be cake.

So, leaving the pair behind to deal with administrative matters, I began to wander. With each step, I took care to notice when the heat coming off my ring dimmed and got hotter. The library was huge, so my meandering earned me a lot of confused looks, and eventually, I snagged a random book from a shelf, acting like a student visiting for academic purposes. Someone who belonged here. With the book in hand, people didn't stare quite as long and moved on more quickly.

I continued looking and after ten minutes doubt crept in. The library was big, but not that big. How had I known to come here, been fairly sure of it and with little effort, but this—finding the opening to a place that was surely close by—was difficult? Heat climbed the column of my neck, into my cheeks. I'd been so certain that this would be easy, and now I'd have to eat my cockiness.

Maybe I need to regroup?

Pausing at the end of an aisle, in a corridor that felt particularly drafty, I nearly retreated into the shelves to fend off the cold. At that very instant, my ring burned like it had when I first set foot in the building.

My heart skipped a beat. How could I be so lucky!? Totally by accident, I was on the right track!

No one was around, so I scanned the corridor with care. Nothing about it appeared special, but perhaps that was the point. Why would anyone hide an entire section of a library, one in which only magical people could enter, in a well-traveled part of the Beinecke?

They wouldn't, and as I studied the ceiling, I noted there weren't any vents there either to explain the strong draft.

Must be magical, too.

I shivered as I stepped into the direct line of the breeze. The temperature dropped a few more degrees. Though there were a few gleaming research desks in this area, all larger than others I'd passed too, I sure as hell wouldn't study back here. Not without a fur-lined parka.

With the ring on my hand still burning, I relied more on my magic. It had been humming in the background since I began the search—doing what my ability intuitively did, but I didn't seem to be as accurate as when wards were not involved.

Still, I would be stupid not to rely on my entire arsenal. With a deep inhale, I pushed my power to work harder.

A sudden yank behind my breastbone gave me immediate feedback. My magic told me to turn right, so I followed the silent instructions, strolling slowly. When I came across a vast expanse of empty wall, one where no desk sat—though that would have made sense—I grinned.

That had to be it. However, before I proclaimed that I'd found it, I needed to be sure. Wisteria didn't seem like she'd be big on second chances.

Gently, I placed my hand on the wall and pushed my seeker powers into it. It responded, rebounding into me before pulling me harder. As if I needed it, the ring burned hotter too. So hot that I let out a hiss and removed the piece from my finger. A red line rimmed my skin. If I'd let that go on, soon I'd have a permanent burn mark.

"It's here," I murmured. "Has to be."

"Is that your final answer?" a voice called from behind me.

I turned to find Wisteria at the end of an aisle of books, her hands folded in front of her while she waited for my reply. She hadn't made a sound as she approached.

"This is it," I declared boldly. "The entrance."

For a never-ending moment, the hedge witch studied me, but the moment her lips curled up, victory sailed through me.

"You're correct." Wisteria motioned for someone off to the side to join, and Tobias appeared, smiling at me. "Tobias has done all that he must to ensure your admittance. Now, let's go inside and see if we can find that gem."

The librarian joined me at the wall, and placing her palm flat on it, she motioned for me to do the same. So, I did.

CHAPTER TWENTY-THREE

A jolt of unfamiliar magic shot through me, and a gasp parted my lips.

"Hold still," Wisteria instructed.

Once again, I did as she asked, wondering if the wall would fall away, and if that happened, would others see the empty space? Wisteria didn't seem at all worried by that prospect, so I doubted it.

As it turned out, I was right. All that happened was the surrounding area blurred, as if it wasn't solid.

"Walk forward," the librarian commanded. "Into the wall."

I did as she said, and immediately found myself in another library that looked nothing at all like the Beinecke.

"Whoa. Old-school." Something moved and I gaped, as a candle encased in a lantern floated out of an aisle and toward us. "Aren't you scared those will crash into the shelves and break? The candle could burn down the library!"

Wisteria chuckled. "They're well enchanted—nothing of the sort will occur."

Well, yeah. I mean, candles can't normally fly!

"Right," I said, trying to sound less like a new-to-magic chump. "This looks so different from outside the wall."

"The Beinecke is lovely, but we have many members who prefer things done the traditional way. Myself and my dear Bellamy included."

"As do I," Tobias agreed, appearing magically from behind. "Now, Meredith, I believe that if you're to find the stone, you'll need your powers. Wisteria told me she does not know where your mother hid it—only that your family was given free rein to safeguard the gem here." He raised his eyebrows, as if to say, *'that's a big deal'.*

"They told me a story with such dire implications that I could not refuse them anything," Wisteria whispered. "I was bound to a secrecy so strong a witch of my powers could never break it. My husband is also bound. Even if we knew, neither of us would be able to hint at its location. You will have to discover its hiding place and what it means in your own time."

Nodding, I turned to face the room. This library, along with clearly being magical, appeared so old world and rich, every bit of furniture was made of dark woods and there were even those green library lamps I always saw in movies.

My moonstone ring remained warm, but not so hot that it would burn me, so I slipped the band back on my finger, hoping for gentle guidance.

Studying the area, I walked down the main center aisle of the library, a path that bisected a row of six shelves. As I passed, I read the topics one might indulge in within the mystical section.

Demonology.

Vampire Bloodlines.

Potions.

Mythical Objects.

I stopped when my ring burned hotter. Following the pull of my magic, I pivoted left to an aisle labeled Oracle Visions and Prophecies.

Was that a sign?

My stomach clenched so tightly it masked my magic's pull for a moment. I hoped not. Being the 'chosen one' or whatever else through a prophecy was so not my jam. I wanted to do my part in finding these stones, sure. After all, I had been the one to unleash the Pearl of Hell on the world, but I didn't need to be the only one to save it. In fact, I really hoped that wasn't the case.

Too much pressure.

Suddenly, the ring seared the skin of my finger, and this

time, it was far hotter. I yelped and yanked it off again, swearing at the band for betraying me.

"You don't have to be so intense!" I hissed. "I get the picture!"

"What happened?" Tobias stood at my side a second later, leaving Wisteria to wait at the end of the aisle.

I glared down at the circle of metal and the moonstone it displayed. "The damned thing has a mind of its own. It's burning me at random."

"Perhaps it senses it will be whole soon and does not want to wait?" The elderly hedge witch called out, an eyebrow raised.

Yeesh. It wasn't just the ring that was impatient.

Tobias's lips twitched. "Let me know if I can help."

"Thanks," I said, appreciating the support even if I had to do this myself.

Hesitantly, I slipped the mercurial ring back on my finger. When it didn't blast me with heat again, I exhaled. Then, I tuned into my magic.

As if it had been waiting for me to pay it proper attention all this time, the yanking sensation returned with a vengeance, guiding me where I needed to go. It was stronger than it had been before too, which meant that I was close. Very close.

My hand extended, waving in front of the tomes, sensing for the energy that matched that of the ring. As if the stone was also impatient to be found, the air pulsed, sending a shiver of magic through me, and straight to my heart. I shuddered. That was new. Slowly, I turned to the wall of books.

"Here?" Tobias whispered.

"I think so," I replied, equally softly. I kept my hand extended in front of the towering shelves, waving it over the area more slowly and taking time to pause in front of each tome.

When the air pulsed again, this time surging noticeably from a leather-bound book wedged between two monster tomes, I stopped. The book emitting the energy was small, not much larger than a deck of cards.

Carefully, I pried it off the shelf. The front cover boasted rich brown leather, but it was bare—no title to speak of.

"Less exterior decoration is common with older books," Tobias spoke as if he could read my mind. "Open it."

I did, my eyes bulging as they raked over the first page. What I held was a compendium detailing old witching covens.

"Use your magic," Tobias urged, and I got the sense that he was more excited than I was to learn what would happen to the ring once whole.

I held the book in one hand, like a server bringing a tray of drinks and brought the hand with the ring to hover a few inches over the pages. Once I was sure I wouldn't drop the old tome, I turned inward again, and to my utter shock, this time my power acted on the object I held.

The pages of the book flipped on their own accord, all the way to the back.

My eyebrows knitted together while I stared down at the page, mostly text, but with one illuminated illustration. A circle of people, seven of them, danced around a fire, their hands to the sky, and a full moon shining above.

Cupped inside one of the figures' palms, as if they held it for someone to find, was a tiny opal like those on the base of my ring.

As if sensing its missing piece, the moonstone glowed brightly once again.

CHAPTER TWENTY-FOUR

TOBIAS

I DREW IN A SHARP BREATH. MEREDITH HAD FOUND THE MISSING gem, and though it should have been obvious from the indention in the ring, I was shocked to see how small the stone truly was. If they weren't searching for it, one's eyes could easily pass over the opal.

Mine had actually done so.

Months ago, I'd held the very book in her hands, studied it as I searched for a specific lost tome rumored to contain information on the *lapis caelesti*. And though my vision was keen and I was usually quite observant, I did not notice the gem.

The witch barely had to try.

The book had presented itself to her, opened wide and revealed its secrets to the seeker witch.

Momentarily, I wondered if she'd be able to find the book I sought as easily—even without a bit of the text to help guide her magic. The text I sought might illuminate the powers of the other stones, and what would happen when all of them were together. Or perhaps she was simply fated to find this tome and this one only?

"Can we pluck it out of the page? Or will I ruin the book?" Meredith directed the question at Wisteria, and I turned back to the matters at hand. Perhaps later I'd bring up a search for the other tome.

"This is the only time in my life I will sanction the desecration of one of my books," the librarian replied. "Your mother put it here for an excellent reason. I could not deny her."

"At the table, perhaps?" I suggested. "There's less chance of the opal rolling around on the floor if it pops out."

Meredith nodded. "That would be like trying to find a dropped earring back. Good call."

We moved out of the aisle to the nearest table, upon which the seeker set down the book. She stared at it, as if she wasn't sure what to do.

"May I?" I suggested.

"Be my guest. I just don't want to ruin this book—and get you in trouble." She leaned closer, casting a glance back at the hedge witch, who remained a fair distance away, observing but not interacting. "What was that about, anyway? Wisteria made a huge deal about you vouching for me."

She didn't realize that I possessed one lifetime invite and one invite only into this library. Nor would I tell her.

"It's unusual to bring in outsiders," I replied nonchalantly.

Her eyebrows pinched for a moment, but she quickly returned to peering down at the book, apparently willing to accept that reason.

Upon closer inspection, it appeared that Mrs. Stone had seeded the jewel into the page with the paint. The only way to extract the gemstone, would be to chip away the illustration, thereby damaging the image.

I was about to relay my thoughts to Meredith when the witch moved closer, narrowing the distance between us considerably. In that instant, the moonstone, now back on her finger for safekeeping, glowed brighter.

I leaned back, thinking.

The stones wished to be together. What would happen if we merely placed one near the other? Would like attract like? It was generally that way in the natural order of the world, but with this . . . could it be so easy?

Would the seeker's mother have made it so? Surely, she would not find pleasure in ruining a book on her kind. Perhaps she'd even taken extra precautions to protect it.

"Meredith, might I see your ring?"

For a heartbeat, she hesitated, but thought better of it, slipping it off her finger and handing it to me.

"I'll return it," I assured her.

A forced chuckle left her throat. "I guess I'm protective of the ring. Didn't even realize it until you asked."

"As you should be. I'm certain this is more than what it seems." That was saying quite a bit, as the ring had helped point us to the library. A normal piece of jewelry, it was not.

"What do you think it can do?"

I paused. "That I'm not sure of, but I want to test something. It might be nothing, but . . ." As I spoke, I moved the ring nearer to the page, and when it was about an inch from the paper, the tiny gem in the illustrated hand moved. The paint, however, didn't budge. Most tellingly for me, however, a faint whiff of honey filled the air. Witch magic—an old spell.

I drew in a sharp breath. "I believe that I've figured it out."

"Whoa," Meredith whispered while I pressed the ring against the paper, right at the spot where the opal should rest in gold. A faint flash of light pulsed, and when I lifted the ring again, the illustrated hand no longer held the stone. The paint was not marred in the slightest, and the tiny gem was once again in its proper position.

"How did you know?" Meredith marveled when I returned her the heirloom.

"I had a hunch your mother would not want to damage this book. Though, to a layperson, it seemed like the paint was doing so, her magic was actually what was keeping the gem in place. She made it so that when placed close enough, the two parts would be attracted to one another and her magic would break."

Meredith slipped the ring back on her finger, and the moment it was in place, another strange thing happened. Light bloomed from it, this time in a kaleidoscope of colors.

Meredith released a soft breath and when the illumination ceased, she raised her hand to admire the ring. "Tobias, look!"

"Extraordinary," I breathed. Before, the stones had all appeared to be small opals. Now only one white remained.

The rest were transformed into different gems, which I suspected had been present all along. Magic made them appear homogeneous, hiding their truth.

"Oh, my God," Meredith whispered. "Is that a black pearl?"

"I believe so, and there's still one opal. There are seven, so I believe these now represent the other *lapis caelesti*."

"Agreed." The witch studied the other gems. "The others look like a diamond, emerald, amethyst, sapphire, and a ruby. What are their names? Like the Pearl is of Hell and the Opal is of Heaven."

"That knowledge is lost. We only know that they are stones and the types, not their proper names, what they control, or their powers when the stones come together."

"Hmmm, that's an issue that needs to be remedied pronto."

Her white teeth dug into her bottom lip. "So do you know why the big stone is a moonstone?"

"That, I can't answer either."

"Look at the image," Wisteria called.

We did, and right away, I understood the reference. "The moon."

Meredith released a soft hum. "Maybe this is another clue? It's in a book about covens, so maybe there is an ancient one with a moon-specific name?"

"Likely many," I admitted, regretting that this book did not have a table of contents. "I don't know if your answer will be here, but now that the ring is whole, you realize what this means?"

"I hope it means I'll be able to find Miriam Black, or that it'll help connect me to my past," Meredith confessed. "Still, I want to flip through the pages. I'll note down any covens with the moon in their name. Just in case." She pulled out her phone and opened it to the notes app.

I handed the book over, and Meredith went to work, sitting in a chair and taking in the text page by page. As she read, I watched over her, and Wisteria tidied the surrounding areas. The hedge witch clearly wanted to respect Meredith's privacy, and honor the librarian's code, but I suspected that she was also dying to learn more about the mystery surrounding the Stone family.

You're hardly the only one, Wisteria.

Finally, after a half an hour of skimming the book, Meredith leaned back. "There are too many names that honor the moon to be sure of what I'm looking for, but I have them all listed. Do you think I can research them more in depth here? There must be books on them, right?"

I shot a glance at Wisteria.

"You're Tobias's guest," the librarian replied. "You have access to the library for as long as he is present."

"Tobias? Can we stay for a while?" Meredith asked.

She sounded so excited, there was no way I could say no—not that I'd been planning on it. "I'm with you all day. If you wish to skip your later class and remain here, then very well. I might do a bit of research too."

"Totally do that," she said with a grin before turning to the librarian. "Can you show me the section on covens? Preferably the oldest ones."

The pair veered into another stack of books, and I made my way to the mythical objects' aisle, intent on continuing my studies on the *lapis caelesti*. My gaze raked the shelves, reading titles I'd reviewed already and moving on, looking for something new. Ten minutes passed quickly, and I'd just unearthed a promising tome I hadn't yet studied, when my phone rang.

I pulled the device from my pocket, intent on shutting it off, but when a dozen missed text messages flashed up at me, all from Luca, I answered the phone.

"Where have you been?" the coven master demanded.

"I turned my texts to silent in case I joined Meredith in class."

"Not your ringer?"

"Who calls nowadays?"

I could almost hear the eye roll on the other end of the line. Warranted. *I* called some people, like my sire, but I was over one hundred and fifty years old, and many of my technology habits reflected my age. Most people in S&S texted, so I now expected that form of communication.

"We have a problem," Luca moved on. "Have you seen the news?"

"No. What happened?"

"I fear the madness is spreading in New York. A dozen people have jumped from buildings today."

"In a city of millions. Is that a lot?"

"Tobias, each person leapt at the exact same time."

"Right then." That was unusual no matter the city's size. "The Pearl is in play."

"I believe so. Crime is skyrocketing too, though that could be a result of any number of things. But the newscasters and radio station hosts are beginning to sound frantic."

"We need to check it out."

"My thoughts precisely. I'm calling a meeting, arranging squads. This is an all-hands-on-deck situation, Tobias. Can you be at the coven in twenty minutes?"

I glanced over at Meredith to find her lost in a book about witches. She was smiling, intrigued by something. I hated to tear her from the library, but if there was any chance of finding the Pearl and the Opal, it lay with her.

"We'll be there," I promised and hung up. "Meredith?"

"What's up?"

"I'm sorry to say this, but we need to leave."

She glanced at me, and there must have been something in my expression indicating the seriousness of the situation because she closed her book right away.

"Let's go."

I waved at Wisteria. "Thank you for everything. We'll return soon."

We vanished through the wall, and into the greater Beinecke. Once on the other side, out of earshot of the librarian, Meredith turned to me. "It's happening, isn't it?"

"Chaos has begun in the city," I confirmed. "It's time to act."

I caught the way her thumb rubbed on the moonstone ring, a hitch on her breath as her lips opened. "Finally."

ONE BY ONE, MEMBERS OF S&S GATHERED IN THE SHADOW ROOM. I had yet to spy Luca, but Hans informed me he was somewhere in the tomb, circulating, taking care of matters.

The wizard appeared tense. Something else had happened, or perhaps the violence in the city was worse than when Luca had called the meeting.

Soon, I'd find out.

At my side, Meredith fidgeted. The seeker's time to find the sacred stones had come. No doubt she was nervous.

"You won't be alone," I whispered, wanting to ease her nerves.

"What?"

"Luca won't send you into the city alone. We're going in teams."

"Oh, right."

"I will be on yours." Luca had not said as much, but the thought of not being on her team was simply unacceptable.

When her shoulders loosened, pride bloomed inside me. She liked that I'd be by her side. How far we had come in a few, short days.

"I'd like to be on the same team as Shay and Harper too," Meredith asked. "I . . . need all the support I can get." She blew out a breath. "This is, like, *real.*"

That was putting it mildly. If the Pearl of Hell was in the city, it was also very likely that the Opal of Heaven would be in the mix. After all, the Darkborn seemed to control both sacred stones.

The door to the Shadow Room burst open, and Luca marched inside. Daphne trailed behind him, wringing her hands.

The coven master didn't speak to anyone as he rounded the tables, which were kept in a rectangular formation so that everyone could see everyone else. By the time he took his seat between Hans and me, the room was dead silent, waiting.

"I assume most of you have heard about New York City, and concluded that the Pearl is there."

"Won't the Pearl and Opal be kept together?" Dan asked. The raven-haired bear shifter's laptop sat in front of him in case the coven required him to hack into any systems in the city.

"If we're lucky," Luca admitted. "It's what I'd do, but we can't count on it. The Prince of Wrath might keep them in the same place or separate them. There is strategy to both, and if he trusts his underlings, little to fear."

Hans cleared his throat, and I had no doubt he was thinking of his sister.

"I've just checked the news. The madness in the city is increasing by the hour," Luca added. "We will send in teams of five or six to hunt for the stones and keep order as well as we can." He drew in a deep breath. "But before we divide and leave, there's something you should all know."

A muscle feathered in the coven master's jaw.

"Two things, actually. This morning, Hans discovered that another hedge witch was killed."

Gasps and murmurs circulated the room.

"Yes," Luca muttered, calling our attention. "And to make matters worse, I went to the dungeons and discovered that Josiah escaped."

"What?!" Gus, twin to Dan, exclaimed. "How?"

"We believe his ravens assisted him," the coven master replied. "There was a feather outside the door."

"The bird got out of her cage in the infirmary once." I shook my head, unable to believe we hadn't considered that. "But what about your magic around the cell?"

"The damned bird took care of that too," Luca grumbled. "I use magic, but I also have keys—you know, in case I'm not around and someone else has to extract a prisoner. Earlier, Gus used the key to let Josiah out for further questioning. Obviously, the necromancer took note of where the key was stored and had the raven search for it."

"Where was it?"

"In my office, in a drawer. I'd cracked the window, to let in fresh air, so that bugger had to be watching me all day. Lying in wait to steal the key."

A perfect scheme. No one would take note of that or mark it as unusual. Ravens were commonplace in these parts.

"But how did no one notice Josiah walking out?" Meredith asked. "People seem to be here all the time."

Daphne cleared her throat. "The bird was also around the infirmary when I was brewing a new invisibility potion to replenish my stocks. Josiah must have been listening to the apprentices and I talking as we brewed. Upon Luca's insistence I took stock and discovered one of our bottles is missing."

"The bird could have taken it when she left the infirmary," Luca said. "As we know, Josiah can possess the creatures at any time. Hearing about the potion, well, he would have thought it handy to have around."

So devious. Though I'd had my doubts before, I was becoming more certain that Josiah had murdered Lola. The only motive I could understand was that he was doing this for Sara. Was the person who took her using him?

Luca rubbed the back of his neck. "Josiah could be anywhere by now."

Silence fell in the room and tension mounted so high that my skin prickled.

"And unfortunately," Luca added, "we're in no position to search for him. We have to mobilize teams to New York and discover if it is, in fact, the Pearl causing this madness."

"Inaction will piss off the hedge witches," Gus whispered.

"It pisses *me* off," Luca replied. "But Josiah is a single necromancer, and we're potentially dealing with a Prince of Darkness wielding the Pearl of Hell in one of the largest cities on the planet. Right now, we have to go for the greater of two evils."

CHAPTER TWENTY-FIVE

HANS

I SHIFTED UNCOMFORTABLY IN MY SEAT AND WISHED TOBIAS would hurry the hell up and get to the city.

The vampire insisted my Jeep was 'too big', and parking would be easier with his car. Fine. I could deal with riding in the Stiffmobile.

At least, I'd thought as much until Meredith claimed shotgun, sticking Harper, me, and Shay in a too-small backseat.

Even with Harper between me and Shay things were tense. Every time I spoke to discuss team strategy, the nephilim grew rigid, as if hearing my voice pained her. In these tight premises, I couldn't help but see the reaction.

"I wish we had more teams." Meredith sighed as a newscaster on the radio announced yet another person had leapt off a rooftop to their death. "The faster we can pinpoint the borough the Pearl is in, the better."

"The coven isn't large enough, but the strongest among us will be in the city," Tobias reminded her. "We had to keep a few members in New Haven, in case something occurred there."

No one would say it, but I was pretty sure they all thought something would happen in New Haven. After all, my sister was out as a Darkborn, and she knew I lived there. Would they strike the city I called home in retaliation for me leaving Mother in Hell?

At the thought of her, my fists clenched. Though there was a 50/50 chance of the Darkborn attacking New Haven, I was sure my sister wouldn't be there. She'd go for the big time. It had always been her style. If I was going to see her today, it would be in New York City.

Would I be able to convince her to turn to our side?

"The exit!" Shay shouted, pointing out her window.

Tobias swung the car across the road, which was shockingly empty, turning my stomach. "Apologies. It's been a while since I've been here."

Frustrated, I closed my eyes. Though his car was more reasonable, I should've offered to drive. The vampire was from a different time, and his driving reflected that. Had I been behind the wheel, we would have mobbed into the city ten minutes ago.

"Be on the lookout for parking," Tobias called back once on the exit. "Garage or otherwise."

It took us all of five seconds to discover that it didn't matter where the hell we parked.

Not a single car drove the streets of Manhattan, the wealthiest portion of the city.

"This is . . . different," Harper murmured staring out the window. "It's like a ghost town."

She was spot on. Parking spots were aplenty and even stranger, people had abandoned their cars where they sat in the road. Why? Had they fled on foot? And gone where?

"Dude, stop anywhere," I urged as Tobias scanned the scene with wide eyes.

He complied, pulling to the side. We piled out and grabbed our gear from the trunk—making sure the throwing knives we'd packed were accessible but also hidden in bags that hung off our sides. Who knew if authorities would be out? If they were, we did not want to appear threatening at first sight, but did need to be able to defend ourselves quickly.

Of course, three of us could wield magic as a weapon too. Shit, Harper and Tobias became weapons themselves, but we intended to exercise our supernatural qualifications with restraint. Though in disarray, the city was surely still filled with millions of humans.

We couldn't tell the world about magic, so we had to be careful and use it only when necessary.

"It looks so dead." Harper's gaze swept up and down the streets as we trudged down the sidewalks, first assessing the situation.

"People must be holing up in their apartments," Meredith agreed. "They're scared, and I don't blame them. Crazy shit is happening everywhere."

"That's good for us," I concluded. "Fewer witnesses if we do have to use magic. The Covenant will probably still have a hell of a clean-up job later though."

"For sure. If humans are hiding, they have to have seen stuff they aren't supposed to see," Harper agreed. "I wonder if the Covenant even realizes what's going on yet?"

"That's not our concern," Tobias clarified, turning to our seeker—arguably the most important person in S&S right now. "Meredith, can you sense the Pearl?"

A vibration of magic filled the air. Meredith's power was expanding, growing by the hour. At this show of magic, hope surged through me. Maybe we really had a chance to find the Pearl today. To end this.

And if the Opal was with the Pearl of Hell, all the better.

"I feel *something*," Meredith announced, her tone shocked. "It reminds me of the Pearl, how it felt before I found it the first time. This way."

She led us down the sidewalk, but we made it only one or two blocks when screams filled my ears.

The seeker stilled, casting a glance back at Shay, Harper, and me—the trio that had taken up the rear.

"Continue on," Tobias urged at her side. "Should we need to defend ourselves, we will. But our aim remains the same no matter what we come across."

With a swift nod, Meredith kept walking. At the next intersection, we learned what had caused the sound. Three men with bloodied knives in their hands chased two women. The men were clearly possessed, their eyes glowing red while blood stained the front of their shirts.

"Help!" one woman screamed, waving us down. "Help us!"

Leaping right into action, we ran straight for the possessed men. When they saw us coming, they locked on the girls, eyes gleaming as they veered our way.

A roar burst from Tobias's throat when one of them lunged for Meredith, but the witch did me proud, ripping her dagger from the bag and slicing the man across the arm. His knees buckled from the pain, cracking on the pavement as she ran past him—not missing a step.

Shay stepped up to the plate, dropping beside the man and pushing his torso against the ground. I stopped running, sure that Tobias, Meredith, and Harper, who were already upon the other two guys, had it handled. Among us, Shay was the only one who could cast out a possession. She might need help keeping the man in place.

The nephilim's hands rested on the man's chest, and bright golden magic bloomed out of her, rushing into him. I held my breath, waiting, as a second passed. Two.

Boom!

A cloud of darkness erupted out of the man's mouth, making me stagger back, and leaving the man coughing up a storm.

"You're okay," Shay said, her tone calm as the man writhed.

He gasped as his coughing fit slowed and gripped at his arm, right where the blade cut him. "What happened? Where am I?" He winced, eyes squeezing shut for a moment. "Dammit all to hell! My arm is killing me!"

"Shhh," Shay breathed, and released a faint beam of light, her angelic influence, to calm the guy.

Surely, he still experienced pain, but as her magic took root, he seemed to relax. "Why is there blood on my shirt?"

"You were possessed. And I think you hurt someone." Shay helped him up, but the man stared blankly at her. This would be a difficult matter to accept, but Shay didn't have time to help him through that burden right now. Not to mention that, if we took control of New York, specialized witches would be sent into the city to obliterate everyone's memory of this day, so really, we just needed the guy to move on so we could continue our search. "Do you know where you are?"

"Close to the office." The man looked around us as if confirming what he said was true. "What the fuck happened to the city?"

"Listen to me," Shay demanded. "Can you walk home from here?"

"My apartment isn't far."

"Then go. Stay away from all people. Get home and don't leave until tomorrow."

Startled and confused, the man sprinted away, not even daring to glance back at us. When Shay turned and found me watching, she frowned. "I think the prince might have controlled him with a shade." She paused, her eyes narrowing. "Can you sense him?"

"Prince Orien?"

"Yeah."

The question was a sensible one, though it hurt. No one had asked it yet. "I can't. I can't even sense my mother."

"Oh." Aggravation, as though I was being purposefully unhelpful, lined her features. "Fine. I need to go to the others." She gestured to where Tobias and Meredith had the other two men pinned to the ground, waving at her.

I let her do what she needed to do, annoyed at myself for not being able to sense the prince, even if I didn't want to, and frustrated with Shay for lumping me into the same categories as super powerful demons.

She still saw the worst in me.

And so did I.

"Done with the last exorcism!" Shay called out, and I turned in time to see a previously-possessed man dash around the corner and disappear. The other was long gone. "Let's move."

The women who were being chased had already left too, so we pressed on with Meredith in the lead, following her magic.

"I think . . ." The seeker stopped at another intersection, "it was here. Like not recently, but its presence is still here."

CHAPTER TWENTY-FIVE

"Is the trail clearer than before? Or less so?" Tobias asked.

For a moment, Meredith studied a street pole, eyes narrowed. "Clearer. Whoever held it, touched that."

"What?!" Harper ran over to the pole, and her green eyes popped open wide as she sniffed the metal. "Smells weird. Dark. Like sulfur."

Meredith and I locked eyes. Sulfur, like Hell.

"Get a good whiff then," I suggested. "Maybe you can help Meredith track the Pearl that way?"

"I'd appreciate any help," Meredith agreed. "We can't mess this up."

Harper brought her nose closer to the pole and inhaled.

As she did, I updated our location through the coven's chat group, scanning for the other teams' whereabouts. Everyone else had made it to their boroughs and were searching. Many had sent updates claiming that they'd already fought off demons. So far, no one had been injured, thank the Goddess.

I glanced up from my phone to assess this area better and provide a report. The deeper we plunged into the city, the more desolate and abandoned it looked. Ten feet away, bags of groceries littered the ground, as if someone dropped them to run.

Had a Darkborn mob come through here? Were the humans running from possessed humans? Or was something else causing New York to look ever more barren?

When I glanced at Shay, I found that she was also glaring at the empty streets, her fists clenched. Perhaps she was having the same realization as me. She alone could pull darkness from people. If too many were infected, she wouldn't be able to handle them all.

As if she felt me watching her, the nephilim turned, catching my eye. Her nose wrinkled, disgusted by me, and feeling like dirt, I focused on the chat again, giving the other teams a rundown of what we'd experienced. Luca was in the next borough over and, knowing that our team would most likely be the one to find our quarry, had insisted that we stay in communication as often as possible.

I'd just sent the text when a sound called my attention.

"Are those *wolves*?" Meredith asked, her tone high pitched.

Wolves!? Shoving my phone into my pocket, I glanced up, found what she was looking at—a group of at least twenty animals were running down the street. Squinting, I stiffened.

Aw, shit.

"Hellhounds!" I yelled, the pack coming ever closer. "And they've locked in on us. Run!"

"But—what about the trail I was following?!" Meredith cried back.

"Do as he says," Tobias snarled, pulling her from where we'd been lingering.

Our group broke into a sprint down the street, turning one corner and then another, trying to shake the beasts off. The snarling sounds grew louder, the monsters from the underworld were gaining.

"What can they do?" Meredith yelled.

"One bite will cause a person to wish they were dead," Tobias replied, not out of breath in the slightest.

I didn't often feel jealous of vampires, but their ability to perform athletic feats without getting winded was one of the qualities I envied.

"Like shade poison?"

"Way worse," I spat. "Like rabies, but more painful."

"We can't run forever!" Shay shouted. We were all in shape. To work for S&S physical fitness was a requirement, but she was right. We'd run out of steam before the pack of monsters. And we couldn't hide and let the pack roam. They'd surely tear a human to shreds.

They might have already done so. I swallowed thickly.

Hiding was out. We had to fight, but first, we needed to secure a position of advantage. Swiftly, I scanned the street in front of us.

"There!" I shouted.

At the end of the next block, a wreck had created a five-car pileup. One of the vehicles involved was a delivery truck, partially perching atop three cabs, one sedan, and, to my horror, a sweet-ass Lamborghini. Willfully ignoring the destroyed sports car, I focused on the flatbed, the perfect elevated place to fight, giving us an advantage. "On top of the truck!"

"How?!" Meredith yelled. "Dude, I'm strong, but I don't know if I can pull myself up to that!

"I have you," Tobias assured her.

The rest of us would be fine. Though she didn't usually use them in public, Shay had wings. Harper, as a wolf, was more athletic and agile than other women, and I knew the right spell to give me a quick boost.

As we closed in on the pileup the snarls and occasional barks grew even louder. Against my better judgment, I tossed a glance over my shoulder and a stream of curse words flowed from my lips.

The pack of hellhounds had closed the gap. They were only fifty or so feet away, close enough that I could see their eyes gleaming red. Much closer than I'd thought.

"When we get to the top, draw your weapons!" I screamed, calling on a burst of speed to help me gain momentum in the leap.

As I approached the pileup, I visualized where I wanted to land and hoped to the Goddess this would work. *"Gailua."*

I shot up, the magic propelling me and sending me straight for the top of the delivery truck. From the corner of my eye, I caught white wings beating—Shay.

I landed, and three thumps followed. Meredith's cry of surprise told me we were nearly all there, but when I spun, my pulse spiked. Harper was still on the ground, scaling the other cars like a beast, but the hellhounds were right behind her. How had they gotten there so fast?!

One nipped at her feet, and she barely avoided its teeth. "Harper! Launch yourself toward us!"

Without missing a beat, the wolf jumped, even though it was far too soon for her to make it to the top on her own.

"Gailua!" I yelled, and my spell caught her, shooting the wolf toward us.

"Incoming!" Harper shouted. "Stop me!"

Shay was on it, her wings unfurling as she rose and caught her roommate, saving her from simply flying over the truck and landing on the other side.

The pair touched down on the moving truck's roof right as the first hellhound launched itself at the vehicle, which shook so violently that my knees buckled.

"How much do those things weigh?" Meredith gasped, trying to steady herself while another hellhound came at us, ramming into the metal sides of the truck.

"Forgot to google that on my way here," I shouted. "Every-one, attack!"

Busting out her knives, Harper began hurling them while Meredith, Shay, and I relied on magic to fight back. Though Meredith had little experience defending herself with magic, the girl did me proud. Her blazes of light seared into the hellhounds' eyes, blinding them so Harper could plunge the daggers into their skulls. And, unsurprisingly, Tobias hurled each of his blades with frightening accuracy.

One by one, the vicious creatures fell as we remained in our safe, elevated position. When Tobias hurled a dagger at the final beast, sinking it in its skull, I dropped my hands, able to let my guard down for a moment.

Or so I thought.

One feral beast had sneakily rounded the back of the truck and took that moment to attack, landing on the roof with us.

I spun. "Watch out!"

Shay stood closest and the hellhound snapped at her wing. Thankfully, she dodged quickly, lifting into the air and out of reach.

The creature wasted no time in lunging for Harper, and I went on the defense, visualizing a shield for protection. *"Baestu!"*

My barrier wrapped around the wolf, and Tobias attacked, zooming up behind the hellhound and twisting its neck until the bones cracked.

"Bloody monster," Tobias muttered and released the beast of the underworld so that it collapsed onto the roof of the truck. For a moment, we all stood there, staring at the creature.

"Damn, those things are freaky!" Meredith exclaimed, her tone wobbly.

I had to agree. I'd read up on the beasts, seen images of them in books, but never come face-to-face with one in real life. No one had. Where had Wrath been hiding his monsters while he waited to attack the human world?

"More will come," Tobias spoke ominously, "and now that we know they live in this realm, it would be smart to have an antidote on hand to negate their bite. Someone should take a saliva sample, so the healers can get working on that when we return to New Haven. Did anyone bring a vial?"

"I have one," Harper answered, reaching into her bag and pulling out a metal tube. "Can the saliva touch my skin?"

"Yes," I assured. "But be careful not to get it into your bloodstream. Are you cut?"

"No."

"Then you're good."

Harper knelt next to the beast, her nose wrinkling in disdain. "Stinks."

"It's from Hell," I agreed, and regretted the words.

My mother hailed from there and despite my own unease about being Hellblooded, I did love her, and she didn't smell. I doubted any of the royals did. They might rule the underworld, but in most ways they were separate from the creatures in their domain.

"While Harper is doing that, let's retrieve the weapons," Tobias said, leaping off the truck.

Shay, Meredith and I followed and our quartet began pulling the daggers from the hellhounds' heads. The first blade came out with a disgusting sucking sound, the second took more muscle, but eventually, it popped out of it.

Clamoring over a few cars, I reached a third hellhound corpse on the edge of the pack. It had taken two blades to do this one in, and they'd sunk deep. I placed my foot on the creature's head and pulled. When it came loose, blood spurted out, splattering all over my pants.

Fucking sick, I thought not because I worried over blood but this particular blood stank and now the rank scent of hellhound covered me. I reeked of sulfur.

I looked around for something to wipe the blood off, if that was even possible. Not only did I hope that it reduced the smell, but less blood on my clothes meant less chance of infection if I got cut later.

"That happened to me too," Meredith called out. "There are napkins in the truck. Wipe up what you can."

"Thanks." I pivoted to return to the delivery truck, but stopped before I even took a step.

At the end of the block, black ribbons twisted and spun out of an alleyway.

Nicoleta.

All sense left me, and I sprinted for the alley, ignoring the sounds of my covenmates' cries for me to stop, to go back.

The ribbons continued to spin, but as I reached the alley, they retreated down the lane, disappearing over a fence. My teeth gritted together.

So, my sister wanted to play? Well, I did too, but for a different win. I'd play her games to save her soul from the darkness.

Bring it on. I launched myself over the fence and chased after the ribbons.

CHAPTER TWENTY-SIX

MEREDITH

I stood there, amidst the rubble of the wreck, stunned still as the black tendrils of Nicoleta's magic lured our teammate away.

"Hans!" I screamed, hoping to get through to him, to stop him, but he didn't stop, didn't turn around, he didn't even freaking flinch in my direction.

I swallowed the lump rising in my throat. Did Nicoleta have him under her spell? The idea made my stomach tighten. Hans had said his sister was an excellent manipulator.

"What. An. Idiot." Harper groaned. "That has to be a trap."

Oh right. The others hadn't seen this. They had no idea what the younger Novak could do.

"It's his sister's magic," I replied, but then thought better of it. "Unless lots of demons have that kind of magic?"

"No one can be certain of that," Tobias offered, coming up alongside me. "Pureblooded demons have been gone from this world for decades. Or so we thought."

"She isn't all demon though." I pointed out. "She's like Hans—wizard Dad and demon Mom."

"Yes, but his mother is *Lilith*," Harper countered. "Lucifer's bride is as strong as the Princes of Darkness."

I'd heard that before, but as I hadn't come across a Prince of Hell, I didn't really know what it meant. Probably, that I should be scared, but all I cared about was making sure that Hans was safe—with us.

"We should follow him," I suggested, beginning to go the same way as Hans. I didn't make it far when the tug behind my breastbone stopped me cold.

Crap. The Pearl. The single item I was here to find. My seeker instinct said it was located in the exact opposite direction Hans had gone.

"Rooms? What's wrong?" Shay asked.

"I sense the Pearl," I admitted. "It's almost like it's calling to me."

The others exchanged a look.

"What?" I asked uneasily.

"We kind of backtracked from where you felt it, so that doesn't sound right," Harper said. "But if you're sure, we have to follow the urging of your power. Getting that stone, hopefully both *stones*, is our priority."

Not Hans. The words hung in the air unsaid.

"It seems that the other teams have had no luck." Tobias stared down at his phone.

I hadn't checked the coven chat. There had been no need because Hans stayed on top of it. With him gone, that task fell to Tobias.

"But we can't leave Hans," I argued, agreeing with Harper, but torn because I'd seen what his sister could do, how insane she was. "*Someone* has to go after him."

"Agreed, but that person will not be you, for you must seek the Pearl." Tobias gave me a look that made it all too clear he was sticking with me, and a warmth rose through my veins. "Harper?"

"I can scent the Pearl," she replied hesitantly, because that left only one other person.

I turned to the nephilim. "Shay. I know you're upset with him, but *please*. His sister is violent and cruel."

My part-angel roommate closed her eyes, an internal war going on in her heart. Lengthy seconds passed until, finally, a sigh parted her lips. She opened her eyes again.

"Fine. I can fly anyway, so it will be faster." She shot a look at Tobias, as if daring him to comment on her use of wings. When he did not, she added. "Once I find his dumbass, I'll fly us both to find you three."

I hoped when that time came, we weren't inside a building and no longer visible, but I didn't say that. Splitting up wasn't ideal, but right now it was unavoidable.

"We're wasting time," Harper announced. "Let's go."

Shay's wings stretched out and beat, lifting her into the air. "Catch you guys later," she said and soared off in pursuit of Hans.

Sure that she'd find him, I turned in the direction the pull was coming from, ready to do my part.

"I'm going to shift," Harper announced. "Can someone take my pack? That way you can use the knives, if you need."

Tobias grabbed the messenger bag and slid it over his chest, settling the bag on his empty hip so the blades would be accessible.

Magic filled the air, lifting goosebumps on my arms. I'd never witnessed my roomie change like this.

Swiftly shifting, Harper transformed right before my eyes

into a wolf with reddish brown fur. She was larger than I would have thought, like she'd put on at least fifty pounds of pure muscle in the transformation.

The magic that laced the air during her shift settled, and apparently ready, she let out a soft yip, trying to get my attention but not call others to us.

"Okay, let's haul ass." I turned in the direction that my internal compass pointed.

While I followed the pull of my seeker magic through the city streets, Tobias and Harper stayed quiet so I could concentrate. Up and down countless blocks, through alleys, and even into a few deserted shops we walked. A lingerie store. An electronics repair joint. A pizzeria that reeked of garlic.

Only after we'd been searching for nearly an hour and had just exited a destroyed diner, did I stop and run my hand through my hair, my frustration nearing boiling.

"I can still feel it, but it's not getting closer." I paused, letting that sink in. "I think whoever is carrying it isn't staying in one place. What does that mean?"

"Perhaps that they're trying to lay a false trail?"

My lips parted. That made sense. I wasn't familiar with the city but at one point, I felt like I was going in a circle.

"You must dig deep, Meredith," Tobias said. "They do not know we have a seeker so this is merely to anger us and throw us off. But you can pinpoint the stone's location if you focus. You should be able to sense the stone itself above all the paths others laid."

I did as Tobias suggested, digging deeper into myself, into my magic, than I ever had.

Back in the day, I'd referred to my power as intuition. While a part of me still found that fitting, it no longer quite covered the extent of what I felt inside me. My ability both led me and seemed to need to be directed.

So, I listened harder than was usually necessary, until another pull, this one strong as hell, yanked behind my sternum.

"It's that way," I pointed.

"Central Park is in that direction," Tobias said. "And many elegant locales that would likely draw a prince."

"The tug inside me is stronger," I said. "I say we check it out."

Harper yipped in agreement.

Tobias nodded. "Stick close together then. There are many places to hide in the park, and even more in the surrounding buildings."

As we ran down the city blocks—somehow even more deserted than the places we'd already been—I found my emotions shifting strangely.

Before, I'd wanted to get the Pearl, but really, I would rather not see the Prince of Hell at all.

Now, however, my hope that we'd come across Prince Orien grew. I found myself wanting to battle him. To pay him back for all the fear he'd instilled in me. For making me a villain—the reason that the world was in danger. For breaking into my vault!

My fists clenched into balls and the skin on the back of my neck tightened with anger.

Yes, I wanted a piece of that demon! I wanted to show him who he was dealing with, that I could defeat him.

I want his blood.

I blinked, my train of thought broken, and slowed. Where the hell had that come from? And why was my chest so tight? Why did I feel like I might explode at any second?

"Meredith?" Tobias slowed alongside me, and Harper followed suit. "Are you okay?"

"No." My fingers pressed against my temple, a strange, uncomfortable pressure building there. Inside I felt hot and sticky, like my blood had turned to oil and its influence was spreading anger and hate through me. It made no sense. What was happening?

"I feel funny," I said when Tobias inched even closer, clearly worried. "Like I want to wring someone's neck. I actually had the thought that I wanted *blood*. That has never happened before." I snorted. "And I've dealt with some real assholes, so that's saying a lot."

Harper's growl reached me, and I turned to find her hackles raised and eyes glowing. "Something wrong, Harp?"

She shook her head, like dogs did when they itched, but Harper did so with more violence. Then, mid-shake, she began to shift. When she stood before me as a human, her eyes were wide with fear.

"I felt that way too." Harper chewed her bottom lip. "For a moment, I even felt an urge to leap at you, Mer. That's why I shook, to get it out of my head, but it didn't work, so I had to shift—to become less deadly."

"Oh." I took a step away.

"It's gone now," Harper assured me. "I'm in control but it was getting stronger the closer we got to the park. Something is off about this area."

Tobias's jaw ground from side to side. "I suspect there's a perfectly good reason for that. You're sensing the power of the Prince of Wrath. We're closing in on him, and in all likelihood, the Pearl. This must be one of his defenses."

I gaped. "He can make people feel wrathful?"

"It's a rumor from the past that, apparently, is true,"

Tobias admitted. "The Princes of Hell can directly manipulate people to do one sin, the one they represent. I believe, since you are experiencing such emotions related to wrath. He must have distributed his influence all around the area he's staying in. What better way to control people than to create havoc?"

Well, crap. How was I going to control myself? Those feelings had been strong, they'd spiraled me. It would do no good to take on a Prince of Darkness when I was under *his* influence. And I couldn't be sure that would not happen again.

"We cannot take you in there," Tobias cautioned, on the same line of thinking that I was veering toward. "Possibly, we'd all be affected. Me, more slowly, as I don't require breathing to live, but we cannot venture forth. Not like this."

"Agreed." Harper pulled out her phone, and her fingers flew over the keyboard. "I texted the other groups and told them about this area, so no one comes this way and gets lost in the sin. But how in the world are we going to get the Pearl if we can't go near Prince Orien without losing our shit?"

"We need to seek a coven with a warder," Tobias answered. "Someone who can create a specific protection around our person. I know of covens in the area, though I cannot say with any certainty that such a member is in their midst."

My jaw tightened. We were so close! The sensation of the tugging behind my breastbone, strong and insistent, assured me of that. For the first time since arriving in New York, the Pearl was somewhere within our reach. And now we had to backtrack because the Prince of Wrath was far more powerful than anyone had anticipated.

I huffed. "What covens do you—"

Harper's phone rang, and she nearly dropped it from shock. S&S members had agreed not to call each other while we were in New York. It was too likely that the ringing might draw attention.

"It's Luca," she announced. "He must have already read my message. Hopefully he knows of a coven that can help." She answered the call and put her phone to her ear. "What's up, Luca?"

Though I couldn't hear what he said, Harper's eyes widened with each second.

"Got it. Thanks." She hung up. "Luca agrees that we need protection. He has someone to shield us and says she's close by."

At that instant, Harper's phone vibrated. She glanced down, pulling up a map. "Like *super* close. He just sent me the address and we're a couple of blocks away. We can be there in five minutes, tops."

"Where will the others go?" I asked. Surely, the other teams would be redirecting our way now that we knew Orien was in this area.

"There are covens in the other boroughs. They'll seek them out for protections and then converge in the park. Hopefully, we'll all get there around the same time."

"Is this woman a lone warder?" Tobias asked.

"Uh, why would that matter?" I asked.

"Covens recruit warders. So it's rare that they're lone practitioners of magic," Harper explained when my eyebrows knitted together. "And no, she's not a warder, but a mage."

Tobias blinked. "Is she the one Luca claims he trusts with his life? The one with access to his magical safe?"

"He didn't say," Harper replied. "But we should get going. Wrath's influence is trying to wriggle its way into me again."

I turned inward and discovered the same could be said of me. I hadn't even noticed it, but now that I did, I squirmed.

The sensation was uncomfortable, hot and sticky, and building with each second, I stood there. It was time to move on before it took me over. "Lead the way."

Phone in hand, Harper maneuvered us through the semi-post-apocalyptic landscape of New York. With each step we took away from Central Park, Wrath's influence dimmed, eventually falling away entirely.

"We're here." The wolf stopped in front of a door to a fancy apartment building. "Now I need to–"

The door to my right squealed open an inch.

"Your names," a sharp, feminine voice demanded from the darkness.

The vampire shifted to stand in front of Harper and me. "Tobias, Meredith, and Harper. Who are you?"

"Get inside."

No one moved.

"I'm Luca's friend."

The mention of the coven master's name was all we needed. We darted through the door and found ourselves face to face with a short, curvy woman with raven-wing hair and dark brown eyes. She dressed elegantly in a black sheath, which, considering what was going on outside her door, felt out of place. If I had to guess, I'd put her at about fifty, though the youthful glint in her eyes hinted that she was probably spry and active for her age.

"Follow me," the woman instructed and bolted to the stairwell.

Trailing her, we climbed five flights of stairs, entering the hallway to the fifth, and top, floor in silence. When we got to her door, she placed her hand above the knob. Magic poured from her palm and the door swung open. Swiftly entering, she waved for us to follow.

Only when the door was closed once again did she speak. "Which one of you is Meredith?"

"Me." I stepped closer.

Most unexpectedly, the woman closed the gap between us and wrapped her arms around me. I stiffened, though her touch was soft and warm, and she smelled like biscotti straight from the oven.

"If not for you, and those who journeyed to Hell with you, my brother would not be alive," she whispered. "I owe you a debt I fear I can never repay. He is my only true family."

"Luca is your *brother*?"

A soft laugh escaped her as she pulled away. Only then did their similarities sink in. Both had strong Italian features, and the warmest brown eyes I'd ever seen. "He is my twin. I am Ginevra Moretti."

"Oh. I didn't know."

"No one does," Ginevra assured with a shrug. "It would be unwise to flaunt our relationship. Our father is a powerful man, and we have half-siblings in Isila who would positively love to do away with us, and any claim we might have to power in the other realm."

She spoke so lightly about the matter, as if she were saying that her siblings didn't want to share a Coke with her.

"You're also the mage he trusts with his magical safe," Tobias concluded, bringing up the enchanted vault the coven master used to store dangerous artifacts.

"I am. And obviously, you are bound to secrecy on that matter." The mage tilted her chin. "He wishes for me to protect you, but I must watch over my brother and that which he holds dear first."

"None of us will say a thing," Tobias vowed. "You have our word."

CHAPTER TWENTY-SIX

"I promise," I agreed, and Harper echoed me.

That brought a smile to Ginevra's face. "Thank you. Luca surely knows that. He wouldn't have directed you here if he did not trust you. Now, tell me what is happening out there," she gestured to the window, "in that land of horrors."

We gave her the rundown.

Once we were done, the mage went to her cabinet, bringing out a bottle of liquor and drinking straight from the bottle. "A Prince of Hell? His sin creeping over the city? Altering minds and hearts? I never imagined such a thing."

"You should leave the city," I urged.

"Not while my brother is here," the mage argued, taking another swig. "Which means I must get you three shielded as best I can, for the sooner you find your quarry, the better."

Ginevra walked across her apartment to another cabinet and began pulling out items.

While she worked, I looked at my friends.

"What's going to happen to the city after this ends?" I spoke as if that were a given, because daring to imagine any other scenario scared the piss out of me.

"The Covenant will have a hell of a time clearing this up. Witches, fae, mages—anyone who can modify memories— they'll all be working overtime," Harper replied. "I'm not sure it will be enough."

"Nor am I," Ginevra commented, mixing a blue liquid in one vial with another so that the product glowed green. "Never in all my years have I witnessed a scene such as this one. And unlike my brother, I spent decades in Isila."

I had so many questions about the other realm, but now wasn't the time for them. Maybe, if we lived through the day, I'd indulge myself.

"One more thing."

The mage's hand hovered over the cabinet again before she plucked a bottle of dried petals from the case. With deft, slender fingers, she retrieved three petals and placed them in the vial, then slipped her thumb over the top and shook. The green color changed again, this time to a light violet.

There wasn't much potion in that vial. "Will that be enough?"

"It's incredibly potent," Ginevra assured me. "You only need a sip each." As she spoke, the air around her hands and the vial shimmered. The hairs on my arm rose.

"How long will it last?" Tobias asked. "Luca wasn't forthright with details."

"A day," Ginevra replied and when I gaped—because the invisibility potion had only lasted an hour—she smiled. "Mage magic differs greatly from the power of witches."

"Why?" There were obvious differences, of course. Mages' magic was far more versatile. Luca could do practically anything. And according to Hans, mages lived for centuries, but I didn't understand the basis of their differences.

Ginevra shrugged. "My kind live, and most are born, in a world of pure magic. I can't say for sure, but I believe witches are further from the source of pure magic. Not that your kind cannot be powerful and have specialties that mages do not possess. Seeking, for example. Overall, however, mages hold more power." She sighed. "Though being away from Isila dims it."

I got the distinct impression that she wished to return to the other world. Was it her malicious family holding her back?

"Here we are." Ginevra extended the vial to us. "One sip each, and it will shield you from anything affecting your mind and emotions."

"Not our physical bodies?" Harper asked. "Like not a shield?"

"For maximum potency, I chose to be specific to the Prince of Wrath's powers. His influence over your minds."

"We thank you for it." Tobias took the vial first, drinking straight from it. He winced and passed it to me.

Thinking it would taste awful, I steeled myself, so when sharp but pleasant citrus washed over my tongue, I was surprised. Passing the vial to Harper, I side-eyed Tobias.

"Vampires are particular about their tastes," he explained, premeditating my question.

"About *everything*!" Ginevra countered with a chuckle.

Tobias didn't deny it, and Harper snorted before downing the rest of the potion.

"Thank you," the wolf said, handing the bottle back to the mage. "What's the waiting period?"

"It is already in effect."

"Then we should go," Tobias replied.

"Thanks," I said. "Good to meet you."

"It was excellent to meet you too." Ginevra inclined her head. "And thank you again for saving my brother. If you need anything, ever, do not hesitate to call."

"Will do."

Slipping out of the apartment building, we entered the war zone of New York city once again.

CHAPTER TWENTY-SEVEN

HANS

MY LUNGS BURNED AS I CHASED THE ONYX TENDRILS THAT WOVE through the city, just out of my reach.

Occasionally, the black ribbons would allow me close, but right as I almost touched them, they'd twist out of my grasp, teasing me. The fifth time this happened, my frustration went from simmering to boiling.

What was my sister playing at?

Somewhere in the back of my mind, my team surfaced, the people I'd abandoned, but their memory and my guilt over leaving them were distant—unimportant . . .

That wasn't like me.

Nicoleta's manipulating me.

The idea slammed into me, and for the first time since I'd taken off like a crazed man, I stopped running. Chest heaving, I shook my head, trying to rid myself of her presence, of her magical influence, which had grown stronger than I'd ever known. Hell, I'd run off on my own thinking I was going to save her. That I'd do something good.

She was using my character traits, what she guessed I'd do,

against me. Making it so I wouldn't see anything else—like reason.

That I should never have left my squad.

Why didn't I consider this before? She wanted me to come after her! To abandon my squad!

How did she get in my head without me knowing? My teeth gritted together, and again, I attempted to force her out, to be the only one in my mind once more.

The effort expelled was great, but a few seconds later the clouds in my mind parted. Finally in full control of myself I spun, scanning the area.

Nothing was recognizable, which was no big surprise. I'd run far. Was I even still in Manhattan?

"*Fuck!*" I roared, unable to keep my fury tamped down.

Yes, I wanted to save my sister. I wanted to give her an option to choose good, but would I have ever risked my teammates for it?

Absolutely not. I was responsible to them, for their lives, as they were to me. I'd not considered that when Nic used her manipulation magic on me and as a result, totally screwed up.

Pulling out my phone, I tried to text the team, but before I could, a figure dropped out of the sky right in front of me. I grabbed one of my daggers.

"You're a hard guy to catch up to," Shay huffed, stopping me short of attacking.

I blinked, taking in the nephilim, her windswept hair, the color in her cheeks from flying. "You followed me?"

"Did you think we were going to let you go? In this?" She gestured at the destruction, the desolate streets and pileups of vehicles nearby, pushing back strands of wayward hair as she did so.

"What about the stones?" I asked. "Are the others going for them?"

"They're on their way now, and we're to meet them. I can fly us both if yo—" Shay grabbed at her neck as a black ribbon slithered around it and tightened.

"No!" I grabbed the ribbon. "Nicoleta!"

I couldn't see my sister, but this was her magic. She had to be close.

"Nic!" I roared as the ribbon tightened around Shay's slender neck. "Let her go!"

"Why, Brother?" My sister's dangerous voice, the sweet one she only used when she was pissed, rang around us. "You so kindly brought me an angel! My lord will love to play with her."

The thought of a demon prince 'playing' with Shay sent my blood boiling. I ceased trying to pry the ribbon off and took more drastic measures, placing my hand above the black magic.

"*Disol,*" I ordered.

The tendrils dissolved, as they had so many times when Nicoleta and I played with our powers.

Nicoleta's guttural scream ripped through the air. "How could you!"

Shay coughed, but didn't hesitate. Her hand went right to one of her daggers, unsheathing it with grace. The other hand lit up gold with angelic power.

"Where are you, Nic?" I called out, still searching for her. "You don't have to do this. You have other choices—"

"I told you not to call me that!" My sister appeared, sweeping out of an apartment complex, dressed in black leather pants and a black crop top Father would not have approved. The only thing on her person that vaguely resembled the girl I'd grown up with was our grandmother's necklace—one of the only heirlooms our family possessed. Seeing it made me all the more determined to bring Nicoleta back. I'd save my sister from the demon prince's influence if it was the last thing I did. I had to—for her, for me, for our father who'd done his best to raise us despite what we were.

"Bitch," Shay hissed, her voice raspy from the strangulation.

Nicoleta barked out a cruel laugh. "I thought angels were forbidden from talking nasty? Are you a half breed too? If so, the Darkborn might have a place for you. With conditions, of course."

"Screw your conditions!" Shay blasted gold light at my sister.

My insides clenched, but Nicoleta saw the attack coming and sprung out of the way with such dexterity that it became clear that she'd been training hard for this battle. This life.

For a Prince of Darkness to rule.

How long had she been working toward this goal?

For how long had I not known my sister?

"Ladies, please." I inserted myself between the two women. Shay lowered her hands, and sure that *she* wouldn't be the one to do anything hasty, I turned to my sister. "Nicoleta, I know you're pissed at me. And I deserve that, but I have an offer I don't think you're going to be able to refuse. Or even want to resist."

My sister's black eyes narrowed to dangerous slits. "There's nothing you can give me I don't already have within reach."

"Safety. Prosperity. Your family back." The last slipped off my tongue, the kingpin in my argument. Or so I thought.

What a mistake.

Ribbons burst from her core, shooting toward me. "You failed to get our mother the first time, you idiot! Why would I trust you?! You're not my family anymore!"

"Nic! I—"

"Defend yourself!" Shay growled, sliding in front of me before the ribbons could strike and spraying golden magic at the tendrils, which turned to harmless smoke.

Nicoleta snorted. "This bitch has to do your dirty work? Pathetic." She spun and shards of black shot out of her, spraying toward us with the speed of bullets.

"*Ezku!*" I yelled, ready this time.

A shield billowed out in front of us, stopping the shards. The few that slipped through my protection turned to harmless sand.

"Witch spells!" Nicoleta screamed. "Weak! If you're really going to do this, Brother, use your *real* power!"

"Hans, no," Shay whispered. "If you do, I can't—"

"I won't," I growled, not wanting to hear what she'd say. I *never* used my demon magic and wasn't tempted. That part of me needed to die, and it needed to take my sister's darkness with it. "Split."

Shay's blue eyes remained locked on me for a second longer, before she unfurled her wings to lift into the air. Nicoleta tracked Shay as the angel disappeared over the roof.

"She left you, huh?" my sister snorted, a hard smirk on her lips. "Giving you up for a lost cause? Does she not see that you're infatuated with her?"

My heart, which had been thundering in my chest, ground to a halt. "What the hell are you talking about?"

"You and the angel. The way you look at her, Hans. It's *so* obvious." My sister rolled her eyes.

"You've got it all wrong," I argued.

"I doubt it, but I'm not surprised you didn't figure it out. You always were the stupidest Novak. You—"

Gold magic rained down, shutting my sister up. In quick succession, she performed three backflips to land under the apartment awning so that Shay's attacks fell harmlessly to the cement.

Without hesitation, I rushed my sister. She might not be willing to see sense, but if I knocked her out then I could take her to New Haven.

Father is going to kill me, but I gotta do what I gotta do.

She'd be safe in the coven's dungeons. Surely, when another option was laid before her, when Luca talked to her in that calm, convincing way of his, then Nicoleta would sway sides.

That was what I thought, but the instant my sister turned her dark, hardened gaze on me again, doubt crept in.

Again, her ribbons appeared, this time forming swords that seemed to stretch on forever. Face full of spite, she swung them at me.

"Sister!" I tried again, bobbing and weaving out of harm's way. "We'll hide you!"

"Not before I leave your mangled body in the nearest alley!"

Another blaze of gold came from above. A warning Nicoleta did not heed as she stomped out from the safety of the awning, right up to me, and swung her freakish sword right at my neck.

I bent backwards, limbo-style, and spun to the ground, catching myself with both hands right as a sword sliced into the ground a few short inches from my face.

The cement split open, black smoke hissing from what should have been impenetrable rock.

"You have *no idea* what I can do, Brother. No idea what he's taught me. He was my mentor. My real family!"

"He wants to use you!" I roared, scurrying backward, putting space between us. "You're Lilith's daughter! You might be as powerful as him. Don't let him use you!"

Her laughter was almost manic with belief in her lord. "So what?! I want to use him *too*. To rule."

Another swipe of the sword, and this time it shot outward, again coming right for my neck. Somehow, I dodged the attack once more, and as I did so, another blast of angel magic showered down on my sister. This time, Shay landed a direct hit. Her golden magic spread over Nic, like oil, coating her skin a gold shine that pulsed rhythmically.

My sister shrieked and fell to the ground, her weapons and attacks on me forgotten as her body convulsed.

What the fuck? Shay's magic was strong, but I'd never seen it do anything like this.

Aghast, I looked up, found the angel watching with wide eyes, no longer attacking. "Shay! What's going on?!"

"I don't know!" Shay called back, and a lump lodged into my throat.

Nicoleta writhed on the ground, the angel magic still shimmering and pulsating on her skin. I couldn't live with hurting my sister, with killing her.

What kind of big brother was I?

"Nic . . . what's going on? What can I do?"

In answer, she tore herself from the ground, twisting toward me and in that instant the golden light evaporated. An animalistic growl ripped from Nicoleta's lips.

I took a step back, fear slithering through me.

My sister's eyes, usually black as night, were crimson. Her

skin, normally pale and smooth, had become red and even from here I spotted lines of gray traveling her arms.

Her veins were gray? But why? Was that all from Shay's magic? Or was it a result of Nic breaking Shay's hold over her?

"What's going on, Nicoleta? *Please*, let us help you!"

"I need no help," she growled, and ribbons spiraled from her, but this time they dug into the ground, sending black smoke up again. "I need *nothing* from you, Brother. The next time I see you, you better watch your back because that's when you'll get what's coming to you."

The cement beneath my sister dissolved, and the black smoke engulfed her until I could no longer see her.

"Nic! Where are you? Please! Let us help!"

Instead of a reply, gritty smoke rushed me. An acrid stench that reminded me of the bowels of Hell filled my nose, and I collapsed to my knees, eyes stinging.

"Hans!" Fire flashed in the blackness. Shay was wielding her flaming sword—a weapon best suited to fighting up close—in case Nic rushed her. "Where are you?"

"Here!" The word came out strangled, and weakly I waved my hand, barely able to see through the smoke.

The fire flashed closer, then disappeared as fingers gripped mine, and another hand tightened around my palm. "Hold tight."

My arms stretched out, until my toes left the ground and I was hanging in the air, lifted by Shay.

"Wait!" I rasped, but the word didn't come out right. I twisted, trying to see below. "My sister!"

"She's gone," Shay said. "Stop moving! I have to get you away from this smoke!"

What?! How?

A second later, my feet touched down on the ground. Shay's hand released mine and I coughed, trying to force the horrible stench of my sister's dark magic from me. Two deep breaths, three, and finally, I could breathe normally once more. Slowly, I opened my eyes and found that I was on a rooftop.

Shay stood in front of me, rubbing the skin of her hand, which was bright red.

"What happened to you?" I asked.

"That's where I touched you. Where the smoke licked my skin." She shook her head. "I don't know why you're so worried about me. You should look at yourself."

Lifting an arm to my face, the hairs on my nape stood on end. My skin wasn't just red, the veins that ran beneath were dark. Not black, but gray.

What the hell had Nicoleta done to us?

"Where is she?" I shoved to my feet, surprised to find that my skin didn't hurt, and since my veins didn't explode or do anything crazy, I figured I was all right. "Your power did something to her."

"I know," Shay admitted. "But I don't know why it affected her that way. And clearly, hers did something to me—to us. A similar irritated reaction, except for your veins."

"Hers too. I saw them turn gray before I couldn't see her any longer."

"Any idea why?"

"None." Not only had I never sported gray veins, but I'd sparred with Shay many times before. In all those sessions, her power had never done anything like what it had done to Nic.

"Nicoleta!" I called out as I peered over the side of the building, into the street.

"I told you, she's gone. The ground swallowed her up."

Swallowed her up? What the actual fuck?

"How?" I spun.

"I thought you might know."

"All I know is that she's accepted her dark power while I blocked mine. My sister's demon magic is advanced far beyond mine. She's right, I don't know half of what she can do. What she's capable of."

"She might have made a deal with Prince Orien," Shay warned. "Hellblooded people aren't common, but I've seen a few. Never one with powers like hers though. She's no weak girl, Hans. Your sister is a tempest just waiting to rage out of control."

I closed my eyes, fearing that Shay was right.

CHAPTER TWENTY-EIGHT

TOBIAS

Central Park grew ever closer, and with each step, the tension edging my spine ratcheted up another notch. We had ventured beyond the location where we'd first turned around, and so far, I sensed nothing, no sensation of wrath trying to claw its way into me. Though it had not affected me the first time either, so I couldn't be sure it was not there.

Was the sin affecting the witch and the wolf? I studied them, but noticed nothing amiss. When the greenery of the park peeked through the buildings, announcing our impending arrival, I figured it prudent to flat out inquire as to how they were managing.

"How do you ladies feel?" I looked to Meredith first, then Harper, who had yet to shift to her four-legged form in case the shielding-potion did not work as expected. We did not need a shifted wolf succumbing to the sin of wrath and lashing out.

"Fine," the witch replied and lifted her dagger, which she'd been carrying at the ready since we left the apartment. "I should have felt stabby by now, but I don't. I'm scared and anxious, but otherwise normal."

"Yup. I think the potion is working," Harper confirmed, never halting from scanning the road. "Hopefully the other teams arrive soon, and their protections are as good as ours."

"I'm sure Luca will be swift," I said, feeling the same as the wolf.

"So glad we met Ginevra," Meredith breathed. "Now we can figh—"

"Oh, darling," a voice, deep and brimming with power, rang from all around. "You truly think you can fight *me*?"

"Shit!" Harper shouted and shifted to a wolf while I spun, searching the area.

Meredith stayed in place, blade in hand, poised to strike. "Who are you?"

"The question is, witch, who are *you*?" Smoke billowed from the end of the street, blocking our view of Central Park as it rolled our way in threatening black clouds.

"Anyone know what that is? Should we run?" Meredith asked. "We're still alone."

"Hold your ground," I gritted. The smoke, while threatening, was too theatrical. Whoever this was, and I had a good idea of who we were probably dealing with, wished to frighten us.

We could not allow it.

The smoke rolled ever closer, expanding, and filling the entire street as it neared. Faint growls emitted from within, hinting the Prince of Wrath, should he truly be in the cloud, was not alone.

"Prepare to fight many," I warned, not sure Meredith's witch ears could hear the growling. "He is not alone in there."

"I'm ready to chop whatever comes out of *that* into little demon cubes." The witch's eyes narrowed on the smoke.

A laugh barked out of me at precisely the same moment the cloud came to a stop, some twenty feet away, and vanished.

A devil of a man, dressed in a modern all-black suit, appeared. Feathered wings expanded from his back, black as the night sky in an open ocean. Black horns swept back from his forehead, glinting in the late afternoon light. Behind the man hovered six demons, all of varying sorts, none very human looking—all grotesque.

"Brave," the prince intoned, mercurial gray eyes flashing. "I respect that you did not run."

"And why should we care about that? Who the hell are you?" Meredith sneered. Of course, she had to have a hint, but wanted to be sure.

"No longer am I in Hell," the man replied with a smirk. "Haven't been in some time, much to the *wild* annoyance of my dear brothers, I'm sure. But I do rule there, even in my absence."

"If you talk this much, and don't bother answering questions, I doubt they're annoyed that you left." The rebuttal earned Meredith a dangerous smile laced with venom.

"I am Prince Orien, mortal. Or just Wrath. It's not my given name, but I do quite like the ring of it."

"*Just Wrath,*" Meredith spat out the name as if it disgusted her. "You've got to be kidding me."

"Not in the slightest." His lips curled dangerously. "And don't act like my favorite sin doesn't worry you. After all, you've guarded yourself from my power."

"We have," I interjected. "And you should know there are more of us coming. All capable fighters. We're here for the Pearl and the Opal. You'd do well to relinquish them."

"Or what?" The prince laughed. "Vampire, I'm as difficult to kill as you."

"There are always ways to end an immortal life."

"Certainly, but since there are only three of you now, and . . ." he gestured back to his minions, "seven of us, I shall take my chances. That is, unless you'd like to cross over? I could use more Darkborn followers for what's coming. Particularly one with your talents, witch. Sweet Nicoleta has told me much about your abilities."

"*Fucking finally!*" Meredith let out a long breath of relief. "Now that we've received a real invite, I'd love to join your cult."

I twisted to find her expression deadpanned, and my lips curled upward. Cheeky bugger.

The Prince of Wrath was not as amused and the sharp planes of his cheeks turned three shades redder.

"Fine, witch. Decline my grace. It matters not. We'll use your power, whether you are with us or not, and when we're done with you . . . Well, then you'll learn what Hell is *really* like."

"Don't think so, douche-canoe." Meredith hurled her blade at him, striking the prince in the chest. "Not going back."

He exhibited not a modicum of pain, not even as he gripped the hilt and pulled the dagger out slowly. Right away, the wound healed. "Oh, but I think you are."

With a snap of his fingers, the demons behind the prince charged, teeth gnashing and claws flailing.

I didn't recognize the type of devils that were coming at us, and that was a danger. What if, like the hellhounds, they transmitted a horrible disease? Or their blood was poison like the shade?

One was still a fair way away when it launched itself at

Meredith. In that moment, the questions I once harbored vanished. Only one thought remained.

Protect what's mine.

Lunging at the demon, I collided with his brutish body, tumbling to the ground. Teeth snapping, the beast tried to bite into my face, but I was too fast. I reached up, gripped at its temples below a pair of stubby protruding horns, and tore the creature's head clean off.

"Tobias!" Meredith yelled. "You alright?"

When I looked up, dread and fear cut through me. A bloodied demon body lay at her feet but she wasn't safe yet. While she scanned my face, the Prince of Wrath went straight for her.

"Behind you!" I yelled.

Meredith spun as I hauled myself up to aid her. I couldn't help but feel both proud of her bravery, and aching to rip out the prince's heart if he so much as scratched her skin.

I prowled closer, watching the witch arch her dagger high. Not swayed in the slightest, the Prince of Wrath ran forward, though he didn't see Harper coming from the side.

The wolf launched at the prince, her sharp teeth sinking into his arm. A roar emitted from the devil, and two streams of dark magic surged out of him.

One slammed straight into Meredith, and time slowed as she soared through the air, her body crashing into a building. She went limp and fell to the ground.

"Nooo!" I pivoted, desperate to get to her, but it was no use. Ribbons of darkness wrapped around me, pinning my arms to my torso.

As the Prince of Wrath used his ribbons to reel me in like a sailor pulling a fish from the depths, I searched for Harper, only to find her passed out against a building too.

Fucking hell! He'd knocked both my partners out in one go. Where were the other teams? Had they been unable to find covens with warders?

Luckily, we had already dispatched all six of the prince's minions before he shot my teammates down, so no one could injure the witch or the wolf further. Not as long as I distracted the prince.

Before I could come up with a plan to save them, Wrath and I were eye-to-eye. A smart strategist, he kept me at arm's length so I couldn't bite him. But I spied an advantage. I was still close enough for me to use my one remaining power.

"Release me," I demanded, drawing on my compulsion ability.

Wrath's eyes dimmed and glassed over. For a millisecond, the grip of his black tendrils around me loosened. Then, his eyes returned to normal as the prince shoved my compulsion from him, claiming his mind once more. The tendrils cinched ever tighter around my torso.

"With influence like that, you must be a Laurent."

When I sneered, he smirked, already knowing the answer. "You weren't exaggerating when you called your trio capable fighters." The prince shook his head. "I'll admit, I didn't believe you. Humans so often overstate their power and strength. I won't make that mistake again. I—"

A bolt of energy raced along my back, electrifying me, and a scream wrenched from my throat as the black binds fell to the ground. The shock took down the prince too, and he bellowed in pain, releasing me to the clutches of gravity.

"Tobias, move!" a voice called as I thudded against the cement.

Shots of pain blasting through me, I rolled away from Wrath, until I was far enough to stagger to my feet.

"Over here!"

My head snapped toward the voice, to find that Luca and his team had arrived. Another was right behind them. It had taken them longer than we'd hoped to acquire protection from Wrath's sin, but they were finally bloody here.

"Out of the way!" the mage ordered, seconds before he unleashed another stream of magic. It flooded the street, aiming for the Prince of Darkness.

I darted to the side, away from harm, but couldn't help looking back, taking great glee in the expression of horror crossing Wrath's face.

A mage, especially one as powerful as Luca, was not to be crossed. Particularly, when Wrath had no backup.

In that instant, Orien seemed to realize the same thing, for black smoke poured from his hands, thick and fast. It enveloped him, partially obscuring him from view and when Wrath clapped his hands together, the smoke expanded, swallowing him whole and billowing out again.

It flowed over me, the stench acrid, nearly choking me as it burned my skin. Somewhere in the distance, the others coughed loudly.

"Wait it out!" I yelled. "It will dissipate."

Although his cloud took longer to disappear than it had when the prince arrived, the smoke did eventually clear, leaving me standing in the street, demon corpses all about, but no Prince of Wrath to be found.

"Tobias." Luca came up behind me. "Are you alright?"

"I am." Spinning around, I searched for Meredith. I'd gotten disoriented in the fight, wasn't quite sure where I was. When I found her, relief swelled within me. Coven members were assisting and two others squatted near Harper too. Thanks to the wolf's quick healing abilities, she was already sitting up, blinking heavily. "Are they okay?"

"Too soon to tell," Luca admitted. "Let the others assess the damage. Tell me what happened."

Though I wished to go to Meredith's side, I did as the coven master commanded, sparing no detail. "Thank you for sending us to Ginevra," I finished. "Her potion probably saved us. Your secret is safe."

"If I didn't trust each one of you implicitly, I never would have compromised her."

"Luca!" someone called from the side. "You should see this!"

The coven master exhaled. "Thank you for assuring me, though, Tobias."

"Always," I replied, and we split, Luca going to assess a finding, while I strode to Meredith's side.

When I reached her, she was once again conscious and sitting up. She shooed those tending to her away and met my stare.

"We scared him off?"

"We did."

"But no stones?" Meredith frowned.

"Unfortunately, not."

"Why didn't he use them?"

"I don't know," I admitted. "Perhaps he wanted to show off what he could do . . . either way, I'm sure Wrath had them, but he left when Luca appeared."

Her eyebrows knitted together. "Why?"

"Demons and mages do not live in the same realms, and while demons fear angels more, Luca's kind is a close second on their list of magicals to avoid. Mage magic is versatile and deadly."

"Too bad there aren't more mages around here then."

"Or that they're not as powerful as our leader," I added, knowing full well some mages wouldn't have succeeded in scaring off the prince. Luca's bloodline and his commitment to the study of magic made him tremendously powerful. "How do you feel?"

"Like I got the shit knocked out of me, but other than an aching head and shoulder, okay, I guess."

"Eloquent as always."

"I save all my grace for you."

Her sass helped me relax a touch more because it meant that she really was fine, and held out a hand. "Can you walk?"

"Let's find out."

She took my hand, our fingers twining together in a way that sent shots of electricity up my arm that stole my breath. I suspected the same thing happened to her, for Meredith's eyes widened.

"Umm," Meredith breathed, coming to stand mere inches from my person. So close, I could feel the heat of her skin, could count her eyelashes. "Thanks for the lift."

"You're welcome," I replied, doing my best to ignore her distracting jasmine and pine scents that threatened to cloud my head. "I'm sorry I didn't defend you better."

"It wasn't your job," she paused, "not really. We didn't succeed in our job."

Her eyes dropped to the ground, and unable to help myself, I hooked the underside of her chin with my finger, lifting her face to mine again.

She's beautiful.

"We didn't get the stones," I agreed, struggling not to act

on the emotions rushing through me, demanding that I take her lips in mine. That I claim this woman.

Mine

I swallowed, fighting down the thought. "But we know for certain who our enemy is now and what they're capable of. It's a step in the right direction."

Meredith's gaze blazed into mine, her pink lips parted, and for one insane second, I gave up fighting and dipped my face toward hers.

"Okay, teams!" Luca called out, shattering whatever spell was left between us.

I exhaled, thankful for the grounding his voice provided and leaned away. At my motion, Meredith took two steps back, her breathing deeper, though her stare was still locked on me, a turmoil of emotions swirling in those mis-matched eyes.

"The Prince of Wrath might be gone, but the city is still in disarray," Luca called out, clearly oblivious to the near-kiss he'd interrupted, thank the bloody saints my mother had prayed to. "People are hurt, and some are still possessed. I've contacted Hans and Shay and they're on their way. If you find a possessed person, text Shay right away. She'll find you. Anyone else, help where you can." He clapped his hands, signaling that we could get a move on.

Not about to let her out of my sight, I turned to Meredith. "Would you like to sear—"

A trio of screams, one of them youthful, cut off my words.

Meredith whirled. "That came from deep inside the park!"

"Looks like we know where to start," I said as Luca, and a few others, ran by us toward Central Park.

Meredith and I took off after them. She was slower than usual, but given that she'd sustained a head injury, that didn't surprise me. It only made me resolve to keep watch on her.

When we got to the green space in the middle of the city, most of the teams had already dispersed, searching for those who needed help. The screaming, however, stopped, leaving me uncertain about which way to go.

"One sounded like a kid to you, right?" Meredith asked.

"It did."

"That sign says there's a playground this way," she said. "Let's try there first, and hope the kid is just scared because their mom is missing."

I went with her, hoping against hope we would only find an abandoned child, waiting to be reunited safely with a parent. That would not be ideal, and certainly traumatizing for the kid, but considering the city had been infested with demons, far worse scenarios were sure to exist.

The moment the playground came into sight, and the hedges and fences obscuring its insides became obvious, I rounded the witch. "Let me go in first. You were recently injured."

She blinked and her mouth parted. Unable to stop myself, my eyes dipped to her lips.

"Okay, sure."

"I . . ." *Can't bear to see you hurt again.* "We're a team, so we need to look out for one another. S&S code," I finished, pushing down the lust rising inside me.

"Right," she replied, though she didn't sound like she bought it. Did she sense the air heating between us too?

"Stay here."

"I'll come in *when* you give me the all-clear."

I snorted and faced the park. Meredith would not be bossed around, and to be honest, I didn't mind as much as I should. I was getting used to the sassy, stubborn witch. Perhaps, annoying as they were at times, I even liked those qualities about her.

My keen senses took over, checking the surrounding area. The aromas I associated with children—sugar, dirt, and the chemical tang of sunscreen from their mother's applications— laced the air heavily as if someone, or multiple someones, were in the area. But all was quiet. If someone was inside, they were likely hiding, terrified by the monsters in their city.

I unlatched the gate and let myself inside. A quick scan revealed no children, but among the park's varied equipment there were many tunnels to hide. More importantly, there were no demons in the area that might attack. We could take our time searching.

"Meredith," I called back. "All is clear. You—"

"Tobias!" Meredith screamed.

I whirled to see the seeker witch lifted in the air by a winged demon.

CHAPTER TWENTY-NINE

MEREDITH

"Let me go!" I thrashed in the demon's talons as the beast soared higher and higher.

Over light posts, we flew, and then took a sharp turn upward to skim the roofs of skyscrapers. Going so fast my eyes started to water, the destroyed city flew by below, the cars resembling ants.

On second thought, maybe I don't want to be let go. Falling would mean certain death, so I stopped moving, stopped insisting the monster drop me.

"Where are you taking me?" I screamed into the wind.

The ugly, horned creature with a bull-like face growled and tightened its grip. Sharp talons dug into my shoulders, and a hiss parted my lips as pain spiraled through me. Before, at least I'd been able to move. Now? No way, bucko. Not if I didn't want to lose my arm.

"Dude!" I yelled when I caught my breath again. "Lay off! I need my arm!"

In response, the demon only growled once again.

Could it talk? Something told me it was too stupid for such

things. Would a stupid or a smart demon be more dangerous? Either way, it probably wasn't acting alone. Did Wrath send it?

Where was this thing taking me?

Seeing as I wasn't going to get an answer from the beast, I bided my time for when we landed, trying to figure out how I'd attack fast enough to escape. I still had weapons in the bag I carried, so the moment he released me, I'd have to get to them quickly.

Our sudden descent interrupted my thoughts. I glanced down to find that the demon was approaching, not the ground like I'd hoped, but the top of a building.

We were going in for a rooftop landing. And fast. Waaaay too fast.

"Shit!" I screamed as my captor hurtled toward the building, apparently not accounting for the fact that it carried a human parcel that, if smashed into the wall, would likely die.

At the last minute, though, the beast jerked upward so that the soles of my feet skimmed the rooftop, rather than my body crashing into the wall. When we touched down, my trembling feet flat against the roof, a gravely sound that might have been laughter rolled out of the creature, and fury rose inside me.

"Oh, you're so funny, aren't you? Well, what do you think about this—" I yanked my arm from the devil's talons and instead of just injuring myself further, I actually succeeded. Not wasting a second, I reached for my daggers, ready to fight the horned monster off with one arm.

"I think not." A door banged open and before I could wrap my hand around cold steel, the bag ripped away from my body to soar across the rooftop and disappeared over the edge.

"What the hell!"

"Immobilize her, creature!"

The demon kicked me to the ground, but I caught myself and rolled away from him. A heartbeat later I sprang back up like a jackrabbit, spinning toward the new enemy.

A man, tall and gangly, strode in my direction, his hand extended, his head shaking. "Idiot beast. I'll do it."

The next thing I knew, my hands were bound magically behind me. No! I'd wasted my chance to escape!

Still, I could run, but the new guy was blocking the door. So I did the only thing I could do and sprinted to the side of the roof, trying to put distance between me and the magic-worker.

"And where will you go?" he drawled. "You have no wings."

I blinked. Obviously, he was correct, and I had no way out, but how would he know that? Wrath knew I was a seeker, but wasn't it possible I was of mixed heritage? Like Nicoleta? She was a witch and demon and had wings.

My questions were cut short when the door to the rooftop opened again and a short, muscular woman wearing a long black trench coat appeared. Trailing a half step behind her was another guy.

"Josiah!?" His name came out strangled.

"I-I'm sorry, Meredith."

That was all he said. All he needed to say. In those words, it was clear to me that Josiah was a traitor to the coven. He'd escaped confines in the tomb because he'd been guilty of killing Lola and that other witch. Had he also been the one to send word to burn the lucimisia crops that had made the journey to hell necessary? How did the acts benefit one another?

"Why?" I demanded.

"They took Sara."

"And I will keep her, until you deliver." The woman spoke with such confidence that it became clear she, not the tall man, was the leader.

Somehow, she seemed familiar too.

"Who are you?"

"Meredith, you wound me," the woman replied. "You don't recognize me?"

Sort of. I'd never seen her face, but those ice-blue eyes . . .

"We've never met," I replied, because being wishy-washy would sound weak, and while I might be in a position of weakness, *I* was not weak.

"Oh, but we have, Meredith Stone," the woman assured. "Many, many times." Her hand dipped into the pocket of her trench, pulling out something.

My stomach pitted. It couldn't be.

But the moment the mask slipped over her face, the moment those ice-blue eyes blazed from behind a shield of black planes, I knew.

"The Ringmaster," I forced out, fear lacing my voice.

"Surprised?" the woman asked. "Most people are."

"This isn't your voice."

"Of course not. Think, Meredith." She ripped off the mask. "I control criminals. Billions of dollars pass through my enterprise. Power flows to and from me—a woman at the top of her game. Why would I not disguise myself? Not use a synthesizer? Did I not insist that you, of all those in my employ, utilize disguise during jobs? Why would I not do so too?"

She had. Many times, the use of a disguise had saved me.

"But when you pulled me off the street, you were a man." I remember the day like it was yesterday. The man approached, still in a mask, but the body had undoubtedly been male. That was a moment I thought was my salvation, soon became a house of horrors that I wanted desperately to escape.

"A hired body, and nothing more," the woman replied. "That man wore an earpiece, doing what I told him to do, to say. I was not there in body, but rest assured I was always there pulling the strings as that masked puppet got you set up and prepared you to work for me."

And then, I never saw him again. Not in person. I'd been placed in a home with other thieves in training, watched over by a hard as nails couple in the Ringmaster's employ. They did as the boss said, doled out missions, and punishments, just as the Ringmaster wished.

The scars lining my back prickled as the memory of the day the cane had cracked open my skin returned with vengeance. All that pain because my boss felt I hadn't done my job properly.

"Don't feel stupid," the Ringmaster continued. "Few know my secret, and those who find out . . . well . . ."

They were soon dead.

Did Josiah and the other guy realize what awaited them?

"Not these two," the Ringmaster said, catching me. "I need someone to train my magic, and Josiah will be useful for when I wish to grow my powers. He lives, as does Sara, for as long as I wish."

A twisted expression crossed Josiah's face. I didn't understand why the Ringmaster took Sara to use Josiah, but assumed Sara refused to give the woman what she wanted.

Harper had called Sara a pacifist, and apparently, she could remain that way as long as her boyfriend did the dirty work of stealing magic.

The trio stopped to stand in front of me. The demon that brought me here was still off to the side, waiting for a command. This seemed to be proof that my old boss had always known about the supernatural.

"So, are you a Darkborn?" I asked. "Here to usher in a demon prince?"

The Ringmaster barked out a laugh. "God no. Though I have been privy to the magical underworld for some time, I've not had much access. And I'd never encountered the Darkborn before, though I did find that group's willingness to trade and work together very useful."

"What does that mean?"

"After Denz came slinking back to me, a man appeared at my door. He wanted Denz to work for him, but I recognized the man was something special."

She had to be referring to the vampire who had changed my ex-partner.

"He was powerful, and though I'm often in positions with leverage, this man reeked of something different. Something not human. Of strength and a rare pedigree of might—like one who did not cower, nor did he do business with the weak. He *dripped* with possibility. I took a chance and told the man he could have Denz, *if* he gave me a servant. And information."

Her hand landed on the gangly man's shoulder.

"The servant came easily. The other not so much, but I persevered. My new partner invited me deep into a world I'd only glimpsed before. One that intrigued me in a way I had not experienced in years. I wanted a piece, and the man, though he clearly was not used to dealing with humans, said he would help me. But there was only one way for me to be truly of this world, to have power that even my wealthiest, most influential clients will never possess."

Stealing magic from supernaturals.

"You targeted Lola," I whispered.

"I did, and that other witch. For practice." The Ringmaster spoke of their deaths like they were nothing. "Her magic would have been good to test myself with. But you have been my true target for some time, Meredith."

"Me?"

A hard and cruel smile curled her mouth.

"I suspected you were different. It was why I always kept a close eye on you—and, of course, gave you the choicest jobs. After I lost Denz to my business partner, I sent a team to look for you. They found you—with *a coven*, of all things. After that, it took a bit of research, discussions with my new connections, and blackmail . . ." She cast a glance at Josiah. "But I figured out what you were. That you possess a particular breed of magic explains so much, don't you think?"

Like how I'd always been the best thief in her employ. The first to find lost objects even when we had almost nothing to go on. The one with the best track record.

"You've always been smart, so now I'm sure you see, Meredith, what's to happen? It's time to call in your debts."

At her tone, ice trickled through me.

Ambition glinted in her ice-blue eyes. "And since you ran, your debt to me has grown. I'll accept only one form of payment—your power." Her attention shifted to Josiah, the light glinting off the slender line of her skin as the sun set. "If you want to save your loved one's neck, it's time to get to work, necromancer."

CHAPTER THIRTY

GUNNER

"This has gotta be it." I stared through the rain splattered windshield as we came upon a drive barely wider than our car, and overrun with ferns. "Don't you think, Si?"

"I guess so," the fae replied. "Seeing as we've passed by it three times, there might be other properties that we missed. This area is difficult to navigate."

He was right. The roads were dinky as all get out, and there was too much vegetation. Not much light either. I could sense that magic blanketed the area too, hiding something. Unfortunately, the magic was spread out for miles, which made it hard to judge where the magic worker themselves might be hidin' out.

"The weather ain't helpin' one bit," I added, glancing at the darkened sky. As a fae, Si had to feel the magic too. That didn't need to be said.

"This rain is supposed to last through the night." Silas pulled up the drive, a narrow gravel road, and tucked the car out of the way of oncoming traffic before turning to me. "Should we wait until tomorrow to check it out?"

Tempting...

A beer, and the pretty curvy server manning the inn's pub were callin' my name. And yet, even with all those comforts and promises, I didn't want to give up yet.

Damn near twelve hours it had taken us to get to England, drive to the remote village in the north of the country, and find someone who'd give us directions to the area where Miriam Black lived. Not that they'd heard the woman's name, but they knew the area. We had to take what we could get, round these parts.

Overall, I considered myself a pretty laid-back guy, but retreatin' now felt bad. Like giving up for good. Plus, I couldn't shake the hunch that if we came back tomorrow, we might not find this place again.

"Nah. The boss gave us a job," I reminded. "Let's check 'er out."

Silas sighed. "We'll have to walk down the drive. The car won't fit."

"Yeah, sorry 'bout that." I'd been the one to insist on the largest sedan the rental agency had. I was a big dude, so I didn't like to be cramped in those tiny hybrids. Though, truth be told, I wasn't sure one of those Mini Coopers would even fit down this way.

"Don't apologize to me." The fae snorted. "I have magic that will keep me dry, but you'll get wet."

"I'll shift. Won't mind it as much that way."

"And what if Miriam isn't supernatural, and I show up with an enormous wolf? What do we tell her?"

"For one, it's damn near certain she's magical if her name was on the *Le Bastion* paperwork. I doubt they have a single human client. Besides that, you think she'll notice a wolf, but won't say something about magic keepin' the water off your head?"

Silas didn't reply, instead opening the door and stepping into the pouring rain. Following him, we tramped along the narrow lane. I squinted through the rain. Sniffed too.

"Don't see any lights. You?"

"None," the fae affirmed. "But a few feet down the lane and magic laces this area even more heavily than it did on the street."

I inhaled more deeply and caught what he meant. Sweetness filled the air, fixin' to burst with witch magic. "You think it's for protection?"

"It has to be, and that has me worried. If this is where Miriam lives, she's far from . . . well, everything. Why are so many wards necessary out here?" He paused, swallowed. "We must proceed with caution, Gunner."

"Will do, Si." With that, I shifted into my wolf form.

When I was younger, right after puberty, the process of shifting—which consisted of cracking and rearranging of bones, the rapid growth of black fur, and the sharpening of my already keen senses—used to hurt. Nowadays, it was nothing but a release that I reveled in.

I was my wolf, and my wolf was me. Take one away, and you might as well, lay me in my grave.

Once the process completed, I stared up at Silas, who nodded. We prowled forward, ready for anything.

With each step, I listened and scented the air. The property was lush with vegetation, reminding me of my pack's forest acreage in North Carolina. Wetter, though, and a damn sight colder too.

But the cold and wet drenching my fur was the least concerning of the differences between this place and my pack's land. The farther we got down the road—which narrowed more every few yards—the sweeter the air smelled. The heavier and more menacing the power.

Witches lived here, that much I was sure of, though they seemed to have hidden themselves far away.

From what though?

Why would someone want so much protection when they lived in the middle of nowhere? A few simple wards should have done the trick.

But no . . . finding this place had been like finding a runt pup running loose in the woods. Hoping to get the answer to those, and a dozen other questions, we kept on goin', searchin'.

It wasn't until we'd walked at least a half a mile that I caught sight of what could be a house through the dense foliage. Since Silas was no wolf, and we couldn't mind-link, I let out a low rumble to get his attention. The fae looked at me, and I jerked my head toward the lights.

He squinted, his soft inhale punctuated the sound of raindrops falling in puddles. "That has to be a mile away."

Same thing I was thinkin'. Also thought that the magic in the air was tryin' to sway me to want to turn around.

Interesting bit of magic they got there.

"Isn't it odd for someone to have such a long driveway?" Silas sounded anxious. "Perhaps we should wait until morning, Gunner? Don't you want to go back to the inn, get a beer?"

That sneaky fae was trying to tempt me!

Didn't take much. Usually, a cold brewski would work, but not today—I wanted to make *some* progress. Even if it was just seeing the house, to make certain it was real. Because the magic in the air was making me question things, for true.

Ignoring him, I kept on walking, and because S&S had a code to never leave your partner behind, Silas followed.

"You better be sure of this, wolf."

I wasn't sure of much in this world. My family. My pack. That I worked for a good guy and with good people. Also, that the Old Ones had blessed me. This creepy ass lane? I wasn't sure of this place, not one bit, but I'd made a promise to check it out, and do that I would.

When a twenty-foot-tall gate suddenly appeared out of thin air, not fifteen yards in front of us, I stopped.

Cautiously, I scanned the road, the forest that surrounded us, even up in the trees. No one was around. The gate was magical, and we had triggered it somehow.

"Gunner," Silas breathed. "They don't want us here. My gut is telling me we're taking this too far."

Again, I prowled forward to the gate, walking along it. The metal barrier extended into the woods, and though I didn't follow it far in either direction, I guessed it would extend all the way around the house we saw twinklin' away in the distance. After all, half-assing magical protections didn't make sense.

I returned to where Silas stood, craning my neck to look up at the fence. Had it been a six-footer, even a ten-foot-tall fence, I might have jumped it. This height, though? There was no way I'd be able to leap over that sucker. Not in this form, anyhow.

Knowing there was only one way, I shifted back to my human aspect.

"It's iron." Silas hung back. "I sense it and won't be able to touch it."

"Maybe I can climb it?" I suggested, ignoring the strong 'go away' aura coming from the fence. "Then I'll go to the house and get someone to let you in?"

He didn't respond.

"We gotta try, Si. Don't you take chances on your missions?"

"Of course," the fae snapped, sounding more annoyed than worried. "It's just that this feels so wrong . . ." He shivered. Was he feeling that sense to leave too? Was it stronger on him? "We can return later, Gunner. I'm getting a strong sense that we should."

Yeah, I was pretty sure that the magic in the air was repelling him. I needed to find a way in and fast.

"How 'bout you stay here, and I'll check it out." Stubborn as a tick on a hound, I approached the fence. Hesitantly, I reached out, touching the iron, and half expecting it to ignite to deter people.

What happened was so much worse.

One moment, Silas and I stood in the woods in front of a fence, open space spreadin' for miles behind us. The next, a cage descended from nowhere, slamming into the sodden ground and trapping us within cold bars.

"Well, shit," I muttered as Silas scurried to the middle of the cage, wincing. Fae couldn't abide iron so it had to be made of that metal too if he was reacting like that.

I stared out at the trees, preparing for someone to emerge. If the cage appeared out of nowhere, it stood to reason that someone had put it there. Or, at least, I hoped they had.

I waited, and when no one appeared right away, doubt crept through me.

"Who's out there!" I roared. "We aren't here for trouble! We need to talk!"

Rain continued to pummel my face, to pour, the only

soundtrack to our situation. With each passing second, my muscles hardened. Being caged didn't suit an alpha wolf.

"Silas, can your magic do anything?"

"If that were the case, I would have done something by now."

"Worth the ask. I'm gonna see if I can bend the bars."

"You'll do no such thing," a female voice, sharp as a whip, cut through the night.

I spun to find a trio of women, all at least in their seventies, had snuck up on us. How, I wasn't sure, but I applauded that. It wasn't easy sneakin' up on a wolf.

"Do you live here?" I asked. "We don't mean you any trouble, ladies, but we're lookin' for someone."

"Are you of the seven?" the woman in the middle asked. Her gray hair was matted down, and rain dripped off her chin, though it didn't seem to bother her any.

"The Seven?" I cocked my head. "Don't think so."

"You'd know." She sniffed. "And if you're not of the Seven, then you're an intruder and we have no use for you." She looked at the other two. "Shall we call Jon-Jon? Or leave them there to rot, sisters?"

What the hell?!

"My dear ladies." Silas found his voice and stepped forward, all courtly manners and fae charm. "I apologize for our entry onto your property. We should have waited—"

"You shouldn't have come *at all,*" the middle one argued. "Can you not feel the magic telling you to turn away?"

"Fine," I spat, not about to tell them that we did feel the magic, and I was pigheaded. "Then let us out. It's not like we're gonna get over this fence anyhow."

A crow's laugh escaped the woman on the left, setting my

teeth on edge. "Are you deaf? We have no intention of letting you go."

Nah, I wouldn't accept that. We could get out of this. There might be a way.

My mind latched on to one thing. Meredith was supposed to find a woman named Miriam. Could one of these crones be her? If so, was Meredith one of the Seven? Whatever the hell that meant.

It was time to find out.

"You should let us go, because I think I know who one of the Seven is that you're talkin' about." I tilted my chin up in defiance. "But if we don't make it back home, she won't come here. She'll know it won't be safe."

Bluffin'. That was what I was doing. Meredith would come, I was sure of it. Witch like her wouldn't rest until she did, but these ladies didn't know Meredith from Adam. Thankfully, I'd learned the fine art of bluffin' from my Pa and judging by how the old ladies' faces lit up, my skills hadn't failed me.

"You know one of the Seven?" the middle woman asked, her tone totally different. Interested. Almost greedy. "Are you sure? What's their name?"

"Pretty sure. Her name is Meredith Stone." I didn't miss when the witch on the right clutched her heart. Or when the one on the left looked to the sky, her lips moving fast, as if their prayers had been answered.

And I certainly didn't miss when the middle crone waved her hand, and magically, the cage disappeared. The gate opened.

"Come," the middle witch said. "You two might be useful after all."

ALSO BY ASHLEY MCLEO

<u>The Winter Court Series: Crowns of Magic Universe</u>

A Kingdom of Frost and Malice

A Lord of Snow and Greed

<u>Coven of Shadows and Secrets: Crowns of Magic Universe</u>

Seeker of Secrets

Hunted by Darkness

History of Witches

Marked by Fate

Kingdoms of Sin

Bound by Destiny

<u>Spellcasters Spy Academy Series (Magic of Arcana Universe)</u>

A Legacy Witch: Year One

A Marked Witch: Internship

A Rebel Witch: Year Two

A Crucible Witch: Year Three

The Complete Spellcasters Spy Academy Boxset

<u>The Wonderland Court Series (Magic of Arcana Universe)</u>

Alice the Dagger

Alice the Torch

<u>Standalone Novels</u>

The Alchemist of Silver Hollow (Magic of Arcana Universe)

<u>Fanged Fae Series - A Bonegates sister series</u>

Blood Moon Magic

Faerie Blood

The Bonegate Series - A Fanged Fae sister series

Hawk Witch

Assassin Witch

Traitor Witch

Illuminator Witch

The Royal Quest Series

Dragon Prince

Dragon Magic

Dragon Mate

Dragon Betrayal

Dragon Crown

Dragon War

The Starseed Universe

Prophecy of Three

Souls of Three

Rising of Three

ABOUT THE AUTHOR

Ashley lives in the lush and green Pacific Northwest with her husband, their dog, and the house ghost that sometimes makes appearances in her charming, old home.

When she's not writing urban fantasy and portal fantasy novels she enjoys traveling the world, reading, kicking butt at board games, and frequenting taquerias.

For all the latest releases and updates, subscribe to Ashley's newsletter, The Coven. You can also find her Facebook group, Ashley's Reader Coven.